P9-DOH-805

PRAISE FOR

Wolfsbane and Mistletoe

"The fifteen contributors provide fresh, interesting tales with no losers, and [the stories] star some of the more famous series characters, like Sookie Stackhouse in 'Gift Wrap' by Harris and radio talk host Kitty in 'Il Est Né' by Carrie Vaughn. Fans will enjoy this fine anthology."   —*Alternative Worlds*

"Fifteen exceptional authors are brought together to make *Wolfsbane and Mistletoe* a captivating collection. From stories of urban fantasy to those edged in horror, this anthology offers a fun and sometimes gory variety. Edited by Charlaine Harris and Toni L. P. Kelner, *Wolfsbane and Mistletoe* offers up the Christmas spirit in a wonderfully wicked way. Each story is written as a stand-alone, but among them readers will find entertaining additions to some of the most followed series."   —*Darque Reviews*

"I can easily recommend this to fans of the paranormal, werewolves, [and] Santa Claus, and for people who just like stories."   —*BSCreview*

"The expertise of fifteen wolfishly inspired authors is dished up into a combination of stories that run the gamut from funny to downright creepy. There's a little something for every taste—literally!"   —*Romantic Times*

PRAISE FOR

Many Bloody Returns

"In this anthology, thirteen talented writers have found clever ways to intertwine two seemingly disparate themes: vampires and birthdays . . . entertaining and worth reading. This excellent collection will appeal to the growing legion of paranormal fans."   —*Library Journal*

"[An] anthology no paranormal fan should miss. From the sad and poignant 'The Wish' to the truly bizarre 'The Mournful Cry of Owls,' each story is entertaining and engaging."   —*Romance Reviews Today*

Ace Anthologies Edited by
Charlaine Harris and Toni L. P. Kelner

MANY BLOODY RETURNS

WOLFSBANE AND MISTLETOE

DEATH'S EXCELLENT VACATION

WOLFSBANE
AND MISTLETOE

Edited by
Charlaine Harris
and Toni L. P. Kelner

ACE BOOKS, NEW YORK

Flagstaff Public Library
Flagstaff, Arizona

THE BERKLEY PUBLISHING GROUP
Published by the Penguin Group
Penguin Group (USA) Inc.
375 Hudson Street, New York, New York 10014, USA
Penguin Group (Canada), 90 Eglinton Avenue East, Suite 700, Toronto, Ontario M4P 2Y3, Canada
(a division of Pearson Penguin Canada Inc.)
Penguin Books Ltd., 80 Strand, London WC2R 0RL, England
Penguin Group Ireland, 25 St. Stephen's Green, Dublin 2, Ireland (a division of Penguin Books Ltd.)
Penguin Group (Australia), 250 Camberwell Road, Camberwell, Victoria 3124, Australia
(a division of Pearson Australia Group Pty. Ltd.)
Penguin Books India Pvt. Ltd., 11 Community Centre, Panchsheel Park, New Delhi—110 017, India
Penguin Group (NZ), 67 Apollo Drive, Rosedale, North Shore 0632, New Zealand
(a division of Pearson New Zealand Ltd.)
Penguin Books (South Africa) (Pty.) Ltd., 24 Sturdee Avenue, Rosebank, Johannesburg 2196,
South Africa

Penguin Books Ltd., Registered Offices: 80 Strand, London WC2R 0RL, England

This is a work of fiction. Names, characters, places, and incidents either are the product of the authors' imaginations or are used fictitiously, and any resemblance to actual persons, living or dead, business establishments, events, or locales is entirely coincidental. The publisher does not have any control over and does not assume any responsibility for author or third-party websites or their content.

Collection copyright © 2008 by Charlaine Harris, Inc., and Toni L. P. Kelner and Tekno Books.
A complete listing of individual copyrights can be found on page 341.
The Edgar® name is a registered service mark of the Mystery Writers of America, Inc.
Cover art by Lisa Desimini.
Cover design by Judith Lagerman.
Text design by Kristin del Rosario.

All rights reserved.
No part of this book may be reproduced, scanned, or distributed in any printed or electronic form without permission.
Please do not participate in or encourage piracy of copyrighted materials in violation of the authors' rights. Purchase only authorized editions.
ACE and the "A" design are trademarks of Penguin Group (USA) Inc.

PRINTING HISTORY
Ace hardcover edition / October 2008
Ace trade paperback edition / November 2010

Ace trade paperback ISBN: 978-0-441-01762-1

The Library of Congress has cataloged the Ace hardcover edition as follows:

Wolfsbane and mistletoe / edited by Charlaine Harris and Toni L. P. Kelner.—1st ed.
        p. cm.
    ISBN 978-0-441-01633-4
  1. Werewolves—Fiction. 2. Horror tales, American. 3. Christmas stories. I. Harris, Charlaine.
II. Kelner, Toni L. P.

    PS648.W37W65 2008
    813'.0873808375—dc22   2008030837

PRINTED IN THE UNITED STATES OF AMERICA

10 9 8 7 6 5 4 3 2 1

Flagstaff Public Library
Flagstaff, Arizona

To the furry critters who've added so much to our lives,
and not just on the full moon:
poodles, ferrets, boxers, mice, guinea pigs, and large white cats.
Yummy treats all around!

CONTENTS

INTRODUCTION

We were so fired up by the good reception given *Many Bloody Returns* that we could hardly wait to begin assembling another anthology. Since we'd given the previous contributors two elements for their stories (vampires and birthdays), we decided we'd stick with a winning format. Coming up with the two elements for our second outing was a lot of fun; in fact, probably too much fun, considering that we spent entirely too much time e-mailing each other with preposterous ideas. Zombies and Arbor Day, anyone?

After we'd settled on the saner combination of werewolves and Christmas, we compiled our ideal list of contributors with even more glee. To our delight, almost all of them agreed. J. K. Rowling was busy with some other series, but almost everyone else was able to fit a short story into his or her schedule.

We hope you all enjoy this collection as much as you enjoyed our first outing. We love seeing what talented writers from several genres can come up with when they're given the same two building blocks. Read and enjoy.

CHARLAINE HARRIS
TONI L. P. KELNER

Gift Wrap

Charlaine Harris

Charlaine Harris is the #1 New York Times bestselling author of the Sookie Stackhouse novels and the Harper Connelly series. She's been nominated for a bunch of awards, and she even won a few of them. She lives in southern Arkansas in a country house that has a fluctuating population of people and animals. She loves to read.

It was Christmas Eve. I was all by myself.

Does that sound sad and pathetic enough to make you say, "Poor Sookie Stackhouse!"? You don't need to. I was feeling plenty sorry for myself, and the more I thought about my solitude at this time of the year, the more my eyes welled and my chin quivered.

Most people hang with their family and friends at the holiday season. I actually do have a brother, but we aren't speaking. I'd recently discovered I have a living great-grandfather, though I didn't believe he would even realize it was Christmas. (Not because he's senile, far from it—but because he's not a Christian.) Those two are it for me, as far as close family goes.

I actually do have friends, too, but they all seemed to have their own plans this year. Amelia Broadway, the witch who lives on the top floor of my house, had driven down to New Orleans to spend the holiday with her father. My friend and employer, Sam Merlotte, had gone home to Texas to see his mom, stepfather, and siblings. My childhood friends Tara and JB would be spending Christmas Eve with JB's family; plus, it was their first Christmas as a married couple. Who could horn in on that? I had other friends . . . friends close enough that if I'd made puppy-dog eyes when they were talking about their holiday plans, they would have included me on their guest list in a heartbeat. In a fit of perversity, I hadn't wanted to be pitied for being alone. I guess I wanted to manage that all by myself.

Sam had gotten a substitute bartender, but Merlotte's Bar closes at two o'clock in the afternoon on Christmas Eve and remains closed until two o'clock the day after Christmas, so I didn't even have work to break up a lovely uninterrupted stretch of misery.

My laundry was done. The house was clean. The week before, I'd put up my grandmother's Christmas decorations, which I'd inherited along with the house. Opening the boxes of ornaments made me miss my grandmother with a sharp ache. She'd been gone almost two years, and I still wished I could talk to her. Not only had Gran been a lot of fun, she'd been really shrewd and she'd given good advice—if she decided you really needed some. She'd raised me from the age of seven, and she'd been the most important figure in my life.

She'd been so pleased when I'd started dating the vampire Bill Compton. That was how desperate Gran had been for me to get a beau; even Vampire Bill was welcome. When you're telepathic like I am, it's hard to date a regular guy; I'm sure you can see why. Humans think all kinds of things they don't want their nearest and dearest to know about, much less a woman they're taking out to dinner and a movie. In sharp contrast, vampires' brains are lovely silent blanks to me, and werewolf brains are nearly as good as vampires', though I get a big waft of emotions and the odd snatch of thought from my occasionally furred acquaintances.

Naturally, after I'd thought about Gran welcoming Bill, I began wondering what Bill was doing. Then I rolled my eyes at my own idiocy. It was mid-afternoon, daytime. Bill was sleeping somewhere in his house, which lay in the woods to the south of my place, across the cemetery. I'd broken up with Bill, but I was sure he'd be over like a shot if I called him—once darkness fell, of course.

Damned if I would call him. Or anyone else.

But I caught myself staring longingly at the telephone every time I passed by. I needed to get out of the house or I'd be phoning someone, anyone.

I needed a mission. A project. A task. A diversion.

I remembered having awakened for about thirty seconds in the wee hours of the morning. Since I'd worked the late shift at Merlotte's, I'd only just sunk into a deep sleep. I'd stayed awake only long enough to wonder what had jarred me out of that sleep. I'd heard something out in the woods, I thought. The sound hadn't been repeated, and I'd dropped back into slumber like a stone into water.

Now I peered out the kitchen window at the woods. Not too surprisingly, there was nothing unusual about the view. "The woods are snowy, dark, and deep," I said, trying to recall the Frost poem we'd all had to memorize in high school. Or was it "lovely, dark, and deep"?

Of course, my woods weren't lovely *or* snowy—they never are in Louisiana at Christmas, even northern Louisiana. But it was cold (here, that meant the temperature was about thirty-eight degrees Fahrenheit). And the woods were definitely dark and deep—and damp. So I put on my lace-up work boots that I'd bought years before when my brother, Jason, and I had gone hunting together, and I shrugged into my heaviest "I don't care what happens to it" coat, really more of a puffy quilted jacket. It was pale pink. Since a heavy coat takes a long time to wear out down here, the coat was several years old, too; I'm twenty-seven, definitely past the pale pink stage. I bundled all my hair up under a knit cap, and I pulled on the gloves I'd found stuffed into one pocket. I hadn't worn this coat for a long, long time, and I was surprised to find a couple of dollars and some ticket stubs in the pockets, plus a receipt for a little Christmas gift I'd given Alcide Herveaux, a werewolf I'd dated briefly.

Pockets are like little time capsules. Since I'd bought Alcide the sudoku book, his father had died in a struggle for the job of packmaster, and after a series of violent events, Alcide himself ascended to the leadership. I wondered how pack affairs were going in Shreveport. I hadn't talked to any of the Weres in two months. In fact, I'd lost track of when the last full moon had been. Last night?

Now I'd thought about Bill *and* Alcide. Unless I took action, I'd begin brooding over my most recent lost boyfriend, Quinn. It was time to get on the move.

My family has lived in this humble house for over a hundred and fifty years. My much-adapted home lies in a clearing in the middle of some woods off Hummingbird Road, outside of the small town of Bon Temps, in Renard Parish. The trees are deeper and denser to the east at the rear of the house, since they haven't been logged in a good fifty years. They're thinner on the south side, where the cemetery lies. The land is gently rolling, and far back on the property there's a little stream, but I hadn't walked all the way back to the stream in ages. My life had been very busy, what with hustling drinks at the bar, telepathing (is that a verb?) for the vampires, unwillingly participating in vampire and Were power struggles, and other magical and mundane stuff like that.

It felt good to be out in the woods, though the air was raw and damp, and it felt good to be using my muscles.

I made my way through the brush for at least thirty minutes, alert for any indication of what had caused the ruckus the night before. There are lots of animals indigenous to northern Louisiana, but most of them are quiet and shy: possums, raccoons, deer. Then there are the slightly less quiet, but still shy, mammals; like coyotes and foxes. We have a few more formidable creatures. In the bar, I hear hunters' stories all the time. A couple of the more enthusiastic sportsmen had glimpsed a black bear on a private hunting preserve about two miles from my house. And Terry Bellefleur had sworn to me he'd seen a panther less than two years ago. Most of the avid hunters had spotted feral hogs, razorbacks.

Of course, I wasn't expecting to encounter anything like that. I had popped my cell phone into my pocket, just in case, though I wasn't sure I could get a signal out in the woods.

By the time I'd worked my way through the thick woods to the stream, I was warm inside the puffy coat. I was ready to crouch down for a minute or two to examine the soft ground by the water. The stream, never big to begin with, was level with its banks after the recent rainfall. Though I'm not Nature Girl, I could tell that deer had been here; raccoons, too; and maybe a dog. Or two. Or three. *That's not good,* I thought with a hint of unease. A pack of dogs always had the potential to become dangerous. I wasn't anywhere near savvy enough to tell how old the tracks were, but I would have expected them to look dryer if they'd been made over a day ago.

There was a sound from the bushes to my left. I froze, scared to raise my face and turn in toward the right direction. I slipped my cell phone out of my pocket, looked at the bars. OUTSIDE OF AREA, read the legend on the little screen. *Crap,* I thought. That hardly began to cover it.

The sound was repeated. I decided it was a moan. Whether it had issued from man or beast, I didn't know. I bit my lip, hard, and then I made myself stand up, very slowly and carefully. Nothing happened. No more sounds. I got a grip on myself and edged cautiously to my left. I pushed aside a big stand of laurel.

There was a man lying on the ground, in the cold wet mud. He was naked as a jaybird, but patterned in dried blood.

I approached him cautiously, because even naked bleeding muddy men could be mighty dangerous; maybe *especially* dangerous.

"Ah," I said. As an opening statement, that left a lot to be desired. "Ah, do you need help?" Okay, that ranked right up there with "How do you feel?" as a stupid opening statement.

His eyes opened—tawny eyes, wild and round like an owl's. "Get away," he said urgently. "They may be coming back."

"Then we'd better hurry," I said. I had no intention of leaving an injured man in the path of whatever had injured him in the first place. "How bad are you hurt?"

"No, *run,*" he said. "It's not long until dark." Painfully, he stretched out a hand to grip my ankle. He definitely wanted me to pay attention.

It was really hard to listen to his words since there was a lot of bareness that kept my eyes busy. I resolutely focused my gaze above his chest. Which was covered, not too thickly, with dark brown hair. Across a broad expanse. Not that I was looking!

"Come on," I said, kneeling beside the stranger. A mélange of prints indented the mud, indicating a lot of activity right around him. "How long have you been here?"

"A few hours," he said, gasping as he tried to prop himself up on one elbow.

"In this cold?" Geez Louise. No wonder his skin was bluish. "We got to get you indoors," I said. "Now." I looked from the blood on his left shoulder to the rest of him, trying to spot other injuries.

That was a mistake. The rest of him—though visibly muddy, bloody, and cold—was really, really . . .

What was wrong with me? Here I was, looking at a complete (naked and handsome) stranger with lust, while he was scared and wounded. "Here," I said, trying to sound resolute and determined and neutered. "Put your good arm around my neck, and we'll get you to your knees. Then you can get up and we can start moving."

There were bruises all over him, but not another injury that had broken the skin, I thought. He protested several more times, but the sky was getting darker as the night drew in, and I cut him off sharply. "Get a move on," I advised him. "We don't want to be out here any longer than we have to be. It's going to take the better part of an hour to get you to the house."

The man fell silent. He finally nodded. With a lot of work, we got him to his feet. I winced when I saw how scratched and filthy they were.

"Here we go," I said encouragingly. He took a step, did a little wincing of his own. "What's your name?" I said, trying to distract him from the pain of walking.

"Preston," he said. "Preston Pardloe."

"Where you from, Preston?" We were moving a little faster now, which was good. The woods were getting darker and darker.

"I'm from Baton Rouge," he said. He sounded a little surprised.

"And how'd you come to be in my woods?"

"Well . . ."

I realized what his problem was. "Are you a Were, Preston?" I asked. I felt his body relax against my own. I'd known it already from his brain pattern, but I didn't want to scare him by telling him about my little disability. Preston had a—how can I describe it?—a smoother, thicker pattern than other Weres I'd encountered, but each mind has its own texture.

"Yes," he said. "You know, then."

"Yeah," I said. "I know." I knew way more than I'd ever wanted to.

Vampires had come out in the open with the advent of the Japanese-marketed synthetic blood that could sustain them, but other creatures of the night and shadows hadn't yet taken the same giant step.

"What pack?" I asked, as we stumbled over a fallen branch and recovered. He was leaning on me heavily. I feared we'd actually tumble to the ground. We needed to pick up the pace. He did seem to be moving more easily now that his muscles had warmed up a little.

"The Deer Killer pack, from south of Baton Rouge."

"What are you doing up here in my woods?" I asked again.

"This land is yours? I'm sorry we trespassed," he said. His breath caught as I helped him around a devil's walking stick. One of the thorns caught in my pink coat, and I pulled it out with difficulty.

"That's the least of my worries," I said. "Who attacked you?"

"The Sharp Claw pack from Monroe."

I didn't know any Monroe Weres.

"Why were you here?" I asked, thinking sooner or later he'd have to answer me if I kept asking.

"We were supposed to meet on neutral ground," he said, his face tense with pain. "A werepanther from out in the country somewhere offered the land to us as a midway point, a neutral zone. Our packs have been . . . feuding. He said this would be a good place to resolve our differences."

My brother had offered my land as a Were parley ground? The stranger and I struggled along in silence while I tried to think that through. My brother, Jason, was indeed a werepanther, though he'd become one by being bitten; his estranged wife was a born werepanther, a genetic panther. What was Jason thinking, sending such a dangerous gathering my way? Not of my welfare, that's for sure.

Granted, we weren't on good terms, but it was painful to think he'd actually want to do me harm. Any more than he'd already done me, that is.

A hiss of pain brought my attention back to my companion. Trying to help him more efficiently, I put my arm around his waist and he draped his arm across my shoulder. We were able to make better time that way, to my relief. Five minutes later, I saw the light I'd left on above the back porch.

"Thank God," I said. We began moving faster, and we reached the house just as dark fell. For a second, my companion arched and tensed, but he didn't change. That was a relief.

Getting up the steps turned into an ordeal, but finally I got Preston into the house and seated at the kitchen table. I looked him over anxiously. This wasn't the first time I'd brought a bleeding and naked man into my kitchen, oddly enough. I'd found a vampire named Eric under similar circumstances. Was that not incredibly weird, even for my life? Of course, I didn't have time to mull that over, because this man needed some attention.

I tried to look at the shoulder wound in the improved light of the kitchen, but he was so grimy it was hard to examine in detail. "Do you think you could stand to take a shower?" I asked, hoping I didn't sound like I thought he smelled or anything. Actually, he did smell a little unusual, but his scent wasn't unpleasant.

"I think I can stay upright that long," he said briefly.

"Okay, stay put for a second," I said. I brought the old afghan from the back of the living room couch and arranged it around him carefully. Now it was easier to concentrate.

I hurried to the hall bathroom to turn on the shower controls, added long after the claw-footed bathtub had been installed. I leaned over to turn on the water, waited until it was hot, and got out two fresh towels. Amelia had left shampoo and crème rinse in the rack hanging from the showerhead, and there was plenty of soap. I put my hand under the water. Nice and hot.

"Okay!" I called. "I'm coming to get you!"

My unexpected visitor was looking startled when I got back to the kitchen. "For what?" he asked, and I wondered if he'd hit his head in the woods.

"For the shower, hear the water running?" I said, trying to sound matter-of-fact. "I can't see the extent of your wounds until I get you clean."

We were up and moving again, and I thought he was walking better, as if the warmth of the house and the smoothness of the floor helped his muscles relax. He'd just left the afghan on the chair. No problem with nudity, like most Weres, I noticed. Okay, that was good, right? His thoughts were opaque to me, as Were thoughts sometimes were, but I caught flashes of anxiety.

Suddenly he leaned against me much more heavily, and I staggered into the wall. "Sorry," he said, gasping. "Just had a twinge in my leg."

"No problem," I said. "It's probably your muscles stretching." We made it into the small bathroom, which was very old-fashioned. My own bathroom off my bedroom was more modern, but this was less personal.

Preston didn't seem to note the black-and-white-checkered tile. With unmistakable eagerness, he was eyeing the hot water spraying down into the tub.

"Ah, do you need me to leave you alone for a second before I help you into the shower?" I asked, indicating the toilet with a tip of my head.

He looked at me blankly. "Oh," he said, finally understanding. "No, that's all right." So we made it to the side of the tub, which was a high one. With a lot of awkward maneuvering, Preston swung a leg over the side, and I shoved, and he was able to raise the second leg enough to climb completely in. After making sure he could stand by himself, I began to pull the shower curtain closed.

"Lady," he said, and I stopped. He was under the stream of hot water, his hair plastered to his head, water beating on his chest and running down to drip off his . . . Okay, he'd gotten warmer everywhere.

"Yes?" I was trying not to sound like I was choking.

"What's your name?"

"Oh! Excuse me." I swallowed hard. "My name is Sookie. Sookie Stackhouse." I swallowed again. "There's the soap; there's the shampoo. I'm going to leave the bathroom door open, okay? You just call me when you're through, and I'll help you out of the tub."

"Thanks," he said. "I'll yell if I need you."

I pulled the shower curtain, not without regret. After checking that the clean towels were where Preston could easily reach them, I returned to the kitchen. I wondered if he would like coffee, or hot chocolate, or tea? Or maybe alcohol? I had some bourbon, and there were a couple of beers in the refrigerator. I'd ask him. Soup, he'd need some soup. I didn't have any homemade, but I had Campbell's Chicken Tortilla. I put the soup into a pan on the stove, got coffee ready to go, and boiled some water in case he opted for the chocolate or tea. I was practically vibrating with purpose.

When Preston emerged from the bathroom, his bottom half was wrapped in a large blue bath towel of Amelia's. Believe me, it had never looked so good. Preston had draped a towel around his neck to catch the drips from his hair, and it covered his shoulder wound. He winced a little as he walked, and I knew his feet must be sore. I'd gotten some men's socks by mistake on my last trip to Wal-Mart, so I got them from my drawer, and handed them to Preston, who'd resumed his seat at the table. He looked at them very carefully, to my puzzlement.

"You need to put on some socks," I said, wondering if he paused because he thought he was wearing some other man's garments. "They're mine," I said reassuringly. "Your feet must be tender."

"Yes," said Preston, and rather slowly, he bent to put them on.

"You need help?" I was pouring the soup in a bowl.

"No, thank you," he said, his face hidden by his thick dark hair as he bent to the task. "What smells so good?"

"I heated some soup for you," I said. "You want coffee, or tea, or . . ."

"Tea, please," he said.

I never drank tea myself, but Amelia had some. I looked through her selection, hoping none of these blends would turn him into a frog or anything. Amelia's magic had had unexpected results in the past. Surely anything marked LIPTON was okay? I dunked the tea bag into the scalding water and hoped for the best.

Preston ate the soup carefully. Maybe I'd gotten it too hot. He spooned it into his mouth like he'd never had soup before. Maybe his mama had always served homemade. I felt a little embarrassed. I was staring at him, because I sure didn't have anything better to look at. He looked up and met my eyes.

Whoa. Things were moving too fast here. "So, how'd you get hurt?" I asked. "Was there a skirmish? How come your pack left you?"

"There was a fight," he said. "Negotiations didn't work." He looked a little doubtful and distressed. "Somehow, in the dark, they left me."

"Do you think they're coming back to get you?"

He finished his soup, and I put his tea down by his hand. "Either my own pack or the Monroe one," he said grimly.

That didn't sound good. "Okay, you better let me see your wounds now," I said. The sooner I knew his fitness level, the sooner I could decide what to do. Preston removed the towel from around his neck, and I bent to look at the wound. It was almost healed.

"When were you hurt?" I asked.

"Toward dawn." His huge tawny eyes met mine. "I lay there for hours."

"But . . ." Suddenly I wondered if I'd been entirely intelligent, bringing a stranger into my home. I knew it wasn't wise to let Preston know I had doubts about his story. The wound had looked jagged and ugly when I'd found him in the woods. Yet now that he came into the house, it healed in a matter of minutes? What was up? Weres healed fast, but not instantly.

"What's wrong, Sookie?" he asked. It was pretty hard to think about anything else when his long wet hair was trailing across his chest and the blue towel was riding pretty low.

"Are you really a Were?" I blurted, and backed up a couple of steps. His brain waves dipped into the classic Were rhythm, the jagged, dark cadence I found familiar.

Preston Pardloe looked absolutely horrified. "What else would I be?" he said, extending an arm. Obligingly, fur rippled down from his shoulder and his fingers clawed. It was the most effortless change I'd ever seen, and there was very little of the noise I associated with the transformation, which I'd witnessed several times.

"You must be some kind of super werewolf," I said.

"My family is gifted," he said proudly.

He stood, and his towel slipped off.

"No kidding," I said in a strangled voice. I could feel my cheeks turning red.

There was a howl outside. There's no eerier sound, especially on a dark, cold night; and when that eerie sound comes from the line where your yard meets the woods, well, that'll make the hairs on your arm stand up. I glanced at Preston's wolfy arm to see if the howl had had the same effect on him, and saw that his arm had reverted to human shape.

"They've returned to find me," he said.

"Your pack?" I said, hoping that his kin had returned to retrieve him.

"No." His face was bleak. "The Sharp Claws."

"Call your people. Get them here."

"They left me for a reason." He looked humiliated. "I didn't want to talk about it. But you've been so kind."

I was not liking this more and more. "And that reason would be?"

"I was payment for an offense."

"Explain in twenty words or less."

He stared down at the floor, and I realized he was counting in his head. This guy was one of a kind. "Packleader's sister wanted me, I didn't want her, she said I'd insulted her, my torture was the price."

"Why would your packleader agree to any such thing?"

"Am I still supposed to number my words?"

I shook my head. He'd sounded dead serious. Maybe he just had a really deep sense of humor.

"I'm not my packleader's favorite person, and he was willing to believe I was guilty. He himself wants the sister of the Sharp Claw packmaster, and it would be a good match from the point of view of our packs. So, I was hung out to dry."

I could sure believe the packmaster's sister had lusted after him. The rest of the story was not outrageous, if you've had many dealings with the Weres. Sure, they're all human and reasonable on the outside, but when they're in their Were mode, they're different.

"So, they're here to get you and keep on beating you up?"

He nodded somberly. I didn't have the heart to tell him to rewind the towel. I took a deep breath, looked away, and decided I'd better go get the shotgun.

Howls were echoing, one after another, through the night by the time I fetched the shotgun from the closet in the living room. The Sharp

Claws had tracked Preston to my house, clearly. There was no way I could hide him and say that he'd gone. Or was there? If they didn't come in . . .

"You need to get in the vampire hole," I said. Preston turned from staring at the back door, his eyes widening as he took in the shotgun. "It's in the guest bedroom." The vampire hole dated from when Bill Compton had been my boyfriend, and we'd thought it was prudent to have a light-tight place at my house in case he got caught by day.

When the big Were didn't move, I grabbed his arm and hustled him down the hall, showed him the trick bottom of the bedroom closet. Preston started to protest—all Weres would rather fight than flee—but I shoved him in, lowered the "floor," and threw the shoes and junk back in there to make the closet look realistic.

There was a loud knock at the front door. I checked the shotgun to make sure it was loaded and ready to fire, and then I went into the living room. My heart was pounding about a hundred miles a minute.

Werewolves tend to take blue-collar jobs in their human lives, though some of them parlay those jobs into business empires. I looked through my peephole to see that the werewolf at my front door must be a semipro wrestler. He was huge. His hair hung in tight gelled waves to his shoulders, and he had a trimmed beard and mustache, too. He was wearing a leather vest and leather pants and motorcycle boots. He actually had leather strips tied around his upper arms, and leather braces on his wrists. He looked like someone from a fetish magazine.

"What do you want?" I called through the door.

"Let me come in," he said, in a surprisingly high voice. *Little pig, little pig, let me come in!*

"Why would I do that?" *Not by the hair of my chinny-chin-chin.*

"Because we can break in if we have to. We got no quarrel with you. We know this is your land, and your brother told us you know all about us. But we're tracking a guy, and we gotta know if he's in there."

"There was a guy here, he came up to my back door," I called. "But he made a phone call and someone came and picked him up."

"Not out here," the mountainous Were said.

"No, the back door." That was where Preston's scent would lead.

"Hmmmm." By pressing my ear to the door, I could hear the Were mutter, "Check it out," to a large dark form, which loped away. "I still gotta come in and check," my unwanted visitor said. "If he's in there, you might be in danger.".

He should have said that first, to convince me he was trying to save me.

"Okay, but only you," I said. "And you know I'm a friend of the Shreveport pack, and if anything happens to me, you'll have to answer to them. Call Alcide Herveaux if you don't believe me."

"Oooo, I'm scared," said Man Mountain in an assumed falsetto. But as I swung open the front door and he got a look at the shotgun, I could see that he truly did look as if he was having second thoughts. Good.

I stood aside, keeping the Benelli pointed in his direction to show I meant business. He strode through the house, his nose working all the time. His sense of smell wouldn't be nearly as accurate in his human form, and if he started to change, I intended to tell him I'd shoot if he did.

Man Mountain went upstairs, and I could hear him opening closets and looking under beds. He even stepped into the attic. I heard the creak its old door makes when it swings open.

Then he clomped downstairs in his big old boots. He was dissatisfied with his search, I could tell, because he was practically snorting. I kept the shotgun level.

Suddenly he threw back his head and roared. I flinched, and it was all I could do to hold my ground. My arms were exhausted.

He was glaring at me from his great height. "You're pulling something on us, woman. If I find out what it is, I'll be back."

"You've checked, and he's not here. Time to go. It's Christmas Eve, for goodness' sake. Go home and wrap some presents."

With a final look around the living room, out he went. I couldn't believe it. The bluff had worked. I lowered the gun and set it carefully back in the closet. My arms were trembling from holding it at the ready. I shut and locked the door behind him.

Preston was padding down the hall in the socks and nothing else, his face anxious.

"Stop!" I said, before he could step into the living room. The curtains were open. I walked around shutting all the curtains in the house, just to be on the safe side. I took the time to send out my special sort of search, and there were no live brains in the area around the house. I'd never been sure how far this ability could reach, but at least I knew the Sharp Claws were gone.

When I turned around after drawing the last drape, Preston was behind me, and then he had his arms around me, and then he was kissing me. I swam to the surface to say, "I don't really . . ."

"Pretend you found me gift-wrapped under the tree," he whispered. "Pretend you have mistletoe."

It was pretty easy to pretend both those things. Several times. Over hours.

When I woke up Christmas morning, I was as relaxed as a girl can be. It took me a while to figure out that Preston was gone; and while I felt a pang, I also felt just a bit of relief. I didn't know the guy, after all, and even after we'd been up close and personal, I had to wonder how a day alone with him would have gone. He'd left me a note in the kitchen.

"Sookie, you're incredible. You saved my life and gave me the best Christmas Eve I've ever had. I don't want to get you in any more trouble. I'll never forget how great you were in every way." He'd signed it.

I felt let down, but oddly enough I also felt happy. It was Christmas Day. I went in and plugged in the lights on the tree, and sat on the old couch with my grandmother's afghan wrapped around me, which still smelled faintly of my visitor. I had a big mug of coffee and some homemade banana nut bread to have for breakfast. I had presents to unwrap. And about noon, the phone began to ring. Sam called, and Amelia; and even Jason called just to say "Merry Christmas, Sis." He hung up before I could charge him with loaning my land out to two packs of Weres. Considering the satisfying outcome, I decided to forgive and forget—at least that one transgression. I put my turkey breast in the oven, and fixed a sweet potato casserole, and opened a can of cranberry sauce, and made some cornbread dressing and some broccoli and cheese.

About thirty minutes before the somewhat simplified feast was ready, the doorbell rang. I was wearing a new pale blue pants and top outfit in velour, a gift from Amelia. I was feeling self-sufficient as hell.

I was astonished how happy I was to see my great-grandfather at the door. His name's Niall Brigant, and he's a fairy prince. Okay, long story, but that's what he is. I'd only met him a few weeks before, and I couldn't say we really knew each other well, but he was family. He's about six feet tall, he almost always wears a black suit with a white shirt and a black tie, and he has pale golden hair as fine as cornsilk; it's longer than my hair, and it seems to float around his head if there's the slightest breeze.

Oh, yeah, my great-grandfather is over a thousand years old. Or thereabouts. I guess it's hard to keep track after all those years.

Niall smiled at me. All the tiny wrinkles that fissured his fine skin moved when he smiled, and somehow that just added to his charm. He had a load of wrapped boxes, to add to my general level of amazement.

"Please come in, Great-grandfather," I said. "I'm so happy to see you! Can you have Christmas dinner with me?"

"Yes," he said. "That's why I've come. Though," he added, "I was not invited."

"Oh," I said, feeling ridiculously ill-mannered. "I just never thought you'd be interested in coming. I mean, after all, you're not . . ." I hesitated, not wanting to be tacky.

"Not Christian," he said gently. "No, dear one, but you love Christmas, and I thought I would share it with you."

"Yay," I said.

I'd actually wrapped a present for him, intending to give it to him when I next encountered him (for seeing Niall was not a regular event), so I was able to bask in complete happiness. He gave me an opal necklace, I gave him some new ties (that black one had to go) and a Shreveport Mudbugs pennant (local color).

When the food was ready, we ate dinner, and he thought it was all very good.

It was a great Christmas.

* * *

The creature Sookie Stackhouse knew as Preston was standing in the woods. He could see Sookie and her great-grandfather moving around in the living room.

"She really is lovely, and sweet as nectar," he said to his companion, the hulking Were who'd searched Sookie's house. "I only had to use a touch of magic to get the attraction started."

"How'd Niall get you to do it?" asked the Were. He really was a werewolf, unlike Preston, who was a fairy with a gift for transforming himself.

"Oh, he helped me out of a jam once," Preston said. "Let's just say it involved an elf and a warlock, and leave it at that. Niall said he wanted to make this human's Christmas very happy, that she had no family and was deserving." He watched rather wistfully as Sookie's figure crossed the window. "Niall set up the whole story tailored to her needs. She's not speaking to her brother, so he was the one who 'loaned out' her woods. She loves to help people, so I was 'hurt'; she loves to protect people, so I was 'hunted.' She hadn't had sex in a long time, so I seduced her." Preston sighed. "I'd love to do it all over again. It was wonderful, if you like humans. But Niall said no further contact, and his word is law."

"Why do you think he did all this for her?"

"I've no idea. How'd he rope you and Curt into this?"

"Oh, we work for one of his businesses as a courier. He knew we do a little community theater, that kind of thing." The Were looked unconvincingly modest. "So I got the part of Big Threatening Brute, and Curt was Other Brute."

"And a good job you did," Preston the fairy said bracingly. "Well, back to my own neck of the woods. See you later, Ralph."

"'Bye now," Ralph said, and Preston popped out of sight.

"How the hell do they do that?" Ralph said, and stomped off through the woods to his waiting motorcycle and his buddy Curt. He had a pocketful of cash and a story he was charged to keep secret.

Inside the old house, Niall Brigant, fairy prince and loving great-grandfather, pricked his ears at the faint sound of Preston's and Ralph's departures. He knew it was audible to only his ears. He smiled down at his great-granddaughter. He didn't understand Christmas, but he understood that it was a time humans received and gave gifts, and drew together as families. As he looked at Sookie's happy face, he knew he had given her a unique yuletide memory.

"Merry Christmas, Sookie," he said, and kissed her on the cheek.

The Haire of the Beast

Donna Andrews

Like Meg Langslow, the ornamental blacksmith heroine of her humorous mystery series from St. Martin's Press, Donna Andrews was born and raised in Yorktown, Virginia. These days she spends almost as much time in cyberspace as Turing Hopper, the Artificial Intelligence Personality who appears in her technocozy series from Berkley Prime Crime.

Although Andrews has loved fantasy and science fiction since childhood, during her years at the University of Virginia she grew fond of reading mysteries—particularly when she should have been studying for exams. After graduation, she moved to the Washington, D.C., area and joined the communications staff of a large financial organization, where for two decades she honed her writing skills on nonfiction and developed a profound understanding of the criminal mind through her observation of interdepartmental politics.

Among her less savory hobbies is toxic horticulture, or gardening with poisonous plants. Last year's crop of wolfsbane was particularly fine.

"Why on earth would you want to be a werewolf?" I asked.

"Why not?" Tom said. "I mean, don't you think it would be cool?"

"Cool?" I repeated. I tried to keep my tone neutral, but brothers and sisters learn to read each other.

"Okay, maybe you wouldn't, but I'd love it," he said, through another mouthful of spaghetti. "Imagine being able to turn into a wolf, and run free through the forest. Having a sense of smell a thousand times keener than we do. Night vision. Wolves are cool."

He was waving his beer in his enthusiasm, and spilling rather a lot of it.

"Wolves don't run free anywhere closer than Canada," I said, as I tried to mop up behind him. "Here in Virginia, if you see a wolf, it's either in a cage or a rug in front of someone's fireplace. They probably get shot at a lot, those free-range wolves. And unless it works way different than in the movies, it's not that you can turn into a wolf—you can't help it at the full moon. Take it from me, unavoidable monthly biological transformations are no picnic."

"I knew you wouldn't understand," he said, sounding a little sulky. "You have no sense of adventure."

"You're really going to try this?" I said, gesturing at the battered old book that lay on the table between us. "And what do you need my help for?"

"The spell's written in this really antique language," he said. "I thought you could help me figure it out."

I shook my head—in exasperation, not refusal. I pulled the book closer to my side of the table and wrinkled my nose. It smelled musty, with faint undertones of matches and rotten eggs.

"Don't get spaghetti sauce on it," he warned. "Professor Wilmarth would kill me if I messed it up."

"I'm surprised he let you borrow it," I said. "Or did he?"

Tom managed to have a really big mouth of spaghetti when he heard my question, and took his time chewing.

"You stole it," I said. "Tom!"

"I borrowed it," he said finally. "He's got a million of these old gri-moires; he won't miss this one for a few days. I figured you could help me translate it. I mean, you did live with a leading medievalist for five years."

I bit back a sarcastic comment. I'd learned the hard way that telling the truth about Phil, my ex, only sounded like sour grapes. So when people mentioned how brilliant he was, how well his career was going, how happy he was with his new girlfriend, I just nodded and smiled. No one would believe me if I told them how much of the research for Phil's dissertation I'd done. I wasn't the same book-smart-but-street-stupid kid who'd agreed to support him while he got his Ph.D., only to get dumped when it was time for me to start mine. The new girlfriend could have him, whoever she was—and my money was on a bright young graduate student who could replace me as his researcher.

"I'm surprised you didn't ask Phil to help you with this," I said aloud. "Since he's such a leading medievalist and all."

"If I was still talking to him, maybe I would," he said. "I told you—after what he did to you, I try not to have anything to do with him."

Yes, he'd told me, but I hadn't necessarily believed it. Though if he brought this crazy idea to me instead of Phil, perhaps I should.

"Besides, Phil would just laugh and tell me not to meddle with forces beyond my comprehension," Tom added.

Now that sounded like something Phil would say. In fact, I was almost certain Tom was quoting him. And it explained one thing that had been puzzling me—how Tom had found a grimoire with a were-wolf spell in the first place. Phil. The son of a bitch had probably dangled the grimoire in front of Tom's nose, translated just enough to get him really hooked on the idea, and then refused to help him. Phil had always known just how to play Tom.

"Look, if you can't figure it out—" Tom began.

"I can figure it out," I said. "But I can't do it tonight—in case you freshmen haven't noticed, first semester grades are supposed to come out Monday, and I have papers to read and grades to turn in if I want to keep my TA assignment."

"But you'll do it," he said.

"I'll try."

Tom's good humor returned. I brought out the plate of brownies—one of his favorites—and we talked about other things for the rest of the meal.

"Don't forget about the spell," he said, as he was putting on his coat. "I don't suppose you could just photocopy the right page so I can take the book back now?"

Back to Professor Wilmarth? Or back to Phil?

"No," I said. "I might need the rest of the book. What if when I finally translate the spell it says, 'Then add a pinch of bat powder—see recipe on page forty-three.'"

"Yeah, right."

"Seriously, with something like this, you sometimes have to study a word or phrase in context. A whole book is a lot more context than a couple of pages. I need the whole book."

"Okay," he said. "But be careful with it."

"I will," I said. "See you Thursday."

"Thursday?"

"Christmas dinner? Turkey and trimmings?"

"Oh, right," he said. "I almost forgot it was so close. Thursday, then."

Had he really forgotten it was so close to Christmas? Or was he deliberately ignoring the approach of what would be only the second holiday without our parents?

Of course, knowing Tom, maybe he was just laying the grounds for pretending he'd forgotten to shop for my present.

I watched as he strolled down the driveway from my garage apartment back to the street. In the main house, Mrs. Grogran's evil little Lhasa Apso—the Lhasa Raptor, as we called him—heard Tom's footsteps and barked furiously for at least fifteen minutes. I hoped Mrs. Grogan had peeked out and seen it was only my brother leaving. I didn't think my lease would really let her turn me out for having late-night male visitors, but she could make my life a living hell while we fought it out.

I returned to grading the student papers. Not my favorite way to spend a Friday night, but at least if I got them out of the way, I could enjoy the rest of the weekend. I polished the last one off by eleven, finished the data entry into the departmental grading system a little before midnight, and went to bed.

But not, alas, to sleep. The moon was still almost a week from full, but it shone straight through my window, and when I finally got up to pull the shade down and block it out, I realized even that wouldn't help my insomnia.

I went back out to the kitchen and opened Professor Wilmarth's grimoire again. I felt a curious reluctance to touch the stained leather cover, and my stomach turned slightly at the faint smell of sulfur.

I remembered that the archaic name for sulfur was brimstone. Maybe I should have photocopied the relevant pages after all and made Tom take the nasty thing away.

Nonsense. I made myself turn to the werewolf spell, and as so often happens, I got caught up in the project. I looked up after what I thought was only a few minutes of reading and realized that day was breaking.

Just as well. I had to look up a few things in the university library.

By Saturday evening, I was pretty sure I'd puzzled out the werewolf spell. In fact, I'd puzzled out nearly all the spells in the book, some of them a lot more useful sounding.

Mixing up the powder needed for the werewolf spell would be challenging, since most of the ingredients weren't FDA approved. I'd figured out that djinn's eggs were mandrake roots. The devil's trumpet was datura, or jimson weed. And I was reasonably sure that when the werewolf spell called for "the haire of the beast," it wasn't some archaic equivalent of "hair of the dog." It meant real wolf hair.

The herbs were bad enough, but grinding up wolf hair and eating it? Yuck.

Tom could probably dig up a wolf pelt somewhere, but what if hair from a dead wolf didn't work? Worse, what if it turned him into a dead wolf at moonrise?

Not that I necessarily believed the spell would work. At least half the herbs needed for the powder were strong hallucinogens. A few sprinkles of the stuff and you wouldn't need to be a werewolf to howl at the moon.

Too many sprinkles would kill you. And annoying as he could be, I didn't really want Tom dead.

Phil, now.

Okay, it was a crazy idea, but I decided to take Phil as my guinea pig. I'd use a nonlethal dose of the various toxins, so if the spell didn't work, the powder would give him only a few stomach cramps, and I could tell Tom I told you so.

And if it did work, it wouldn't be Tom hauled in by Animal Control and maybe waking up in a cage.

Sunday afternoon I gathered my ingredients. Most of them I had to get from a pair of ex-students who'd dropped out during the sixties and now ran a highly unconventional herb farm out in the mountains twenty miles from town.

Sunday evening I mixed the powder and baked it into some brownies—one of Phil's favorites as well as Tom's. Mixed up a few other useful-sounding concoctions from the grimoire while I was at it. If the werewolf spell worked, I'd give some of them a try.

Once the brownies had cooled, I wrapped them up in some paper with jolly Santa Clauses all over it and attached a gift tag that said, "Merry Christmas, Professor Phil!" I made the dots over the *i*'s into hearts. He'd probably think some lovestruck coed had left them on his porch in the middle of the night.

When I got back from my late-night delivery, I cleaned up all my herbs and tools and hid them in Mrs. Grogan's garage. In her late husband's fishing box, which hadn't been opened in a decade.

I kept the radio on nonstop for the next few days, so I'd hear right away if the campus station reported a popular young medieval history professor succumbing to food poisoning. But all I heard was the usual endless carol marathon.

Christmas Day arrived, and with it the full moon. Though moonrise wasn't until 4:52 P.M. I'd checked. The hours crawled by.

At least I had some distraction. I'd invited Tom for dinner. I fixed the traditional spread—turkey, dressing, mashed potatoes, the works. I was hoping Tom would be too focused on the food to nag me about whether I'd made progress on his spell. But if not, I'd tell him what I'd done. Maybe enlist him to go over with me to Phil's neighborhood later, to see if the spell worked.

But Tom was strangely distracted. Twitchy. He kept shifting in his chair and scratching his arms and legs. He wasn't even eating much.

"What's wrong with you anyway?" I finally asked.

He shrugged.

"Don't feel so great," he said.

"Do you want a beer?" I asked. "Or a Coke?"

"Maybe some water?"

If Tom turned down both hops and cola, he really must be ill. I went out to the kitchen and filled a glass with ice and water.

When I came back, Tom was writhing on the floor.

And howling. The pieces fell into place.

"You've been visiting Phil, haven't you?" I said. "You went over there and ate some of the brownies."

He must have felt really awful. He didn't try to lie—just nodded, and clutched his stomach.

"It serves you right," I said. "I was going to test your stupid spell on Phil, to see if it worked before letting you try it."

Even through his pain, I could see his face brighten.

"Is that what this is?" he gasped. "I'm turning into a wolf?"

"Not exactly."

He convulsed one more time, then screamed as his body contracted and flowed in strange ways. I winced and closed my eyes for a second.

When I opened them again, I saw a rather bedraggled Lhasa Apso quivering on the floor, with Tom's abandoned clothes scattered around him.

"I couldn't really scare up wolf hair on such short notice," I said. "I figured dog hair would work for the test."

Tom opened one eye to glare at me. Then he curled his lip and growled feebly. Even in dog form, he was pretty easy to read.

"Don't give me that," I said. "This wouldn't have happened if you'd stayed away from Phil."

He whimpered. He got up, a little shaky on his feet, and turned around in a half circle as if trying to get a better look at his tail. Then he looked up at me and whined.

"Oh, don't worry," I said. "I can fix it."

He wagged his tail slightly, and cocked his head to one side as if asking how.

"I found a recipe for a potion that makes whatever state you're in permanent. So all we have to do is wait till the moon sets. About seven tomorrow morning. You'll be human again, you can drink the potion, and you won't have to worry about changing into a furball next month."

He wagged his tail with enthusiasm.

"So you stay here for a while," I said. "Finish your dinner and get some sleep."

I threw a couple of pillows on the floor, and put a plate of turkey beside them.

"I'll be back as soon as I can," I added.

He yelped slightly, and tried to grab the leg of my jeans.

"Sorry," I said, pushing him away as gently as I could. "You'll be fine here. Just don't bark, or Mrs. Grogan will call Animal Control. Keep quiet, lie low, and we'll fix you up tomorrow morning."

He whined and cocked his head to the side again.

"Me?" I said. "I'm going over to Phil's house. He'll be getting his dose of the permanence potion a little earlier than you will."

On my way out, I stepped into the garage and snagged an old dog lead. Mrs. Grogan was going to love her Christmas present.

Lucy, at Christmastime

Simon R. Green

Simon R. Green has just hit middle age, and is feeling very bitter about it. He has published over thirty novels, all of them different. His series include the Forest Kingdom books, the Deathstalker books, the Nightside books, the Secret Histories books, featuring Shaman Bond, the very secret agent, and his new series, the Ghost Finders. He has lived most of his life in a small country town, Bradford-on-Avon. This was the last Celtic town to fall to the invading Saxons in A.D. 504. He has also worked as a shop assistant, bicycle-repair mechanic, journalist, actor, eccentric dancer, and mail-order bride. He has never worked for MI5. Don't believe anyone who tells you otherwise. He is, however, secretly Superman.

You never forget your first; and mine was Lucy.

It was Christmas Eve in the Nightside, and I was drinking wormwood brandy in Strangefellows, the oldest bar in the world. The place was crowded, the air was thick with good cheer, the ceiling trailed long streamers of the cheapest paper decorations money could buy; and as midnight approached, the revellers grew so festive they could barely stand up. Even so, everyone was careful to give me plenty of room as I sat on my stool at the bar, nursing my drink. I'm Leo Morn, and that's a name you can scare people with. Of course, my Lucy was never scared of me, even though everyone told her I was a bad boy, and would come to a bad end. Lucy sat on the stool beside me at the bar, smiling and listening while I talked. She didn't have a drink. She never does.

The music system was playing "Jingle Bells" by the Sex Pistols, a sure sign the bar's owner was feeling nostalgic. Farther down the long (and only occasionally polished) wooden bar, sat Tommy Oblivion, the existential private eye. He was currently doing his best to convince a pressing creditor that his bill might or might not be valid in this particular reality. Not that far away, Ms. Fate, the Nightside's very own leather-costumed transvestite superheroine, was dancing on a tabletop with demon girl reporter, Bettie Divine. Bettie's cute little curved horns peeped out from between the bangs of her long dark hair.

The Prince of Darkness was sulking into his drink over the cancellation of his TV reality show; the Mistress of the Dark was trying to tempt Saint Nicholas with a sprig of plastic mistletoe; and a reindeer with a very red nose was lying slumped and extremely drunk in a corner, muttering something about unionization. Brightly glowing wee-winged fairies swept round and round the huge Christmas tree, darting in and out of the heavy branches at fantastic speed in some endless game of tag. Every now and again one of the fairies would detonate like a flashbulb, from sheer overpowering joie de vivre, before re-forming and rejoining the chase.

Just another Christmas Eve, in the oldest bar in the world. Where dreams can come true, if you're not careful. Especially at the one time of the year when gods and monsters, good men and bad, can come together in the grand old tradition of eating and drinking yourself stupid, and making a fool of yourself over past loves.

Alex the bartender noticed my glass was empty, and filled it up again without having to be asked. Since he knows me really well, he usually has the good sense to insist I pay in advance for every drink; but even nasty mean-spirited Alex Morrisey knows better than to disturb me on Christmas Eve. I saluted Lucy with my new drink, and she smiled prettily back. My lovely Lucy. Short and sweet, pleasantly curved, tight blonde curls over a heart-shaped face, bright flashing eyes and a smile to break your heart. Wearing the same long white dress she'd been wearing just before she left me forever. Lucy was . . . sharp as a tack, sweet as forbidden fruit, and honest as the day is long. What she ever saw in me, I'll never know. She was sixteen, going on seventeen. Of course, I'm a lot older than her now.

I only ever see her here, on Christmas Eve. I don't have to come here, tell myself every year that I won't; but I always do. Because no matter how much it hurts, I have to see her. *Silly boy,* she always says. *I forgave you long ago.* And I always nod, and say, *I don't forgive me. And I never will.*

Were we in love, really? We were very young. And everything seems so sharp and intense, when you're a teenager. Emotions surge through you like tidal waves, and a sudden smile from a girl can explode in your heart like a firecracker. Immersed in the moment, transfixed in each other's eyes like rabbits caught in the glare of approaching head-lights . . . Yes; she was my first love, and I have never forgotten the time we had together.

All the things we were going to do, all the people we could have been . . . thrown away, in a moment of madness.

I reminded Lucy of how we first met; standing on a railway station late at night, waiting for a train that seemed like it would never come. I looked at her, she looked at me, we both smiled; and next thing I knew we were chatting away as though we'd known each other all our lives. After that, we were never apart. Laughing and teasing, arguing and making up, walking hand in hand and arm in arm because we couldn't bear not to be touching each other. Running through the thick woods under Darkacre; drinking and singing in a late-night lockup, even though we were still underage, because the owner was an old romantic who believed in young love; and later, slow dancing together on the cobbled street of a back alley, to the sound of sentimental music drifting out of a half-open window up above.

You never forget your first love, your first great passion.

I was jolted out of my mood, as Harry Fabulous lurched out of the crowd to greet me with his best salesman's smile. He should have known better, but Harry would try and sell a silencer to the man who was about to shoot him. Always affable and professionally charming, Harry was a con man, a fixer, a specialist in the kind of deal that leaves you counting your fingers afterwards. Always ready to sell you something that was bad for you, or someone else. A hard man to dislike, but worth the effort. He went to sit on the stool next to me, and then froze as I fixed him with my stare. I smiled at him, showing my teeth, and he went pale. He eased back from the stool, holding his empty hands out before him to show how sorry and harmless he was. I let him go. My time with Lucy was too precious to interrupt with the likes of Harry Fabulous.

I remembered running through the woods, chasing Lucy in and out of the tall dark trees as she ran giggling before me, teasing and taunting me, always just out of reach, but careful never to get so far ahead I might think she didn't want to be caught. It was late at night, but the woods were lit up with the shimmering blue-white glare of a full moon. The whole world seemed to come alive around me as I ran, rich with scents and sounds I'd never noticed before. I felt strong and fast and indomitable, like I could run and run forever.

Lucy ran ahead of me, in her long white dress, like a ghost fleeting through the trees.

The moonlight filled my mind, and boiled through my body. My senses were so sharp now they were almost painful. I'd never felt so alive, so happy. The change swept over me like a red rolling tide. Bones creaked and cracked as they lengthened, and I didn't care. Fur burst out of me, covered me, made me whole. My mouth stretched out into a long muzzle, so I could howl my thanks to the full moon that gave me birth. I hardly even noticed as I fell forward and continued to run on four feet. I was a wolf, under the glorious moon, doing what I was born to do. The ancient imperative of the hunt was upon me. I forgot about Leo Morn, forgot about Lucy. I ran howling through the trees, maddened by the moon and the exhilaration of my very first change. The real me had finally burst out of its human cocoon, its human trap; released to run and hunt as I was meant to.

I ran and ran, driven on by the marvellous strength and speed of my new four legs, lord of all I surveyed; as though the whole world and everything in it was nothing more to me than prey.

I shot back and forth, questing between the trees, crested a ridge, and threw myself down onto the prey cringing below. I slammed it to the ground, and tore out its throat with one easy snap of my jaws. The blood was hot and wet and wonderful in my mouth. The prey kicked and struggled as I tore it apart, but not for long. I feasted on the hot and steaming meat, savouring the way it tore easily between my fine new teeth. I ate till I was full, and then raised a leg and urinated over what was left, so no other beast would dare to touch my kill. I licked my blood-flecked muzzle clean, and felt as if I'd come home at last.

When I came to myself again, Lucy was gone.

*   *   *

And now, all these years later, it was Christmas Eve in Strangefellows; and the crowd was singing a carol, or something like it. The night was almost over. I didn't tell Lucy what I'd been thinking about, but I think she knew. She only ever looks sad when I do. But it's all I can think about, on this night of all nights; the night that separated us, forever. Christmas Eve, when the world seems full of promise; the night I told Lucy I loved her, and that I'd love her forever, forever and a day. I told her there was nothing else in the world I wanted as much as her, and I meant it, then. It was the wolf within that made me a liar. That's why I come here every Christmas Eve, to the oldest bar in the world . . . where sometimes stories can still end in lovers' meeting.

I don't have to show up, but I do, because I promised her I'd love her forever and a day.

The clock struck midnight, the revellers cheered the coming of Christmas Day, and Lucy softly and silently faded away. Gone again, for another year.

When the change first takes you, it's only too easy to mistake one passion for another.

You never forget your first victim.

The Night Things Changed

Dana Cameron

A professional archaeologist specializing in colonial New England, Dana Cameron is also the author of the Emma Fielding archaeology mysteries. The sixth book, Ashes and Bones, *won an Anthony for Best Paperback Original. "The Night Things Changed" is the first story set in her "Fangborn" world; it won an Agatha and a Macavity, and was also nominated for an Anthony for Best Short Story. Having once upon a time lived in Salem, Massachusetts (the setting of this story), she now lives in nearby Beverly with her husband and demanding cats. You can learn more about Dana's work at her website, www.danacameron.com.*

I pounded up the stairs to the roof and slammed open the door; the wintry air lashed my face. My sister the vampire was stretched out on her stomach, nearly naked, under the pale December sun.

She wasn't moving. I knew from her phone call the news was bad, but . . .

"Claudia?" I swallowed; my mouth was dry. "Claud?"

She stirred and opened her eyes blearily. Her face was drawn, she moved stiffly. Claudia relaxed when she saw it was me, fastened the bikini top behind her neck, then sat up.

I turned away, blushing. "Aw, jeez, Claud. Do you have to?"

"What? I'm covered. Gerry, take a pill. No one can see me up here. We picked the place for that very reason."

She was right; evergreen shrubs and dead, leafy vines—a forest of green in the summer—sheltered her place from every side, leaving the roof open to the sky. Despite the crust of snow on the ground, she wasn't even shivering.

It was such a small bikini, though. I kept quiet: she'd think I was being a prude.

"I don't even need to wear a bathing suit when I'm alone," she said, reading my face.

"Yeah, you do, as long as I'm your brother." I *am* a prude; sue me. No guy likes to think about his sister being ogled, especially not when she looked good enough to model that bikini. And I wished she'd cut her long dark hair. It was just too dangerous in a fight.

I changed the topic. "I got your message. I was worried."

She nodded; her shoulders sagging. "A bad one, this morning. It means work for us."

Things had been so quiet lately, it had to happen. "Tell me."

"It was in the emergency room." Claudia "happens" to go through the emergency room a lot, trolling for trouble. "This guy was in for sutures, a cut on his arm he said he got slipping on ice. He was giving Eileen a hard time, and I got a whiff of him. I asked her to send him to me for 'post-trauma assessment.'"

Claudia glanced at me; there were dark smudges under her eyes. She looked beat. "He barged into my office, got angry when I told him he had to wait his turn. Very aggressive, all id, defensive as Hell. Maybe there's a hurt little kid somewhere under all that armor, but he's being led by a really thuggish protector-self."

I hate when she talks like a shrink, but it's how she gets things straight in her own head. "Was he big?"

She nodded. "And he uses it. He doesn't mind threatening people, liked the idea he was scaring me. And then . . . when I stood up to him, he took a swing at me."

I nodded, bristling. She was obviously okay, but I hated hearing this kind of stuff. It was part of our job, and I knew Claudia could take care of herself, but it still chafed. Call me overprotective. "And?"

"He missed. That made him crazy. He tried again." She shrugged. "And then I bit him."

I nodded again; it didn't make me feel much better. If biting had cured the guy, she wouldn't have called me, just saved it for the next time we got together for dinner. "Anyone see you?"

"The door was shut. He knocked me down, then ran out of the office." She paused. "He's a really bad one—"

"We'll get him. We always get the bad guys," I said, confident.

She shook her head. "There was something weirdly, profoundly, wrong about him."

"You're just tired. We always—"

"No, Gerry!" Her sharp tone startled me. "This is different. His reaction . . . I can't get the taste out of my mouth. It's like . . . I could work on him for a year, and still not get anywhere."

Her eyes filled up, and I knew that she'd been thrown for a loop. Professionally and personally, Claudia is a proud person.

"Scootch over," I said. I didn't say any more, just sat down on the lounge and put my arm around her. I resisted the urge to take off my jacket and put it over her shoulders, because the sun was the best thing for a vampire in need of healing, even the weak sun of a Massachusetts midwinter. And besides, I needed my coat myself. I always seem to feel the cold.

Prudish. Overprotective. Chilly. In a lot of ways, we werewolves are just big pussies.

After getting Claudia's promise that she'd take it easy, I took the copy of the file she had and visited the address of "J. Smith."

J. Smith? Proof once again that evil is not creative.

I didn't need to get out of the pickup, but I did. As I figured, the place—a double-decker—was abandoned, my footprints the first breaking the new fall of snow surrounding it. As I nosed around, I picked up lots of strong residual scents, most of them unhappy: drugs and sex, pain and fear. There was something in the background, an ugly smell that made my skin crawl; I didn't know if our guy had been there, but the recognizable odor of Evil called me to Change . . .

Not here, not now. Save it for tonight, when you might be able to do something about it . . .

I reluctantly followed my tracks back to my truck and decided to pick up the trail at the hospital. Construction and early holiday mall shoppers had turned Route 128 into a slushy parking lot, but the F150 handled well with her new snow tires. I tuned the radio to the Leftover Lunch on WFNX and crept toward Union Hospital in Lynn.

I like being a werewolf for the same reasons I liked being a cop. Sure, it's a lonely job and I see life's tragedies, but then I fix them. I help people, I make the world a better place, and I'm good at it. I *like* being one of the good guys. I get a sense of satisfaction I bet your average CPA never gets. Or maybe they do; what do I know? I'm just Gerry Steuben, regular guy, North Shore born and bred, with a CJ degree from Salem State, recently early-retired from the Salem PD. My tax forms say I'm a PI now, but I don't do domestics, insurance fraud, or repo. I'll go to the end of the earth to find lost kids, though, and never charge a cent. But I mostly stick to the family business, which is eradicating evil from the world.

Sounds like I'm full of myself, doesn't it? Not if you know the truth about my type. Our type. The Fangborn, Pandora's Orphans, the ones the ancients called "Hope," supposedly trapped at the bottom of the box. But according to *our* legends, the First Fangborn got out, and it's a good thing they did, too, for when evil was released into the world, so was the means of destroying it. Vampires and werewolves, the first to clean the blood and ease the pain, the second to remove irredeemable evil when we find it. Our instincts are infallible, our senses attuned to evil. True evil—not the idiot who cuts you off in traffic or steals your newspaper—exists, and we're here to fight it. We're the ones evil can't touch, the superheroes you never see, if we do our jobs right. I believe that to the core of my soul, and it's the best feeling in the world.

Imagine the world today if we didn't put the brakes on evil. Funny, since the Fangborn have always been depicted as the most depraved killers in every mythology. My kind aren't the most fertile in the world—there are less than one thousand of us in the United States—and when you normals turned from hunting to agriculture, you started popping out kids like it was going out of style. But we're the children of Hope, so we do what we can, and every bit helps.

As for those myths: It's not the turn of the moon but the call of evil that makes us Change, though I can manage it if I'm pissed off enough. I don't have hair on the palms of my hands, though for a while when I turned thirteen, I was afraid of that happening for other reasons. Claudia says I obsess about anyone touching my stuff, but can you name one guy who isn't territorial? When we order pizza, Claudia always asks for roasted garlic. She relies on the mirror by her front door to remind her to dress like other people when it's cold. She also *claims* she's allergic to silver, but that's because she thinks it looks tacky against her skin.

In reality, we're big on family and secrecy. Me and Claud live in Salem because eastern Massachusetts was where our family was needed, back in the day. Grandpa had a sense of humor about it: "Ven ve move from de old country, I tink, 'Here, dey like tings dat go bump in de night, so ve vill giff dem bumps in de night!'" he'd cackle. I miss the old guy like crazy, but our presence has nothing to do with the witchcraft trials; it was just easier to hide a bunch of Germans with funny habits among the Polish and Russian immigrants in nineteenth-century Salem. Protective coloring is all-important. Around here, not only do you have tales of witchcraft, but there are rumors of a sea monster (a nineteenth-century gimmick concocted by ferry owners and innkeepers), pirate treasures, and haunted houses. What's the occasional sighting of a big dog by moonlight against all that?

The traffic finally nudged its way to my exit and I pulled into the hospital parking lot. Many Fangborn are nurses, doctors, shrinks, cops, even clergy. Any job that gets us close to the public, the people who need protection, is a good job for us.

I didn't even have to roll down the window. The stench hit me from outside the cab of the truck. It was all I could do to keep my hands from turning to claws on the wheel and my human brain focused on parking. I killed the engine as soon as I could, clutching the Saint Christopher medal that's been on my neck since my first Communion. I don't care whether he's a saint; I'm not that religious. My mother gave it to me, and it helps to have something to focus on when resisting the Change. Claudia was right: this guy was a bad one. Smith had escaped her—which was saying something—and then left a trail that a normal could follow, if he'd understood why he was suddenly feeling queasy and irritable. There wasn't a sound of bird or beast anywhere nearby, not even a seagull.

True evil has the smell of rotting meat, sewer filth, sickrooms. Add the feeling you get when you realize something life-alteringly bad is happening, something you can't do anything about, and you'll get close to what I felt. But my senses are a hundred times sharper than yours.

The good thing is that smell brings on the Change and that brings power.

I opened the door cautiously. The wind shifted and I found I could manage without going furry, so I visited the ER. The nurses told me the doc who'd treated "J. Smith" was gone.

I thanked them, then tried Claudia's office. The scent was stronger here, possibly because of his attack on Claudia, but there was something else I couldn't place: it set my teeth on edge. The assistant Claudia shared with the other shrinks told me I'd just missed my sister, that she'd been really shook up by a patient. I feigned surprise—Claudia could get into a lot of trouble for talking about the case with me, much less giving me the file—and said I'd check on her.

I tracked the scent back to the parking lot, where the guys at the valet stand said that a guy had caught a cab dropping someone off, a local company.

Just then Eileen came out, a tart little nurse who'd always had a cup of coffee and a kind word for me when I'd been on the force. Claudia'd said she was the nurse handling Smith's case. We exchanged hellos.

"You heard about Claudia?"

"Yeah." I exhaled, whistling.

"She's okay. Guy was a bruiser. Came in to get stitched up, said it was a slip, but I know a bottle-slash when I see one. Street fight, probably."

I nodded.

"Claudia gave me the high sign, so I sent him along to her. A post-trauma chat, I told him. Oh!" Eileen said, remembering. "It gets better. Weems brought him in. Said he found him in the middle of the street, and hauled him in to get him patched up. Too bad you missed him, you guys could have caught up on old times." She grinned a mean grin; everyone knew Weems and I hated each other.

"My bad luck," I said. I stuck my hands in my pockets. "Apart from this guy, you been busy?"

She shook her head. "Not the past two days. Not even a bumsicle." She glanced at the steely sky. "That'll change. Snow tonight."

I nodded; I could smell that, too. We both knew that between the cold, the holidays, and the law of averages, soon enough there'd be accidents, drunk drivers, domestic disputes, and the homeless who'd freeze to death. The usual.

"Well, the kids will like it." She zipped herself up. "They're out of school after today. Jumping out of their little skins already, the little monsters."

"Oh, come on," I said. "Kids should be excited about Christmas." *I like Christmas. I like the effort people make. I like presents. I like the hope. Like I said, we Fangborn are all about Hope.*

"Yeah, I guess." Eileen looked uneasy, though. "I've got this feeling, Gerry. Everyone's on edge. Maybe it's the low pressure or the full moon, but there's something up. Watch yourself out there."

The ER was always hopping during the full moon. My people aren't the only ones who feel its power.

"I will, thanks. And you take care. Keep up with the patch."

Eileen was startled. "How did you—?"

I grinned. "You've been out here for five minutes and didn't light up." I didn't tell her I could smell the difference in her clothing, see the slight weight gain, feel her nerves humming with the strain of not reaching for that crumpled box of relief . . .

We wished each other Merry Christmas and I left. The trail from the taxi was blasted by the mall traffic and the nearby landfill, so I headed to Ziggy's Donuts in Salem, where the cabbies hung out. It didn't hurt that Annie worked there, a girl I'd been kinda hung up on for a while.

I ordered a jelly-filled because Annie was on the counter. I had been trying to get up my nerve to ask her out on a date. It was one of my New Year's resolutions—from this year. But we chatted while she got my donut, and I didn't say anything dumb, so I counted it a success. Maybe even a sign. I found a seat before I did something impetuous and stupid. I'd have to soon: time was almost running out on my resolution, and I keep my promises.

It's hard, when you're a guy, to ask out a cute girl. I'm okay, I'm not hideous, though personally I think I look better as a wolf. I built my own house when our folks died, I have a decent income and a boat that's paid for, and my place is spotless because I don't like surprises.

But it's even harder, when you're Fangborn, to ask a normal out. The two species can mate, though most of us Fangborn prefer to keep to our own kind. A mixed mating has a lower chance of producing a were or vamp than two Fangborn, but that's pretty low odds, too; how my parents lucked out and got *two*, one of each, I don't know. As far as I understand, it's all about recessive genes, but it doesn't make the initial discussion any easier. "Hey, sweetie? When I said my family was strange, I didn't mean regular, dysfunctional-strange . . ."

My cabbie came in then, sweating profusely, probably thinking he was coming down with the flu; I could smell Smith on him, even though they'd probably only brushed fingers when Smith paid. I waited until the cabbie ordered his coffee—even Annie's smile didn't help him—and then I approached him. He wasn't supposed to tell me where he took his fare, but I slid a twenty across the table and got the address of a no-tell motel on the edge of town. Then I asked to check his cab, to see whether Smith had dropped anything, I said.

"Help yourself," he said, shivering around his coffee cup. "It's open."

I was feeling pleased with myself when Weems pulled up alongside me in the parking lot. As he locked up the cruiser, he didn't speak, but gave me a nod along with the hairy eyeball. I nodded back, and kept moving.

We had never liked each other, and now he harbors the deep suspicion most cops have for PIs. He's always made my hackles rise. I couldn't put my finger on the reason, so I did the best I could to avoid him.

Annie knew him, too. Well enough to know that she could look forward to a full six-percent tip.

I waited until Weems was tearing into his bear claw, then opened the door to the cab—

. . . the screech of brakes before a crash . . . a phone ringing at 3:30 in the morning . . . the gush of blood from a wound that is deeper than you thought . . .

I could barely keep myself standing. I slammed the door, and stumbled back to my truck, not even waiting to calm myself before I fled into the traffic and away from that cab.

"What's next?" Claudia said, when I returned to her condo two hours later. She looked a little better and was now dressed in shorts and a T-shirt that said, I ❤ SPIKE. She was barefoot, making us coffee. I still felt sick and I was freezing just looking at her. Her place is all white wood and glass and bare surfaces, which she calls "clean lines." The Christmas tree and lights looked out of place there, but I was glad of them.

I tried to get myself together. "After I left Ziggy's, I checked the motel. He paid cash, left no forwarding address. No luck at the other fleabags, either. I cast around for a while, but he wasn't doing any walking and I couldn't get anything from car tracks." I didn't tell her I'd driven halfway to New Hampshire before I'd gotten hold of myself, and used my work to keep from spinning into another panic. I wrapped my arms around myself, trying to feel less hollow, trying not to puke watching the cream swirl around the top of the coffee.

She saw me hesitate. "Gerry, what's wrong? You look like seven kinds of Hell."

I pushed the coffee away from me. "Every time I've caught a noseful of Smith, it's almost knocked me off my feet. You were right, he's bad."

"Yeah, bad. But why did I take so long to bounce back after I saw him? And you, you're always psyched up, all bloodlusty and rarin' to go, when you find a bad guy. What's different about Smith?"

"I dunno." I shrunk down into myself, not wanting to talk.

"That's not helpful." She went into psychiatrist mode. "Okay, you can't say what's wrong with *Smith*. What do *you* feel?"

"Claudia—"

"Humor me."

I shivered. She was right, but I really didn't want to discuss it. "Every time I think about Smith, I get sick, I feel confused. It's like the world's upside down, like I'm chasing my own tail—"

I shoved the chair back and bolted for the sink. I made it, just before the donut made a repeat appearance, and turned on the tap while I retched. Much as I wanted it to, the sound of running water didn't block out Claudia's exclamation.

"Oh, my God, Gerry. He's one of *us*."

"He can't be." I wiped off my mouth and turned to her.

"That's got to be it. It explains so much—our reactions, his, the way he went berserk in the office—"

"He's just a psycho," I said. But I knew she was right.

"No, Gerry." She took a deep breath. "He's evil. And he's one of *us*!"

"There's no such thing as an evil Fangborn, Claudia," I said. "Not in all our history."

"Maybe not in our history, but what about our future? I've got to check in with the family, let them know what's going on. Maybe the oracles will have something for us. This is *amazing*—"

A sudden, childish urge hit me. "Claud, don't."

"Don't tell the family?"

I nodded. I just didn't want any of this to be true.

"Gotta do it, Gerry. We can't let Smith get away, and if he's what we think he is, they all need to know. This is *big*."

I shrugged miserably.

She put her hand on my shoulder. "It's scary, yes, the idea of evil appearing in our form, with our powers. It's also a tremendous revelation. Gerry, it can tell us a lot about who we are, maybe more than the geneticists or the oracles can, and it can tell us about the nature of evil. It may even foretell the final battle against evil, Gerry. The one where we *win*. Who wouldn't want to be present for that?" Her eyes were alight and her fangs peeked out with her excitement.

I hated her for being excited, but at least that helped shake off the overwhelming emptiness I felt. Time to man up, Gerry. We're still the good guys—

It's just that the bad guys had never looked like us before.

I nodded. "Okay, you contact the family, and I'll hit the Internet. Smith's out there, and until we get a clue or a scent, we're just gonna have to wait."

We exchanged a look. Sensing the presence of evil is one thing. Being able to find it before it acts is quite another. And the idea of evil in the form of a Fangborn was just plain terrifying.

I went home, and no sooner opened the door than I was attacked by a mass of muscle and fur.

"Beemer, get off!" I peeled the big, brown-striped tom off my shoulder and dumped him on the couch. As a kitten, Beemer jumping from the staircase railing onto me was impressive and cute as Hell. Now that he was in the fifteen-pound class, it was less amusing. To me, anyway. Beemer still thought it was a riot. But even he couldn't cheer me up tonight.

As I heated a shepherd's pie I got over at Henry's Market, I listened to the police scanner, but didn't hear anything that would help. As Beemer washed himself on the leather couch next to me, I drank too much and flipped around the TV—a beaut, 40" plasma, with controls to put the *Enterprise* to shame—but there was nothing to keep my attention. Ditto the Internet and the new issue of *Maxim*. If you wanted proof that my kind are born, not made, just do the math: if we could turn normals, not a single lingerie model would be left unbitten. Trust me.

Frustrated in every sense of the word, I didn't drift off until just before the alarm rang.

Groaning, I got up, dumped kibble into Beemer's bowl, and hit the bricks, not because I had a lead, but because I had a headache worse than any hangover. The memory of evil left unchecked is one of the downsides of the job, and I didn't even want to think about what Smith meant.

I walked by Ziggy's, but Annie wasn't working. The day outside matched my insides: granite gray, cold, depressing. Even the telephone poles were decorated to suit my mood: the neighborhood was papered with missing pet flyers. I knew how I'd feel if Beemer ever went missing:

it'd be a crappy Christmas for the kids worrying about Kitty-Cakes or Bongo or Maxie . . .

Focus on the job, Gerry. Keep it together.

Down by the Willows, I caught a faint scent. The Salem Willows is an amusement park, very small and dated. It's mostly Whack-a-Mole and fried dough stands and rackety rides during the summer. In the winter, it's a wasteland, boarded up and abandoned.

It wasn't abandoned now: Salem PD, state police, and the ME vans were there. My vision and hearing sharpened, and my olfactory nerves went crazy. Smith had been here, not long ago.

Weems was also there. This time, he came right over to me.

"Steuben. Been seeing a lot of you lately." He only reaches my chin, and he's kinda pudgy, so short-man syndrome never helped things between us.

That's why werewolves and vamps have such crappy reputations. The local authorities always notice us sniffing around crime scenes and figure we're the bad guys.

I sipped my coffee. "Been seeing a lot of you, too, Weems. Funny, huh?"

"I ain't laughing." He crossed his arms. "What're you doing here?"

"I'm looking for the guy at the hospital who knocked my sister around."

His face softened, just a little. "Your sister, she's okay."

Suggesting I was not. "C'mon, Weems. I'm trying to catch an asshole here."

"And what're *we* doing?" For an instant, I thought he'd either hit me or have a heart attack. He balled up his fists and turned a shade of red that would have made Santa's tailors envious.

"You know what I mean." I tried to look desperate, no stretch, under the circumstances. "Man, come on. It's *Claudia*."

The stories would have you believe that vampires are incredibly alluring. It's true, they produce a pheromone that seems to make people around them comfortable, which helps vamps in their healing work. Add a good dose of empathy, and yes, vampires hold a definite attraction for normals, who think of it as sexual.

Something about Claudia had long ago hit Weems hard, right between the eyes. She'd hate me throwing her under the bus like that, but if it got me past his defensiveness . . .

I could see that Weems was torn, but he wasn't going to pass up anything that made him look good in front of Claudia. "We got one vic, and it's a wet one. Or it was, a couple of days ago: it's pretty dried up now." Weems looked greenish; he never could stand the sight of blood. "Chest sliced open . . . and the heart removed."

"Jesus." I swallowed. "Got an ID?"

"Homeless guy. My guess, he was either flopping in the shed over there, or he was lured in."

"You said *sliced* open?"

"You're a ghoul, Steuben." He sighed. "ME says a big knife, it looks like. They need more tests."

I nodded. If there was one thing we could agree on, it was the reluctance of the ME to spill details.

He hesitated. "The chest was opened up like . . . ah, jeez. It reminded me of one of those Advent calendars. The skin pulled back square, and the ribs broken to get the heart out."

Maybe he didn't like me seeing him queasy, maybe he just regretted telling me as much as he did, but Weems's face hardened. "Get lost, Steuben. I find you nosing around, you'll be sorry."

"Merry Christmas to you, too, Weems." I left.

"They found a body," I said, after I let myself into Claudia's condo.

Claudia was excited. "Yeah, I know, I just heard it on the news."

It was her day off and while Claud was waiting to hear something solid back from the family—who were going crazy over the news—she was trying to work out a profile for Smith. Maybe she was doing rote work for the same reason I was: to keep from thinking about our world being turned inside out. I still felt like I had the pins knocked out from under me and I hated that uncertainty.

"Down the Willows?" I said, surprised. That was quick.

"No, pulled from the harbor." She frowned. "The woman had been in there about a week. They said 'mutilated,' which usually means something worse."

"So was mine." I told her what I'd just learned from Weems. "They know who she was?"

"A local prostitute, was all they said."

"There's a chance it's not the same guy, not our guy—" I said.

"I'm not willing to bet on that."

"Me, neither."

"He's selecting people on the periphery of society," she said. "Going for those who live under the radar."

I considered where the trail had led me: the abandoned drug den, the dry spell in the emergency room, and—oh, Hell. Three missing cats in one neighborhood was just too much coincidence. I told Claudia. "I guess he's been doing this for a while."

She nodded. "And is escalating. He's refining his ritual, getting bolder, going for less vulnerable, more public targets. It's typical that he started with animals." The look on her face didn't bode well for Smith when we caught him. "Gerry, it's only going to get worse from here. I'm guessing that he's attributing some special significance to the date—the full moon, Christmas . . ."

Suddenly, I knew. "It *is* Christmas," I said. I told her Weems's description of the corpse, what he'd said about Advent calendars. "Doesn't that sound like what you're talking about? Little, uh, treats leading up to the big day?"

She nodded. "Right. Christmas. Good eyes on Weems."

I snorted. "He's my hero." But Christmas was just two days away. "My question is, Why did Smith have to call a cab?"

"He didn't have a car," she answered promptly. "Weems brought him in, right?"

I made a face at her. "But if Smith is responsible for the murders, he must have a car."

"He can't afford to let it go out in public. Too many people could see . . . what?"

"Bloodstains? Cracked window?"

"Too recognizable," she said. "A truck with a business logo on it, contractors, deliveries—"

"Right, it's got to blend in, but not the sort of thing you'd drive for private stuff." I thought a minute, then an idea hit me. "Like a police car. Maybe it isn't Smith! Maybe it's Weems!"

"Gerry. Get real. Weems is your bête noir, and he's a dickhead, but he's not our guy."

"He was at the hospital." I ticked off my reasons on my fingers, *loving* that Smith might just be a garden-variety psycho, his trail confused by Weems. "He was at the donut shop. He's been dogging my tracks all day, and every time I saw him, I felt the call to Change."

"All places you'd expect to see a cop investigating the same case as we are. Have you ever wanted to Change because of Weems before now?" She put her hand on mine; it was warm as toast. "I know you don't like him, but you're getting distracted by this. You've always been so damned sure about everything—"

That was the problem: I couldn't be sure about anything anymore if Smith was Fangborn.

I pulled away. "I don't think so. I think you were picking up on his vibes, the same time you were dealing with some ordinary, run-of-the-mill loony, and that's why you thought it was Smith."

"You're wrong," she said. "Weems has nothing to do with this. I think you want it to be Weems so you don't have to consider that there might be an evil out there we haven't seen before. I get it, Ger: you want things to be cut-and-dried. But now we know . . . it can't be like that."

"Whatever." I turned away.

"Don't dismiss me, Gerry."

You know about that traditional conflict between werewolves and vampires? It's really just a sibling thing.

"Claudia, just because—"

"Sssh!" Claudia was pointing to the TV.

The news was on. A school bus, its driver, and six kids were missing from their daycare center.

* * *

"Okay," I said, "we've got the fake address at the Point, a murder at the Willows, a body in the harbor. Throw in the missing pets, and we have someone with a familiarity with the waterfront. That's a couple of big neighborhoods to cover."

"He needs space, and he needs a place where people won't hear . . . screams." Claudia was looking at the map spread out in front of us. "He's sticking with what's familiar to him, which is good for us, but he's also an organized psychopath, which is bad."

"The houses are too close together, here and here," I said, pointing out two neighborhoods. "That leaves the warehouses in the industrial park down at the Point and the coal plant down here." I pointed to a neighborhood that was near, by water, but on the other side of town, by land.

"A school bus is going to stick out in either place," Claudia said. "Is he going to take them out to sea?"

"If he is, we're pretty well screwed," I said. "Protective coloring— where can you take six crying kids and a school bus where no one will notice?"

We looked at each other, then simultaneously at one of the neighborhoods we had just rejected. A short distance from my own house, separated by large parking lots and a playing field, was the middle school, now empty for the holidays.

It's not that we need the moon to shift, though that helps. It's easier to run around as a wolf when there aren't many people around. It's easier to pick up a faint trail with the dust settled from the day. It's not that we need the moon, but somehow, it makes it easier for me, the same way the sun takes the poison out of vamps like Claudia. You'd have to talk to our scientists who are working out exactly how we Fangborn work, but if you think of it like a vulture's bare head helping to kill the bacteria they pick up, or photosynthesis, taking nutrients from the sunlight, that's probably close. All I know is that Claudia couldn't taste the blood and clean it, cauterize the wound, and numb the memory without sunlight to charge her up. And in the same way—don't ask me how, I'm not one of the geeks—I get recharged by the moon.

Plus, lots of bad guys also wait for night to work. Makes it easier on us all.

The moon was full and low on the horizon as we parked down the street from the school. We ran down the plan again: check the school and then call the cops if we find anything.

Simple, if we were right. If we weren't already too late.

"Got the gear?" I asked Claudia.

She nodded, held up the leash—her excuse for being out with a very large dog—and a charged cell phone. As for me, while I hate what people inflict on their pets—birthday parties, pedicures, Halloween costumes—I will always be grateful for the dog-clothing craze. And grateful to the guy who invented stretch fabrics: my Lycra doggie track suit makes it a heck of a lot easier if I have to Change back to human and don't want to be buck-naked.

Claudia doubled the knots on her bootlaces, tied her hair back, and we went into the schoolyard.

The bus was there, all right, on the side, cold and silent as an empty grave. Sure, school was out and it was night, but who notices a school bus outside a school? The schoolyard had been badly plowed, so there were no clear tracks, but it only took me a minute to find the basement door they'd used, the lock broken.

The reek hit me as soon as we got the door open. This time, I didn't resist the Change.

The rush of adrenaline and endorphins and other hormones blotted out whatever pain shrieking bones forced through evolutionary growth in an instant might bring. Nature wouldn't be so cruel as to put this burden on us without compensation. The bloodlust didn't hurt, either, and it was only Claud's warning hand on my back that reminded me not to howl with the delight of it. Smith's spoor was worse than any I'd ever smelled, overwhelming the traces of new linoleum, old wax, and textbooks. It was nearly unbearable to my lupine nose, but one thought, a bloodthirsty, simple joy, cleared of all human doubt and fear, overwhelmed even that:

It was time to track and to tear.

I stepped out of my boots and glanced up at Claud, who was down on one knee; the reek was hitting her just as badly. It was always harder for her; vamps don't have the same chemical buffer that protects wolves. Her skin took on a violet cast visible even in the shadows, and her eyes were wide and bright. Her facial features broadened, her nose receded, and her fingers lengthened.

She stood up, shook herself, and nodded. As she packed my boots into her backpack, I saw the gleam of her viperish fangs extending, the glint of a streetlight on the fine pattern of snakescale, an armor of supple, thickened skin. Snakes have always been associated with healing and transformation—there's a reason they're on the staff of Asclepius—but they've got a rep for danger, too.

I whined and stared at her neck. Her hand went up, and she found the pearls she'd forgotten to take off.

"Thankths," she said, with a slight hiss. Still largely humanoid, fangs and a forked tongue make speech awkward, but not impossible. She stowed the necklace in her bag, and nodded.

I led the way, as stealthy as a shadow. I cast around, stopped, panted, and tried again, but with no luck. There was no one single track to pick up. Smith'd been here long enough for the basement to be so saturated with his stench that I could barely breathe.

I couldn't detect the children. I hoped we weren't too late.

Claudia nodded. She pointed at the first door, and we both listened. Nothing.

She tried it; locked solid.

The next was an unlocked closet. The stink was there, too, but less. The bus driver was stashed in there. There was a pulse, faint and fading.

Claudia fanged down, called 911. We continued.

The next door opened silently; I could smell WD-40 recently applied to the hinges. No way to tell Claud, but she pointed to the duct tape across the lock, and I nodded. We went in.

The children were there. Even under Smith's foulness, I could tell they were alive. I felt a surge of delight.

They were drugged, only half-awake; a light on the playground offered just enough illumination for a normal to see forms without detail. My nose told me of full diapers, fear, and baby shampoo.

Smith was nowhere around. We went quietly, just in case.

"Hang on," Claudia said. She Changed back about halfway, just enough to keep her powers on deck, but not so far that the first thing the kids saw was a pale purple lady with no nose and very big teeth.

She went over to them quickly. "Hey, you guys? Let's get you fixed up and we'll get you home, okay? My dog Chewie is going to do some tricks for you. He's really big, but he's really, really friendly. Chewie, come!"

That was my cue. I knew to play it dumb and sweet over in the faint light so the kids would focus on me. That way, they'd be less afraid and they wouldn't notice Claudia practicing her leech-craft. I spend my time fighting evil, not practicing party tricks, but whenever I fell over, the kids laughed, so it was okay. And as soon as Claudia got one kid untied, her razor nails dancing scalpels over the duct tape, I was there, his new best friend, and they were so busy patting me they forgot to be afraid. Under the guise of inspecting their wounded hands, she got to work, biting their wrists, narcotizing the pain, neutralizing their terror, sucking out Smith's drugs, dimming their memories. I could sense her body reacting to the blood and emotion she was taking in, her muscles rippling, nearly all trace of humanity lost from her features even as she healed the little ones.

She'd just finished the last one when *he* was on her. Even as I picked up on the fresh scent—snow mixed with spoiled milk and rotting fish heads—Smith rocketed from the shadows, moving faster than anything human.

If I knew he was there, it meant Claudia knew, too. She shoved the kid toward me as Smith landed on her. She rolled with him as far away from us as she could.

In spite of Claudia's ministrations, the kids whimpered. I grabbed the last one by the hood of her jacket and gently pulled her the rest of the way to the group. I stood between them and the brawl, nudging the kids to stand behind me, thankful Disney had removed their fear of large wild animals.

It took everything I had to keep from jumping in and ripping Smith apart, but I had to keep the children safe. And there's not much that can stop my sister when she's pissed and Changed; for all her tweedy skirts and bookishness, she's as much a warrior as I am.

Smith was putting up a pretty good fight and the sonofabitch knew how to use a knife: Claudia would need a week on the roof to recover from this. I was glad of the dark, that the children's eyes weren't as sharp as mine, that they couldn't see the amount of blood that Claudia was letting.

She was winning. Maybe Smith wasn't Fangborn, maybe just some kind of freak human genetic anomaly—

You could practically feel the energy she expended fill the room, almost blotting out the horror of Smith. Righteous violence in the cause of justice—

I let out a low growl; there was *too* much energy, the air was sizzling as if every Fangborn in New England was Changing next to me.

Claudia screamed.

Smith had Changed. An unholy transformation, something never before seen in the world as I knew it: evil taking on the shape of a werewolf.

If I'd had time for rational, human thought, I would have been slowed by what *shouldn't* have been happening, by what was impossible, but the pull to attack was so strong I almost burst out of my skin. I bunched up and launched myself at Smith.

Claudia threw herself out of the way as I bowled the other wolf out of the room. We skidded into the hallway, unable to get a purchase on the cold, polished cement floor. With a scrabble of claws, I was up, but he was just a second faster and knocked me down again, snapping at my eyes. I slashed at his gut and jerked my head out of the way, feeling his hot breath and drool on my ears. I whipped around and grabbed at his muzzle; I was bigger than he was and he almost pulled away before I closed my teeth. I caught him, barely, by the tender tip of his nose and the soft skin under his jaw. Teeth slid through flesh and I held on; he tried to push me away with his front paws, but was more effective with his rear claws, raking across my belly.

I smelled my own blood, but held on for dear life. He couldn't pull out of my grasp without tearing himself and I couldn't let him go.

The door opened and cold air washed over us. I heard a shout and recognized Weems.

He shouted again. I could smell Weems's fear.

Weems drew his pistol. He was going to shoot.

Well, I couldn't let him shoot *me*. I let go and Smith hurled himself at the doorway and Weems.

Thoughts flashed through my head: If Smith landed on Weems, I could grab him before he did much damage. If he knocked Weems out of the way, or took a bullet or six, so much the better for me.

Damn. He bolted right past Weems. He couldn't afford to get caught as a werewolf any more than I could. The prospect of decades of lab experiments made a life sentence at Cedar Junction look like a week at Sandals.

Sweat-soaked polyester, terror, boiled coffee, and roast beef: Weems had had dinner at Big Freddy's. If I planted a dirty, doggy paw in his face as I chased after Smith, I'm sure it was an accident.

Smith was nowhere to be seen as I raced down the street away from the school, but it didn't matter: he was leaving a trail of blood that any Cub Scout could have followed, and his scent was so strong there might as well have been a spotlight on him.

I cut through snowy backyards and vaulted a chain-link fence: Christmas lights lit the snow and the smell of cooking meats and seafood wasn't even a momentary distraction. Another burst of speed brought me down to the historic district on the waterfront, the eighteenth-century houses decorated with candles and garlands.

The tear in my belly was bad; I could feel the shock of the cold air through fur even as my muscle re-knit itself. There was a sharp pain whenever I moved my left hind leg. The icy snow, dirty with sand and road salt, packed itself in between the pads of my paws, slowing me down and throwing off my gait. Blood—mine and Smith's—was matted in my fur, and my jaw ached.

The trail of blood was getting heavier, though: Smith was also slowing down. In spite of my wounds, I sped up, eager to end this.

But part of me hoped Smith would never stop. If he stopped, I'd kill him, and my job would be finished. Then I'd have to think about what was happening. I wasn't sure if my frail human brain could deal with it.

I leapt onto a back porch, tensed, then sailed over the back of the deck onto the sidewalk of Derby Street. I skidded on the icy bricks of the crosswalk, and barely missed getting hit by an Escalade. I yelped, feeling the breeze as the SUV swerved past.

The waterfront opened up in front of me. The heavy clouds parted for an instant and the full moon shone down on the blood that led straight down Derby Wharf, which stretched out a quarter of a mile into the harbor.

Unless Smith wanted to swim in life-sucking cold water toward the winking lights of Marblehead, he had nowhere to go except back to me. I grinned, as only a wolf drunk on power can.

There was no one out, and I was glad; it was usually a place for evening strolls, the marks of lesser canines blazoned against the snow-banks. I padded down the wide gravel path, catching my breath, preparing myself for the last fight.

Smith was smarter than I gave him credit for. He timed his attack for the instant the lighthouse lamp whirled toward me, washing the shadows together and reducing my field of vision.

Keeping my eyes lowered and narrowed, my ears back, I made myself wait until the last moment. Then I sprang at him, just as hard as I could. I caught Smith with his head still up, and seized him by the throat, biting down with every bit of strength I had. His momentum carried him over me, and as he fell, his own weight tore his flesh off in my mouth. Hot blood poured and he dropped dead at my feet.

He might have been a predator with a hero's weapons, but I was a hero with true purpose.

I spat out the fur and gore as the moonlight flooded the wharf and harbor. Steam rose from the wounds of the dead wolf, blood black on the snow. Power from the kill, from having slain one of my own kind, almost knocked me off my feet, and it was possible I was the first one ever in history to have experienced it.

Evil just doesn't exist in the Fangborn. At least, it hadn't before now.

I threw my head back and howled, my inhuman blood singing, the completeness and rightness of my triumph dizzying.

But somewhere in the back of my brain, the part that stays human, I knew it was the last time I'd feel that way.

On Christmas Eve, Claudia found me down in the basement of my house. It's finished with mats on the floors and walls so we can train in private.

"That's some sweat you're working up there," she yelled. She was wearing her T-shirt with the bull's-eye printed over her heart, the one that says, GO AHEAD AND TRY IT, BUFFY.

I was flaked out on the floor in three layers of sweats, my headphones on, music turned to eleven. I considered her statement, then showed her a finger.

She came over to the stereo, cranked it up to fourteen or twenty so I had to pull the headphones off, then she switched off the CD. She glanced at the player.

"*Disintegration*. Nice. And have you been down here since yesterday, moping out to The Cure? I'm going to take my old CDs away from you if you're going to behave like an adolescent."

"I am an adolescent." And I am, by my people's standards. Just a pup.

"I get that. Gerry, you *peed* on Weems's car!"

I shrugged. It seemed like the thing to do at the time.

After I'd returned, still wolfself, to the school, Claudia had sold most of the story to a suspicious Weems. She was out walking her dog when she saw the school bus. Not wanting to feel like a fool if it wasn't the missing children, she'd explored, then found the kids. The kids, still under her chemical thrall, had confirmed it: the scary man's dog had attacked the nice lady's doggie, who chased both the bad guys away. Weems later found Smith's body at the wharf, dead, without a mark on him save for his stitched-up arm.

She knelt beside me. "Gerry, Smith is a shock; I buy that. I was rattled, too. It's scary as Hell. The family computer lists have been lighting up with the discussion, and none of the historians have anything like this. *Ever.*"

"I'm not scared, Claud," I said. "And I get that this is major. It's just that . . ."

I took a breath; it was even harder to say out loud than it was to admit to myself. "I liked knowing that we Fangborn were the righteous ones, and that whatever we hunted was *always* wrong. No doubts, never. I always thought it was the payoff for the work we do." It also meant, no matter what my opinion, that Weems was at least nominally on our side.

She cocked her head. "You mean, in addition to the super-strength, healing, and longevity?"

"Yeah."

"And the rush that comes after the Change?"

"Well . . . yeah."

She frowned. "You're young and you're being greedy and you're forgetting the First Lesson."

I scowled. "'The work is the reward.' You sound like Grandpa."

"There's a good reason for that. He was right." She hunkered down against the wall next to me. "Look, everyone reaches a crisis of faith at some point in his life. For me, it was trying to figure out if we had the right to live outside human law, learning the difference between *law* and *justice*. It's part of the life. It makes us understand what it is to be human, why that's precious and to be protected. Normals never get half of what we have, and go through life in doubt."

"We're not human, Claud. Never will be. And now we get the doubt, too."

She shook her head. "We're closer to them than anything else. Biologically and spiritually. We need that connection. And you know that killing Smith was right, even if he was one of us."

But no Fangborn had ever killed Fangborn before. No Fangborn had ever manifested pure evil before . . . I couldn't turn off the voice in my head.

Claudia talked for a long time about the community of the

Fangborn, duty, honor, and all that crap. I listened. A lot of it made sense.

I nodded. "You're right. I need time, that's all. Thanks."

"No problem. I'm just glad I got here before you got into the Nine Inch Nails." Relief flooded her features, which told me exactly how rocky she thought I looked. "So. You packed?"

"No. It won't take me long." This year, our Christmas present to each other was tickets to Aruba. Expensive, but we both needed the sunshine right now.

She nodded, then eyed me sternly. "But you're gonna go to midnight Mass, right?"

"Probably. I gotta go for a walk, first. Clear my head." I hauled myself up, muscles stiff not from the fight, but from lying around. Any harm I take while wolfself heals rapidly, as long as I remain wolfy, but any hurt I get while in human form reappears when I revert back to human form.

"Good. I'll see you there. And Gerry?"

"Yeah, Claud?"

She wrinkled her nose. "Take a shower, would you?"

I flipped her the bird again, and got my jacket. She smiled as she left, and I knew I had her convinced. That's the good thing about having a shrink for a sister: you learn what they look for and you can give it to them.

Yes, her words made sense. They just did nothing to take away my pain.

I pulled on my duck boots, hat, scarf, and gloves. I probably didn't need so much—it was over thirty degrees—but ever since the fight, I just couldn't get warm.

I walked a long time and found myself at the foot of Derby Wharf. I went out far enough to let the holiday lights of the street fall behind me, until I was alone in the frigid dark. Bloodstains blurred the snow, which had been trampled by the locals looking for the serial killer's savage dog. A fierce hellhound roaming Salem, one more myth in the making.

I watched the lighthouse beam skim the surface of the dark water. Listened to the soft slap of waves against the stone wharf. Anyone with a lick of insight could feel the remnants of the power that had been expended here.

In our family's annals, there was nothing like this, but now I had to wonder: Who else had we missed? Or if this was a really new development, what did it mean? The only thing I knew was that my certainty about my place in the world—my armor and my sword—was shattered.

I felt the silence all around me, city noises muffled by the snow, and tried to find the bottom of the sea of pain I felt. The uncertainty was crushing, the loss of faith like the loss of a limb. I felt broken and made a fool of, mocked by the universe for my belief.

I took a deep breath, the kind you take at the crossroads when the dark man shows up and offers you the world in exchange for your grubby soul. As I watched the obsidian water, I took another breath and realized that if I couldn't manage the leap of faith that Claudia described, then I had to make a leap of another kind.

Down the street from Derby Wharf is a little bar called In a Pig's Eye. It's a local joint; there's no television and they pull the best pints in town.

Annie works there nights.

It was about half full, the folks who were getting one more drink in before Mass and the ones whose family were the other strangers on bar stools.

"Jeez, Gerry, you been sick or something? You look kinda peaky." She set down a coaster in front of me. "Winter Warmer?"

"Thanks. Just . . . out of it, I guess." I suddenly remembered my rank-smelling sweats and two days' growth of beard, and kept my jacket zipped. Hell.

"I bet. I read about Claudia in the paper. You must have *freaked*."

One of the things I've learned to live with is the fact that I'll never get credit for being on the scene, for doing the job. "I worry about her, but she's good at taking care of herself." Then I couldn't resist, sweats or no. "And besides. Chewie wouldn't let anything happen to her."

She put the dark beer down in front of me, a perfect half inch of froth at the top. "No. He's a sweetie."

I felt myself flush, remembering the perfume of Annie's ankles, her hand on the back of my neck as she talked to Claudia one summer night. We'd been coming home from work and I'd still been intoxicated by the kill when we ran into Annie. It's one of my fondest memories. "You like dogs?"

She shrugged. "Depends. Like people, really. You gotta take them one at a time, you know?"

Ask her out, I told myself, ask her out right now, coffee, a drink, anything, or so help me, I'll— "How do you feel about Aruba?" I felt myself go red again: that was not what I meant to say. It was too much, too soon, too pimp, oh shit—

Annie stopped wiping down the bar.

Suddenly, the bottomless water seemed a better choice.

"I'd prefer to start with a drink, maybe dinner," she said slowly. "That is, if you're really, actually, *finally* getting the guts to ask me out?"

"Uh . . . yeah." I swallowed. "That okay?"

"Yeah. But it took you long enough." She glanced at me. "You tough guys, you're all just pussycats. You aren't always a big pussycat, are you, Gerry?"

Mostly I'm a big wolf, I thought giddily. "Never again," I vowed. "How's tomorrow night?"

"Can't." She looked at me funny. "It's Christmas tomorrow, remember? I'm going snowshoeing at Bradley Palmer State Park in the morning."

I wrinkled my brow. An odd tradition, but nice, I s'pose . . .

She blew out her cheeks. "You know I'm Wiccan, right? I like Christmas, but I observe the Solstice."

She looked a little defensive, but I could barely contain myself. I forced myself to take a deep breath. "Trust me when I say that mixed relationships are not a problem for me."

She relaxed, then gave me a look that warmed me instantly, straight through. "If you invite me over for breakfast, I'll ditch the snowshoeing. But I have to leave by noon, because I promised Kelly I'd take her shift at the shelter so she can be with her family."

"Breakfast is at nine o'clock!" I could barely get the words out fast enough.

"Claudia won't mind?"

"Nah. I'll call her when I get home." Claudia had been pushing me to ask Annie out from the first time I'd mentioned her. "She's good people, not an evil bone in her body," Claudia'd said. And Claudia knows bones, good and evil.

"I'll be there." Annie smiled, so sexy I felt my knees go to jelly. "I made a batch of my famous chocolate-chip muffins; I'll bring them."

Into nature, civic-minded, and a cook? I realized I was grinning like an idiot, so I drank the rest of my beer, to keep from proposing to her right then and there, my head ringing with every Christmas carol ever written.

The Werewolf Before Christmas

Kat Richardson

Kat Richardson is the author of the Greywalker paranormal detective novels. She is a former magazine editor from Los Angeles who now lives on a sailboat in the Seattle area with her husband and two ferrets. She rides a motorcycle and doesn't own a TV, so she's only seen one episode of Buffy in her life—poor Kat! On the other hand . . . she has more time for writing and World of Warcraft and working on the Northwest regional board of the Mystery Writers of America. This is her first werewolf story.

'Twas the night before Christmas—well, the late afternoon, in fact, but who could tell at the North Pole in the middle of winter—and Matthias the werewolf was knee-deep in reindeer guts. Really, it was the deer's own fault for having that glowing red nose that had made it ever so easy to pick him out in the gloom. There it had been, like a neon sign saying FAST FOOD and Matt being like Yellow Dog Dingo—always hungry— had taken the opportunity for a quick snack.

It hadn't been as easy as he had expected. Something about the moon magic was really messed up at the North Pole, and he couldn't manage to be quite wolf or man, but an uncomfortable, hairy hybrid of both—but at least he was warm. So he'd vaulted the fence of the reindeer stockade and chased the light-footed lunch to its doom. It was pretty tasty, too: corn-fed.

He'd chowed down with the alacrity you'd expect of a man or wolf who'd been lost in the tundra for most of a week following that stupid, stupid plane crash. That couldn't really be called Matt's fault, either, since the compass and GPS had both been on the fritz when the moon poked its beam through the window. He'd always embraced his wolf nature, and when the moon insisted, he threw himself into the frenzy of the change with the enthusiasm of a pig in a wallow. Well, maybe that had been a bad idea after all. . . .

What had definitely been a bad idea had been going to the North Pole in the first place. What had he been thinking? That people wouldn't mind a werewolf so much up there? That he could be free to be a wolf as much as he wanted and never have to worry about people? That hadn't worked out so well, and when he'd tried to go home by sneaking on the plane and ambushing the crew, things had gone straight to handbasketdom.

He'd been wandering around, half-man, half-wolf, and increasingly hungry since he'd dug himself out of the snow that had buried the plane on impact. The human part of him knew there were weather and satellite monitoring stations near the pole—faking the paperwork for a job at a monitoring station was what had got him to the North Pole in the first place—so he figured he'd find someone or something useful eventually so long as he didn't starve first. Luck or Fate had offered up the reindeer with the funky face and Matthias had grabbed the opportunity with all paws.

He was rooting for "good bits" when the man in red showed up. . . .

He was a medium-sized fellow with a neat, full beard as thick and white as the snow and he had a funny sort of hat that sat on his head in a floppy red peak, something like a small bishop's miter that had gone a bit soft. A black shadow clung to his back and stout black boots stuck out under his long red coat of thick wool trimmed in white fur and held closed by six fancy gold braid things down the front. He held a tall walking stick that looked like a gold shepherd's crook in one red-mittened hand as he stood in the gateway of the stockade and clucked his tongue in disappointment.

"Ahh . . . me. This does present a problem."

Matthias raised his head and growled his best menacing growl. He was stuck in the back corner of the stockade under a half-shed that kept the snow off the manger, and the easiest way out would mean running toward the man in red. His human brain was still a bit groggy and he wasn't thinking as well as he might have had he been a little less wolfy and a little less excited by the kill. He hoped the fellow would just back away so he could hop the fence and follow the man to whatever conveyance had brought him. Then Matt could steal it and get the hell out of the Frozen North. Or at least that was the first plan that suggested itself to his half-lupine brain and it sounded like a good one to him.

But the man held his ground and peered at the werewolf draped in reindeer innards. "Don't I know you . . . ?" the man queried. He held out his free hand and a black book extruded from the shadow behind him and slid into his grasp. He glanced at the pages. "Hmmm . . . Oh, yes. Matthias Vulfkind. Haven't seen you in quite a while, Mattie, and it appears you've been very, very naughty indeed. And now, poor Rudy, too. Ah, what will I do with you?"

Matt stared at the man in red and growled again, forming rough words in his half-human throat even as an entirely human idea began wriggling around in the back of his mind. "Who are you?"

The man in red gave a sad smile. "It has been a while, but you called me Rider and Sunnercla when you were very small and not so shaggy. Do you remember?"

Matthias shook his head. He thought it might be best to just rip the man's throat out and get on with his plans, but the man seemed to calm him in some eerie way and he just couldn't do it. It seemed . . . wrong, which was a concept the werewolf had not bothered with in a long time.

The man shook his head, too. "No? Well, then. I am Nicholas of Myrna. Most people call me Santa Claus now."

Matthias drew back in surprise as the idea in the back of his head popped to the front like a tiny lightbulb exploding. Oh no, it couldn't be. . . . "Father Christmas?"

Santa Claus nodded. "Yes, that too. And Saint Nicholas and Kris Kringle and many other names. And as it is Christmas Eve and you've eaten my lead reindeer, I'm afraid I find myself in a bit of a predicament, Mattie."

The werewolf looked at the bloody carcass of the red-nosed reindeer that lay spread around him and cringed. "Uh-oh."

"Indeed," Saint Nicholas said with a nod. "While it's within my power to raise a child from the dead, I'm afraid it doesn't work on rein-deer. So, it'll have to be you, Matthias Vulfkind."

"Oh no!" Matt howled. He leaped to scramble over the nearest part of the stockade fence and found himself floating in the very thin air of the North Pole's perpetual winter like an ornament from a Christmas tree's bough.

"Oh, yes. Though you are now a man and half a beast, your child-hood memory of me gives me power over you this day." Saint Nicholas held his crozier aloft as if the hook magically held Matthias in the air.

"I'm no deer!" the werewolf objected. "I'm big and I'm hairy!"

"Reindeer are hairy, too. You'll do."

"I'm a predator!"

"The deer won't mind—they've run with stranger creatures than you."

"But I can't fly!" the werewolf barked, which was certainly true when you considered the recent fate of the airplane.

"I can fix that. . . ." said Sinterklaas.

Saint Nicholas reached his free hand into his pocket and brought out a fistful of something that glittered and chimed with the laughter of small children. He flung the stuff toward the werewolf, muttering in Latin—Matt didn't know the words, but he rememberd the sound from his time in Catholic school—and a cloud of sparkling brown dust burst into the air and settled over Matthias.

The dust smelled of cinnamon and brandy and it tasted of ginger-bread and apples, and where it fell into his eyes, Matt saw visions of magical creatures in diaphanous raiment who danced and spun on col-ored ribbons of magic. He sneezed and snorted and shook his fur, whimpered and rubbed his face in the snow, but he couldn't get rid of the stuff or the strange feeling that crept over him. And then the were-wolf was overcome with a giggling, effervescent sensation as if his whole body were made of champagne bubbles. And oh, it tickled! And oh, it itched! And oh, how it made his nose wriggle and twitch and he didn't care for it one bit.

He set up a howl and pawed at the sky, which made him flip into the air and execute a perfect aerobatic loop that would have been the envy of any stunt pilot. He didn't like that much, either, especially when he knocked his head against the stockade railings on his way back down.

"Oh! Oh, what is that . . . *stuff*?" he moaned.

"It's Christmas Cheer," Kris Kringle replied. "It's made of the dust of Christmas cookies, some mulled wine, and a bit of Christmas magic. And cinnamon, because I'm very fond of cinnamon. Perhaps a hint of brandy, too. Just to keep warm, you understand."

"It's nasty!" Matthias whined, pawing at his poor, sensitive nose. He just couldn't get the smell of cinnamon out of it.

"Funny," said Father Christmas, stroking his beard thoughtfully, "I didn't know you were related to Ebenezer Scrooge. . . ."

"Who?"

"Oh, never mind. He reformed. Maybe you can, too."

Matthias growled.

"Now, now. None of that." And with no more than a nod, Santa summoned two elves who seemed to rise up from the very ground on each side of Matthias. They had long pointy ears and pointed chins and slanted, pointy eyes—in fact, they were altogether pointy and pale and rather terrifying. They reminded him of the administrators at the children's home and the nuns who'd rapped his knuckles with rulers and he quailed in remembered fear.

Without a word, the two elves put their hands on the werewolf and guided him out of the stockade and around a stand of firs to the courtyard of a large stone house that Matthias was quite sure couldn't have been there before. In the middle of the courtyard stood a huge, old-fashioned sleigh that was painted bright red with shiny black trim. A horse had been painted just in front of the driver's seat, and as Matthias was led past it, the painted horse turned its head to watch him. The werewolf shivered and turned his gaze to the team of eight reindeer harnessed to the strange vehicle.

He hadn't seen many reindeer before, but he was sure these were the extra-large size. Compared to them, his dinner had been a runt. Had he been on all fours, these fellows would have towered over him; shambling as he was, their gleaming eyes were not much below his own. The animals snorted and shook their heads so their crowns of thick, fuzzy antlers menaced the interloper. Plainly, they knew he had noshed on their diminutive red-nosed buddy.

It seemed strange to be in front of the reindeer. As the elves began buckling him into the harness, something clicked in Matthias's brain and he thought, "This time the prey will be chasing me," and a sudden horror came upon him thinking of all those sharp hooves and hard antlers just behind his brushy tail, the owners pawing the air as each and every one of the reindeer ran their enchanted hearts out in hopes of extracting revenge for Rudolph.

His docility dropped away and the werewolf fought and twisted, struggling to get out of the harness that would link him to the angry reindeer team. But no matter how he writhed, snapped, and clawed, he couldn't extract himself from the grip of the elves. In a twinkling he was strapped in tight. Just in front of two huge bucks who snickered and showed him their teeth. Oh, this was going to be a bad night. . . .

The sharp crack of a whip flicked just above his ears and his tormentor in red called out, "Ho, there, Matthias! Pull!" which was entirely unnecessary, as the gunshot sound of the lash had set him instantly bolting forward, baying in fury. The reindeer lurched forward also, clicking their antlers and gnashing their teeth at him as Saint Nick called out, "On Dasher, on Dancer, on Prancer and Vixen, on Comet, on Cupid, on Donder and Blitzen!"

Matthias vaguely rememberd the poem about Saint Nicholas and his reindeer team, but he had never thought about which ones were which. Now he guessed the last were the names of the brutes behind him since they snorted puffs of breath as hot as hell's own on his back and snapped their teeth at his heels. He tried to turn his head and snap back, but the reins held tight in the red-suited tyrant's fists kept him from it. He yipped in frustration and ran as hard as he could, mounting into the sky with every bound.

The sky! At first, he thought he'd lose his lunch as the white land dropped away beneath them and the whole conveyance—reindeer, Santa, sleigh, and all—mounted into the crystalline blackness of the polar night with himself at the front, hauling like a dray horse and howling as he went. But as he pelted through the air, he noticed how fast he was going—faster than he'd ever run on land—and with such little effort! The night sky felt like black velvet against his paws, his nose smelled scents it had never smelled so crisply, and the giddiness of the Christmas Cheer drew a wolfen howl of delight from him.

Santa Claus laughed from his sleigh and shouted, "Marvelous! Pull on, lad! Pull on!"

He didn't need to be urged twice. This was the best running he'd ever had! He dashed on across the gorgeous, moon-kissed night, not even minding the hell-breath of the reindeer at his rear. Tiny twitches of the reins pulled him around, but he hardly noticed, so enamored was he of the fabulous flight of the werewolf.

It was wonderful, like having his own pack rampaging across the sky, and he didn't realize Santa was slowly directing him downward until a snow-crusted cluster of crazy-quilt onion domes hove into view only inches below his scrambling paws. He yipped and skidded as the roofs rose to trip him and the sleigh bumped to an uneven stop on the roof as the man in red called out, "Whoa!"

Picking himself back up from where he'd landed on his nose with his rear paws ahead of his front ones, Matthias glared at Father Christmas. "What's this about?" the werewolf growled.

"It's our first stop, Mattie. Remember that it's my job to deliver gifts to worthy children on Christmas Eve."

"Not *every* child," Matt snorted.

"No, of course not. Just Christian children—and a few corner cases. One must have limits. I couldn't possibly manage every child's holiday wish. Not without help, at least."

And the red-suited saint walked off across the roofs with a sack slung over his back and his uncanny shadow at his heels. The snow swirled up around the man and he vanished into the white glimmer like static on TV.

Matt hunkered on his haunches, thinking, and scratched one ear, keeping a wary eye on Donder and Blitzen, whose attempts to arrange a pincer attack and bite him on the backside were only partially thwarted by the bells on the deer harnesses. The werewolf growled at them and they backed off, blinking and making reindeer smiles like candy wouldn't melt in their mouths.

"Now, now, Matthias. Don't be rude to your teammates," Père Noel chastened him, appearing out of the snow-mist, smelling of apple cider and evergreens, and climbing back into the sled without his sack. The dark shadow flowed across the ground and oozed into the sleigh, too.

The shadow gave him the creeps, but before the werewolf could say anything, the man in the sleigh called out, cracked his whip, and the enchanted deer team—with the wolfman at its head—rose again into the star-spangled night.

But the bizarre sleigh-team leader was thinking as they careened through the sky, and when they landed on the next roof, he asked, "How do you know which children are worthy?"

"I keep a list, you know," Sinterklaas replied. He motioned to the shadow beside him and it solidified into a thin, angular, hook-nosed man with a dark mien and black clothes. He looked a bit like the elves . . . but large and evil. The man's eyes glittered red in the gloom that surrounded him as he handed over the big black book.

Matt's hackles rose at the sight of the dark man and he let out an inadvertent whimper of fear. A childhood horror stirred in his mind and he cowered under the man's burning gaze.

Saint Nick patted the book. "In here are recorded all the children over whom I watch. Those who are good are given gifts. And those who are not . . ."

"Get beatings and coal and sticks," Matt replied, remembering.

"Well, not so much anymore. We've liberalized, so Black Peter here has less to do. Mostly he simply gives wicked children bad dreams or nothing at all. But Pete keeps track, nonetheless."

Matthias slunk to the ground in remembered misery as the Bishop of Myrna and his enforcer walked away from the sleigh with a new bag of gifts. And maybe a nightmare, he imagined, or a smack with a yard-stick as he'd gotten a time or two at the group home. Unpleasant child-hood memories tried to creep out of the mental closet into which he'd locked them long ago and he shivered.

The werewolf had stretched his harness traces to the limit and lain down on the snow in a glaring heap to keep out of the range of reindeer nips when a jerk on the reins pulled him back onto his feet. "Come along, Matthias. Don't be glum. It's Christmas Eve and we've a lot to do before the terminator catches up to us."

The man in red cracked his whip and Matt and the reindeer surged forward instantly, leaping into the sky.

"Terminator?" the werewolf yipped, as he dug his paws into the night. "We're being pursued by a robot assassin from the future?"

Santa laughed. "Oh, no. Of course not! But we are being pursued by the sun. The line where the night becomes day is called the terminator. Right now we are just behind it, but it moves faster than we do, and when it catches up to us, my power ends for the year. The magic of Christmas begins on the morning of the day before Christmas and ends on Christmas Day. We had best be back on the ground at Christmas House before then, or we'll fall from the sky and no amount of Christmas Cheer will save us. So, now, dash away, dash away, dash away all!"

And he cracked the whip again. Matthias and the reindeer put on a burst of speed and raced into the night toward the next stop. And as they ran through the holy night, the werewolf thought very long thoughts.

It was curious, Matthias mused, that Christmas had such power and yet it lasted such a short time. Hadn't there been a whole season of it when he was a child? The traditional joy hadn't been present so much after a while—not after his parents died and he bounced from one children's home or foster home to another—but he was quite sure there'd been weeks of delicious odors, songs, and glittering decorations, even at the charity boarding school run by the Sisters of Mercy.

He was surprised he could remember anything good about the place. He hadn't thought of it in years. He had willed himself not to think of it, in fact; for that was where the bad things first began to happen and that was where he'd first met Black Peter. Oh yes, now that his mind was turning over the stinking depths of his memories, he remembered the terrifying dark figure with the hooked nose and the blazing red eyes.

The dark man had come late on those childhood Christmas Eves. He'd come with switches and cudgels, towing nightmares that overwhelmed the joy of the morning's paltry gifts—hand-me-down clothes and rough toys in generic paper and ribbons. The gifts hadn't even had names on them, just green ribbons for boys and red ones for girls and cryptic marks in the paper corners, which Matthias had figured out indicated the sizes of the secondhand shirts, pants, or shoes inside. Under the hands of some of his caretakers, bruises or horror had not been new to Matthias over the years. The small daily abuses, the neglect, the cruelty of children, and the worn-down rote charity of exhausted adults had made his young life too bleak for tinsel to rectify.

As he'd grown older, the whole holiday thing—his whole life—had become terribly depressing and the Season of Light had seemed shabby and dim. He'd gotten into fights, talked back to the nuns, and cheated on his schoolwork and exams—not just at Christmas but all the time. He kept himself warm in his anger at the world that seemed to hate him—it was better than the constant chill of fear and despair.

The year he'd pushed Lindsey Strathorn down the chapel steps on the third Sunday of Advent had marked his first visit from Black Peter. He'd only been reaching for her braids to give them a yank, but it had been too tempting to give a little shove instead—just a little shove. . . . He hadn't *meant* to break her arm—it wasn't really his fault.

The year he'd started smoking had been the last time he saw the bleak specter of the fiery-eyed man. He'd woken to the rustle of someone's garments in the dark and the thud of a stick against the bedpost. Matthias had jumped from beneath the covers and run screaming into the chapel, turning over the ranks of burning votives and cursing God and the nuns as he bolted out into the snowy Christmas night.

Wandering in the snow-drifted streets in his pajamas, he'd fallen in among wolves of the human kind and pushed his past aside forever, burying it in the darkest part of his mind, along with the death of his parents and the sight of the burning chapel.

At first he had been just the youngest predator in the human pack, but he'd fought and bit and clawed and gouged his way up until he met a bigger, meaner wolf than he was; an inhuman beast that still walked upright like a man. Maybe, he thought, it had been inevitable that he'd end up a werewolf. He hadn't minded. Actually, he'd kind of liked it and taken to it with ferocious glee. He'd had enough of being hungry and poor and hated for no reason at all. He'd be a wolf and he'd never be hungry or cold and no dark man would beat him. And if somebody hated him, they had good reason, and if they feared him—even as a tale in the dark of night—so much the better.

He'd rejected everything he'd learned from the Sisters of Mercy so thoroughly that he hadn't believed there was a Saint Nicholas. The fellow in the sleigh didn't look that much like the jolly fat man of American soda commercials and sidewalk collection kettles—more like the European figurine his German-speaking parents had put on the mantel—so who could blame him for not recognizing the man? Well, he wouldn't make that mistake again. Yet here the fellow was and he had the power to let Matthias fly through the air—if only for one night a year and in the company of bad-tempered reindeer who held grudges. He seemed to have a great many powers and that was interesting. Very interesting indeed . . .

They paused again on a rooftop made of moss-shagged wooden shingles. From below, Matt could detect the odor of sleeping babies and Christmas cookies with hot tea. He watched Kris Kringle closely this time as he stepped down from his sleigh and walked across the rooftops to vanish in a flurry of snow and a sparkle of icy glitter. Matt wasn't quite sure how the trick was done, but he had an idea.

When the jolly old elf and his not-so-jolly companion returned, Matthias cleared his throat and asked, "Just how many children do you visit every year?"

"A few thousand. I'm not sure of the exact number."

"Why not all of them? I thought that's what you did."

"That would be impractical," the red-clad saint replied with a sad nod. "These days I make personal visits only to certain children—the ones for whom hope, charity, and comfort are the greatest need."

"What about the rest?" Matt growled. "Don't they deserve that stuff, too?"

"Of course they do. But I've a great many helpers and no need for me to try and visit every child. There are over six billion people on the planet now, you know."

"That many?"

Santa nodded. "That many. Of course, many of them don't believe in me and I cannot enter where there is no memory or belief in me—even just the memory of belief, as you have, Mattie. Atheism and pragmatism have cut into my old territory, and of course, there's also commercialism."

"Doesn't that bother you?"

"Oh no. Who do you think started it? All that Christmas buying frenzy and advertising—the commercialism of Christmas that so many decry—has lightened my workload tremendously. Every hopeful, believing child who receives a gift bought by their parents and labeled 'From Santa' is still, in a way, receiving a gift from me. It's the Spirit of Christmas that's important, not the size or the origin of the gift."

"Seems like a con job to me," Matthias muttered.

Sinterklaas stroked his beard and climbed into the sleigh. "Seems to be working out all right. I hadn't taken you for such a traditionalist, Mattie."

"I'm not," the werewolf growled and started to say more.

Santa Claus shook his head and picked up the reins. "We can talk as we go, but we have a great deal yet to do, my furry friend. Trot on!" And he snapped the reins, urging the team up into the sky once more.

They ran between the stars and the earth, and Matthias paused a moment to snap at a bit of stardust that sprinkled from above and hauled the sleigh up and around into a huge, swooping loop—just to see if the red-coated man and his load of gifts would fall out. But Saint Nicholas only clung like a limpet to his seat and laughed, "Ho, ho, ho! Excellent, Mattie!"

As they raced ahead of the terminator, the weather became damp and misty, though none of the team or the driver seemed bothered by the cold. The fog, however, was a different matter.

"Oh dear," muttered Sunnercla. "Now I do miss Rudolph—that nose of his lit the way through even the densest fog. I hope we won't get lost in this murk."

"I have a nose," Matt objected.

"And it's lovely, but it's not exactly casting light in the darkness, dear boy. How will we find the houses of the deserving children if I can't see them?"

"I'll bet I could smell them out," Matthias said.

"Really? Well . . . most of them do leave me cookies but there're a lot of cookies around this time of year."

"And hope. You said your special children have hope."

"Yes. And belief. But those don't have a smell."

"Oh yes they do," the werewolf said, remembering. "Hope smells like despair before it goes sour. Belief smells like candle wax and incense. And I smell that right now." He also smelled the odors of sleeping children and gingerbread and fir boughs near a wood fire. He was sure that only a house full of Christmas could smell like that—all the others had—but he didn't say so. Rider had his tricks, but so did Matthias and he wasn't going to let on that the Christmas Cheer had made his nose as magical as his flying paws.

"Indeed?" asked Sinterklaas. "Then lead on!"

Putting his nose to the scent, the werewolf snuffled and trotted through the air, following the smell down and around, skirting through ranks of tall buildings, over the tops of trees, and finally to a rooftop where the team paused for Santa Claus to run his errand.

As they waited, the reindeer looked at Matthias out of the corners of their eyes and muttered among themselves. They still didn't like him, but at least they weren't trying to bite him anymore.

When the man in red returned, he walked right up to the deer team and began distributing cookies from his pockets. "There you go, my good friends. You've worked very hard, so it's time for a treat—there's still much yet to do, though, so eat up!" He walked up to Matt and held out a gingerbread man. "That was excellent work, Mattie. I saved the best one for you."

The werewolf sniffed at the cookie and sneezed. "I'd rather have the children—they're tastier. If you can go in all these houses and do all of this, why do you settle for cookies and milk? You could have anything. If I could do that, I'd definitely eat the brats in their cribs."

The Bishop of Myrna frowned, saying, "I couldn't do that. I'm the patron saint of children—I could never hurt them."

"But you let Black Peter punish them. Just like you did me."

"You were awfully naughty, Mattie. Children need correction once in a while—to learn what is right and what is not. All parents know this. You had no parents and no one to help you know when you'd done wrong."

"I had foster parents and a schoolful of nuns to correct me."

"Apparently not enough—considering. And after all I'd done for you . . . Well, water under the bridge now. We'd best be going."

Saint Nicholas scratched him behind the ears and walked back to the driver's seat with the shadow of Black Peter slinking along behind. For just a moment, the dark man showed his face and winked at Matthias and gave an evil grin.

Annoyed and a little afraid, but feeling a post-Rudolph emptiness, the werewolf gobbled down the gingerbread man in two bites—it certainly wasn't as good as reindeer, but it would do. Then the sleigh was on its way again, with Matthias still sniffing and leading them through the fog.

They'd visited several more fog-bound buildings and were just emerging from the mist above a frozen lake when a mournful sound drifted up to the sleigh from the ice below.

"Whoa, Mattie!" called the man in red. "Find that noise!"

Cocking his ears, the werewolf listened for the thin cry. There it was . . . the chilled voice of someone alone on the ice, freezing and crying. Matthias plunged toward the sound of the weakling, thinking of the times he'd hunted to similar cries of distress, cutting the weak and injured from herds of animals—and men.

The reindeer pulled with all their strength to match the powerful leaps of their leader and they dashed down to the ice-bound lake, circling lower and lower until they touched as lightly as eiderdown onto the cracked surface of the ice. A small figure lay on the ice beside a fissure in the surface. Next to the still body, a wavering form wailed its distress.

Matthias wouldn't have imagined the red-clad saint could move so fast, but Saint Nicholas bailed out of the sleigh when it was barely stopped and ran across the treacherous ice to the child lying beside the hole. He knelt down and scooped up the dead child, cradling its blue face against his red woolen shoulder.

"Peter!" he cried. "Black Peter, you wretch, bring the book and my crozier!"

Matthias sniffed at the wailing ghost of the little boy. "What happened to you?" he asked.

The young ghost sniffled and blinked at him. "A man offered me a ride home from school, but we never went home. He hurt me and then he left me out here. I prayed and prayed for someone to come. . . ."

"Bit late . . ." Matt growled.

"Never say that, Matthias!" Saint Nick scolded. "Not on Christmas." He held out his hands to Black Peter, who offered him the big black book and the gold shepherd's crook.

The patron saint of children looked at the sad little ghost and opened the book. "There, now, José, we'll make it right."

Matt craned his neck to look over the man's shoulder at the book. He could see a creamy page that had but a single name penned on it in wet, red ink—José Maria Antonio Guttierez. As he looked, Santa Claus began to speak, long Latin phrases that shivered in the air and the ground shook as he raised his stick in his free hand. The words broke into sparkling shards that swirled and glittered, falling on the page and on little José, making the red ink run.

Still Sinterklaas intoned the strange words and the ink shimmered, turning brown, then yellow. . . . The ghost gasped and so did the boy in the saint's arms.

The glimmering words that filled the air blazed into white light and the red-coated man brought his crozier down. It touched the little boy with a sound like distant cannon and a shout of angels and the air itself was afire!

Matthias jumped back and the little boy in Santa's arms coughed and opened his eyes. Matt looked for the ghost but it was nowhere to be seen. He looked at the book and saw that the name on the page was now written in gold ink that gleamed as if it were a coin newly minted.

José looked up and gasped, "Papa Noel . . ."

"Merry Christmas, José," said Father Christmas. He glanced at

Matt and Black Peter, then back to the boy. "You're a long way from home, but we'll get you back."

The man and his shadow bundled the boy into the sleigh, and Matthias and the reindeer team hauled the conveyance into the sky once again, soaring miles to the south, over rivers and fields, over the craggy red and yellow spires of New Mexican canyons, to touch down on the grass of a playing field while Kris Kringle took the boy back to his home. He handed him back into the care of his dazed, tearstained parents, who didn't seem to realize how far their child had traveled or that they were talking to the real Santa Claus and not just some seasonal department store employee.

Black Peter grumbled, brushing at the book as he stood beside Matthias and watched from a distance—no one wanted to explain the presence of a magical sled with eight reindeer and a werewolf in its traces and certainly not a black shadow of a man with burning red eyes.

"Now, I'll never hear the end of it," Black Peter muttered.

"Huh?" Matt grunted. "End of what?"

"You'll find out. . . ." The dark man looked quickly around and then flipped open the book and pointed at it. "Here, take a look, but read fast, the bishop is coming back."

Matthias glanced down and saw his own name on the page. There were three gold stars beside his name—which was a filthy brown with tiny hints of gold at the edges—and then a little red X followed by more gold stars, and then a handful of black check marks that stopped abruptly with a big black X. The werewolf could guess what the stars meant—those were the years of his youth, surely—and the black X must have marked the year he rejected Christmas.

"What's that mean?" he asked, poking his paw at the red X.

Black Peter grinned—his teeth looked like knives and Matt felt a shiver of dread at that smile. "That's when you died, little Mattie."

"But I'm not dead! And I don't remember being dead. . . ."

"Think of what you've just seen—"

A hand in a red mitten snapped the book closed and Saint Nicholas took it away from his dark companion.

"Now, now, Peter, don't scare poor Mattie. He's done very well tonight. That name was jet-black before this night started, and you and I shall have to discuss how that blackness came about. . . ."

Matthias growled at Rider. "Tell me about the X!"

Grandfather Frost sighed. "That's a long story and the sun is catching up to us. I think it should wait for another time, so we're not stranded here on Christmas Day."

"I won't be stranded," Matthias snapped. "I don't need a magical team of reindeer to fly me home—I am home—or close enough." Matt hunched his shoulders, raising his hackles and bristling as he crouched close to the ground, poised to leap at the man in the red suit—completely forgetting about the harness.

Saint Nicholas glanced at the eastern sky, then back to the werewolf. Matthias couldn't see any difference in the color of the night, but he supposed that came with practice—like the trick of getting into houses.

"Very well," Santa said. "You know that I am the patron saint of children and that is because of what this evil man did." He pointed to Black Peter, who glowered. "When I was Bishop of Myrna, three young boys from one of the villages went missing. They were all good friends and mischievous little scamps so at first no one was too worried about them, thinking they'd be back as soon as whatever adventure they had conceived was done. But they didn't come home and their families began to worry. There had been famine in other villages and many people were hungry and many more were desperate. The city was suffering the most, for there were too many mouths to feed on the food the villages and ships could supply.

"I had bought some grain for the city from a ship's captain. His cargo was meant for a powerful lord farther down the coast, but he sold the grain to me out of pity, which moved the heart of God. A miracle was given to him so that his grain was replaced for his goodness and he did not suffer punishment by his master for coming home shorthanded.

"The people cried in joy over the grain, but among the cries of joy I heard the cries of the sad parents for their missing children. And another sound came to my ears as well—the voices of the missing boys themselves, praying for their lives, for their families.

"So I followed the sound of those prayers and they led me to the home of a butcher—a fat, evil butcher named Ruprecht," the saint added, glaring at his shadow, "who had tricked the boys into his home, then killed them and chopped them to bits. He put the bits into his salting barrel and meant to sell them to the hungry people of the town as salt pork. The arrival of the grain had delayed the butcher's plans and so I found the murdered boys and raised them from the dead and sent them home to their families. Ruprecht became my assistant to atone for his sins. He keeps my list and he punishes the wicked children so that they won't grow up to be like him. I prefer to call him Peter, now, so he won't be reminded so much of his evil past, but perhaps that has been a mistake," the saint added, glaring at the dark man.

"So you see that I have the power to bring children back to life—but only once and only on Christmas. When you were three, Matthias, your family was killed in a house fire on Christmas Eve. I couldn't save your parents, for I don't have that power, but I brought you back. You'd always been a good little boy."

"And you brought me back for what?" Matthias roared. "So I could be an orphan and hated for it? Blamed for surviving while my parents died? Bounced from home to home? Starved and poor all the time? That was your gift to me—your only gift, I might add! In all those years you never brought me a present!"

The reindeer shied and shuffled in the snow and snorted in fear as the werewolf howled his fury.

Saint Nicholas spread his arms, calming the deer, then looked to Matthias, frowning. "You didn't get them? I brought them every year. They were such little things but I thought you knew—I couldn't let them be too obvious—but they were there. The way your shoes always fit better than anyone's. The red coat when you were five with the fire engine in the pocket—"

"I never got a fire engine! There never was a red coat!" The reindeer jumped with nerves and the sleigh rattled as Matthias bayed and raged. "The shoes pinched and leaked. The nuns beat my knuckles until they bled and we all went to bed hungry every night but Christmas Eve—and that was only because people brought us their unwanted food. You raised me from the dead just to leave me in hell—what sort of saint are you?"

Hagios Nikolaos glanced at Black Peter. "And what do you know about this?"

The punisher of wicked children only shook his head and said nothing. But there was a glint in his red eyes. . . .

"We shall speak of this again, Black Peter. Mark my words." Then Sunnercla turned from him and put his arms around the furious werewolf, trying to gentle the savage beast by muttering soft words. Matthias ripped and tore at the man in red, biting and gouging and howling with anger and despair, but every injury he inflicted healed again almost as fast as he gave it.

At last the werewolf put his head down, exhausted, on the snow. Santa Claus sat down beside him.

"I'm so sorry, Matthias. So sorry," he said. "I can only save a child once. After that, you have to save yourself. You were a good child and I never understood why you went bad. Then you ceased to be a child at all and I didn't know what had become of you for such a long time. I have many duties besides Christmas—patron of many things—and I suppose I didn't look hard enough for you. But you weren't a sailor or a baker or a prisoner and I didn't think you'd keep a shop or move to Greece. None of my other spheres of influence seemed very likely to benefit you, either—and that was my fault for not looking harder. Then, tonight, here you were and I had another chance. I have tried to help you. Now, Matthias. Now I do truly need your help."

"I don't want to help you. I think my Christmas Cheer has worn off," Matt muttered.

"But don't you like running through the night sky?"

Actually he did, very much, but he only shrugged, not trusting the old red-coated fake.

"Do you really want to strand the sleigh and the reindeer here? To disappoint all the other children I have to visit tonight? Would that be fair?"

Matt grumbled. He didn't care—well, he didn't. But maybe a little more running through the sky . . .

"I don't know," he muttered. "You weren't very fair to me. What do I get out of it?"

He could tell Rider didn't like that, but he figured he had the fellow by the short fur now. The sunrise *was* inevitable and the terminator crept toward them inexorably. If the Bishop of Myrna wanted to get home before it caught them, he'd have to make a deal.

Saint Nick heaved one more sigh and got to his feet. "All right. . . . You've got me over a barrel, Matthias. What's your condition?"

The werewolf sat up and shook his fur back down, grooming a little just for the delay. Then he said, "I want the recipe for Christmas Cheer."

"Christmas Cheer? But that only works once a year!"

"That's all right. I can be content with running through the skies once a year. It's not bad."

"Is that all?"

"Yup. Well . . . and directions out of the North Pole because that place is crazy."

Santa stroked his beard and said, "All right. It's a deal. So long as you get us back to Christmas House before dawn."

"And the recipe had better work!"

"I guarantee it will—on my word as Father Christmas. But only on Christmas Eve, remember."

"That's fine." The werewolf stood back up in the harness and shook his fur into place. "Give me a little more Christmas Cheer for right now and let's go!"

Another handful of the glittering magical dust was presented and drizzled over him while Saint Nicholas muttered his magic words. Then the man in red and his dark henchman settled themselves in the sleigh and Matt and the reindeer took off.

They raced against the creeping sunrise, dashing for the last of the houses full of worthy, sleeping children, and every time they stopped, Matthias paid close attention to what Père Noel did. He always put his mittened hand to his face, said something, and then vanished into the snowy uproar of Christmas magic at work.

Finally Matthias asked, "How do you do that? The chimney trick, that is? How do you get in and out?"

"Mattie, we don't have time for a long discussion. We're running a bit late as it is."

"I'm not. I have all the time in the world."

"Oh, all right, I'll tell you. If I say the right words and breathe in a pinch of Christmas Cheer, I can pass through anything—I become the Spirit of Christmas itself for a few minutes. It doesn't last very long, so I have to make my trips quickly or work the spell again."

"Oh! So that's what that poet-fellow meant in the 'Night Before Christmas'! I thought he just meant you were winking at him."

"Poet-fellow . . . Oh, you mean Clement Moore who wrote 'A Visit From St. Nicholas.' Yes, yes . . . 'laying a finger aside of his nose . . .' That's what it was," Saint Nick agreed.

"Ech . . . snorting cookie dust," Matt said with a shudder. "That's disgusting." Though not quite as disgusting as some of the things he'd done in wolfskin, Matthias thought. Then he grinned a smug, wolf grin; it was just as he'd suspected.

"Well, the job's not all sugar plums and Christmas cake, Mattie."

Was it his imagination, or did the old saint seem tired and cranky? Surely Santa didn't get grumpy. . . . He was supposed to be perpetually jolly. But it was getting pretty late and even the reindeer had given up any extra expenditure of energy. Matt had noticed they had stopped trying to bite long ago and begun to pull along willingly with him, not just to show him up or get revenge. Maybe they were starting to get used to him, after all, and that was just fine with him.

Matt shrugged and waited for the crack of the whip or the flick of the reins to signal it was time to move once again, and they took to the sky in a flurry of hooves and paws.

As they finished their rounds, the edge of the sun flared on the eastern horizon like prairie fire. Saint Nicholas turned the team sharply north and urged them to run for their lives into the polar darkness. And run they did, for they were now airborne and the nighttime terminator was as deadly as any assassin robot. If the sun touched them, they would tumble to the ground with all the aerodynamic grace of flung rocks.

They dashed for the north with their hearts in their mouths, ripping at the blue-black sky with their hooves and paws. Matthias could feel the bubbly sensation of the Christmas Cheer fading, dulling the brightness of color, stealing the extraordinary scents from his nose, and letting the chill of the perpetual winter touch him even through his thick wolfen pelt. He pulled and pulled, ran and ran, sinking toward the earth. . . .

And stumbled to the snowy ground with a thud and a tumble. The reindeer skidded to a stop behind him, tugging him to a sliding halt with the weight of their bodies. He picked himself up, shaking off the snow, and looked around. He could see the edge of Christmas House and the elves trotting across the snow to help them. He breathed a sigh of relief.

The elves clustered around them, unharnessing the team, dragging away the sleigh, helping Matthias out of the modified straps of his own harness. They led the reindeer back to their stockade and helped Santa Claus—who seemed suddenly very old and frail—toward the house. Matthias trotted after them.

"Would you like a bite to eat or a hot drink, Mattie?" the Bishop of Myrna asked as they flopped down in front of a roaring fire in his living room.

"Oh, no. I should get going."

"Are you sure? It's been a long, hard night—you did very good work."

Matt scratched himself, yawned, and stretched, then stood up. "It has been a long night, but I'd rather be on my way. After you give me my present, that is."

Saint Nicholas frowned, but he got up and left the room, returning with a piece of paper and a small bag that he offered to the werewolf. "Here it is. The bag has the recipe and a few ingredients you may have difficulty finding out of season. Make it up fresh in the morning of the day before Christmas and it should be just fine. The directions out of the North Pole's influence are on the paper." He looked a little wistful as he added, "I do wish you'd stay a little while, though. We might have much to talk about. . . ."

"No thanks," Matthias replied. He took the bag and the paper and carried them off into the darkness of Christmas Day.

*   *   *

The next year, as Christmas Eve lengthened toward night, Matthias was lying in the snow behind a stand of fir, watching the activity in the courtyard of Christmas House. His nose was full of the scents of cinnamon and brandy, and the flavor of gingerbread and apples lingered on his tongue. Visions of magical creatures in diaphanous raiment danced and spun on colored ribbons of magic before his eyes as the elves below dragged out the sleigh and polished the harness. They wouldn't know what hit them. . . .

Oh yes, Matthias had made his plans meticulously; he'd mixed up the Christmas Cheer and he'd retraced the route to the North Pole and now he need only wait. He knew all the old saint's tricks, and this year, when the red-coated hypocrite came out to the stockade, Matt wouldn't be dazzled or taken by surprise. This time he'd jump on the Bishop of Myrna and rip his throat out. Then he'd take his place in the sleigh and rampage through the Christmas Eve sky from house to house, and he wouldn't be settling for milk and cookies. . . .

Behind him, in the gloom, a shadow formed and flickered a knife-blade grin, and dark hands checked the book where the gold-tinged name *Matthias Vulfkind* turned ashy black. Something horrible laughed and was cut off short. . . .

Another voice spoke from the darkness. "Black Peter, you have a lot to answer for."

Matt jerked around, looking for Saint Nicholas, and found instead a huge white wolf. Its fur was as thick and as white as the snow and the look in its eye was both kindly and disappointed. From its jaws hung a thread of black shadow that writhed and spat red sparks of ire. The Nicholas wolf spat Black Peter onto the ground and put a paw upon the writhing shadow, then chuckled a wolfy chuckle. "Oh, Matthias . . . As a child I gave you a second life, as a wolf I gave you a second chance, but here you are again. Do you need more flying lessons?"

Matthias could only stare.

"What? Didn't you know I'm also the patron saint of wolves? Mattie, my boy, what shall I do with you . . . ?"

Fresh Meat

Alan Gordon

Alan is the author of the Fools' Guild Mysteries, published by St. Martin's Minotaur Books, continuing the adventures of Theophilos, a thirteenth-century jester. Titles in the series include Thirteenth Night *(now available from Crum Creek Press),* Jester Leaps In, A Death in the Venetian Quarter, The Widow of Jerusalem, An Antic Disposition, The Lark's Lament, The Moneylender of Toulouse, *and the recent* The Parisian Prodigal. *Alan sold his first short story to* Alfred Hitchcock Mystery Magazine *in 1990. Since then, he's had numerous mystery, fantasy, and science fiction stories in* Hitchcock, Ellery Queen Mystery Magazine, Asimov's Science Fiction, *and several anthologies. By day, Alan is a criminal defense attorney with the Legal Aid Society of New York, with over a hundred trials to his credit. He lives in New York City with his wife, Judy Downer, an editor, and son, Robert. He is a graduate of Swarthmore College, where he received the William Plumer Potter Award for Fiction, and the University of Chicago Law School.*

"Your order's ready, Mister Lehrmann," called Bert, emerging from the back room wiping his hands on a bloody towel. "Two sides of beef, so fresh they were mooing yesterday."

"Thanks, Bert," said Lehrmann. "That should keep us through the twenty-sixth. Okay if I bring the van around back?"

"No problem, Mister L," said Bert. "What are you doing for Christmas? Family coming over?"

"I'm expecting some tonight. Maybe."

"That's nice," said Bert. "Nothing like having family on Christmas Eve. Let's see, you just paid me for the month, so we'll put this on your tab for January, okay?"

"Works for me," said Lehrmann, signing the proffered receipt. His nose crinkled happily as he scanned the display case.

"Those lamb chops look good," he said. "Maybe I should get the dogs a treat for Christmas. Got a lamb you haven't cut up yet?"

"Sure thing," said Bert, adding it to the invoice.

Lehrmann stepped outside to where the cargo van was parked, the LEHRMANN'S GUARD DOGS ad on both sides. He pulled it around to the loading dock where Bert was already waiting with the beef and lamb on a dolly.

"Those dogs eat better than most people," commented Bert as Lehrmann hauled the meat into the van. "Not that I'm complaining to my best customer. You really think they should get fresh, raw meat every day?"

"Part of their training," said Lehrmann. "The bloodier, the better. Brings out the hunter in them."

"Sure wouldn't want to run into one of your puppies on the job," said Bert.

"You really wouldn't," said Lehrmann, slamming the rear doors shut. "See you Monday, Bert. Have a good Christmas."

Lehrmann raised and trained his dogs in a converted warehouse ten miles out of town, not far from the woods. A large, white sign marked the turnoff onto the farm road that led to it. The Spinellis came in at two for their last training session with Waldo. They were a family of four, living in one of the McMansions in the new development. The Doberman sensed them before he could even see them, and started baying a greeting.

"Waldo, hush," Lehrmann said to the dog, and he quieted down immediately. Lehrmann opened the cage and attached the lead to Waldo's collar, then brought him out to the training pit while the other dogs watched with professional interest.

"Afternoon, folks," he said. "Everyone ready?"

"Ready as I'll ever be," said Mr. Spinelli nervously.

"Hi, Waldo," said Sally, the fearless eleven-year-old, and Waldo wagged his tail. Sandy, her little brother, watched from behind her, his thumb in his mouth.

"You can hang out for a few minutes while I get my padding on," said Lehrmann. "Here."

He tossed the reward bag to Mr. Spinelli, and the lead to Mrs. Spinelli, who gave a quick whistle. Waldo immediately sat at her feet.

"Good dog," she said, patting his head.

Lehrmann strapped the quilted padding over his arms and torso, then faced them.

"Any time," he said.

"Waldo, come," commanded Mr. Spinelli, unclipping the lead from the dog's collar, and the dog followed him as he walked around. "Good dog. Waldo, perimeter."

Waldo ran around the edge of the pit.

"Waldo, here," said Mrs. Spinelli. The dog made a beeline for her. She looked at Lehrmann. "Are you sure about this?"

"Go ahead," smiled Lehrmann.

"Waldo, arm," she said, pointing at Lehrmann.

Waldo turned into a snarling, speeding set of teeth, hurtling toward Lehrmann. The dog leapt, and his jaws closed around the padding on the trainer's shoulder.

"Waldo, here," said Mr, Spinelli.

The dog relinquished his hold immediately and returned to the family.

"Good dog," said Mr. Spinelli.

"Don't forget the meat, Daddy," said Sally.

"Good dog," repeated Mr. Spinelli, handing him a chunk of beef from the reward bag.

Waldo wolfed it down.

"Dog biscuits won't do?" asked Spinelli as Lehrmann stripped off the padding.

"You want to keep him on your side, make it fresh meat," said Lehrmann. "You do want to keep him on your side, don't you?"

"Oh, yes," said Mrs. Spinelli.

"You've invested time and money to get not just a guardian, but a companion and a friend," said Lehrmann, coming forward to rub Waldo's neck. "A long time ago, dogs found us, and learned how to protect us. In exchange, we learned how to feed them, and we fed them well.

Co-evolution. Any dog can be trained to attack strangers, but a great dog, like Waldo here, won't be attacking strangers. He will be defending you, because you're his family and he loves you. Remember that."

"We will," promised Mr. Spinelli.

"Let me get him his new collar," said Lehrmann. "Waldo, come."

Waldo swallowed the last of his food, and followed Lehrmann to his office in back. The trainer took out a thick, black leather collar and put it around the dog's neck. Waldo looked at him attentively.

"Sorry you can't be here for Christmas, Waldo," said Lehrmann. "But you get to spend it with your new family. They are good people, and they will treat you well. Make me proud."

The dog nodded, and Lehrmann planted a quick kiss on the top of his head.

"Here's your Christmas dog," Lehrmann said as he brought Waldo back out.

"And here you are," said Mr. Spinelli, handing him a check.

"We'll bring him back for visits," said Mrs. Spinelli.

"I'd like that," said Lehrmann. "It's been a pleasure."

Waldo woofed at him once as they took him to their car.

"Merry Christmas!" cried the children.

Lehrmann waved, then closed the door and turned back to the rest of the dogs. They looked at him in anticipation.

"Playtime," he called, pressing a switch on the wall, and the doors all swung open at once.

The dogs burst out of the cages and charged madly into the pit, racing and colliding with each other. There was a mad pileup at one end as several skidded into the padding on the curve, launching a number of wrestling matches. As they played, Lehrmann went methodically through the cages, cleaning each thoroughly. Then he went into the walk-in refrigerator and hauled out one of the sides of beef. Using an electric butcher's saw, he hacked it into dog-sized portions. He laid them out in individual bowls, then came back out to the arena.

"Chow!" he called, and the dogs abandoned their melee and raced to their cages. He closed the doors, then began distributing the bowls.

While the dogs ate, Lehrmann hauled out an artificial Christmas tree and began stringing lights over its branches.

From the woods at the rear of the warehouse, a man watched through a pair of binoculars, catching glimpses of Lehrmann as he passed by the windows, his arms full of wreaths and ribbons.

"Very festive," muttered the man.

He was wearing a ribbed black sweater that was fine for the Georgia winter, along with black jeans and boots. A ski cap covered his hair, but his chin and jaw were covered with a matted, gray beard. His legs were thick and powerful.

He had been keeping his vigil from the woods the entire day, making sure that Lehrmann would be alone tonight. He had watched the Spinellis leave, knowing they were the last customers before Christmas, and smiled. His palms itched. He wiped them briefly on his sweater, then scratched the right one with the corner of his belt buckle. He looked through the binoculars again. Lehrmann was hanging a wreath on each of the dogs' cages.

"Very festive indeed," said the man.

The dogs made this one a challenge. He couldn't risk breaking into the warehouse and planting any bugs. He had used a combination of a long-range listening device that bounced an infrared beam off the windows, and a monitor that picked up any nearby cell phone signals. The arrangement still left gaps in the sound. And any time one of the damn dogs started barking, the infrared could have been a flashlight for all the dialogue he was picking up.

Lehrmann was unfolding a six-foot cardboard Santa Claus and hanging it on a wall.

"Now, that one is just plain tacky," said the watcher.

The cell phone monitor chirped. He squatted down and turned the volume up.

Lehrmann picked up his cell phone from his desk.

"Lehrmann's Guard Dogs," he said.

"Hi, Sam," said a familiar voice, and he clutched the phone hard for a moment. "You still there?"

"Hello, Mona," he said.

"It's Christmas Eve, Sam," she said. "I thought you might like some company."

"I've got company," he said.

"You know what I mean," said Mona. "Dogs don't count."

"Man's best friend," said Lehrmann. "Didn't you know that?"

"Only when the man has no woman," said Mona. "You're in Georgia, Sam. Not Alaska. Georgia. A man in Georgia doesn't need to spend the only Christmas Eve of the year with a bunch of dogs."

"You been drinking, Mona?"

"It's going to be a beautiful night," she continued. "Crisp and clear, with a full moon. A full moon on Christmas Eve, Sam. That doesn't happen that often. Maybe we'll see Santa's sleigh flying across it. Yes, I have been drinking, Sam. I'm alone in Georgia on Christmas Eve, and I'm drinking. Can't I come over? You shouldn't be alone with a bunch of dogs."

"Dogs are loyal, Mona," he said. He wished immediately that he hadn't.

She was silent. He thought for a moment that she had broken the connection, but then he heard her crying.

"How's Nicky?" he asked, awkwardly changing the subject.

"Nicky's a great, big, warm, wonderful pal," she said. "I am going to cuddle with Nicky tonight. I could be with you, roasting marshmallows in the fire . . ."

"I don't have a fireplace," he said.

"Please let me back into your life, Sam," she said softly. "You can't shut me out forever."

"Good night, Mona," he said. "Merry Christmas."

He broke the connection.

The man in the woods checked his watch, then glanced up at the sky. The sun was nearing the horizon. It would be an hour until nightfall.

He looked through his binoculars to see Lehrmann sitting disconsolately at the desk, staring at his cell phone, then turning it off.

"Poor Sam," said the watcher. "Full moon and empty arms."

An alarm signal went off, and Carson, an eight-year-old German shepherd, looked up.

"Easy, boy," said Lehrmann. "Still got an hour. Plenty of time. Finish your dinner."

The dog went back to his meal, but kept glancing up at the windows.

She was drinking early today, thought Lehrmann. God knows that the holidays will do that to a person. Hell, he was all shook up from a two-minute conversation with her, and he was the sober one.

"Hell of a time to call, Carson," he said, and the dog grimaced sympathetically.

Lehrmann thought back to when she'd first walked through his front door. What was it, three years ago? Three and a month. It was mid-November, and he was training a Rottweiler, a ten-month-old female.

The woman was slim, brunette, and built like a runner. Her clothes were carefully casual in a way only large amounts of money could accomplish. She had ruby drops dangling from each ear, with more strung along a gold necklace that plunged between her breasts.

He was playing tug-of-war with the Rottweiler, using a broomstick wrapped in several layers of cloth. The dog had clamped on tight, and was digging its claws into the mat, trying to pull the broomstick out of Lehrmann's hands. She looked like she might succeed. The woman leaned forward, resting her hands on the wall of the pit, and watched.

"Here!" Lehrmann said suddenly.

The Rottweiler looked up at him, but refused to relinquish the broomstick.

"Here!" Lehrmann commanded her again.

The dog reluctantly let go, and moved to sit by Lehrmann's right foot. She stayed there, a resentful glare on her face.

"Good girl," Lehrmann praised her, and he handed her a small piece of beef. "Can I help you, ma'am?"

"If I'm not interrupting," said the woman, smiling. "Is that raw beef?"

"It is," said Lehrmann.

"Then you won't mind if I don't shake hands just yet," she said.

"I have been known to wash them on occasion," said Lehrmann. "Give me a minute. You could shake the dog's paw while you're waiting."

"Will she do that without attacking me?" asked the woman.

"She won't attack unless she's told to," said Lehrmann. "At least, that's how it's supposed to work."

"I'll chance it," said the woman, coming into the pit. She squatted down to face the dog. "Hello. My name is Mona Havelka. What's yours?"

"This is Nicky," said Lehrmann. "Nicky, shake."

The Rottweiler immediately held out a paw, and Mona shook it.

"Very pleased to meet you, Nicky," she said.

"Here, give her this," said Lehrmann, holding up a piece of beef.

Mona took it and held it out for Nicky, who took it carefully from her, then licked her hand.

"No point in standing on ceremony now," said Mona, holding her hand out to Lehrmann. "Are you the owner?"

"Sam Lehrmann," he said, shaking it. "Pleased to meet you. Let me show you where to wash up."

He escorted her to a washbasin in a tool room in back and tossed her a bar of soap.

"Guests first," he said, turning on the taps. "Hope you don't mind sharing."

"A gentleman," she said, scrubbing her hands thoroughly. "And such a romantic spot, too."

"You'd be surprised," he grinned as she handed him the soap. "So, how may I help you?"

"I came to see a man about a dog," she said as he washed up.

"I'm the man," he said. "What kind of dog have you got in mind?"

"Someone to protect me when I'm sleeping."

"Apartment or house?"

"A town house," she said. "In town."

"You looking for something with more bark or more bite?" he asked as they walked back into the main room.

She looked at him, and the smile left her eyes.

"I want a bark that will put the fear of God into anyone stupid enough to break in," she said. "And a bite that will send anyone stupid enough to ignore the bark straight to Hell."

He rested his chin between his thumb and forefinger, and pondered her request for a moment.

"I have this really vicious dachshund that might fit the bill," he said.

She stared at him in disbelief.

"No, seriously, I've been trying to get rid of the little bastard for years," he continued, his nose crinkling for an instant.

"An attack dachshund," she said, starting to laugh.

"Well, pretty much an ankle biter," he conceded. "But let him get a running start, and that baby will take out a decent chunk of thigh."

"Really," she said. "I had no idea."

"It's the element of surprise," he explained. "Gets them every time."

"Be serious now," she said.

"All right," he said, opening the gate to the pit. "Nicky, here."

The Rottweiler bounded up and sat before them expectantly. Lehrmann looked into the dog's eyes, then back at Mona's.

"This one," he said. "This one is your dog."

Lehrmann went back into the refrigerator, removed the lamb, and placed it on the butcher block. Then he took the saw and simply cut it in half. He put one part back in the refrigerator, then carried the other to a large empty cage set back from the others and placed it inside. He made sure there was plenty of water, then went back to his office, where Carson was waiting, idly scratching his ear with his hind paw.

"You done?" Lehrmann asked.

The dog nodded. Lehrmann let the dog out of the office, then went around the building, checking the locks.

"How did you get to be so good with dogs?" she asked him one night as they lay in bed together. Nicky was downstairs, exiled to her dog bed as usual when he stayed the night.

"I grew up with them," he said. "And when I started raising them, they grew up with me. We just got to know each other better than most humans and dogs do."

"But the training," she persisted. "They respond to you like nothing I've ever seen."

"Something in my voice, I guess," he said. "I probably have all these auditory cues I use without even being aware of it."

"And they pick up on them," she said. "Maybe you've gotten it all wrong. Maybe the dogs are the ones who trained you, not the other way around."

"Could be," he said, letting his fingers trail gently down the curve of her body. "I never thought of it like that before."

He let his hand wander and explore, and she arched her back.

"How did you get to be so good with me?" she gasped, and he drew her to him in response.

"We're tight," he said to Carson as he punched in the numbers on the last lock and pulled the door shut. "Carson, patrol."

The dog began loping about the building.

The watcher pulled out his cell phone and pressed a single button.

"Did you get the security code?" he asked quietly.

"Affirmative."

"Good," said the watcher.

He broke the connection and waited impatiently. He had been

spending the day in a state of forced calm, but now, with the moment so close, he was nervous, jumpy. You would think that the killing urge would die out over the years, he thought. That the rage would gradually fade given time. Time that heals all wounds. A laughable notion in his case. With each kill, the wound seemed to rip open more, the bloodlust increased, and the only thing he could think about was the next one. Maybe Lehrmann would satisfy the urge for a while. He thought he might. Lehrmann was going to be a good one. Lehrmann was his Christmas gift to himself.

Edwards lay prone in a cornfield, watching the front of the warehouse until he saw Lehrmann go back inside. Then he crawled backward through the dried stalks until he could get to a crouching position unobserved. Still staying low, he scuttled to the rear of a barn where the surveillance van was parked. He tapped twice, then three times, on the side door. It slid open, and he clambered inside.

Kenner was behind the wheel. Hidalgo was in the back, monitoring the police radio.

"Any of that coffee left?" asked Edwards.

"In the pot," said Hidalgo. "Make it quick. It's almost time."

Edwards poured himself a cup, threw in three sugars and some creamer, and stirred it. He drank it in two gulps, then began putting on the padding.

"Did you guys ever feel like we work for a crazy person?" he asked.

"Sometimes," said Kenner. "Then I see my paycheck and the feeling goes away."

"And he's not so crazy," said Hidalgo.

"What makes you think so?" asked Edwards, tightening the straps to make sure nothing crucial was exposed.

"Because he's making you go in first," explained Hidalgo.

"You got a point," said Edwards. "Ever feel like I've become a crazy person?"

"That we do," said Kenner, checking his watch, then his gun.

*　*　*

Lehrmann went back to the large cage and checked his watch. Fifteen minutes. He stripped off his clothes and hung them from a pair of hooks. Then he took off his watch and placed it on a table so that it faced the cage. He checked the timer on the lock, then stepped inside and pulled the door shut. The lock engaged.

Carson came by and sat in front of the cage.

"It's locked," said Lehrmann, shaking the bars to prove it. "Thanks for checking, buddy. I'm good."

The dog woofed once, then resumed his patrolling.

The clanging of the cage echoed through the watcher's earpiece. He smiled.

"Next," he said softly.

At the Spinelli house, Waldo made a thorough inspection of every room. Then he heard a whistle, and galloped down the stairs to the front hallway.

Sally was waiting for him with his leash.

"Time for your walk, Waldo," she said, clipping it to his collar. "Mom? I'm taking Waldo for a walk around the block."

"Sweetie, it's getting dark," called her mother from the kitchen. "Don't be too long."

"Ah, come on, hon," said her husband. "Think who's with her. She'll be the safest girl in the neighborhood. Take your time, kiddo. Show Waldo who's friendly and where the weirdos are."

"'Kay, 'bye," she called, leading him out the front door.

Lehrmann looked through the bars at his watch. Five minutes. He sat cross-legged in the middle of the cage and took deep slow breaths. He held his hands out at his sides, palms up.

Outside the windows, the sky turned to night.

"Om," he chanted. "Om."

The change always started inside his chest as his rib cage expanded. The surrounding muscles resisted for a moment, then began to stretch and re-form to accommodate the larger shape.

"Om," he continued. "Om."

It spread up through his shoulders and neck, and down through his pelvis as the bones shifted, making crackling noises like twigs popping on a fire. The hair was sprouting now, thick, coarse, and gray.

"Om," he said, clinging to the sound, concentrating all of his being in the chant.

The arms and legs were at it now, the claws bursting through his fingers and toes. That pain was always the worst. The chant was coming out hoarsely. He was choking on it, but forced it out. Then came the jaws thrusting forward, the teeth, the fangs.

The mind.

"Om," he whimpered.

He wanted to howl.

Just one howl.

What harm could one little howl do?

Let it out.

"Om!" he shouted.

He took a deep breath.

"Om," he chanted. "Om."

He sensed the other dogs watching him down the row of cages. Fascinated. Envious.

His heartbeat slowed back to normal. Whatever the hell that was.

Carson came by and sat, looking at him.

"I'm good, buddy," said Lehrmann. "Want to hand me the remote? Let's see what's on cable tonight."

Carson went over to the table where the remote control sat next to the watch. He picked it up gently with his teeth and brought it over to the cage where the werewolf sat, scratching his back. He put it on the floor, then nudged it between the bars with his nose.

"Thanks, buddy," said Lehrmann, picking it up and turning on the monitor mounted on the wall outside. He tore off a chunk of the lamb carcass and shoved it through the bars to the dog. Carson grabbed it and went back on patrol.

The usual Christmas fare. Repeats of specials he had seen dozens of times before. He flipped through them. There was the Island of Misfit Toys, and Linus wrapping his blanket to shore up that pathetic little tree. He growled with displeasure and turned it off.

"Oh, I love this one!" she cried. "Best 'Christmas Carol' ever!"

They were cuddling on the couch downstairs, a bowl of popcorn and a pitcher of bourbon-laced eggnog on the coffee table. Nicky was curled up on the far end, forcing them together. He wondered if that was her intent.

"The Mister Magoo one was the best," said Lehrmann.

"Never saw that one," she said.

"They used to show it when I was a kid," he said. "The Ghost of Christmas Future scared the crap out of me."

"That's no surprise," she said. "The future always scares you."

He looked at her.

"Where did that come from?" he asked.

"Oh, come off it, Sam," she said. "It's Christmas Eve. Our third together. Only we're not completely together, are we?"

"I'm over here most nights, aren't I?"

"Yes, but I'm a greedy little bitch, Sam," she said. "I want them all. Where were you Tuesday night?"

"I was home."

"Now, that's simply a lie," she said. "I called you at home, and you didn't answer. And when I drove by, no one was there."

"Wait, Tuesday. You're right, I wasn't home. I was at the warehouse most of the night. Waldo wasn't feeling well. He's this new Doberman puppy, and—"

"I called your cell, Sam."

"Battery was dead. I forgot to recharge it."

"And I went by the warehouse, Sam."

He was silent for a moment.

"You did," he said.

"I most certainly did," she said. "There was a light on, but no one answered the door."

"I may have dozed off," he said. "I'm surprised Carson didn't start barking. He must have known it was you."

"You know," she drawled. "I bet if Carson could speak, he could tell a lie way better than any drinking buddy ever could."

"I don't have drinking buddies," he said.

"You going to tell me what's going on?" she asked.

"Why are you doing this tonight of all nights?"

"Because I am tired of being with a man who won't be with me, Sam Lehrmann," she said. "I am tired of you keeping secrets from me. I can't live with a man who keeps secrets."

"Everyone has secrets."

"That is true. But I want you to trust me with yours, Sam. I want to know that you trust me."

He took his hands and placed them on her shoulders.

"There are things about me that no one can know about," he said.

"I do understand the concept of secrets, Sam," she said sharply. "I don't care if you're an escaped convict, or practice vivisection on hitchhikers, or you're a Mets fan. I just want to know the truth."

"I'm not a Mets fan," he said. "I'm not a convict, and I almost never practice vivisection on hitchhikers."

"Tuesday night, Sam. I want to know where you were."

"I was at the warehouse, Mona, and that's God's own truth for you."

"Alone?"

"Just me and the dogs. Not another human being around."

"And what were you doing there?"

"Nothing that concerns you," he said.

"You concern me," she said.

"I love you and I trust you," he said. "Now, I am asking you to trust me when I tell you that there is something about me that I cannot possibly talk about with you, or with anyone else. But it doesn't affect how I feel toward you, or—"

"Get out," she said wearily.

"What?"

"Get out, go away, don't come back," she said. "Get out of my house, get out of my life. I don't have many good years left, Sam, and I am sure as hell not going to waste them on you. Get out."

"It's Christmas Eve, Mona," he protested.

"There is no more room at this inn, Sam," she said. "And there ain't no manger waiting for you in back. Get out. And if you run into the Three Wise Men, ask them why they think they're so smart when they ain't got any women in their lives."

He stood up, walked to the door, then looked back at the woman and the dog on the couch. The dog was looking at him. The woman wasn't.

"You take good care of her, Nicky," he said.

The dog nodded. He left.

It was just as well, he thought. Stupid of him to even try. But it had lasted longer than he could have hoped, and he was beginning to dream of having . . .

Having what? A normal life?

Sure. That could happen.

The watcher met his men in front of the warehouse. Edwards waddled forward, his hands now encased in a pair of thick leather gloves. Hidalgo punched in the security code on the keypad while Kenner stood with his gun at the ready. The light on the keypad turned from red to green. Edwards took a deep breath, turned the knob, and went through the door.

Carson was on him before he had gone two steps, ripping through the padding on his right leg like it was made of crepe paper. Kenner leaned through the door, sighted carefully, and pulled the trigger once. Carson whined for a second, then went limp.

Edwards looked down at his leg. Blood was seeping through it.

"Damn," he said admiringly. "That's one sumbitch of a dog."

The watcher came in as the others fanned out around him, weapons at the ready. He nodded in satisfaction.

"Let's go," he said.

Arnie, the dachshund at the end, sensed them first, and let out a furious bark that set off those dogs that were awake and woke the ones that weren't. The combined bays, howls, yips, and snarls echoed off the metal roof of the warehouse at a deafening level.

Lehrmann was on his feet, his paws clapped over his ears.

"Everyone be quiet!" he roared.

The dogs ceased immediately, except for the dachshund.

"Arnie, will you please shut up?" said Lehrmann.

Arnie trailed off after one last token woof of protest.

"Thank you, Mister Lehrmann," said the watcher, strolling into view. His men spread out behind him, their guns pointed at Lehrmann's cage.

"What did you do to Carson?" asked Lehrmann.

"He's asleep," said the watcher. "Unharmed, but asleep. Unlike my man, who is somewhat harmed but very much awake. I trust that Carson had all of his shots?"

"Yeah," said Lehrmann. "I'm gonna have to get him more if he bit one of you guys."

"Cute," said the watcher. "Why do you call him Carson?"

"I named him for Johnny," said Lehrmann, standing toward the rear of his cage with his arms folded. "He's my late-night dog."

"How do you do it?" asked the man. "How do you get through the change so calmly?"

"What's it to you?" asked Lehrmann.

"Curiosity," said the man. "Werewolves are a hobby of mine."

"Meditation, relaxation techniques," said Lehrmann. "Nothing fancy. You just set your mind to it."

"Yet you keep yourself caged. Why?"

"First hour is always rough," said Lehrmann. "Just a precaution."

"Yes, I've watched you go through it for a couple of months, now," said the man, pulling out a small notebook. "The timer is set to release you at precisely one hour after sunset. Then you usually watch television until midnight, then go to sleep. Fascinating life you lead."

"Keeps me out of trouble," said Lehrmann, glancing through the bars at the watch on the table.

"Don't bother," said the man. "You still have half an hour until the lock opens. I'm surprised you don't have a backup switch for emergencies."

"That's Carson's job," said Lehrmann.

"Unfortunate," said the man.

"Yeah, I've got to figure out something better," said Lehrmann. "Never figured on the backup needing a backup. So, you gonna tell me who you are?"

The watcher smiled.

"I'm the Bogeyman," he said.

A German shepherd named Max was making the rounds at the factory where he lived. He looked up suddenly, then loped to a small hole in the chain-link fence that only he knew about. He wriggled through quickly, then galloped off into the night.

Sally and Waldo were three blocks from her house when he became agitated and strained against the leash, nearly pulling her off her feet.

"Waldo, come!" she said.

He looked at her resentfully.

"What's wrong?" she asked.

He whined. She squatted to look into his eyes. She studied them for a long time, then reached down to unclip his leash.

"All right, but you have to come back soon," she said. "I don't want either of us to get into trouble."

*　　*　　*

Mona stood at the doorway of her town house, a tumbler in her hand and Nicky by her side. She looked up at the full moon and shivered.

"Go to him," she whispered to Nicky, and the dog took off down the street.

"You got a name, Bogeyman?" asked Lehrmann.

"That's Mister Bogeyman to you," said the watcher. "Or you can call me Taylor."

"That your real name, Taylor?"

"It is."

"Well, Mister Taylor, how about you letting me know what you're doing here. I am assuming this isn't a social call."

"I have come to kill you, Sam," said Taylor, taking a tranquilizer gun handed to him by Hidalgo.

"Then I would prefer you call me Mister Lehrmann," said Lehrmann. "I don't fancy being on a first name basis with you at the moment."

"Fair enough," said Taylor.

"There is the question of why," said Lehrmann. "You one of those guys who is sexually impotent and only gets off on killing werewolves?"

"Are there many of those?" asked Taylor curiously.

"You hear things," said Lehrmann.

"No doubt," said Taylor. "No, this is a little tradition of mine this time of year. The last full moon before Christmas, I hunt and kill one werewolf."

"Wouldn't it be more fun if you stuck with the mistletoe and a little caroling?" suggested Lehrmann. "Chestnuts roasting on an open fire, and all that?"

"My sister was killed by a werewolf," said Taylor. "Christmas Eve, twenty-two years ago."

"I'm sorry," said Lehrmann. "You know it wasn't me."

"But I don't know that," said Taylor. "Not that it matters, not that I care. Even if you're not the one who killed my sister, you probably got some blood on your paws somewhere along the line, even with your nifty little yoga techniques."

"Most of us don't kill humans," said Lehrmann. "Unlike humans."

"Nevertheless, one of you did," said Taylor. "And she was very dear to me."

"I'm sorry for your loss, I truly am," said Lehrmann.

"Are you about to beg for your life?" asked Taylor.

"Would it do me any good?" asked Lehrmann. "Has it ever done anyone any good?"

"Not so far," said Taylor. "But there's always a first time."

"Yeah, well, in that case, fuck you," said Lehrmann.

Taylor pointed the tranquilizer gun through the bars and shot him in the leg.

"Ow," said Lehrmann, staring down at the dart. He pulled it out and threw it on the floor. "So the plan is you tranquilize me and then hunt me down?"

"No, the plan is I kill you slowly," said Taylor. "How does the leg feel?"

"Like it has a needle stuck in it, you fuck," said Lehrmann. "You better hope that shit works fast, because if I'm—"

He stopped as the burning sensation kicked in.

"Hurts, doesn't it?" observed Taylor. "At least, I hope it does."

"What was in the needle?" asked Lehrmann, his heart racing.

"A sizable dose of aconite," said Taylor. "The pain is nasty, but then comes the numbness."

"Aconite," repeated Lehrmann.

"From the plant *Aconitum vulparia*," said Taylor, watching him intently. "Commonly known as—"

"Yellow wolfsbane," said Lehrmann.

"Of course you would be familiar with it," continued Taylor. "Folklore says that it's fatal to werewolves. The truth is, it's fatal to pretty much everybody. Nasty little neurotoxin in a pretty yellow flower that will kill you even if you only pick it up barehanded. I grow my own. Very carefully."

"How long does it take?" asked Lehrmann.

"The amount you just absorbed will kill a man in about an hour," said Taylor. "From my experience, and I can't say that I have a large enough sample to conclude this scientifically, about ninety minutes to two hours to kill a werewolf, depending on the strength of the werewolf."

"That gate opens long before that," said Lehrmann. "And I am pretty damn strong."

"A daunting prospect if you could walk," said Taylor.

The werewolf sagged to one knee.

"The literature describes the sensation as numbness spreading through the body, eventually stopping the heart," said Taylor. "The symptoms are said to be fairly unpleasant. Again, in my experience, that is a gross understatement. Werewolves seem to be particularly susceptible to it. And the best part—do you want to know the best part?"

"Not really," said Lehrmann.

"The best part is that you will be conscious until the very end."

"You bastard," muttered Lehrmann, trying to stand and failing.

"What is lovely about this particular kill is that the full moon fell on Christmas Eve again," said Taylor. "Only the second time that's happened since my sister's death, given the vagaries of the lunar cycle and the solar calendar. In honor of the holiday, I thought I should make this one special."

"Lucky me," said Lehrmann.

"No doubt, the irony of being helpless in a building full of guard dogs has already struck you," said Taylor.

"Sure has," said Lehrmann.

"Such beautiful animals," said Taylor. "And you treat them so well. I thought that we would give them a little Christmas treat."

Hidalgo and Edwards carried in the butcher's block and the electric saw. They placed it by Taylor, then stood back, weapons at the ready.

"Once you are sufficiently paralyzed," said Taylor, "I am going to take this dandy little saw of yours and chop you into dog food, piece by piece. And you will be conscious until the moment your heart stops. You had better pray that it stops quickly. Then I am going to feed you to your own dogs. Mind you, the aconite in your bloodstream isn't going to do them any good, but that's the risk with fresh meat."

"You sick fuck!" shouted Lehrmann.

"You are going to be the death of the creatures you love most dearly in the world," said Taylor, squatting to see him better. "More than that pathetic lush who wasted herself on you."

Boss?

Lehrmann almost didn't sense it.

Boss?

Nicky? he thought.

There was a dissonance of thoughts, then Nicky hushed the others.

Me, Max, and some new dog, says he just got placed today.

Waldo.

"Mister Lehrmann, are you still with us?" asked Taylor.

Lehrmann moaned in pain.

"Not as strong as he thought," commented Edwards.

Boss, how many are there?

Four, thought Lehrmann.

We can take them. They left the door open.

No. They're armed.

Others will be here. One hour, maybe less.

I don't have an hour, thought Lehrmann.

The lock beeped and clicked, and the gate swung open. He tried to lurch forward, but neither leg was working.

"It's reached the lower spine, and it's working its way up," said Taylor. "Give him a few minutes. He can still swing those arms."

"Suits me fine," said Edwards. "I already got one bite tonight."

Too bad the gate was working so well, thought Lehrmann. If it had jammed, at least the other dogs would have been spared their last meal.

The other dogs.

Nicky, do you know where the switch to the cages is?

No. That was put in after I left.

I do, thought Waldo.

Can you reach it?

*   *   *

Outside the door, the Rottweiler and the German shepherd looked at the Doberman. He bared his teeth.

Taylor looked at his watch.

"We should start now," he said. "I don't want him to die without feeling it."

He looked down at the werewolf, who was breathing hard.

"Mister Lehrmann," he called. "Please don't struggle when we pick you up. You may be strong, but we outnumber you."

"Other way around," gasped Lehrmann.

Waldo shot across the arena, gathered himself, and leapt, crashing into the switch on the wall, then falling in a heap on the floor. The doors to the cages sprung open. There was a brief moment while everyone was silent and looking at each other.

"Playtime," said Lehrmann.

For all the pent-up rage and primal savagery of the pack, it was Arnie the dachshund who was the first out of his cage, baying and scampering on his short legs as hard as he could. The others took his cue and crashed into the room ahead of him. Of the four men, only Hidalgo managed to get a shot off before a pit bull clamped down on his wrist. The gun fell from his hand as he screamed.

A minute later, the hand fell from his arm.

The dogs piled on top of the four men, clawing and gouging whatever they could reach. Arnie, the last in, jumped as high as he could and sank his teeth into Taylor's thigh. The watcher, staggering under the weight of five dogs, uttered a piercing shriek, then fell.

Nicky came in, surveyed the scene, then came over to where Lehrmann lay on the floor. She looked into his eyes, then licked his paw.

"Nice to see you, too," he said. "Is everyone okay?"

Waldo's a little woozy from jumping into the wall. He's a good dog. I like him.

"Tell Max to get him home," he said. "Then help me get to the tool room."

She ran off, and he started to drag himself across the floor with his arms. Nicky came back, saw him, and gave a quick bark. Several of the larger dogs separated themselves from the carnage and ran to help. Together, they pushed the werewolf along the floor until he was inside the tool room. He tried to pull himself up, then collapsed.

Mona drove her Prius extremely carefully. She worried that she might be driving too carefully, a sure tip-off to any patrolling cop that she was anything but sober.

Somehow, she made it to the farm road without inflicting any damage. As she turned on to it, her headlights picked up a pair of dogs loping toward her. She stopped the car and stared. A German shepherd and a somewhat dazed Doberman looked back at her. The Doberman bared his teeth. Then she could have sworn that the German shepherd recognized her. He growled softly, and the two dogs resumed their journey past her.

She drove on until she reached the warehouse. The front door was open. A strange cargo van was parked in front. She reached under her glove compartment and grabbed her gun. She got out of her car and walked quietly to the door. She listened for a moment, then stepped inside.

Immediately she was ringed by a pack of snarling dogs, many with their teeth and muzzles bloody, but before any of them could make a move, a familiar bark greeted her.

"Nicky!" she cried, and the Rottweiler bounded up to her.

The rest of the pack ceased their menacing and trotted back into the other room.

"Nicky, where's Sam?" she asked.

The dog whined and ran to the entrance to the tool room. She ran after her, looked inside, and screamed.

There was a wolf lying on the floor—no, larger than a wolf, larger than the biggest wolf who ever lived, with fangs that were bared and claws that could slice through tree trunks, and she raised her gun and was about to shoot when it rolled its eyes in her direction and whimpered.

"Sam," she cried out, dropping the gun and throwing herself down to hold him tight.

"Mona," he breathed hoarsely. "Medicine cabinet. Box labeled ATROPINE."

She leapt to her feet and flung open the cabinet. The box was on the lower shelf. She opened it and saw three syringes, their needles capped.

"How many and where?" she asked, kneeling to hear him.

"Two," he gasped. "Right in the heart. Then wait five minutes and give me the third if there's no response."

"Your heart," she said, feeling the matted fur on his chest.

"Same place it always was," he said. "Don't hit a rib."

She pulled the cap off the first needle and felt along his ribs under the chest until she located the gap. She took a breath, then jabbed the needle deep into his chest and pressed the plunger until it could go no farther. He grunted with pain. She removed it, repeated the process with the second, then leaned down and wrapped her arms around him.

"What if the third one doesn't work?" she asked.

"Then I'm dead," he whispered.

Sally was standing on the spot where Waldo left her, his lead in her hand. She gave a cry of relief when she saw him, then stopped when she saw the German shepherd by his side. Waldo came up and sat by her feet.

"Are you all right?" she asked.

He nodded, still groggy. She looked at the other dog.

"Are you a friend of his?" she asked.

The dog nodded.

"Did Mister Lehrmann train you?" she asked.

The dog nodded again.

"My name is Sally," she said. "Very nice to meet you."

The dog nodded once more, looked at Waldo, then ran off.

"Merry Christmas!" she called after him. She clipped the lead onto the Doberman's collar and went home.

* * *

"Ahh!" he cried.

"Sam, do you need the third injection?" she asked.

"Just pain," he gasped. "Pain's a good sign. Means the nerves are coming back."

He made a fist several times.

"Help me sit up," he asked.

She reached her arms around his body and pulled.

"God, you're heavy," she said, wrestling him to a sitting position against the wall.

"I think it's going to be okay," he said. "My heartbeat sounds good."

"But you're a werewolf," she said.

"Atropine doesn't cure that."

"But you're a werewolf," she repeated.

"Yes."

"What the hell just happened? What was the atropine for?"

"Antidote for aconite," he said. "I always keep it around for special occasions like this."

"What the hell is aconite?"

"It's a poison," he said. "Word got around that someone's been going after us—"

"Us? There are more?"

"You'd be surprised."

"You got that right."

"So anyway, I got some atropine just in case some nut job decided to throw some wolfsbane in my direction. And that's pretty much what happened."

"Wolfsbane," she said, confused. "Wait. Where is the nut job? There's a van outside—"

She jumped up, grabbed her gun, and charged back out.

"Mona!" he called after her. "Don't go in there!"

She appeared in the doorway a minute later, the blood draining from her face, the gun dangling limply at her side.

"I'm going to go outside and be sick for a while," she said numbly. "You wait here."

By the time she came back, he was breathing easily and bending his knees.

"I brought some eggnog," she said. "And some marshmallows. Do werewolves eat marshmallows?"

"Don't see why not," he said.

He pulled himself to his feet and staggered a little.

"How did you know I was in trouble?" he asked.

"I didn't," she said. "Nicky knew somehow. Dog telegraph, I suppose."

"How did you know to let her go to me?" he asked.

She looked into his eyes. Still Sam's eyes.

"I guess I responded to her auditory cues," said Mona. "That happens in a close relationship."

He took her hand between his paws and pressed it to his chest.

"So, this is the big secret," she said as they walked together out of the tool room. "All those nights you avoided me were when the moon was full. I never picked up on the pattern."

"Didn't see any way of telling you," he said.

"All things considered, that's understandable," she said. "I'm sorry I didn't understand it at the time."

"It's Christmas Eve," he said. "I think a little forgiveness is in order. Both ways."

"Okay," she said.

"Dogs, playtime's over!" he called.

They came up to him, and he knelt before them.

"Thank you," he said. "Thank you all."

Tails thumped on the floor.

"Dogs, cages," he said, and they turned and went to their beds. He pressed the switch, and the cages closed.

"What are you going to do about those men?" she asked, rubbing Nicky's neck.

"I'll put what's left of them into their van, and drive it down to the old quarry pond," he said. "I should be able to sink it in there."

"Won't you be leaving fingerprints?"

He held up his paws.

"I don't have fingerprints right now," he said. "And if they find a hair, they'll just think it was a wolf."

"Want me to mop up while you're gone?"

"No," he said. "I'll do that tomorrow."

"Hell of a way to spend Christmas Day."

"Could have been a whole lot worse," he said. "You get a fire going outside."

"A fire?"

"For the marshmallows."

"Hey, Mister Lehrmann," said Bert as Sam came in. "How was your Christmas? Did your family make it over?"

"Yes, they did, Bert," said Lehrmann. "Everything worked out fine."

"And did the dogs enjoy their Christmas lamb?"

"They did," said Lehrmann. "I'm sure they would thank you if they knew how. It's like I said, Bert. There's nothing like fresh meat for a dog."

Il Est Né

Carrie Vaughn

Carrie Vaughn survived her Air Force brat childhood and managed to put down roots in Colorado. She lives in Boulder with her dog, Lily, and too many hobbies. A graduate of the Odyssey Writing Workshop, she's had short stories published in such magazines as Realms of Fantasy *and* Weird Tales. *Most of her work over the last couple of years has gone into her series of novels about a werewolf named Kitty who hosts a talk radio show for the supernaturally disadvantaged. "Il Est Né" takes place right before the third book,* Kitty Takes a Holiday.

Hugging himself, shivering, David curled up under the reaching bows of a pine tree. A moonlit drift of snow glowed silver just a few feet away, outside his shelter. More snow was falling, and he was naked. If he simply relaxed, he wouldn't be that cold. But he was afraid. More afraid every time this happened.

He didn't know where he was, but that didn't bother him so much anymore. And how strange it was, that something like that didn't bother him. *That* was what bothered him. Not knowing, not remembering, had become normal. He didn't know where he was, but he knew exactly how he got here. It was getting harder to claw his way out of this space, to keep this from happening. He was losing himself.

The fire had taken him again. Blood rose and changed him. In a helpless surge, another body of fur and teeth, claw and sinew overcame him. The hunter, the wolf. He couldn't stop the Change. He could flee, stumbling into a wild place where no one would see him, where he wouldn't hurt anyone. Better that he stay here, because the pull was getting harder to resist. Easy to say that this was where he belonged, now.

Sometime in the last year, since this curse had landed on him, his thinking had switched. He wasn't a human who turned into a wolf.

Instead, he was a wolf trapped in human skin. The wolf wanted to run away forever. Might be easier, if he just never returned to human. But he did.

At some point, he drifted back to sleep and woke to bright sunlight gleaming off the snow. Blinding, almost. It would be a beautiful day, with a searing blue Colorado sky, crisp snow, chilled air. And he couldn't really sit here under a tree, bare-ass naked, confused, and depressed, all day.

Ultimately, that was what drew him back to civilization. He was still human, and the human grew bored. He'd walk, find a road, a town, steal some clothes. Figure out the date and how long he'd been out of it this time. Wander in the company of people, until the fire took him again.

Just because Kitty couldn't go home for Christmas didn't mean she had to be alone.

At least, that was the reasoning behind forcing herself to spend part of the day at a Waffle House off the interstate. It was the holidays, you were supposed to spend them with family, with voices raised in celebration, toasting each other and eating too much food.

Not that any of that was happening here. It was her, a couple of truckers, the waitress, the cook, a glass of middling nonalcoholic eggnog, and Bing Crosby on the radio. All in all this was one of the most depressing scenes she'd ever witnessed.

She was reading Dickens while sipping her eggnog. Not the obvious one, which hadn't lasted long, but *Bleak House*. The title seemed appropriate, and at three inches thick would last her a good long while.

Just a couple more hours, she thought. Long enough to have supper in the company of other people—no matter that no one had said a word to each other in half an hour. Then she'd go to her rented room, call her family to wish them happy holidays, and go to bed.

The music cut off, and Kitty looked up, ready to complain. The Christmas carols had been the only thing making this place bearable. How pathetic was that, clinging to old-school carols piped through the speakers of a cut-rate stereo? Behind the counter, the waitress pulled over a footstool and used it to reach the TV, sitting on a shelf high on the wall. She popped a VHS tape into the built-in slot.

As if she felt Kitty watching her, she—Jane, according to her name tag—looked over her shoulder and smiled.

"*It's a Wonderful Life*," Jane said. "I play it every year."

Oh, this was going to make Kitty *cry*.

The fact that Jane had spent enough years here to make it a tradition, not to mention she had the movie on videotape rather than DVD, somehow added to the depressing state of the situation. That could have been a lot of Christmases. Jane wasn't young: wrinkles formed around her eyes and lips, and her curling hair was dyed a gray-masking brown. Waitressing at Waffle House didn't seem like much of a career. A stop-gap maybe, a pay-the-bills kind of job on the way to somewhere else. It wasn't supposed to become your life. No one should have to work at Waffle House on Christmas every damn year.

Kitty set her book aside and leaned back in the booth to get a better view. There were worse ways to kill time. She'd watch the movie, then blow this popsicle stand.

Amazing what people left on their clotheslines in the dead of winter. It was a small-town characteristic he'd come to depend on. Blue flannel shirt, worn white T, wool socks. He wasn't desperate enough to steal underwear and went without. He found baling twine in a trash can and turned it into a belt to hold up a pair of oversized jeans. The work boots he found abandoned behind a gas station were a size too small. He didn't look great. He looked homeless, with shaggy brown hair and a five o'clock shadow—five o'clock the next day. He *was* homeless. He only bothered because he felt he ought to. Walk through town and remind himself what it was like to be human. He *wanted* to be human. Wearing clothes reminded him. He'd loved his job—raft guide in the summer, ski instructor in the winter. Stereotypical Colorado outdoor jock. He and some of the guys wanted to start their own rafting company. He was going to go back to school, get a degree in business—

Not anymore.

David cleaned up as well as he could at the gas station restroom. The nice thing about stealing clothes off a clothesline—at least they were clean. He scrubbed his face, his hands, slicked back his hair, guessed that he didn't smell too awful. Squared his shoulders and tried to stand up straight. Tried to look human.

He regarded himself in a cracked mirror and sighed. He wasn't a bad-looking guy. He was young. He should have had his whole life ahead of him. But he looked at himself now and only saw shadows. His eyes gave off a shine of helplessness. Hopelessness. Their brown seemed more amber, and something else looked out of them. He was trapped in his own body. He washed his face again, trying to get rid of that expression.

He could usually find an evening's work somewhere, washing dishes or sweeping up, if someone felt sorry enough for him. Enough to pay for a meal—a cooked, human meal. He hadn't yet resorted to panhandling. He'd rather run wild in the woods and never come back.

Near the interstate, the minimalist main street of this small town seemed quiet for an early evening. No cars drove by, only a couple were parked. The only place open, with its sign lit up, was the Waffle House at the edge of town.

The smell of the town seemed strange after his days in the forest. His nostrils flared with the scent of oil, metal, and people. An inner voice told him this wasn't his place anymore. He ought to flee. But no—he was here, he'd make a go of it. Trying to soften the tension in his shoulders, willing himself to stay calm, he headed to the restaurant.

The bell hanging on the door rang as a man walked in. What do you know, another angel gets his wings.

Kitty glanced over to see him, but his scent reached her first: wild, the musk of lupine fur hiding under human skin. In instinctive response, her shoulders tightened with the motion of hackles rising. She sat up, her hands clenching, the ghosts of claws reaching inside her fingers.

He was a werewolf. Just like her.

He froze in the still open doorway, his eyes wide. Clearly, he'd scented her as well, and was shocked. He looked like he might bolt. Their gazes locked, and Kitty's heartbeat sped up. A stare was a challenge, but this wasn't right, because the guy almost looked terrified. Like he didn't know what to do.

"You want to close that, honey? You're letting the warm air out." Jane smiled over the counter at the guy, and that broke the tension.

Kitty looked away—another bit of wolf body language, a move that said she wasn't a threat, and she didn't want to fight. She forced herself to settle back—and could sense him relax a notch as well, lowering his gaze, turning away. She desperately wanted to talk to him. What was he doing here? She didn't know of any werewolves within a hundred miles.

Which was part of what brought her here.

The man—young, disheveled, wearing ill-fitting clothing and a haunted expression—slouched inside his flannel shirt and moved to the counter.

He spoke softly to Jane, but Kitty held her breath and made out what he said. "Uh, yeah. I'm a little hard up, and I was wondering if there was anything I could do to earn a cup of coffee and a pancake or something."

Jane smiled kindly. "Sorry, there's nothing. This is our slowest night of the year." The man looked around, at faded tinsel garlands strung around the walls, at the movie playing on the TV, and blinked at Jane in confusion. "It's Christmas," she said.

He glanced at the TV again with a look of terrible sadness.

This scene pushed all Kitty's curiosity buttons. The urge could not be denied.

It was all she could do not to rush straight at him, but if he'd been startled and tense at her just looking at him, she could imagine what that would do. He was on edge—more wolf than human almost, even though full moon was over a week away.

She walked toward him, her gaze down and her posture loose. He backed up a step at her approach. She tried to put on a pleasant, non-threatening face.

"I'm sorry, I don't mean to interrupt, but you look like you could use a cup of coffee. Can I buy you one?" She laced her hands behind her back. He started to shake his head, and she said, "No strings, nothing funny. Consider it a Christmas present from another one of the tribe who doesn't have anywhere else to go." She glanced at Jane, who smiled and reached under the counter for a cup and saucer.

"Hi. I'm Kitty." She offered her hand. Didn't really expect the guy to shake it, and he didn't. It wasn't a wolfish gesture. She'd never seen a lycanthrope look so out of place in human clothing.

He took a moment to register the name, then pursed his lips in a sti-fled laugh. He actually smiled. There was a handsome guy under the hard times. "I'm sorry, but that's the funniest thing I've heard in a while."

She wrinkled her nose. "It gets a little old, believe me."

"How did a were—" He cut himself off when Jane returned with the pot of coffee.

"Why don't we go talk about it?" Kitty said, nodding back toward her booth.

A moment later, they were sitting across from each other, each of them with fresh cups of coffee. Jane also brought over a plate of pan-cakes. David gazed up at her sheepishly, blushing. Embarrassed, Kitty decided. He didn't like the charity. But he drowned the pancakes with syrup and dug into them.

Around bites, he finished his thought. "How did a werewolf end up with a name like Kitty?"

"The better question is, How did someone named Kitty end up as a werewolf? That's a long story."

"It's almost as bad as a werewolf named Harry."

Perish the thought. "Oh my God, your name isn't—"

"No," he said, ducking his gaze. "It's David."

"Well, David. It's nice to meet you. Though I have to say, I wasn't expecting to see another one of us walk through the door. Are you from around here?"

"No. I've been on the road awhile."

"That's what I thought."

He hadn't yet taken a sip of his coffee, but he wrapped a hand

around the cup, clinging to it like he could draw out its warmth. He
hunched over, gazing out at the world with uncertainty. He probably
didn't realize how odd he looked, coming out of the cold without a
coat. Werewolves didn't feel the cold as much.

Looking at the tabletop, he said, "I've never met another one. Not
ever. But I could tell, as soon as I walked in here I could smell you and I
knew. I almost walked right back out again."

"What, let a little old thing like me scare you off?" She'd meant it as
a joke, but he flinched. She willed him to relax. His hand around the
mug squeezed a little tighter. He set his fork down and pressed his fist to
the table.

His voice was taut. "You seem so calm. How do you do it?" His
gaze flickered up, and the look in them was stark. Desperate.

She froze, nerveless for a moment. Is that how she looked? Calm?
She was exiled from her pack, driven from Denver by the alpha werewolves, and so was spending Christmas at a Waffle House in a desolate
corner of the state and not with her family. She felt like she was on the
verge of losing it. Without an anchor. She'd lost her anchor—but David
had never had one.

"What about the one who turned you?"

"I was camping by myself, something . . . something attacked me. It
looked like . . . I remember thinking, this is impossible, there aren't any
wolves here. I knew something was wrong when I woke up, and I didn't
have any wounds, no scars, and I didn't . . ."

He stopped, swallowed visibly, clamped his eyes shut. His breathing
and heart rate quickened, and his scent spiked with fur and wild, wolf
trembling just under his skin.

He didn't know how to control it at all, she realized. He hadn't had
anyone to teach him. He'd been running as a wolf recently. Probably
woke up with no idea where he was—no idea that it was Christmas,
even.

Suddenly, her own situation didn't seem so bad.

"Breathe slowly," she whispered. "Think about pulling it in. Keep it
together."

He rested his elbows on the table and ran his fingers through his hair. His hands were shaking. "I turn all the time. Not just on full moons. I can't stop it. Then I run, and I don't remember what happens. I know I hunt, kill whatever's out there—but I don't remember. I try to stay away from people, far away. But I just don't remember. I don't want to be like this, I don't—" His fingers tightened in his hair, his jaw clenched, teeth gritting. His wolf was right on the edge. Always right on the edge.

"Shh." She wanted to touch him, to steady him, but didn't dare. Anything might set him off. And wouldn't that be a Christmas to remember? Werewolf rampage in a Waffle House in southern Colorado . . . He might have done okay by Jimmy Stewart, but she'd like to see Clarence the angel fix that mess.

He looked at her. Square on this time. "How do you do it? What's your story?"

"I had a pack," she said. "They found me right after it happened to me. Like you, in the woods, attacked. But they took care of me. Told me what had happened, taught me how to deal with it."

"Does that happen?"

"Yeah, it does. There are probably more of us out there than you think. We keep quiet, stay hidden. At least, most of us do." And that was more story than she should probably go into at the moment.

"Where are they? Your pack."

Her smile turned wry. "I left. Or got kicked out. Depends on who you ask."

He looked crestfallen. The concept of a pack—the idea that he might not be alone—seemed to have heartened him. But that opportunity had once again become remote. "I didn't know. How was I supposed to know something like that was possible? I've been so alone."

What were the odds that his wandering brought him here, to her, perhaps the one werewolf in all the world who'd listen to his problems and want to help?

She said, "It doesn't have to be like that. You can control it. You can lead a normal life. Mostly normal, at least."

"How?" he said, teeth clenched, voice grating. Like she'd told him he could fly to the moon, or dig a hole and find a million dollars.

"You have to really want to."

Donning a smile that was more grimace, he glanced through the fogged window, to a graying, snowy parking lot. He spoke with sarcasm. "You make it sound so easy."

"I didn't say that. It's not easy. I spend a lot of time arguing with my inner wolf."

"So do I. I lose."

"Then you have to figure out how to start winning."

He chuckled. "You ever think about going into the self-help business?"

She almost asked him if he listened to the radio much, or watched TV recently. Obviously he hadn't, or he would have already said something about her talk radio show.

She smiled slyly at the tabletop. "The idea had occurred to me."

David seemed calmer. Once or twice, Kitty had been accused of talking too much. But she found that talking improved almost every situation. Talking could make a lone werewolf on the run feel a little less lonely.

Jane marched in from the kitchen, straight toward the TV. Frowning, she pressed a cell phone to her ear. "Okay," she said. "What channel?"

She pulled her stool under the TV again and stopped the tape. A cheerful Donna Reed cut off mid-sentence.

In place of the movie, Jane turned on a news station, turned up the volume, then moved away to watch.

A young news reporter was standing in a winter landscape, a windblown field in the foothills nearby, a few stray snowflakes drifting around her. She was lit with a harsh spotlight and speaking somberly.

". . . series of gruesome murders. The violence of these deaths has authorities concerned that the perpetrator may be using an attack dog of some kind. Police would not give us any further details. Authorities are asking residents to stay inside and lock their doors until the killer is apprehended."

Behind the woman, a crime scene was in full swing: three or four police cars, an ambulance, many people in uniforms moving purposefully, and what seemed like miles of yellow caution tape. The camera caught sight of a spatter of blood on the ground and a filled body bag before the scene cut away.

A male reporter in a studio repeated the warning—stay indoors— and a scroll at the bottom listed the information: five deaths within the space of an afternoon, violence indicating a highly disturbed, animalistic killer.

Jane folded her phone away, hurried to the door, and locked it. "That's just a few miles up the road from here. I hope nobody minds," she said, regarding her customers with a nervous smile. No one argued.

He said he Changed, hunted, and didn't remember.

For a long moment, Kitty stared at the stranger across from her. Nervously, he looked away, tapping his fingers, slumped in the plastic booth like he didn't fit in the confined space.

She shouldn't have automatically been suspicious, but David's situation raised questions. Where had he come from? What had he been doing before he woke up and found—stole—the clothes he was wearing? Was it possible? The only thing she knew: David was a werewolf, and werewolves were capable of violent, bloody murder.

"Get up," she said to him, growling almost. She didn't like the feeling rising up in her—anger, which stirred her Wolf. Quickened her blood. Had to keep that feeling in check. But she'd offered him friendship and didn't want that to have been a mistake.

"What?" he said, voice low.

"Come on. In back. We have to talk." She jerked her head toward the bathrooms, down a little hallway behind her. Glaring at him, she stood and waited until he did likewise. She stormed into the back hallway, drawing him behind her.

Kitty pulled him into the women's restroom. If anyone noticed, let them think what they would. Keeping hold of his collar, she pushed him to the wall. Working on sheer bravado, she tried to act big and strong. He could throw her across the room if he wanted to. Trick was not to let him try. Dominate him, play the alpha wolf, and hope his instincts to defer to that kicked in.

"Where were you before you showed up here?" she demanded.

Whatever attitude she'd been able to pull out worked. He was almost trembling, avoiding her gaze. Mentally sticking a tail between his legs.

She hadn't been sure she could really pull it off.

"I was walking," he said. "Just walking."

"And before that?"

"I was out of it." He grew more nervous, looking away, scuffing his shoes. "I turned. I don't really know where I was."

"What do you remember?"

"I never remember very much." His voice was soft, filled with pain.

She understood what that was like—remembering took practice, control. Even then the memories were fuzzy, inhuman, taken in through wolf senses. He didn't have any of that control to begin with.

"Did you hunt?" she asked, hoping to spark some recollection. "Did you kill?"

"Of course I did! That's what we do, what we are."

He tried to pull away, cringing back from her touch. She curled her lip in a snarl to keep him still.

"Think, you have to think! What was it? What did you kill? Was it big? Small? Did it have fur?"

He growled, his teeth bared, and an animal scent rolled off him.

She'd pushed him too far. She almost quailed. She almost backed down. His aggression was palpable, and it frightened her. But she fought not to let that show. Stood her ground. Being alpha was a new feeling for her.

"So you could have killed someone," she said.

He pulled away and covered his face with his hands. She barely heard him whisper, "No. No, it's impossible. It has to be impossible."

He didn't know. Honestly didn't know. Now, what was she supposed to do about that?

She tried again, calmer this time. Pulled out whatever counseling skills she'd picked up over the last year.

"Try to think. Can you remember images? Scents, emotions. Some clue. Anything."

He shook his head firmly. "I don't know what it's like for you, but I don't remember anything. I don't know anything!"

"Nothing?"

"It's a blank. But you—how can you remember? You don't actually remember—"

"Images," she said. "The smell of trees. Night air. Trails. Prey." A long pause, as the memory took her, just for a moment. A flood of emotion, a tang of iron, euphoria of victory. Yes, she remembered. "Blood. Now, what do you remember?"

He dug the heels of his hands into his temples and dropped to a crouch. Gritting his teeth, setting his jaw, he groaned, a sound of anguish. Every one of his muscles tensed, the tendons on his hands and neck standing out. He was shaking.

She worried. He was alone, out of control, and over the edge. She knelt by him and touched the back of his head—simple contact, chaste, comforting. "Keep it together," she said. "Pull it in. Hold it in. Breathe slower. In . . . out." She spoke softly, calmly, until he matched his breaths to the rate of her speech. Slowly, he calmed. The tension in his fists relaxed. He lowered his arms. His face eased from a grimace to a simple frown.

She stroked his hair and rested her hand on his shoulder. "It's possible to keep some control and remember."

"I used to have a life," he said. "I just want my life back."

She didn't know what to say. Of course he wanted his life back. So much easier if everything could go back to the way it was. Nearly every day she thought of it. But if you wanted that life back, you had to fight for it. Fight for that control, every day.

"What am I going to do?" he said, voice shaking, almost a sob.

"Nothing," she said. "We wait."

If he hadn't done anything, nothing would come of this. Nothing would lead the police to him. But she didn't want to even suggest that much. In case he had done something, and the police did come for him.

David took a moment to recover after Kitty left the bathroom. Not that a moment alone would help. He felt fractured. The parts of his being had scattered, for months now.

He didn't understand her at all. She was like him—the same, another monster, a werewolf. And yet she was completely different. So . . . with it. And he didn't understand how she did it. How she looked so *calm.*

If he couldn't remember what had happened, maybe he could learn what happened some other way. He couldn't sit here waiting for the cops to find him and haul him away. Not that they could. The moment he felt danger, he knew what would happen—he would turn, and run.

He stepped to the end of the hall that tucked the bathrooms away from the restaurant. Kitty had returned to the booth. The waitress poured her more coffee, which she sipped. Hunched over the table, she looked out with a nervous gaze. He could see the wolf in her, intense brown eyes flickering to every movement, watchful, alert. Part of him was afraid of her, her strength and confidence. She'd had him cowed in a second.

She believed he was a murderer, and he couldn't deny it. Couldn't say that she was wrong. He couldn't be sure that she wouldn't call the police. He'd only known her for an hour. She might be a monster like him, but she also seemed like the kind of person who would tell the police. A law-abiding werewolf. He never would have believed it.

He had to prove that he didn't do it.

From the hallway, he ducked and slipped to the back of the kitchen, moving quickly so Kitty or the waitress wouldn't see him. She'd think the worst.

One guy in the kitchen, a Latino wearing a white apron, looked at him. "Hey—"

David didn't slow down but ran straight through the kitchen, unlocked the back door, and slipped out. Outside, he paused, taking deep breaths of chilly air through flaring nostrils. Night had fallen, gray and overcast. A light snow fell. A dusting of it would mask scents.

Thinking like a hunter, a wolf—he shook his head to clear his vision of the haze that covered it for a moment. Couldn't let the wolf take over. Had to stay human. What had Kitty said? Keep it together.

His breathing slowed. He straightened his back and felt a little more human.

The lot behind the restaurant was lit by a single, fuzzy orange lamp. Only one car was parked here. Snow coated it, so it had been here awhile.

Beyond that lay an interstate wasteland: scrub-covered verges, cracked parking lots and frontage road, ancient gas stations. Cars hummed on the distant freeway, even on Christmas.

A set of flashing lights traveled along the frontage road. David took off at a run after the police car.

In less than half an hour, he reached one of the murder scenes.

He caught a scent—blood, thick on the ground. A hint of rot, meaning guts had been spilled. Not fresh, the slaughter had lain open to air for a while.

Human blood. Somehow, he recognized it.

But did he recognize this place, this situation? Or was it a false memory? Did he recognize the scene from the newscast?

Moving low, almost on all fours, touching the ground with his hands every now and then to keep his balance as he ran, he approached the site. He kept out of sight, hiding among the dried vegetation, banked with crusted snow. *This would be easier on four legs. As wolf.* He fought to ignore the voice whispering at him, clawing at him. He wanted to keep his awareness.

Police cars blocked off a place where a pickup truck had pulled over along the road. Yellow tape fluttered, marking off almost an acre of land around it. A half dozen people moved around the space, bent over, studying the ground.

David stopped and lay close to the ground, hidden, and studied the area as well as he could. Three body bags on stretchers lay by an ambulance. The pickup truck's doors were open, lights shining around it. Its interior was covered in blood.

Did he even know what he was looking for here? What he hoped to find? He had to admit, he didn't know. He just wanted to see the bodies. See that it had been guns or knives that had done this, spattered all that blood over the truck. Not teeth and claws.

But he could imagine a scenario: Driving along the road, this family, or maybe group of friends, saw a huge wolf loping alongside them.

Curious, they stopped to watch, because wild wolves weren't found here. Maybe they stepped out to take a picture. And it wasn't a wolf, and he was drawn by the promise of easy prey, of slaughter—

He buried his face in his arm to stop the vision. He choked on a sob, because his mouth was watering. At the same time, he wanted to vomit.

That wasn't a memory. Just overactive imagination. He couldn't remember. *Couldn't.*

He imagined Kitty's voice telling him to slow his breathing, to hold the panic at bay. To keep it together.

Crawling on his belly, infantry-like, he inched forward to get a better look.

Kitty expected David to follow her back to the booth, after he settled down. They'd wait for news, hope for the best.

Surely he'd remember *something* if he'd killed someone. Surely. But who could say? For all her bluster, she knew so little about it.

Minutes passed, and he didn't return. Not that she could blame him if he'd decided to avoid her. Maybe stay in the bathroom, hiding from everyone. This whole spending the holidays with people thing left something to be desired.

Finally, she went back to the bathrooms to check. He wasn't in the women's anymore. For the best, probably. She knocked on the door to the men's. "David?" she called, and got no answer. She opened the door a crack, peered in. Empty. So where had he gone?

From the back hallway, the kitchen was visible, all stainless steel surfaces and stove tops. The single cook on duty leaned on a counter, looking out at the TV. And on the other side of the room was a door to the outside.

Her heart thudded, contemplating what he was doing. She'd been stupid, confronting him like that. Now she'd driven him off. Who knew what he would do, an out-of-control werewolf roaming the countryside?

Of course, now it was up to her to clean up the mess. Or at least keep it from getting worse.

Crouching to avoid drawing the cook's attention, she dashed across the kitchen and went through the door, which was already unlocked. As if someone had been this way already. Outside was freezing. But her blood was warm, Wolf running through her, firing her senses. Scent, sound, feel—she searched for his trail by the way the hairs on the back of her neck tingled. She felt the heat of his footsteps on the ground.

Breaking into a jog, she followed his trail, the faint touch of his scent, like a taste in the back of her throat. She let a bit of Wolf bleed into her consciousness. A bit of the hunter, tracking one of her own.

She shouldn't have been surprised to find the trail leading straight toward what was clearly a crime scene of epic proportions. Flashing blue and red flared out over the countryside, turning the darkness into a surreal disco parody. The snow fell heavier now, large flakes burning on her skin. They glittered in the lights. She'd forgotten her coat, but hardly noticed; she was sweating from the exertion.

Not wanting to get caught, and certainly not wanting to answer questions about why she was out here, she dropped to the ground. She assumed David had done the same, since she couldn't see him silhouetted against the lights. Instead, she saw what must have been dozens of cops milling inside a taped-off area.

And she smelled blood. Great quantities of reeking, rotten blood and bile. People hadn't just died, they'd been shredded. Her human sensibilities gagged. The Wolf merely catalogued the information: several bodies, human, gutted, and they'd been out awhile. Carrion, Wolf thought. Kitty shook the thought away.

Had they been dead long enough for David to have been the culprit? Almost, she turned around and went back, because she didn't want to know.

Just a little bit farther, though. If she could smell the bodies, she ought to be able to catch a scent of what did this to them. Since she couldn't get close, she concentrated on the land around them. If something had killed them here, then that same something had to have fled. The trail might have been covered with snow now, but she might find a trace of it.

She smelled David.

Pausing a moment, she tasted it, fearing what it meant. But no, this was fresh. Still warm. The touch of him on the air was more human than wolf. He was in human form. His trail didn't have the reek of a predator who'd just devoured prey.

Ahead, she saw him, a dark figure stretched out on the ground, collecting bits of snow in the wrinkles of his clothes. She was in the perfect position to sneak up on him and pounce. In fact, her hands itched, the claws wanting to come out, Wolf wanting to grab this opportunity.

And wouldn't that be a complete and utter disaster? She refrained, not wanting to give him a heart attack—or a good excuse to turn wolf at this particular moment.

"David," she called in the loudest whisper she could manage, creeping up until she was beside him.

Despite her caution, he flinched and twisted back to look at her. Then he sagged with relief.

"What are you doing here?" he hissed back.

"Following you. Have you found out anything?"

He took a deep breath. "I don't think a werewolf did it. There'd be some trace of it, wouldn't there?"

There would. She'd smelled the aftermath of a werewolf-killed body before, and he was right—if David had done it, they'd be smelling blood, bodies, and *wolf*.

"Yeah, there would," she said.

He slumped and made a sound that was almost a sob. He'd come out here for no other reason than to reassure himself.

Tentative, she touched his shoulder. Leaned close to him in a wolfish gesture of companionship. "It's okay. It's going to be okay. Let's go back now." Back to the warmth, light, virgin eggnog, Jimmy Stewart, and a wonderful life.

"If I didn't do this," David said. "Who did? *What* did?"

"That's for the police to find out."

Something seemed to have taken hold of him. Some newfound determination. Like the evidence had given him confidence—proof that he wasn't an out-of-control ravening monster.

"We ought to be able to find something out," he said. "We can smell the trail. The police can't do that. If we can, shouldn't we help—"

"'With great power comes great responsibility.' Is that what you're thinking?" she said with a smirk.

Looking away, he frowned. "It can't hurt to try."

She wanted to apologize. She shouldn't tease him.

"So," she said. "You feel like a hunt?"

He stared out to the murder scene. He might have had a human form, but crouched there, his gaze focused, body tense, ready to leap forward in an instant, his body language was all wolf. She felt the same stance in her own body.

"Yeah," he said. "I do."

Together, they took off at a jog, keeping clear of the cordoned-off area and the circle of lights that marked it.

Prowling out of sight of the police, they found a trail, the barest scent of blood on the air. Probably not so much as a drop was left on the ground for the police to find. But it was there, lingering, fading rapidly because of the falling snow. If they were going to do this, they needed to hurry.

They ranged back and forth along the same half-mile stretch of prairie leading away from the road, looking for the sign they'd discovered: blood on the air, and oil, like the person they were looking for worked in a garage. There was something undefinable—something she as a human being couldn't describe. But the wolf inside her knew the flavor of the smell. This was a predator they were looking for. A taste of aggression rather than fear, like there'd be with prey. The feeling put her on edge. She was sure, though: the murderer was human.

A few miles from the interstate, another set of police cars gathered around a house at what looked like a junkyard. Acres of wrecked and rusting cars lined up on the land around it, roped in by strings of barbed-wire fencing. The familiar ring of lights and yellow tape bound the house. And the tang of blood and slaughter drenched the air. This scene was more recent than the other.

"What is this?" Kitty whispered. "Is some guy roaming the country-side murdering people he just happens across?"

The thought of a crazed murderer running around out here didn't frighten her; she was a werewolf. Unless his weapons were silver, he couldn't hurt her without really working at it. Even so, this was turning into one of her more harebrained adventures.

"What are we going to do if we find the killer?" David said.

"Call 911?" Then she grumbled, "Ignoring for a moment the fact that I didn't bring my cell phone and I'm betting you don't have one . . . we tell the police what?"

"I don't know. I thought you were the one with all the answers."

Ha. Why did everyone think that again? Just because she ran her mouth more often than not was no reason to actually put any *faith* in her.

She had no desire to get closer to this murder scene, and the killer's trail was fading.

"Let's go," she said, and took off at a jog. After a moment's hesitation, David followed her.

Made her wonder, just for a moment, what it would be like to have a pack again. The thought made her lonely, so she shook it away. The thing now was to find this killer. Figure out a way to throw him at the cops. Or to stop him, if it came to that.

The guy was on foot. If he had left footprints, the falling snow covered them. They tracked by scent alone, but the smell of human blood was strong. Not exactly subtle. Nothing about these murders was subtle. Kitty could tell that much by the police response, without even seeing the bodies. She didn't have to be a trained profiler to tell these were unplanned. He was lashing out, haphazard.

David must have been thinking along the same lines. Briskly, they walked side by side, following the trail that the police hadn't found yet. "He's racking up a body count, isn't he? That's what this is about. Whoever he is, he's gone postal."

"Looks that way," Kitty said.

"We're going to have to kill him if we find him, aren't we?" David said.

"No." She shook her head. "I don't want to get in the habit of killing people. Even if they are bad guys. I don't think you want to get into that habit either."

He pursed his lips and nodded sharply.

When they spotted another house up ahead, lit by the yellow circle of a lamp by the door, Kitty's stomach sank. They'd found his next target.

It wasn't really a house, but a weather-beaten single-wide mobile home, white aluminum siding rusting at the edges, sitting by itself at the end of a long dirt road. The minimum of what could be called a homestead. But it had a fenced-in yard with spinning plastic sunflowers sticking out of the snow, and a TV dish attached to the roof, which was outlined in colored holiday lights. Somebody loved this place and called it home, and the killer had headed right for it.

She tugged on David's arm and broke into a run. Dodging around the fence, they went to the front door. The place seemed peaceful. Soft, shaded light shone through the fogged windows. Faintly, the sound of Christmas carols played on a radio, muted. Maybe nothing was wrong. Maybe they'd made a mistake.

They hesitated at the base of a trio of steps leading to the front door. Their breaths, coming fast after the effort of running, steamed in the chill air. David glanced at her.

"What do we do?" he whispered.

"We knock on the front door," she said, shrugging. "If nothing's wrong, we can sing 'Jingle Bells.'"

He actually chuckled. The boy was coming around.

She mounted the steps first, raised a fist to knock on the door—and saw that it already stood open a crack. *Shit.*

Then she thought, what the hell, and pushed open the door all the way.

Her nose flared with the scent of blood at the same time she saw the spray across the linoleum floor of the entryway before her.

Wolf's senses sprang to the fore, the instinct to Change and defend herself ripping through her gut. She swallowed back bile and forced that feeling down, told herself to keep it together, stay human, keep that beast locked away. Her gut clenched, but she didn't shift.

Still, she looked over the scene with a hunter's gaze, and a growl burred in her throat.

Standing over his prey, the man looked at Kitty with surprise. He was tall and thin—unnaturally thin, like he hadn't eaten well in some time. His clothes hung oddly on him. He wore a green canvas jacket, white T-shirt, threadbare jeans. All shone wet with blood. He was covered with red, presumably from his previous two stops. She could smell violence on him, illness, like an animal that had gone out of control, that no longer worked by instinct, but by madness, striking out at everything. His pale eyes gleamed with it. His ear-length hair was matted, uncombed, and an uneven beard grew around his slack mouth. His whole body was rigid.

He loomed over two people, a middle-aged man and woman, husband and wife probably, who lay in the middle of what passed for a living room—a plush sofa shoved up against one wall and a large TV in the opposite corner. They were both a little worn-out and overweight, both wearing jeans and T-shirts—they matched the trailer, Kitty thought absently. They were trussed up like a holiday meal. That was the only way Kitty could think of it. Each had wrists and ankles bound fast in front of them with thin twine. Both were gagged with strips of cloth, so tightly their teeth were bared, their lips stretched back in grotesque smiles. Their eyes glared large and white with fear. Bloody marks shone on their heads, as if the killer had subdued them by hitting them with something. But they were alive, trembling, pressing themselves away from the killer even while bound.

He'd started with her, slashing her arms, spilling blood everywhere. He held an eight-inch-long serrated knife, dull-looking, something that might rip like the teeth of an animal. It dripped blood onto the floor.

The scene froze as the killer regarded Kitty and David.

Wolf, the voice of wild instinct, spoke to Kitty: *Can't show fear, can't show terror, then he'll know he's stronger and he'll attack, he'll kill. We must be stronger, we must dominate, we are alpha here.*

Wolf was right. Kitty wanted to scream, but she didn't. Instead, she looked him in the eye. Glared. Bared her teeth a little. He was in the wrong here. He must be made to relent—to show his belly. Cow him before they had to fight it out.

Beside her, David was doing the same. His fingers were curled, stiff, as if showing claws. For a moment, she worried. Much more of this, and he'd shift. Hell, they both might. And maybe that wouldn't be so bad—no way could this guy escape from a couple of werewolves with full-on claws and teeth.

The killer took a step back. He sensed something, obviously. The aggression, the challenge. The fact that these were a couple of monsters standing in front of him, no matter how harmless they might look. But he didn't know how to read the signs. He didn't know how to respond. A wolf would either return the challenge or back down—slumped shoulders, lowered gaze. Make himself small and helpless before them, to show that they were stronger.

This guy twitched, feet stepping in place. His grip tightened and retightened around the handle of the knife. His gaze shifted between them, the door, his captives, the knife in his hand, and back. He didn't know where to look, where to go, what to do. His eyes were wide, shocky, and his lips trembled.

Then he asked a strange question.

"What are you?"

I'm your worst nightmare, Kitty wanted to mutter in a bad accent. But she didn't. She wondered what he saw in them, though—two people with wolves staring out of their eyes, tense and glaring like they were ready to rip his throat out. The guy ought to be scared.

She had to swallow a couple of times before she could speak instead of growl.

"You're not going to do this anymore. You're not going to get away with what you've already done."

After staring at her for a moment, he bit his lip and made a noise that almost sounded like a giggle.

What had she thought he would do, put the knife down and his hands up and wait for the cops to get here?

He stepped toward her, and Kitty braced to defend herself—kicking and scratching his eyes out if she had to. She wasn't worried about the knife. It was stainless steel, not silver. He'd have to just about cut her head off before it would do real damage.

Not that it wouldn't hurt a whole lot in the meantime.

David moved to intercept him. His shoulders were bunched up, like hackles raised, and his glare seemed to bore through the killer. In response, the man stumbled back, clutching the knife with both hands and pointing it defensively. The knife was shaking, just a little.

Hell. Maybe she could just talk him out of it.

"You're going to put the knife down now," Kitty said, her voice low, rough. "You're not going to kill anyone else. We won't let you."

Then, unbelievably, he started crying. Didn't make a sound, but tears spilled from his eyes. Kitty thought, something drove him to this. Something pushed him over the edge and he couldn't cope, and he was psychotic enough to begin with that he did this. This was something else that could happen when you didn't have a place to go home to at Christmas.

Wolf wouldn't let her go soft, though. Wolf didn't have an ounce of sympathy for a predator who slaughtered for no reason, who didn't recognize territory, who didn't obey the rules. Wolf could spot the signs and see what was happening right before the killer tensed and raised his knife to attack. Shouting, he made a mad plunge for the door, ready to slash his way past her and David.

She'd have let him go. They could call in an anonymous tip, let the cops go after him. They'd saved these people—wasn't that enough?

But David stopped him.

She thought he was shifting, that he'd lost it and his predator had burst forth to meet this human predator in challenge. The killer lunged forward, ready to stab down and cut his way through to the door.

David ducked and tackled him. Planted his shoulder under the guy's ribs and shoved. Werewolves were stronger than people. David threw more power into the move than appeared possible. The killer swung sideways and banged into the flimsy plywood wall dividing the living room from the kitchen.

David didn't shape-shift. His wolf hadn't taken over. He used the wolf's power and managed to stay in control, though he was breathing hard, and his teeth were bared.

He didn't let the killer recover. Pouncing, he pinned the guy to the floor, tossed the knife away, and leaned a rigid hand on his neck, pressing down with all his weight. The killer sputtered, gasping for air, thrashing, but he couldn't escape David's strength.

So maybe he wasn't entirely in control of himself.

"David," Kitty said. David flinched, startled, and glared at her, something amber and animal lurking in his eyes. He was *barely* under control. "Keep it together. You don't have to kill. Just keep it together."

"Then what do we do?" His voice was a growl.

"We'll leave him for the cops."

Kitty waited until he nodded, until his muscles relaxed, until he stopped looking like a wolf in human skin, before she knelt by the victims. But when she approached them, they screamed around their gags.

"No, no, I'm not going to hurt you," Kitty murmured. Once again, she wondered what she and David looked like from the outside. Were their eyes glowing or something? Maybe they were. Her senses were on a trip wire.

She moved slowly, and the husband let her work off the gag and the cords on his wrists. "Do you have rope or duct tape or something?" she asked.

He nodded quickly. "Kitchen. By the sink." Then, just like the killer had, he asked, "What are you?"

That question again. And those wide, fearful eyes.

"Doesn't matter," she said. She went to the kitchen and found a length of clothesline in the drawer by the sink.

Kitty helped David tie up the killer. They probably tied him much tighter than he needed to be. But she didn't want to take chances.

"I don't want to have to answer questions for the cops," David said.

"That's okay," Kitty said. "I don't think we should stick around." She turned to the couple, who were now free of their cords. "Call 911. Get help."

"Thank you," the man said breathlessly. "Thank you, thank you—"

"Thank us by not telling the cops about us. Okay? The guy got sloppy. You did this yourselves. Okay?"

Both of them nodded frantically. They kept looking at the bound killer like they expected him to attack. But he lay limp, staring unblinkingly at nothing. He whined with every breath. Like a hurt wolf.

In a moment, the man was talking on the phone, and Kitty and David stood by the door. She had a weird urge to say, "Merry Christmas," or something before they left. The woman was looking back at her, cradling her torn and bloody arms in her lap, gasping for breath. But smiling. Just a little.

Kitty smiled back, then pulled David out the door with her.

They trudged back to town, led by the sounds of cars on the freeway and the faint glow of lights through the misty air. Snow was falling picturesquely. Her feet, and the rest of her, were soaking wet. David was using the snow to wash blood off his hands.

He looked at her. "Why the hell are you smiling?"

Kitty was grinning so hard she thought her face would break.

"Why am I smiling? Because we totally saved those people. We're werewolf superheroes! We're Batman and Robin! That's so awesome!"

Then again, that might have been the adrenaline talking.

Almost, David wanted to howl at the night sky, in joy and triumph. He'd almost shifted. He'd almost gone over the edge. Attacking that guy had come instinctively. It had been like hunting. But he came back from the edge. With Kitty's help, he pulled himself back and stayed human. And that felt powerful.

The glaring yellow sign of the Waffle House shone like a beacon over the snow-covered prairie. Like the Star of Bethlehem over the manger. David felt a surge of relief when he and Kitty came back in sight of it. Civilization. A roof and hot coffee. Glorious.

No telling how much time had passed since they left. They crept in through the still unlocked kitchen door. The cook was gone. Both of them were soaking wet from running in the snow. At least it made the blood he'd gotten on him less noticeable. Almost, he could think about the blood without wanting to turn wolf.

Kitty rubbed her arms and shook out her shirt, squeezing water out of the hem. "Not the smartest thing I've done recently," she muttered. "The one time I didn't bring a change of clothes . . ."

David resisted an urge to reach out and hug her. From affection. From happiness. How long had it been since he'd been happy? Despite the adventure, the running, tracking the killer, and the violence of what he'd witnessed, the urge to turn wolf had faded, a whisper rather than overwhelming thunder. He'd taken a step toward asserting his dominance over that part of his being. The world looked brighter because of that.

Jane, the waitress, came in. "There you are. I thought maybe you'd ducked out on me, but your coat and bag are still here, and you weren't in the bathroom. I was starting to worry . . ." She narrowed her gaze. "What are you two doing back here?"

David opened his mouth but couldn't think of what to say. It was Kitty who announced cheerfully, "Oh, you know. Looking for mistletoe."

He blushed, which must have lent some truth to her excuse, because Jane quirked a smile and left again.

"Sorry," Kitty said. "But people tend not to ask more questions if you tell them you've been fooling around."

He wanted to burst out laughing. "Does this sort of thing happen to you a lot?"

"You'd be surprised."

He had a feeling he wouldn't.

Out front, they returned to their booth. Other customers glanced at them, but no one looked unduly concerned. The TV was still tuned to local news. The same reporter stood by what looked like the same snowy roadside, speaking grimly at the camera. Similar text scrolled along the bottom listing details: five murders and two attempted murders at three different locations. But instead of "serial killer on the loose," the text now read, "serial killer caught."

Then he listened. "Police apprehended the suspected murderer just a little while ago. He appears to have been overpowered by his latest would-be victims, both of whom were injured in the encounter and taken to a local hospital. The police have made a statement that they cannot speculate on the exact series of events, and the lone survivors of these horrific events are not talking to reporters."

So maybe they were safe. The witnesses wouldn't remember them. No one would come looking for them. Just a couple more monsters in the night.

He and Kitty got refills on their coffee and made a little toast. "To Christmas," Kitty said. He just smiled. He'd faced down a killer. Captured a killer, and kept his own killer nature locked inside him. Now that he knew he could do it, he wondered if it would become easier. Wondered if maybe he could go home again. He thought he knew what Kitty would say if he mentioned it to her: He'd never know until he tried.

Maybe it wasn't too late to go home for the holidays.

"Thank you," he said to Kitty.

She glanced away from the TV. "For what?"

"For helping me. For teaching me. For making my day a little more interesting. For giving me hope."

She shrugged and gave a surprisingly shy smile. "I didn't do much but get in trouble. As usual."

"Well, thank you anyway. I think I'm going to go back home. See if I can't get my old job back. See if I can't cope with this a little better. I think I can do that now."

"Really?"

He shrugged. "I'd like to try. Not much future for me waking up naked in the woods every couple of days."

"Not unless you're in an industry with a lot of X's in the job description." He had to laugh. "Just remember to breathe slowly," she said.

"Yeah." He started to get up.

"You're going right now?"

"I'm going to make some calls." He gestured to the front door and the pay phone outside.

"Do you need money or something? For the phone."

"I'll call collect. This is the one night a year I know my folks will be home. It's . . . it's been a while since I've called. They'll want to hear from me. I can get some money wired, then catch a bus for home."

He finished standing, because he really was anxious to get going. Anxious to test himself. She seemed put out. She really wanted to help, and it heartened him that people like that were still out there.

"Here, take this." She dug in her bag and pulled out something, which she handed to him. A business card. "That has all my info on it. Let me know if you need anything."

"Thanks."

"Good luck." Smiling, she watched him leave.

He was at the pay phone before he took a good look at the card. It was for a radio station: KNOB. Her name: Kitty Norville. And a line: Host of *The Midnight Hour*, The Wild Side of Talk Radio. She hosted a talk radio show. He should have guessed.

He hadn't talked to his parents in months. Not since he'd run away. He'd done it to protect them, but now, dialing the operator, he found himself tearing up. He couldn't wait to talk to them.

He heard the operator ask if they'd accept the charges. Gave him his name, and he heard his mother respond, "Yes, yes of course, oh my God . . ."

He said, his voice cracking, "Hi, Mom?"

Thankfully, Jane turned the news off when the reporter started repeating herself.

The movie was long over. The carols were back, all the ones Kitty knew by heart. Jane must have had the same compilation album that her parents played when she was growing up. Funny, how it wouldn't be Christmas without them.

One of her favorite tunes came on, a solemn French carol. A choir sang the lyrics, which she had never paid much attention to because she didn't speak much French. But she knew the title: "*Il Est Né le Divin Enfant.*" *Il Est Né*. He is born.

She dug in her bag and found her cell phone. Dialed a number, even though it was way too late. But when the answer came, Kitty heard party noises in the background—her parents, her sister, her niece and nephew, laughter, more carols—so it was all right.

She said, "Hi, Mom?"

The Perfect Gift

Dana Stabenow

Dana Stabenow was born in Anchorage and raised on a seventy-five-foot fish tender in the Gulf of Alaska. She knew there was a warmer, drier job out there somewhere and found it in writing books. Her first science fiction novel, Second Star, *sank without a trace, her first crime fiction novel,* A Cold Day for Murder, *won an Edgar® Award, her first thriller,* Blindfold Game, *hit the* New York Times *bestseller list, and her twenty-seventh novel and eighteenth Kate Shugak novel,* Though Not Dead, *comes out in February 2011.*

"They're overgrazing their range."

"True."

"If we don't reduce their population, there'll be fuck all left to hunt."

"Also true," Neri said.

"They savaged us the last two times we tried to establish some control over their activities, to the point that the population of the various packs is now seriously out of balance."

"No one is arguing with you, Lucas," Mannaro said.

"Then why are we pussyfooting around here?" Lucas had a long, strong nose, a square jaw, and cheekbones by Praxiteles, although Mannaro thought his countenance exhibited an almost regal lack of animation. Austerity was not usually a characteristic of the young, and Mannaro thought it only made Lucas appear ever so slightly pompous. "We have to make a decision," Lucas said, "and the sooner the better." His attitude said all too clearly that they had left it too late as it was.

Wulver leaned forward. His broad Scots' accent would have been impossible to understand if he hadn't spoken so slowly and with such deliberation. There was no doubt the board understood the seriousness of the issue before them. "One caveat, however. Do we really want to start a shit-storm of this magnitude just before Christmas?"

He looked at the head of the table. Mannaro, impeccably coifed and immaculately tailored, sat very much at his ease, an attitude belied by the restless brilliance of a pair of shrewd dark eyes, which lingered on Neri for a considering moment. She was worth the attention, a long-limbed blonde with creamy skin that flushed easily, heavy-lidded blue eyes, and a lush red mouth that hinted to most men of soft kisses and lazy Sunday afternoons.

Mannaro knew his niece rather better than most men, however. There was nothing soft or lazy about Neri. "Wulver makes a good point," he said. "The last two times the Board of Game proposed a hunt, there was an outpouring of sentiment—and may I say, sentimentality—from the larger community. E-mails, letters, and phone calls poured into the commissioner's office. 'Predators are a necessary part of the food chain.' 'Predators are a vital and beautiful part of the balance of nature.' 'These predators cull only the weak and infirm, thereby keeping the prey herd healthy and viable, which in turn keeps the predator population healthy and viable.'"

He held up a hand. "I know, you've heard all this before. Very well. We are agreed that action is necessary, are we not?"

There were nods from around the table. "We are also agreed that this pack is out of control. Reluctantly, we agree that the sole action left to us is elimination. Such a draconian decision is arrived at only after repeated attempts at remedial action, all resulting in failure of effect, and after extensive deliberation over what will benefit the greater good."

Again, no outward dissent.

Mannaro looked at Wulver. "But Wulver is also correct in that every time we propose controlling the population, there is a backlash of epic proportion, and as the controlling body we're left hanging out there all alone, the target of every rights group with an in-house attorney. And he makes a very good point in that the season will exacerbate reaction community-wide."

"But something has to be done," Lucas said. "Their actions have become too widespread to safely ignore. Any more publicity will result in full-scale vigilantism, putting the greater population at risk. It's not like it hasn't happened before."

"Indeed." Mannaro inclined his head in a graceful acceptance of the challenge that Lucas' near snarl had flung down. "What we need is to turn this action into a gift. So let me put it to you. Who will this action benefit, other than ourselves?"

He was looking at Neri as he spoke. "To whom," he said, "may we offer it as something befitting the season? As, say, the perfect gift?"

She met his eyes for a startled moment before comprehension came.

And then she laughed, a full-throated sound of amusement, with an underlying excitement sharp enough to cut.

Mannaro smiled, content.

The Alaska state troopers in Anchorage worked out of a five-story rectangular building with a dull gray exterior and an interior cut into matching gray cubicles. Littered surfaces of metal desks were lit by fluorescent tubes, every third or fourth one burned out.

Lobison thought it worked as a metaphor for the job, although it would have been as much as his life was worth to use a word like *metaphor* in here. He dumped four packets of creamer and six packets of sugar into his coffee mug and went to his desk, where the stack of case files had not miraculously diminished overnight.

His partner was already at work, sleek head bent over a series of crime scene photographs, the graphic nature of which made the human in him wince away and gave even the cop in him pause.

"Morning, Ben," she said.

"How do you do that?" he said. "I didn't make a sound. You must have ears like a cat."

She looked up and fluttered her eyelashes. "Maybe I just have a sixth sense for big good-looking doofuses."

They'd been partners for a year and their working relationship had evolved into a low-key flirtatious raillery that never overstepped the rule of no departmental fraternization. Romanov was so hot she sizzled, but Lobison had too much respect for the job to hit on his partner, or that's what he told himself whenever his imagination went into overdrive.

"I think that's doofusi," he said. He sat down across from her and pointed at the photographs. "Why are you looking at those again? It's not like the MO is going to change if you stare at them long enough."

"I know." She sat back and rubbed her eyes with thumb and forefinger. "How many have there been now? Twelve?"

"Thirteen," he said grimly, "if you count that kid in Chickaloon, and I do."

"Thirteen deaths by exsanguination over the past eleven months," she said, "in each case caused by massive trauma to the throat."

"As in they had their jugulars ripped out," Lobison said. "Don't pretty it up. The ME's considered opinion is that each victim was attacked by an animal, perhaps a dog, maybe a wolf or a bear, possibly even a wolverine. That I might actually believe, wolverines are nasty little sons of bitches. But since most of the soft parts of the bodies are missing and presumed eaten, the ME hasn't been able to get a good imprint of the teeth."

She leaned back in her chair and folded her arms, a quizzical look on her face. "You still don't think it is an animal, do you?"

"Where is this alleged animal?" He waved a hand at the photographs. "We've got crime scenes ranging from Girdwood to Wasilla, including Bird Creek, Indian, Spenard, Muldoon, Mountain View, Eagle River, Peters Creek, Palmer. No one single sighting of the animal or animals in question reported by any of the witnesses interviewed. The attacks always occur at night, always on a full moon, and don't those jackals in the media just love that." He paused. "Tonight's a full moon."

She glanced at him. "Yeah? So?"

"Ask any EMT or any emergency room nurse, they'll tell you. All the stats go up during a full moon, robbery, rapes, murder, drive-bys, domestic disturbances, you name it. People get squirrelly around the full moon."

"You know that's just a self-perpetuating prophecy," she said in a singsong voice, as if she were reading out of a manual. "Because people say the full moon makes people squirrelly, people get squirrelly during the full moon. Ask any shrink."

"Yeah, yeah." He shifted uncomfortably, as if his jacket were suddenly too tight across the shoulders. Truth was, he was always twitchy during the full moon, and he didn't like it. He was a cop, he dealt in the real, the tangible, what he could see and hear and touch. It was humiliating, especially in front of his partner, who also happened to be an attractive member of the opposite sex, to admit to a belief in what amounted to a fairy tale.

"It was even clear the night of the Eagle River attack," he said, bringing them firmly back to the subject. "That and the full moon made visibility so good you could read a newspaper outside. The victim was found almost immediately by a couple who were camping up the trail and who heard the attack and came to investigate, and they didn't see anything. We haven't found any tracks, no one's heard any howling or growling, there's no scat or hair." His mouth tightened into a grim line. "And they're too much alike."

"The bodies?"

"Yes. Same killing blow, or bite, at least so far as the ME is willing to commit himself. All the soft parts gone, face, throat, breasts on the women, belly, thighs. No dental impressions left in the bones. To me, that kind of similarity argues, I don't know, an intelligence, if you will, behind the killings. Which makes them murders in my book."

She raised a skeptical eyebrow, but before she could reply the phone on her desk rang. "Detective Romanov. Yes. Yes." She scribbled something down. "I'm sorry, and why should we go all the way out there?" Her eyes widened and she snapped her fingers at Lobison. *Line two,* she mouthed at him.

"Yes," she said into the phone, "but you have to understand, these are horrific crimes. We would require serious proof before we could make an arrest. We can't just show up and kick in the door. What makes you think these people are responsible?"

Lobison called for a trace and then as quietly as possible switched to line two. "It's up to you now," the man was saying, his voice rough-edged and a little garbled. "I've told you who they are and where they are. They're sick, murderers, they're cannibals is what they are! You have to stop them!"

"Yes, but sir, please, tell me your name! Sir!"

There was a click. She looked at Lobison, who switched lines again and spoke briefly. He hung up and shook his head. "Not long enough to find a location, other than in state. And he was using a voice disguiser, I'm betting. What did he give you?"

She ripped the note from the pad and handed it across the desk. "Get your boots and parka. He says the so-called Wolf Murders are the work of a family in the Valley named Vilkachek."

The Vilkachek homestead was down a snow-covered, one-lane gravel road that wound back into the Chugach foothills. It was large, two stories, and old enough to be one of the houses built by one of the farm families who came to the Valley in 1936 as part of the WPA project to settle the territory. It had a wraparound porch with a broad set of steps leading up to it, and it was set in a grove of black spruce that had been encouraged to creep right up to the windows, obscuring the view within. Deliberately? This far out in the boonies, there was no need for a privacy screen. The nearest neighbor was five miles away.

Lobison spoke softly into the mike clipped to his vest. "Ferguson, all set around back?"

Two clicks replied in the affirmative. He drew his weapon and looked at Romanov. "Back me up?"

She already had the silver nine-millimeter automatic in a business-like grip. "Go," she said.

The wind came up and the trees sighed and creaked in response, sifting through the light of the moon just cresting Pioneer Peak. Even on the crusty snow, Romanov moved so silently behind him that he was compelled to look around once to see if she was still there. Her face moved into the shadow as he turned, so that for a fanciful moment he thought he saw her eyes gleam and her hair coarsen from its usual sleek knot into a ruffled pelt, and then the wind moved the boughs aside and she was once again Romanov, the partner who had his back.

They approached the front of the house, the snow frozen hard underfoot so that there was no postholing to give them away. There was a light in one of the front rooms upstairs, and the reflected glow of another somewhere at the back of the first floor.

Lobison set one tentative foot on the bottom stair.

As if it were a signal, someone fired from the house, a shot he first felt as a burning past his cheek. Immediately afterward he heard the instantaneous report, so close it sounded like cannon fire.

Lobison fell into an instinctive dive and rolled, coming to his feet again behind the trunk of a tree, shaking snow from his eyes. Romanov shouted something, and almost simultaneously there was a crash of glass and breaking wood from the back of the house. There were yells and screams and more shots.

"Ben! Are you all right!"

"I'm okay, you?"

"I'm good!"

And that was all the time they had for conversation as another shot hit the tree he was standing behind. It tore away a chunk of bark and he flinched away, and in that same instant the house exploded with a thunderous roar, blowing out the walls and bursting into an immense ball of flame. The wind whipped up and fanned the flames higher and the heat was so intense that even from behind the tree the force of it pushed him into retreat, hands half raised in a futile effort to ward it off. His heel caught on a thick root and he fell hard and clumsily.

As he fell, the wind tossed the branches between him and the burning house. Shadows cast by the moon formed and broke and formed again. For just an instant he thought he saw a four-legged form, dark and somehow elegant, leaping through a top-floor window to the roof of the porch. From the porch it leapt in a dark, fluid continuation of movement to the ground, and melted into the trees as if it had never been.

*   *   *

"A stray bullet hit the propane tank at the back of the house," the chief of detectives said. "Kaboom."

"Jesus," Lobison said. "Our bullet, or theirs?"

"Don't know," the chief said firmly, "and don't want to know, so don't ask again."

Lobison felt dizzy, disoriented, and generally pissed off. It was, he felt, a reasonable response to nearly being blown up. Romanov, by contrast, looked barely ruffled, the moonlight giving her an ethereal, otherworldly glow. God, she was so gorgeous it made him want to bite.

Her eyes widened as if she could hear his thoughts, and he looked away and cleared his throat. "How many bodies?"

"Eight," the chief said, "but they're still counting crispy critters in there, and they will be for a while. It was a pretty efficient explosion. If anyone was in the house, they're dead."

Next to him Romanov said quietly, "The local cops say there were twenty-three family members spread over three generations, all residing at this address."

"Three generations?" Lobison said.

"No children," Romanov said, answering what he'd meant rather than what he'd said. "The youngest of them was twenty-three. They evidently . . ." She hesitated, seeming to search for the correct word. "It appears that each generation evidently married early and had children very young."

In some distant part of his brain Lobison was relieved at the news, but it felt as if he had received it at a distance, one step removed from himself. He shook his head again, not in disbelief but in an attempt to shake off his disorientation. His stomach growled, loud enough for Romanov and the chief both to hear. That was nuts, he'd had a Pop All-Dark at the Lucky Wishbone just before they'd headed out, he couldn't possibly be hungry.

Romanov looked at him and he felt the weight of her considering gaze. He shook his head a third time, almost angrily. The scent of her perfume seemed to increase in intensity, so that he could smell nothing but her.

The chief took Lobison's demeanor as remorse over the slaughter. "I wouldn't weep any real tears one way or another," he said. "We found this." He held out a dented metal box. "Explosion blew it out one of the windows. Looks like trophies from all thirteen victims. Your partner's already ID'd some of them."

Lobison took the box automatically, looking inside it, recognizing a ponytail holder, an earring, a pitiful jumble of personal objects that held no meaning except to the loved ones left behind.

"One for the books," the chief said. "A whole family of serial killers. I put it in NCIC and the Feebs are practically pissing in their pants. They're sending up a profiler from Quantico on the red-eye. A whole family," he said again, marveling, and then brightened. "I guess the family that preys together stays together." He laughed at his own joke and elbowed Lobison. "'Preys together?' Get it?"

"Jesus," Lobison said again, only this time it was a whisper. "The guy who called. He was telling the truth. It was them."

"Damn straight it was," the chief said. "The way I see it, we're damn lucky that stray bullet caught the propane tank and fried the whole bunch of them. This way we've got the perpetrators of thirteen bloodthirsty murders dead to rights—" He laughed again. "And we don't even have to bring them to trial. Not to mention, you both get gold shields." He grinned. "It's the gift that keeps on giving, Sergeants. Merry Christmas." He looked over Lobison's shoulder. "Oh, crap."

"What?" Romanov followed his gaze. A Channel 2 truck was pulling into the yard.

"Who called us?" Lobison said. "Who tipped us off?"

"Who cares?" the chief said, straightening his tie. "I'll take these assholes for you." He winked at them. "You two head on home. Sleep in, come in late. Reports on my desk tomorrow by end of shift."

"Yes, sir," Romanov said.

The chief headed for the television crew, and Lobison registered the logo on the side of the van for the first time. "Shit," he said, and pulled out his cell. "I've got to call my family before this hits the news. They're always expecting to see me dead or dying on film at ten."

Romanov was amused. "Your family worries about you on the job?"

"You have no idea. Especially my brothers." He hit the speed dial and held the phone to his ear. "All six of them."

He didn't notice how still she went at his words. "You have six brothers?"

"Yep," he said grimly, "and it doesn't help that I'm the youngest."

Romanov drifted closer to him, too close. Her arm brushed his and that scent, floral deepening to musk, grew even stronger, to the point that he could smell nothing but her. Over the increasing roar in his ears he heard her say, almost dreamily, "You never told me you were a seventh son."

He forced a laugh, at the same time contriving to take a small step away from her. He was startled and embarrassed to find that he was abruptly, rudely, achingly hard. "Everyone bursts into song when I do, so I don't much. Hey. What're you doing?"

This as she reached for his cell phone and closed it. He sensed a presence at his shoulder and his head snapped around. A dark man in a very sharp suit that looked very much out of place on a back road in the Valley seemed to coalesce out of the forest. There was nothing in his appearance to alarm Lobison, but when he found himself backing away, head down, rolling his shoulders, he realized that he was, in fact, alarmed. There was something menacing, something even threatening about the stranger, he didn't know what, but he hadn't survived this long as a cop by ignoring the heebie-jeebies when they announced themselves at this volume. He pressed his arm against the comforting weight of the nine millimeter in the shoulder holster. "Who are you?" he said brusquely. "What do you want?"

"It's okay," Romanov said, her voice soothing. "This is my uncle. This is my partner, Uncle Mannaro, Ben Lobison."

"Sir," Lobison said, with a quick, unfriendly nod. He could feel the hair on his neck standing straight up. "No offense, Romanov, but what the hell is your uncle doing at a crime scene?"

"Detective Lobison," the uncle said in greeting, with what would have been a charming smile if his canines had been a little shorter. As it was, it looked as if he was about to bite into something. And was looking forward to it.

"Did you hear?" Romanov said to her uncle, her voice very soft. "He's a seventh son."

"I heard."

"What the hell does my being a seventh son have to do with anything?" Lobison said.

She licked her lips, lips that looked fuller, almost swollen, over white, sharp teeth that looked suddenly as sharp as her uncle's. Her lids drooped over heavy eyes, her gaze fixed on his face. Lobison felt heat begin low in his belly and radiate up and out over his whole body. He pulled open the front of his parka, the crisp, cold air welcome against his skin.

"Your birthday's on the twenty-fourth of December, isn't it, Ben?" she said.

"Really," her uncle said, and gave Lobison an appraising look. "Well, well. Why didn't you tell us, Neri?"

"I didn't know he was a seventh son," she said, without taking her eyes from Lobison. "The birthday by itself didn't seem worth mentioning."

"You think that old wives' tale is true?"

"I think," Romanov said, her head tilting back, a slow smile spreading across her face, "that all we have to do is wait."

They were both looking at him with the same narrow-eyed intensity, Romanov still too close, her nearness making Lobison want to pace. The wind increased, the boughs creaked, the moon was bright enough to cast shadows. Lobison was uncomfortably aware that he was still hard. He hoped Romanov's uncle didn't know, but come to think of it he didn't really care that much if Mannaro did. His clothes felt too tight, and he felt too hot in them, too hot in his skin. He glanced at the moon, and away, the light too bright for his eyes.

"Why now?" the uncle said. "Why tonight? He's, what, late thirties? Why hasn't he changed before?"

"The first time we change with our pack. Maybe he needed a pack to change." Romanov shrugged without taking her eyes from Lobison's. "There'll be time to figure that out. Later."

"Detective," Mannaro said, "just as a matter of curiosity, are your parents still living?"

"Look," Lobison said, "I'm not exactly in the mood for twenty questions. I'm tired and I'm filthy and my ears are still ringing from the explosion and I'm hungry—"

"You're not just hungry," Mannaro said, his voice understanding, almost caressing. "You're ravenous."

Lobison felt his stomach rumble again, this time as if in response to the words. He stared from Mannaro to Romanov. "What's going on?" he said, and he could barely recognize his own voice in what growled out of his throat. "What the hell is happening to me?"

"Uuuuuuuncle," Romanov said, and without warning Lobison knew that she wanted him as badly as he wanted her. He wanted to jump on her, tear her clothes from her body, feast on her flesh. The saliva flooded his mouth, he had never been so hungry, so edgy, so needy.

The uncle glanced up at the full moon, and back at Romanov. "Soon, Neri."

"Noooooow," she said. It was almost a howl, and Lobison felt that howl in the very marrow of his bones. He could smell her, her arousal, her need, he wanted to feed, to sate this abrupt, pounding need, he wanted to take. She was his, this night she was only his. He would take, he had to, it was no longer a choice, if indeed it ever had been one. He took a step forward, breath coming fast now, close enough to nuzzle her throat, close enough to smell the blood pounding beneath her skin, close enough to bite.

Mannaro looked at the two of them standing so close to each other, and laughed, a knowing sound, an invitation into the dark. "The tribe increases. Who knew? The gift that keeps on giving." He looked at the chief of detectives, who had intercepted the Channel 2 reporter and was leading her in the opposite direction. "All right," he said. "Now."

The three of them melted into the trees, Lobison joining the others as if by instinct. His eyesight was suddenly so acute that impressions rushed in to overwhelm him. An owl perched on the branch of a tree blinking its knowing eyes. A hare crouched in a hollow, its white coat almost indistinguishable from the surrounding snow but he could see every twitch of a whisker, hear every flick of an ear, taste the rich, red blood, feel the crunch of bones between his teeth.

Once among the trees it seemed natural to strip the clothes from his body, to drop to his hands and knees, only they were paws now, paws with long, sharp claws that dug strongly into the snow, that claimed the earth and made the wild his own.

Mannaro put his nose in the air and howled. Now an elegant black wolf, his call was deep, mellow and compelling. It reverberated inside Lobison's skull, swamping every other sound and sense, an imperative call he could not ignore.

Mannaro was answered immediately by Romanov, on four legs long and slender, white fur silver in the moonlight. The howl tore apart everything Lobison thought he was and the moonlight rebuilt him into something else, an untamed being of beauty and grace and hunger.

Romanov howled once more, a long, drawn-out call of yearning. Her head dropped and she looked at him, blue eyes unblinking.

He looked back, feeling that howl in every sinew and bone, in every hair of the thick gray pelt that now covered his body. He could smell her, almost taste her, the seductive, singing scent of her musk. He wanted her in a way he had never wanted her before, had never wanted anything ever before, wanted with a savage need that rode him like a demon, relentless, unmerciful, inevitable, undeniable.

She sprang at him, nipping at his shoulder, her teeth stinging, and vanished into the trees.

The smell of his own blood flooded his nostrils. In the next instant he was after her.

Christmas Past

Keri Arthur

Keri's an Aussie gal who grew up sharing her life with dragons, elves, vampires, werewolves, shapeshifters, and the occasional talking horse. Which worried her family to no end. Of course, now that she's actually making a living sharing her life with the aforementioned creatures, they no longer contemplate calling the men with the short white coats. When not at her keyboard, Keri can be found in front of the TV, or taking her two dogs for a walk.

Normally, I love Christmas.

I love decorating my scrawny little tree with tinsel and ornaments, and hanging Christmas lights in every available corner of my one-bedroom apartment. I love making eggnog and baking Christmas gingerbreads, and the way Christmas cheer suddenly fills the usually dour offices of the Para-investigations squad. I even liked battling the Christmas hordes to get the latest "must-have" present for my niece and nephews.

And I'd been looking forward to all that and more this year to make up for the crappiness that had been last year's Christmas. But it was all starting to go sour again, and it had a whole lot to do with my current situation.

For a start, it's hard to feel very Christmassy when you're standing in an elf costume in the middle of a snowstorm freezing your ass off.

And okay, it wasn't *exactly* a snowstorm—more like a steady sprinkling of the wet white stuff—but when I was dressed in a silly green outfit that wasn't even fur-lined like a Santa costume would have been, and wearing stupid pointy shoes that jingled annoyingly every time I moved, it might as well have been a storm. Warmth just wasn't happening.

But the snow wasn't the worst of it. I could probably have handled the snow and the cold and the non-appearance of anything resembling a bad guy, if it weren't for the six-foot, broad-shouldered, dark-haired presence standing deep in the shadows of a doorway ten feet to my left.

That presence just happened to be Brodie James, werewolf expert and chief investigator for the Para-investigations squad. Owner of a killer smile and a body designed to inspire lust.

And the man who had dumped me without warning precisely one year ago.

I blew out a breath and rang the bell with more force than necessary. The cheery sound pealed out across the darkness, but did little to attract the attention of the strangers who scurried past. On a night like this, all anyone wanted to do was get inside. Giving to charity wasn't even hitting their radar.

Hell, the fiend who was murdering Christmas collectors probably had more sense than to come out on a night like that.

Which meant my standing there as bait was every bit as useless as it was feeling.

"Ring that bell any harder, and you'll probably break it," Brodie said, his warm, rich voice filled with amusement.

It was a sound that had filled far too many of my dreams over the last year.

I didn't answer him. I might have to work with the rat on this case, but I didn't have to talk to him any more than necessary. I suppose I just had to be thankful he'd been out of the state on other cases for the better part of the year. I would have had to ask for a transfer if I'd had to deal with him day in and day out.

And that would have been a damn shame, because I actually liked being a part of the squad. When I wasn't standing out in a snowstorm freezing my ass off, that was. And it was certainly a job that suited my talent for sensing "evil" in people—human or not. The squad was a small division of the FBI, and we handled any case that held even the remotest hint of paranormal activity. Humans might have accepted the presence of vamps, werewolves, and the other things that went bump in the night, but they sure as hell didn't like getting involved with them. And the cops were very quick to handball anything mystical.

Of course, I was human myself, but my talents had always made me feel like an outsider within my own race. Although Brodie dumping me so suddenly hadn't exactly made me feel wanted by the non-humans.

"You have to talk to me eventually," he said, shifting position slightly. His rich, spicy aroma stirred through the cold air, bringing on memories of the long nights I'd spent in his arms, breathing in that very same scent.

I rather violently rattled the tin at a woman running past. She shook her head without even looking at me. It was just as well I wasn't a proper collector—the children's charity wouldn't be doing very well out of me.

"What if I say I'm sorry?" he added eventually.

"What if I tell you I don't care?" I snapped back, kicking myself mentally for actually breaking my vow of silence, but unable to hold back the words regardless.

"I wouldn't believe it."

I turned around, eyeing the darkness that held him so completely. "Last Christmas, I cared. This Christmas, I just want to catch our murderer so I can get out of this stupid costume and the snow that is freezing bits of me off, and go enjoy being with my sister and her kids."

I swung away, presenting my back to him again. Which really wasn't a good thing, because I could still feel his gaze on me. Could feel the heat of it travel up my cold length, warming the ice from my bones and making my pulse skip and dance.

Where the hell was a murdering Christmas fiend when you really wanted one?

"It's nearly midnight," Brodie said. "Given that our murderer hasn't shown an inclination to attack and drain anyone after the magic hour, what do you say to us going to find a café and some coffee?"

"I'd prefer to go straight back to my apartment." Spending more time than necessary in this man's company was *not* a good idea. I might not want to talk to him, but there were bits of me that would have been happy to do a whole lot more.

"Come on, Hannah," he said softly, in that sweet, oh-so-sexy tone that could charm the pants off a virgin. At least, it had charmed the pants of *this* former virgin. "Tomorrow's Christmas Eve. How about showing a little Christmas spirit?"

"Would this be the same Christmas spirit you showed when you dumped me without a by-your-leave?" I said, ever so nicely.

"Ouch," he muttered. Then added, "Did I mention I was sorry for that?"

"I still don't care."

"Did I mention I realize I was an ass, but things got so crazy so quickly—"

"I'm *still* not caring," I interrupted, feeling like a broken record.

Another stranger appeared at the top end of the street. I rang the bell and he looked up briefly, his face ghostly in the darkness. He shook his head and huddled deeper into his coat, before crossing the road and walking down the other side of the footpath. Great, now prospective donors were avoiding me.

That said a whole lot about my appearance. Or my mood.

I took a deep breath and tried to look happy about the whole situation.

I don't think I succeeded.

"Look," Brodie tried again. "I'm a rat, I know, and I don't really have a good excuse for doing what I did. It was thoughtless and inconsiderate and I'd really like the chance to make it up to you."

No, I told my hormones, which were suddenly dancing at the thought of some hot Brodie action. *Remember Christmas past? He's bad for us. We don't like him.*

Unfortunately, what came out of my mouth was, "Why?"

"Because it's Christmas, and because I've missed you horribly."

Of all the damn things to say, I thought, as my treacherous heart did a little sideways lurch. It was just as well parts of me were still holding on to anger, otherwise I'd be putty in his hands. *And oh, wouldn't his hands feel so good.*

"Yeah, you missed me *so* horribly," I replied, irritated at myself, "that you couldn't pick up a phone and talk to me."

"I did," he said mildly. "You hung up on me. Several times."

Oh. Yeah. "That was when I was in my hurt and angry stage. You should have tried once I'd rolled into my not caring stage. You might have had more luck."

"You've been saying you don't care for the last ten minutes, and I'm still having no luck."

"That's because I've now rolled into the no-longer-caring-but-aiming-to-make-you-grovel stage. It's just not your night, I'm afraid."

"Ah," he said, the deepening amusement in his rich tones making my toes curl ever so slightly. "And if I *do* grovel? Will that get you sharing a cup of coffee with me?"

"No, because I can't stand men who beg." The wind chose that moment to blast down the street. I hunched my shoulders against it and wondered if my legs were turning as blue as they felt.

Maybe coffee *was* a good idea.

No. *He's bad for our health and we don't like him, remember?*

Across the street, the pale-faced stranger grabbed the fly-away ends of his coat and wrapped them around his body, his hands so white they almost appeared skeletal.

Gloves, I thought, even as a chill ran down my spine. Had to be. No hands were *that* white, no matter how cold. *Unless you were a vampire.*

My psychic radar hadn't yet sensed anything out of the ordinary, but I'd learned long ago never to ignore the little niggles of wrongness—and that man across the street definitely *felt* wrong.

"Does he smell funny to you?" I asked Brodie softly.

There was a sharp intake of breath, and I had a vision of his nostrils flaring, sucking in the scents of the night and rolling them across his taste buds, sorting and categorizing them. I'd seen him do it a hundred times in the few months we'd been together, and I found it as sexy now as I had then. Which was odd, because until I'd met him, I'd never considered nostrils to be remotely alluring.

But then, the whole package *connected* to this man's nostrils was beyond fine.

"He reeks of booze and cigarettes." Another intake of breath. "And he hasn't washed for a few days, either."

"So he's not the scent you've caught at the last three crime scenes?"

"No." He hesitated. "It's similar, though, meaning he could be related to our killer."

"Being related doesn't mean he knows anything about the killings."

"Doesn't mean he doesn't, either."

The stranger lumbered sideways, crashing shoulder first into a wall. He muttered something I couldn't catch, then glanced over his shoulder.

Our gazes met, and my psychic senses roared to life. There was no life in that blue gaze, but there *was* unlife. And hatred, so much hatred, mixed with anger, and the need to shed blood and taste revenge.

But, deeper than that, there was evil. The sort of evil that likes to rip and tear and drain.

"He may not smell exactly like our quarry," I whispered. "But I'm sure he's connected to these murders somehow."

The words were barely out of my mouth when the vampire snarled. I had a brief glimpse of shattered, broken canines, then he pushed away from the wall and started running. Brodie leapt out of the shadows, stripping off his clothes as he ran, his lean, powerful form shifting, changing, until what was running in front of me was wolf rather than human.

A shiver ran through my soul. I'd seen him do *that* a hundred times, too, and I still found it awe-inspiring.

"Wait for me!"

But of course he didn't. He was a werewolf, after all, and few of them bothered with rules, regulations, *or* half-shouted requests unless it really suited them.

I swore softly and threw the bell and collection box into the shadowed corner where he'd been standing, then grabbed the stakes and his clothes, and ran after him, the bells on my shoes ringing happily across the night with each step. I felt like a one-person Christmas band.

We bolted up the road and around a corner. The suspect was fast, his spindly arms and legs pumping like a runner in a race, his black coat flying out behind him, looking a little like black wings. But for every step he took, Brodie was taking two or three and he was gaining fast.

The vamp skidded left into a side road. Four seconds later, Brodie's sleek wolf form disappeared after him. I was six seconds behind them both, sliding around the corner in a jingle of bells, only to have to suddenly leap over the still-wolf form that was Brodie.

"Where is he?" I said, standing beside him and frowning into the dark and silent side street.

He shifted shape, then said, "I lost him." He held up the stranger's black coat. "This is what I smelled. He was using it to cover his own scent. There's obviously some poor wino out there now freezing his nuts off."

"If he hasn't been drained." My gaze met his. The green eyes were flat and annoyed. "How could you lose him?"

"Because werewolves can't fly."

My gaze went skyward. All I saw was darkness and wet white stuff. "Vampires can't, either."

"Well, apparently no one told *this* murdering son of a bitch that. I should have stayed in human form and shot the bastard." He grabbed his clothes and started dressing.

"Shooting vamps doesn't kill them."

And *this* vamp had an execution order on him. While most non-humans had rights to courts, lawyers, and justice, vamps were the exception. When they killed, an execution order was placed on their heads. No ifs, buts, or maybes. It was our job to serve it—which was the one huge difference between our squad and the rest of the FBI.

"It would have stopped him enough for me to catch the bastard."

"Trouble is, we only have my instincts saying he's connected to our vamp. He isn't our killer, because his canines were smashed and our victims had neat bite wounds."

"If you say he's connected, that's good enough for me." Brodie caught my arm and swung me around, his fingers so warm they just about branded my arm. "But let's get this coat back to the labs so they can double-check. Then once we make our report, we can go get that coffee we were discussing."

"It's going to take more than coffee to make me talk pleasantly to you," I said as we walked—or in my case, jingled—back to his car.

He raised an eyebrow, a smile breaking through the annoyance and tugging at his luscious lips. "What if I add the sweetener of cake?"

I'm an idiot for even considering this. "Depends on the cake."

"Carrot?"

I snorted. "Get real. It has to at least be triple chocolate. With fresh cream."

"Done." He opened the car and ushered me inside, then he bagged the coat while I radioed headquarters, asking them to research flying vamps and where they might have come from. The boss wasn't too happy about us losing our quarry, but hey, when vamps decide to grow wings and fly, there wasn't a whole lot a werewolf and a human could do about it.

Brodie started the car and turned the heater on to full. Cold air blasted down onto my toes, making them feel icier than ever.

"Gee, thanks," I muttered, shifting my feet out of the way.

"It'll warm up in a minute," he said.

"I won't," I said, and wondered even as I said it just how true it was. I mean, he hadn't even gotten serious about trying to seduce me, and here I was about to go for coffee with him. If he went too much further, just how quickly would the ice in my soul melt?

Too damn quickly. The specter of Christmas past, it seemed, wasn't the shield I was hoping it might be, despite all my defiant words earlier.

"How are we going to catch a vampire who can fly? And how can a vamp even manage to do that?" I added, hoping work talk would distract my thoughts from the man sitting far too close.

"It's likely he has shifter in his background. Not all vamps come from human stock, though it is the most common source. And we catch him by spotting him earlier, and chasing him harder." He glanced at me as he ran an amber light. "You got a change of clothes back at headquarters?"

"No." Stupidly, I'd gone straight from home to the stakeout site. "Hopefully, we can get the reports done quickly so I can get home and get warm."

He glanced at me, and the twinkle in his eyes was all too familiar.

Plans were being made, plans that undoubtedly involved me and naked-ness. But all he said was, "How come you didn't sense what he was when he first appeared?"

"Because it doesn't always work like that." I reached around and grabbed my coat from the backseat, wrapping it around my legs blanket-style but feeling no warmer. "I sometimes sense the evil in people very quickly, but it often takes something like eye contact to actually feel what they are." I glanced at him. "But you know all that."

"Last case we worked together, you were getting squat about a guy who'd killed nine people. I thought maybe that was a sign that your psychic gifts were burning out."

Burnout *was* a problem in the squad—though it was often a case of the people burning out more than the actual gifts. So far it had not been a problem for me, but then, simply feeling the evil in someone's soul was a whole lot different from actually sharing their darkest dreams and desires—as some in the squad could.

"It's hard to find the evil in someone's soul when they haven't got a soul," I said. "Just like it's hard to find someone's heart when they haven't got one."

"I have a heart," he said, keeping his gaze on the road. "I just didn't use it very wisely."

Ouch, I thought silently, and looked out the window. We drove the rest of the way in silence. Once back at headquarters, Brodie carted the evidence down to forensics, and I quickly typed up a report. There wasn't much to tell, so it didn't take long. We were in and out inside an hour.

"Now, let's get that coffee," Brodie said, as he opened the car door for me.

"I'd really rather go home," I said, shivering a little despite the ther-mal thickness of my coat. The building may have been heated, but it hadn't done a lot to chase the chill away from my skin. "Besides, I'm wet and I'm dressed as an elf. Not the sort of outfit any respectable per-son would wear to a nice café."

"Nonsense. You look lovely in it." He slammed the door shut and climbed in the other side of the car. "And I promised you cake. I intend to keep that promise."

"Yeah, it would be this one," I muttered.

He ignored me and drove out of the parking lot. I watched the world go by, half of me wanting to play it safe and go home, but the other half—the foolish half—wanting his company, however dangerous that might be to my emotional health. Unfortunately, the foolish half was winning the war.

"Hey, we just passed a perfectly respectable-looking café."

"Is mere respectable going to gain me a smile?"

"Not even triple chocolate cake with fresh cream is going to gain you that, my friend."

"My friend?" He glanced at me, eyebrows raised. "That's better than rat. Or what was it you called me the other day? During that brief moment you deigned to speak to me?"

"I called you a stinking love rat," I muttered. "And let's not make this about what I've done. You're the one who left me, not the other way around."

"And I do believe I have apologized profusely for that." He slowed down for a red light, then added, "And, technically speaking, the term *love rat* does not apply, because I have never loved anyone else."

Again my heart did that treacherous little lurch. *Calm down, stupid. He didn't mean it that way. He left you, remember? That doesn't infer love in any way, shape, or form.*

"That's not what the office talk is."

"You should know better than to listen to office talk. After all, they had us married off within three weeks of us starting to date."

So did I. Of course, we'd only lasted a total of six weeks. I looked away and blinked back tears. Damn it, *this* is why it was a bad idea to speak to him.

He pulled into a side street, and began to slow the car down. Old two-story houses rubbed shoulders with interesting little shops, but none of them resembled a café or anything actually open.

"Here we are," he said, stopping the car in front of a pretty blue and white two-story building.

"And where is here?" I asked, looking up at the window boxes filled with greenery.

"Mom's," he said, and got out of the car.

"What?" But I was talking to thin air. Or thick air, in his case. I waited until he opened my door and added, "I am not going inside to meet your mother."

Especially when she had totally disapproved of me and Brodie going out.

"Well, good, because she's not there. No one is. They're all at my gran's for the night."

He took my hand and tugged lightly. I remained right where I was.

"Then why are we even here? You know how your mom feels about me."

"That isn't a problem anymore, trust me. Besides, you wanted triple chocolate with fresh cream, and my mom bakes the best you'll ever taste. Come on."

He tugged harder, leaving me with little choice. With the bells on my feet ringing joyously, I untangled my legs from my coat and got out.

"We need to get you some decent clothes," he said, his gaze sweeping me critically but still managing to leave me feeling all hot and bothered. "You look rather cold and wet."

He opened the gate and began leading me up the garden path. In more ways than one, I suspected.

"That's because I *am* cold and wet. And I have perfectly decent clothes waiting for me at home. You need to take me back there."

"If I do, you won't come back here."

"So?"

"So, all the progress I've made this evening will go sliding away, and I'll be back to being the rat."

"But you've never stopped being the rat," I said sweetly. "So what's the problem?"

He laughed, a warm rich sound that slid across my skin as sensuously as a caress. He opened the door and waved me inside. I slid past and tried without success to ignore the tangy heat of him. The way my body ached to press forward just that little bit more, and feel all that heat against my skin.

Hello, last Christmas? Remember that? Remember the whole he's a bad man and we don't like him spiel?

I remembered. Unfortunately, I also remembered how good it felt being with him, and no matter how much I told myself I was just setting myself up for more heartache, I couldn't help the need to soak in the warmth of his presence one more time.

You're a sap. And an idiot.

And it's Christmas, and I'm lonely.

It was dark inside the house, but the air was warm and smelled ever so slightly of baking. I sniffed lightly as I hung my coat up on the nearby hook. While the hints of ginger and vanilla were strong, they were underlined by an animal mustiness, and it was a strong reminder that this wasn't any ordinary house. That this was the abode of werewolves.

He caught my hand, his fingers so warm against mine. "This way." He led me up a set of stairs and into a bathroom. "There's clean towels on the shelf above the bath, and a clean robe behind the door."

"Brodie—"

He stopped the words with a short, sharp kiss that left me breathless and yet wanting more. "I'll have coffee and cake waiting downstairs."

And with that, he left me standing there, staring in shock at the back of a door. This night was *so* not going to plan. Well, not to *my* plans, at least. It was becoming a little obvious that he had a whole lot more planned for *his* Christmas than just catching a killer.

I blew out a breath and began to strip off. I had two choices—stay or leave—and as much as I knew it was a stupid move, I wanted the cake, and the coffee, and his company for a little bit longer.

I might well be setting myself up for another crappy Christmas, but it was supposed to be the season of goodwill to all men, wasn't it? And Brodie was definitely a man . . .

And *I* was reaching for straws in an effort to justify the stupidity of my actions.

I shoved the thoughts away and took a shower, then donned my still-wet underwear. I'd rather risk getting a chill than being naked around Brodie. After wrapping myself up in the thick, fluffy gown, I finger-combed my short hair then I grabbed the sodden elf outfit and headed downstairs. Following his scent led me into the rich-smelling warmth of the kitchen.

He was pouring coffee into a mug, and there were two huge slabs of cake already sitting on a tray.

"Where can I dry these?" I asked.

"Are they shrink proof?"

"Well, they didn't shrink on me."

He smiled. It did my pulse rate absolutely no good whatsoever. "There's a clothes dryer through there," he said, nodding toward the door to the right.

I shoved the clothes in the dryer, then headed back into the kitchen. "We eating here?"

He shook his head. "In the living room. It's warmer. You want to grab the cake tray?"

I did, and followed him out of the kitchen and into the living room. A huge log fire was the room's main feature, but it was the Christmas tree that drew my eye. It was big, lush, and totally without decoration, except for the fake snow that adorned the end of the dipping branches. It reminded me of a tree in the middle of a snow-swept forest, and maybe that was the whole point.

"That kind of dwarfs my tree," I said, putting the tray down on the coffee table.

"The tree you had last year had character," he commented, and offered me a mug.

I smiled. "Both that tree and this year's are very sad representations of the Christmas tree."

He sat down on the sofa and patted the spot beside him. I retreated to the fire, standing with my back to it.

Amusement teased his mouth. "So why buy them?"

"Because they looked lonely."

His gaze met mine, green eyes holding touches of amusement and something else. Something that had my pulse skipping. Not lust. Something deeper. Stronger.

"It's a rotten thing," he said softly, "being lonely at Christmas."

I didn't bite. I wanted to, but I didn't. I stepped away from the fire to avoid burning my butt, and picked up a plate of cake instead.

"How are we going to catch this vampire before he kills again?" I spooned some cake into my mouth and felt my knees go weak. Damn, this *was* good chocolate cake.

"The team is still working on possible locations given everything we've seen and I've scented at the crime scenes. If they find something, they'll contact us."

He leaned forward to pick up the other plate of cake, and my fingers suddenly itched with the need to run through his thick, dark hair. I gripped the spoon harder.

"Other than that," he continued, "we just have to hope the bait plan works."

"It's difficult to catch someone when they can up and fly away."

"If it was *that* easy for him to shift shape, he would have flown the coop earlier. Are you going to sit down?"

"Are you going to make any moves on me?"

Again that sexy smile teased his mouth. "Do you want me to?"

Yes, yes, yes. "No."

"Why not?"

I just about choked on my cake. "Why do you *think* why not?"

"Because I'm a rat?"

"That would be a good start."

"Because I forgot to call you for Christmas?"

"And my birthday. And Valentine's."

"That's true. I did, however, buy you presents for both. Does that count?"

Yes. *No.* "Damn it, Brodie, stop. This isn't fair." I shoved the half-eaten cake on the table and thrust my hands into my pockets so he couldn't see they were suddenly shaking.

Because it wasn't fear. It was the need to reach out and touch him, caress him, love him. Just like we used to. Just like I dreamed of on so many of those long nights I'd spent alone.

He placed his plate back down then rose. Only the coffee table

separated us. Only the coffee table stopped me from stepping into the
sweet strength of his arms.

"I know it's not fair," he said softly. "But I never intended it to be."

"But *why*?"

The question was practically torn out of me, and he grimaced.
"Because for the last month I've been trying to talk to you, and you've
barely given me the time of day."

"And that surprises you?"

"No. It's highly frustrating, though."

"Damn it, Brodie, this *has* to stop. I can't . . ." My voice broke a
little. I stopped and took a deep, quivering breath. "I can't go through
another Christmas waiting for you to call but knowing you never will."

He raised a hand and gently brushed my cheek with his fingertips.
His fingers were so warm and felt so good against my skin that desire
surged, making me tremble. And it was tempting, *so* tempting, to press
into his touch. To ask for more than just that light caress.

But that way lay heartache.

I went to step back, away from him, but he must have sensed the
motion. He caught the end of the robe belt and held it lightly. If I
stepped back, the loose knot would undo.

Part of me *wanted* to step back. Wanted to give in to the heat and
power of what still lay between us. But the part of me that was still desperately clinging to sanity and reason made me hold still.

"What if I promise never to make you wait by a phone again?" he
said softly.

My gaze searched his, saw the sincerity and the compassion and the
hunger in the bright depths. I wanted to trust it—trust him—I really
did. But I just couldn't.

"I don't believe in promises anymore. I don't believe in you."

The words hurt him, as I knew they would. But the flash of pain in
his eyes, and the lingering, aching regret in his expression gave me no
sense of satisfaction at all. Because in truth, I didn't want to hurt him,
and I didn't want retribution for all that he'd put me through. Part of
me wanted to know why, but mostly I just wanted to get on with my
life.

A life that didn't involve him. Didn't involve the hurt or the pain that he'd brought into my life.

"I've never promised you anything that I haven't delivered," he said eventually.

Maybe not out loud, but in deed and action you promised me the world. And then you ran away. "You promised to call me the minute you got back from Chicago, Brodie. But you never did."

He blew out a breath and had the grace to look guilty. "There were reasons—"

"It's too late for reasons," I cut in. *Too late for us.*

"I refuse to believe that," he said, leaving me wondering whether he was answering the spoken or unspoken comment.

Then he stepped around the table, wrapped his hand around the back of my neck, and dragged me forward, into his arms. And kissed me.

This time, it *wasn't* a fleeting thing, but rather a long and erotic exploration that had my blood screaming through my veins and my heart threatening to jump out of my chest.

And oh, it was good, so good, to be kissed like that again. Like this moment and I were the only things that mattered to him, the only things that would *ever* matter to him.

It was a lie, of course, but one I was so ready to believe, even if only for this moment. I wrapped my arms around his neck and pressed myself against his long, lean length, until I could feel his every intake of breath. Feel the rigid hardness of his erection pressing against my stomach. Lord, he felt *good.*

His free hand brushed my side, sliding teasingly past my breast. Something akin to electricity flashed through every nerve ending, and a low-down ache leapt into focus. Tiny beads of perspiration skated across my skin—moisture raised by the sheer heat of his body, and my own crazy longing.

I *knew* I should step away, should retreat from the kiss and from all the tangled, unsettled emotions that it raised. But I couldn't. Call me weak, call me a fool, but the reality of this kiss was so much better than the dreams that I could only stand there and enjoy.

It was just as well his cell phone chose that moment to ring, because we both knew where that kiss would have led otherwise.

Brodie growled low down in his throat, a sound that seemed to echo through my lips and body, then pulled away, his breathing harsh as he dragged the phone from his pocket.

"What?"

To say he sounded annoyed would be an understatement. It was probably the closest thing I'd heard to a growl from him when he was still in human form.

His expression got darker as he continued to listen, and I knew without doubt it was work. I took a deep breath to regroup my thoughts and steady my riotous heart rate, then, rather determinately, tied a double knot on the dressing gown. It wouldn't stop him *or* me, but it was the action that mattered. It was a way of reminding my scattered self-control and exuberant hormones that I *did* have a choice, and that I *could* do what was best for me.

Although after that kiss, I wasn't so sure what, exactly, that was right now.

I picked up my coffee and moved back to the fire. I wasn't cold—far from it—but it was the farthest point away from him without getting too obvious about retreating.

He hung up and made another low, growly sound.

"Work?" I said, trying not to sound relieved and failing miserably.

He gave me a dark look. "Yeah, there's been another murder."

My stomach sank. "But it's after midnight."

"I noticed. He obviously didn't."

"Why can't they send someone else? Why us?"

But I knew the answer. The squad was a small one, and this was our case. And there was no such thing as standard hours or being off duty when it came to the Para-investigations squad.

He simply said, "You want to get dressed?"

"I really don't want to wear that elf costume—"

"Well, Mom's clothes won't fit, because she's much bigger than you. So unless you want to wear the robe, we're stuck."

I swore under my breath and stomped out of the room. "We wouldn't have been stuck if you'd just taken me back home like I asked."

"But I wouldn't have had the chance to kiss you if I'd done that, now, would I?"

"Not a snowflake's chance in hell," I muttered. I closed the laundry room door, then quickly pulled the clothes out of the dryer and got dressed. There was a thick pair of woolen socks sitting on top of some clean washing, so I took those and put them on before dragging on my wet shoes.

He was waiting in the kitchen when I opened the door, and his gaze drifted down my length, heating me as quickly as any caress or kiss. "The white socks spoil the look. And they're my brother's."

"Well, your brother just donated them to my cold feet. Where are we going?"

"The cemetery."

"So he didn't attack a collector this time?"

"Nope. Gravedigger."

"They're digging graves at this hour of the night?"

"Death doesn't stop just because it's almost Christmas, you know."

He placed his hand against my back and guided me out of the house. My feet jingled merrily as I clomped down the steps, suggesting a mood I couldn't reach and annoying the hell out of me. So I bent and ripped the stupid bells off.

Silence fell. It was heavenly.

We zoomed through the streets at record speed, and all I could do was thank the stars that there wasn't much traffic about at that hour.

The cemetery's main gates were locked but that wasn't much of a problem to a werewolf. Once he'd broken the lock and opened the gates fully, we drove around to the left, following a road that was lined by bare rosebushes.

"Who reported the murder?" I asked, eyeing the gravestone-filled darkness with some trepidation. Cemeteries were not a favorite place of mine. There were too many ghosts wandering about, and not all of them were the pleasant type.

"It came in anonymously, and they weren't on the line long enough for a trace."

"No caller ID, then?"

"Nope."

"Unusual."

"It could be, but a lot of folks don't want to get involved any more than necessary."

Especially when it came to non-human activities. Still, this time it niggled, and I had no idea why. He pulled to a parking spot and climbed out of the car. I grabbed the stakes and my coat, then followed suit, relieved that I'd torn the bells off my shoes. The jingle would have clashed against the somber feel of the cemetery.

I slammed the door shut and moved to the front of the car. "Where is the body?" I said, my gaze sweeping over the varied headstones sitting in orderly soldier rows. There were no ghosts out there, and for that I had to be glad. I wasn't in the mood for their chatter tonight.

His nostrils flared slightly, then he caught my hand in his and said, "It's this way."

I didn't question his certainty. He was a were, so if there was blood on the breeze, he'd be smelling it. But as we wound our way through the headstones, a chill began to creep across my skin and goose bumps formed.

Something was out there.

My steps slowed. "Brodie—"

"I know," he said softly. "We're being paced at the moment."

"Can you smell what they are?"

"No. They're slightly downwind. But I can hear their steps." He squeezed my hand lightly, but if he meant it to be reassuring, then it failed miserably. "There's only one, so it won't be a problem."

"Maybe not for you, but I'm human." And though I could fight, I still had nowhere near the strength or speed of a non-human. Which was a bummer when it was my job to fight the bad apples amongst them.

"They have to get through me to get to you, and trust me, that's not going to happen."

I couldn't help smiling. Werewolves were so damn confident in their own fighting prowess it was sometimes scary. But at times like this, that was also damn comforting.

The smell of fresh earth touched the cold night air, and within minutes we came across the body. He was lying on his back beside a tractor, right next to a freshly dug grave, and the look of shock frozen onto his face suggested he hadn't even seen his attacker. His neck had been slashed wide open by something jagged, but not much blood had seeped into the collar of his overalls and thick jacket. Someone—probably our vamp with the shattered canines—had sucked it all up.

"Why would he be digging a grave at night? And without a light?"

"There's a lot of non-humans doing this sort of stuff now, and many of them don't need lights to see at night. This guy doesn't smell human." He released my hand and knelt beside the body. "The scent lingering here is the one I chased earlier tonight. But there's also a fainter scent that's the same as the one I found near the other victims."

"So we have two vampires, who may or may not be related, working together." I studied the darkness surrounding us. "You think they could be hiding out here?"

"Wouldn't be the first time vamps have made themselves at home in a cemetery. After all, that's where the legends of vampires rising from graves came from."

"But if our vamp tonight was hungry enough to attack this gravedigger, surely he would have attacked someone earlier? Hell, I was standing there looking more than a little cold and forlorn, and he showed no inclination to attack *me*."

"Maybe he sensed the anger in you, and figured you'd put up too much of a—"

I didn't hear the rest of his sentence, because something long and thin leapt out of the surrounding darkness and came straight at me. I had a brief glimpse of a white face, then he was flying into me, knocking the stakes from my hand and sending the both of us crashing to the ground.

I landed hard enough to leave me winded and briefly seeing stars. Stars that were quickly shattered by the growls of the vampire. His body covered my length and pinned me to the ground and the smell of him—earth and unwashed flesh—filled every breath. He snarled, revealing those shattered bloody canines, confirming our suspicions that he'd been the one to kill the gravedigger. And he intended to feed off me as well.

Not that I was about to let him.

I bucked in an effort to get him off, but he rode me like a bronco and laughed harshly—a sound that was abruptly cut off when my fist smashed into his face. I might be human, but I was strong, and my blow mashed his nose, sending blood flying.

He growled low down in his throat, a sound that was suddenly echoed. Then he was gone from me, tossed into the night like so much rubbish, and Brodie was there, hauling me upright.

"Are you okay?" he said, voice harsh and green eyes afire with anger and concern.

"Yeah, I'm fine—"

"Good. Stay here while I take care of that bastard."

"Brodie, no, wait—"

Once again, I was speaking to nothing more than air. I rubbed my arms and studied the surrounding darkness. Whatever had been watching us before was still watching me now, and the feel of it made my skin crawl. It was an older evil than the one Brodie was chasing, and there was an odd sense of satisfaction coming from it.

I shivered slightly and looked around for the stakes. I found one. I'm sure the other one was out there in the darkness somewhere, but I wasn't willing to go too far to find it. And while one stake might not help if whatever-it-was out there in the darkness attacked as suddenly as the first vamp had, at least holding it gave me some sense of security.

With stake in hand, I knelt down beside the body and studied the poor man's neck. What a mess.

So who'd reported his murder? Did this gravedigger have a partner who'd fled the scene, or was he also lying out there in the darkness with a savaged neck? If so, why hadn't Brodie scented him?

And who the hell was watching me?

I glanced at the surrounding gravestones, my heart pounding rapidly and the taste of fear in my mouth. I might have faced more than my fair share of bad guys over the years, but I was still human. Humans were easy kills for vampires, even one as well trained as me.

God, Brodie, where are you?

Why had he left me alone? Why hadn't he sensed that our other watcher was still out there? Or had his anger at me being attacked blocked out awareness of everything else?

I blew out a breath, and tried to remain calm. But my knuckles practically glowed with the force of my grip on the stake, and every sense I had was tuned in the direction of the thing that still watched.

Still oozed an evil that was making my senses and stomach squirm.

I rose and walked around the body, heading for the tractor, to make sure we didn't have another victim waiting to be uncovered in the cabin.

I didn't get more than five steps when I sensed the approach of evil. Before I could react, he hit from behind, smashing my face into the ground. Suddenly all I could breathe was dirt, and the panic that had already been stirring surged to new heights. I struggled with all my might, but a hand against the back of my head pressed me down harder. A scream rose up my throat, but it had nowhere to go, echoing through my mind instead.

And then his free hand was on me, tearing at my clothes, caressing my skin, his flesh cold and clammy and horrid. I shuddered, fighting his touch, fighting *him*, with all my might, twisting and kicking and punching backward.

He chuckled. A heated, lusty, and totally *evil* sound.

Clothes tore. His fingers forced themselves underneath me, groping for a breast. I shuddered, fighting nausea and feeling more and more desperate for air.

Stake, I thought, and groped blindly around me. My hand brushed against wood, and I grasped it frantically, my fingers tightening around it spasmodically as I lifted my arm and stabbed backward with all the strength I had left.

I hit flesh, felt it give way. He roared in pain and jerked away. Not getting off, but giving me the freedom to move. To breathe. I gulped down air, my whole body shuddering with the effort.

"Bitch!" The sound rode the air, harsh and forced. "For that, I will do you slowly, and then I shall let my brother suck you dry. No easy death for you, little girl."

"Your brother is dead," came a voice so flat, so deadly and so damn cold that for a moment I didn't even recognize that it was Brodie's, "as you soon will be."

Then the weight was off me, and I could move. I forced my trembling limbs into action and pushed up, the now-bloody stake still in my hand as I swung around.

Brodie's powerful fingers were around the neck of a thickset man, and he was holding him off the ground by a good six inches or so. That took more strength than I could ever imagine anyone owning, but he didn't even seem to be exerting himself.

The only sign of effort was in the whiteness of his fingers. Fingers that were ever-so-slowly squeezing the life out of my attacker.

No quick death intended there, whatever he might have said.

"Brodie—"

"No one attacks you and lives," he cut in, his gaze not leaving the thickset man's. "No one."

There wasn't only anger in his voice, but possessiveness. It was the wolf speaking, and the wolf was protecting what belonged to him.

Me.

Normally that knowledge would have made my heart dance, but such a reaction seemed out of place when he was intent on slowly strangling his quarry in the middle of a graveyard. And the fact that this vamp entirely deserved it was beside the point.

"Damn it, Brodie, kill him quickly. You're not him. I don't want you to be like him, or any of the others we kill." Didn't want him to enjoy it, as the protector within undoubtedly was.

His fingers moved, and a loud crack ran across the night. The vamp went limp, and Brodie released him, letting him drop to the ground like so much rubbish.

"God, I'm sorry," he said, his voice soft and suddenly weary as he turned to face me. And the pain in his eyes, the fear still etched in his face, made my heart ache. "I'm so damn sorry—"

I didn't let him finish. I ran into his embrace. Felt his arms wrap around me and hold me so tight. Arms that were trembling more than I was.

"It's okay, I'm here, I'm safe."

"I thought my stupidity had taken you from me a second time." His breath whispered heat past my ear. "I felt your fear echo through me. The thought of a life without you in it hit me, and I panicked. I can't live without you, Hannah. I don't want to live without you."

I broke free of his fierce grip, and stared into the glory of his green eyes. Seeing the honesty there. Seeing the love. Wanting to return it twofold, but still trapped by the hurt of Christmas past. "Yet you walked away for a year. I can't just forget that, Brodie." And while I might have told him I didn't want a reason, that was a total lie.

He sighed, and ran a finger lightly down my cheek. My body trembled in response, and it was all I could do not to step into his embrace again, to forget the past and just enjoy the promise of the present.

But I couldn't. I owed my tear-soaked pillow more than that.

"I was an ass—"

"I think we've both agreed on that point," I said dryly. "The point we need to clarify is *why*."

He thrust a hand through his hair, then said, "We happened very quickly. I just wasn't ready for it."

"So you coped by running away? That's logical."

"Loving a human isn't logical."

"Me being a human isn't a reason, Brodie. It's an excuse. I *need* a reason." Needed to believe he wouldn't do it to me again.

He sighed. "You scared me."

I almost choked on my disbelief. "I scared *you*? You're the big bad hairy monster, not me."

He half smiled. "I never expected—or wanted—to fall in love with a human, Hannah. And my family certainly didn't appreciate the thought of me bringing a human into the pack." He shrugged, his expression a little sheepish. "So I convinced myself it was nothing more than an infatuation, and walked away."

"Just like that," I said, and all the hurt and the pain of that time was suddenly right there in my voice. "So damn easily."

"It wasn't easy. It was *never* easy." He grimaced, and suddenly his green eyes held a loneliness as powerful as anything I'd been feeling over the last year. "You have no idea how many times I picked up the phone to call you. No idea how many times I sat out in front of your place, practicing an apology." He hesitated, and smiled ruefully. "And no idea how many times I came close to interrupting your dates and punching out whatever man you were with. It was that need to destroy the men you were dating that finally convinced me this was no mere infatuation."

"And you never thought to talk to me about any of this?"

"I thought about it, trust me. But it's never easy for a werewolf to admit that they're wrong, especially in the face of such anger and hurt. And the longer I left it, the more certain I became that I'd made the biggest mistake of my life, the more afraid I became that apologizing wouldn't undo the damage and that I might have lost you forever."

"So why are you finally apologizing now?"

"Because I think about you every day, and dream about you every night. We were never a mistake, no matter what I might have thought at the beginning, and what we have will never go away. I love you, Hannah. I need *you*." He let his fingers run over my lips, making them tingle, then dropped his hand. "Please, tell me you'll forgive me. Tell me you'll give me another chance."

I stared at him for a moment, knowing there could only ever be one answer. That there had only ever been one answer from the moment he'd walked back into my life. I might not be able to totally forget the year of loneliness, or the pain he'd caused me, but what we had was worth fighting for.

Rat or not, right or wrong, I wanted this man in my life.

For Christmas.

For ever.

I blew out a breath, and said hesitantly, "I don't know, Brodie."

Tension flitted across his shoulders, and for a moment, utter bleakness shone in his eyes. I let a smile touch my lips, and added, "After all, I didn't even get to finish my chocolate cake. And there's still the matter of the missing Valentine's Day *and* birthday presents to be resolved."

He laughed—a sound so joyous, so happy, that goose bumps ran across my skin. He wrapped an arm around my waist and hauled me close. "What if I promise to bathe you in chocolate cake for the rest of your life?"

I snuggled closer, letting the heat and scent of him flow over my skin and fill every breath. "That might be a step in the right direction."

"And give you two birthday presents for the next ten years?"

"And at Christmas and Valentine's. I'm missing those, remember."

"It's a deal," he murmured, then his lips claimed mine, and he kissed me.

It felt so good, so right. Like I was finally home, right where I belonged.

Christmas past might have been a nightmare, but Christmas present and Christmas future were suddenly looking mighty damn fine.

sa

J. A. Konrath

J. A. Konrath's short work has appeared in over fifty magazines and anthologies. He's responsible for five books in the Lieutenant Jacqueline "Jack" Daniels thriller series, the latest of which is Fuzzy Navel. *He also edited the collection of hitman stories* These Guns for Hire, *and penned the horror novel* Afraid *under the name Jack Kilborn. Visit him at www.JAKonrath.com.*

Robert Weston Smith walked across the snow-covered parking lot carrying a small plastic container of his poop.

Weston considered himself a healthy guy. At thirty-three years old he still had a six-pack, the result of working out three times a week. He followed a strict macrobiotic diet. He practiced yoga and tai chi. The last time he ate processed sugar was during the Reagan administration.

That's why, when odd things began appearing in his bowel movements, he became more than a little alarmed. So alarmed that he sought out his general practitioner, making an appointment after a particularly embarrassing phone call to his office secretary.

Weston entered the office building with his head down and a blush on his ears, feeling like a kid sneaking out after curfew. He used the welcome mat to stamp the snow off his feet and walked through the lobby to the doctor's office, taking a deep breath before going in. There were six people in the waiting room, four adults and a young boy, plus a nurse in pink paisley hospital scrubs who sat behind the counter.

Weston kept his head down and beelined for the nurse. The poop container was blue plastic, semiopaque, but it might as well have been a police siren, blinking and howling. Everyone in the room must have known what it was. And if they didn't at first, they sure knew after the nurse said in a loud voice, "Is that your stool sample?"

He nodded, trying to hand it to the woman. She made no effort to take it, and he couldn't really blame her. He carried it, and a clipboard, over to a seat in the waiting room. Setting his poop on a table atop an ancient copy of *Good Housekeeping*, he got to work filling out his insurance information. When it came time to describe the nature of his ailment, he wrote down "intestinal problems." Which was untrue—his intestines felt fine. It's what came out of his intestines that caused alarm.

"What's in the box?"

Weston looked up, staring into the big eyes of a child, perhaps five or six years old.

"It's, um, something for the doctor."

He glanced around the room, looking for someone to claim the boy. Two people had their noses stuck in magazines, one was watching a car commercial on the TV hanging from the ceiling, and the last appeared asleep. Any of them could have been his parent.

"Is it a cupcake?" the boy asked.

"Uh . . . yeah, a cupcake."

"I like cupcakes."

"You wouldn't like this one."

The boy reached for the container.

"Is it chocolate?"

Weston snatched it up and set it in his lap.

"No. It isn't chocolate."

"Show it to me."

"No."

The boy squinted at the sample. Weston considered putting it behind his back, out of the child's sight, but there was no place to set it other than the chair. It didn't seem wise to put it where he might lean back on it.

"It looks like chocolate. I think I can see peanuts."

"Those aren't peanuts."

In fact, gross and disturbing as it sounded, Weston didn't know what those lumps were. Which is why he was at the doctor's office.

He glanced again at the four adults in the waiting room, wondering why no one bothered to corral their son. Weston was single, no children. None of his friends had children. Being a mechanical engineer, he didn't encounter children at his job. Perhaps today's parents had no problems letting their kids walk up to strangers and beg for cupcakes.

"Mr. Smith?" the pink paisley nurse said. "Please come with me."

Weston stood, taking his poop through the door, following the nurse down a short hallway and into an examining room.

"Please put on the gown. I'll be back in a moment."

She closed the door behind him. Weston stared at the folded paper garment, sitting on the edge of a beige examination table also lined with paper. He set the container down next to a jar of cotton swabs. Then he removed his coat, shoes, jeans, boxer shorts, and polo shirt, placed them in a neat pile on the floor, and slipped his arms through the gown's sleeve holes. It felt like wearing a large, stiff napkin.

Weston shivered. It was cold in the room; examination rooms always seemed to be several degrees too cool for comfort. He stood there in his socks, rubbing his bare arms, waiting for the nurse to come back.

She eventually did, taking his temperature and blood pressure, then left him again with the promise that Dr. Waggoner would be there shortly.

A minute passed. Two. Three. Weston stared at the ceiling tiles, thinking about the hours he'd spent on the Internet looking for some sort of clue as to what strange disease he had. There was plenty of disturbing content about bowel movements, including a website where people actually sent in pictures of theirs so others could rate them, but he'd found nothing even remotely close to the problem he was having.

The door opened, derailing his train of thought.

"Mr. Smith? I'm Dr. Waggoner. Please, sit down."

Weston sat on the table, the paper chilly under his buttocks. Dr. Waggoner was an older man, portly. Bald, but with enough gray hair growing out of his ears to manage a comb-over. He had on trendy round eyeglasses with a faux tortoiseshell frame, and a voice that was both deep and nasally.

"Your blood pressure is normal, but your temperature is 100.5

degrees." He snapped on some latex gloves. "How are you feeling right now?"

"Fine."

"Any aches, pains, problems, discomforts?"

"No. I'm a little chilly, but that's all."

Dr. Waggoner removed some sort of scope and checked Weston's eyes and ears as they talked.

"How long have you been having these intestinal problems?"

"Um, on and off for about three months. But they aren't really intestinal problems. I'm finding, uh, strange things in my bowel movements."

"Can you describe them for me?"

"Like little stones. Or things that look like strips of fabric."

Dr. Waggoner raised an eyebrow.

"Well, I have to ask the obvious question first."

Weston waited.

"Have you been eating little stones or strips of fabric?"

The doctor grinned like a Halloween pumpkin. Weston managed a weak smile.

"Not that I'm aware of, Doctor."

"Good to know. Tell me about your diet. Has it changed recently? Eating anything new or exotic?"

"Not really. I eat mostly health foods, have been for the last ten years."

"Been out of the country in the last six months?"

"No."

"Do you eat a lot of rare meat, or raw vegetables?"

"Sometimes. But I don't think I have a tapeworm."

Dr. Waggoner chuckled.

"Ah, the Internet. It gives everyone a doctorate in medicine."

Weston did the open his mouth and say "aaaaah" thing, then said, "I know I'm not a doctor, but I checked a lot of sites, and the things in my stool, they don't look like tapeworm segments."

"Stones and fabric, you said. Can you be more specific?"

"The stones are sort of white. Some very small, like flecks. Other times bigger."

"How big?"

"About the size of my thumb."

"And the fabric?"

"There have been different colors. Sometimes red. Sometimes black. Sometimes blue."

"How closely have you examined these items?"

Weston frowned. "Not too closely. I mean, I never took them out of the toilet and picked them up or anything. Except for that." Weston pointed to the stool on the table.

"We'll have the lab take a look at that. In the meantime, I'm going to have to take a look myself. Can you bend over the table and lift up your gown, please?"

Weston hoped it wouldn't have to come to this, but he assumed the position while Dr. Waggoner applied some chilly lubricating jelly to his hand and the point of entry.

"Just relax. You'll feel some pressure."

It was a hell of a lot worse than pressure, and impossible to relax. Weston clenched his eyes shut and tried to concentrate on something, anything, other than the fat fingers going up the down staircase.

"You said this began three months ago. Has it been nonstop? Intermittent?"

"Only two or three days out of the month," Weston grunted. "Then it goes back to normal."

"When during the month?"

"Usually the last week."

"Have you . . . Wait a second. Stay still for a moment. I think I feel something."

Which is the absolute last thing you want to hear when a doctor has his hand inside you. Weston held his breath, scrunched up his face. He didn't know which was worse, the pain or the humiliation. Blessedly, mercifully, the hand withdrew.

"What is it, Doctor?"

"Hold on. I think there's more. I'm going in again."

Weston groaned, hating his life and everyone in it. The doctor went back in four additional times, so often that Weston was becoming used to it, a fact that disturbed him somewhat.

"I think that's the last of it."

"The last of what?"

Weston turned around, saw the physician staring at several objects on his palm.

Dr. Waggoner said. "A coat button, part of a zipper, and sixty-three cents in change. Apparently you're not eating as healthy as you think."

Weston blinked, as if the act would make the objects disappear. They remained.

"This is going to sound like a lie," Weston said. "But I didn't eat those."

"I had a colleague who once examined a man who wanted to get into one of those world record books by eating a bicycle, one piece at a time. He removed a reflector from the man's rectum."

"I'm serious, Doctor. I'm not eating buttons or change. I certainly didn't eat a zipper."

"It looks like a fly from a pair of jeans." Dr. Waggoner chuckled again. "I know an old lady who swallowed a fly."

"I didn't eat a fly."

"Okay. Then there's only one alternative. Are you sexually active?"

Weston sighed. "I'm straight. Currently between girlfriends. And the only person who has been up there in my entire life has been you."

Dr. Waggoner placed the objects in a bedpan and said, "You can sit down now."

Weston got off all fours, but preferred to stand. He didn't think he'd ever sit again.

"You think I'm lying to you."

"These things didn't just materialize inside you from another dimension, Mr. Smith. And you probably don't have a branch of the U.S. Treasury inside you, minting coins."

At least someone seemed to be enjoying this. Weston wondered when he'd ask him to break a dollar.

"I'm telling the truth."

"Do you have a roommate? One who likes practical jokes?"

"I live alone."

"Do you drink? Do any drugs?"

"I have an occasional beer."

"Do you ever drink too much? Have blackouts? Periods where you don't remember what happened?"

Weston opened his mouth to say no, but stopped himself. There were a few moments during the last few weeks that seemed sort of fuzzy, memory-wise. He wouldn't call them blackouts. But he'd go to bed, and wake up in a different part of the house. Naked.

"I think I might sleepwalk," he admitted.

"Now we're getting somewhere." Dr. Waggoner pulled off his gloves, put them in the hazardous materials bin. "I'm going to refer you to a specialist."

Weston scratched his head. "So you think I'm eating buttons and spare change in my sleep?"

"They're getting inside you, one way or another. Consider yourself lucky. I once had a patient who, while sleepwalking, logged on to an Internet casino and blew seventy-eight thousand dollars."

"So he came to see you for help with sleepwalking?"

"He came to see me to set his broken nose, after his wife found out. Don't worry, Mr. Smith. I'm going to prescribe a sleep aid for you tonight, to help curb late-night snacking, and the specialist will get to the root of your problem. Sleepwalking is usually the result of stress, or depression."

Weston frowned. "This doctor you're referring me to. Is he a shrink?"

"His name is Dr. Glendon. He's a psychiatrist. My nurse will set up an appointment for you. In the meantime, try to lock up all the small, swallowable objects in your home."

Weston walked home feeling like an idiot. An idiot who sat on a cactus. His apartment, only a few blocks away from the doctor's office, seemed like fifty miles because every step stung.

The sun was starting to set, and Naperville had its holiday clothes on. Strands of white lights hung alongside fresh evergreen wreaths and bows, decorating every lamppost and storefront window. The gently falling snow added to the effect, making the street look like a Christmas card.

None of it cheered Weston. Since his job moved him to Illinois, away from his family and friends in Asheville, North Carolina, he'd been down. But not actually depressed. All Weston knew about depression came from watching TV commercials for antidepressants. He'd never seen a commercial where the depressed person ate nickels, but maybe Dr. Waggoner was on to something.

Fishing his keys from his jeans, he was about to stick them in the lock of the security door when it opened suddenly. Standing there, all four feet of her, was his mean next-door neighbor. Weston didn't know her name. She probably didn't know his either. She simply called him "Loud Man." Every twenty minutes she would bang on the wall between their apartments, screaming about him making noise. If he turned on the TV, she'd bang—even when it was at its lowest setting. If the phone rang, she'd bang. When the microwave beeped, she'd bang. She even banged while he was brushing his teeth.

He'd called the landlord about her, three times. On each occasion, Weston got the brush-off.

"She's eccentric," he was told. "No family. You should ignore her."

Easy for the landlord to say. How do you ignore someone who won't let you into your own door?

Weston tried to step around her, but the old woman folded her arms and didn't budge. She had light brown skin, and some sort of fabric tied to the top of her head. Weston couldn't help staring at her ears, which had distinctive, gypsy-like gold hoops dangling from them. The ears themselves were huge, probably larger than Weston's hands. Maybe if his ears were that big, he'd complain all the time about noise, too.

Her dog, some sort of tiny toy breed with long fur and a mean disposition, saw Weston and began to yap at him, straining against his leash. It had a large gold tag on his collar that read ROMI.

"Excuse me," Weston said, trying to get by.

The old woman stayed put. So did Romi.

"I said, *excuse me.*"

She pointed a crooked old finger at him.

"Loud Man! You keep noise down!"

"They have these things called earplugs," Weston said. "I think they come in extra large."

She began to scream at him in a high-pitched native tongue that sounded a lot like "BLAAA-LAAAA-LAAAAA-LEEEE-LAAAA-BLAAA!" Romi matched her, yipping right along. Weston took it for about ten seconds, and then pushed past, heading for his apartment. The chorus followed him inside.

Though it was early, Weston yawned, then yawned again. He hung his keys on a hook next to the door, switched the TV on to one setting above MUTE, and sat on the sofa. There was dog hair on the carpet, which made no sense, because Weston had no dog.

But the crazy old lady had a dog.

Could she be getting in my apartment somehow?

Panicked, Weston did a quick tour, looking for anything missing or out of place. He came up empty, but to his shame he realized he was picking up everything smaller than a matchbook and sticking it in his pockets. He took these items and placed them in a junk drawer in the kitchen.

For some reason, this act drained him of his last drop of energy, and the sun had barely even gone down. He sat back down on the couch, switched to the SciFi Channel, and closed his eyes for just a few seconds.

A ringing sound woke Weston up. He was naked on the kitchen floor, the sun streaming in through the windows. Weston automatically smacked his lips, checking to see if he could taste anything odd. Then he got to his knees and reached for the phone on the counter.

"Mr. Smith? This is Dr. Waggoner's office calling. Please hold for the doctor."

Weston scratched his chest, listening to Neil Diamond singing to a chair who apparently didn't hear him.

"Weston? This is Dr. Waggoner. How did you sleep last night?"

"Not well," he said, noting his nude body.

"Remember to keep your appointment with the psychiatrist today. And also, it wouldn't hurt to see a dentist as well. We got the lab report from your stool sample. It contained three molars."

"Teeth?"

"Yes. Your teeth. There was also a shoelace, and a silver cross on a necklace. The lab is sending the cross over to my office later, in case you'd like to pick it up. It will be cleaned first, of course."

"Doctor, I . . ."

Dr. Waggoner hung up before Weston could finish, " . . . don't own a silver cross."

He got to his feet and padded over to the bathroom, opening wide for the mirror. Weston wasn't missing any molars. Each of his teeth was in its proper place.

What the hell is going on?

His abdomen grumbled. Weston sat on the toilet and rubbed his temples, trying to make sense of any of this. How could he have swallowed teeth, or a silver cross? Why did he keep waking up naked? What was going on?

He didn't want to look, but before he flushed he forced himself. And gasped.

At the bottom of the toilet bowl were two distinct, unmistakable objects: a gold hoop earring, and a silver tag that said ROMI.

When he stopped running around in a blind panic (which took the good part of twenty minutes), Weston forced himself to the computer and Googled "eating+disorder+neighbor." This led him to sites about anorexia, which certainly wasn't his problem. Next he tried "cannibal" and got hits for bad Italian horror movies and death metal rock bands. "Sleep+eating+people" produced articles about sleeping pills, and "I ate human beings" led to a YouTube video of some drunk Klan member who kept saying "I hate human beings" and apparently posted the video so wasted he misspelled the title of his own rant.

Various other word combinations produced pages about Hannibal Lector, Alfred Packer, Sawney Bean, and ultimately Hansel and Gretel.

While on the site about fairy tales, Weston clicked from the old witch who wanted to eat children to the big bad wolf who wanted to eat children. This took him to a site about the history of lycanthropy, which featured several old paintings of wolf people running off with screaming babies in their mouths. Soon Weston was looking up "clinical lycanthropy," which was a real psychiatric term that pretty much meant "batshit crazy."

Could I really be crazy? he thought. *Do I subconsciously think I'm a werewolf?*

A quick click on a lunar calendar confirmed Weston's fears: The only time he'd had blackouts and found weird things in his poop was during the full moon.

Weston sat back, slack-jawed. He wondered if he should call someone. His parents? A doctor? The cops?

He searched his soul for remorse for eating his mean neighbor and her nasty dog, but couldn't find any.

But he must have killed other, nicer people. Right?

Weston slipped on some shorts and attacked the Internet again, looking through back issues of the local newspaper for accounts of murders or disappearances. He found five.

The first was from yesterday. A hand and partial skeleton found near the River Walk, a popular woodsy trail in Naperville. The prints on the hand belonged to Leon Corledo. His death was attributed to the Naperville Ripper.

How could I have missed hearing about that? Weston wondered. Too much work, probably. And the fact that the news depressed him, so he avoided it. Not to mention the fact that every time he turned on his TV, his recently digested neighbor banged.

Weston read on, found that Mr. Corledo was a registered sex offender. No big loss there. Weston followed the links to articles about the Ripper's other known victims. They included:

Waldemar Daminsky, 66, a local businessman with known ties to Polish organized crime.

Tony Rivers, 17, who was decapitated after robbing a liquor store and beating the owner unconscious.

Ginger Fitzgerald, who had recently lost custody of her daughter for locking her in a closet for a week without food or water.

And Marty Coslaw, a lawyer.

Weston felt zero guilt, and breathed a bit easier. But how many criminals and lawyers did Naperville have? Eventually, he'd run out of scumbags to eat. Then what?

He tried the search term "help for real lycanthropy" and, incredibly, got a hit. A single hit, for a website called *Shapeshifters Anonymous*.

Weston went to the site, and found it to be a home for werewolf jokes. After suffering through a spate of awful puns (Where do were-wolves go on vacation? A Howliday Inn!), he had about given up when he noticed a tiny hotlink at the bottom of the page that read, "Real therianthropes click here."

He knew from his lycanthropy reading that therianthropes were humans who morphed into animals. He clicked.

The page took him to another site, which had a black background and only five large cryptic words on it.

THERIANTHROPES MUST VIEW THE SOURCE

Weston stared, wondering what it meant. Which source? The source of their affliction? The source of their food?

On a whim, he Googled "view the source" and came up with a bunch of websites about HTML programming. Then he got it.

View the webpage source.

He went back to the werewolf page, opened his Internet Explorer toolbar, and under the PAGE menu clicked VIEW SOURCE. The HTML and Javascript appeared in a new window. Weston read through the computer language gobbledygook until he came to this:

&ei=xY0_R6—CZXcigGGoPmBCA"+g}return true};window.gbar ={};(function(){;var g=window.gbar,a,f,h;functionm(b,e,d){b.display=b. display=="block"?"none":"block";b.left=e+"px";b.top=d+"px"}g.tg= function(b)*{real therianthropes call 1-800-209-7219}*

Weston grabbed his phone and dialed with trembling hands.

"Therianthrope hotline, Zela speaking, may I help you?"

"I . . . uh . . . is this for real?"

"Are you a therianthrope, sir?"

"I think so. Is this really a werewolf hotline?"

"Is that what you turn into, sir? A wolf?"

"I have no idea. I black out beforehand, can't remember anything."

"Why do you think you're a therianthrope, sir?"

"I'm finding, um, *things*, in my, uh, toilet."

"Things like bone fragments, jewelry, eyeglasses, bits of clothing, coins, watches, and keys?"

"How did you know?"

"I'm a therianthrope myself, sir. Can I ask where you currently reside?"

"Naperville. Illinois."

"So I'm assuming you just realized you're the Naperville Ripper we've been hearing about?"

"They were all bad people," Weston said quickly. "I'm not sure about the lawyer, but I can make assumptions."

"We've been following the news. He was a defense attorney, defended child molesters. When given a choice, therianthropes usually prefer the wicked over the good. The creatures inside us find evil tastier."

"That's, uh, good to know. So . . . what are you, exactly? Are you a werewolf, too?"

"I'm a weresquirrel, sir."

"When the full moon rises, you turn into a squirrel?"

"Yes."

"A squirrel with buck teeth with a big fluffy tail?"

"That's the one."

Weston wasn't sure if he was supposed to laugh or not.

"Do you shrink? Or stay full size?"

"Full size."

"And you eat people?"

"No, sir. Not all therianthropes are carnivores."

"So, if you don't mind me asking, what do you do when you change?"

"I hoard nuts."

Weston chose his next words carefully.

"Are they . . . *evil* nuts?"

"Sir, I'm going to put your sarcasm down to you being on the edge of a nervous breakdown, so I'll ignore it. Are you interested in getting help for your therianthropy?"

"Yes, please. Thank you, Zela."

"Let me check the meeting schedule. Okay, today, at noon, there's an SA meeting at Saint Lucian's church in Schaumburg, approximately ten miles northwest of you. The secret word to gain entry is *Talbot*."

"What's SA?"

"Shapeshifters Anonymous."

"So I just go there, and they'll let me join them?"

"If you give the secret word. Yes."

"Do I have to bring anything?"

"Donuts are always nice."

"Donuts. I could bring donuts. Will you be there tonight, Zela? I can bring some with peanuts on them."

"That's very thoughtful of you, sir, but I live in New Jersey. And I also think you're kind of a schmuck. Is there anything else I can help you with today?"

"No. Thanks, Zela."

"Thanks for calling the hotline."

Weston hung up, ending what was easily the most surreal conversation he ever had in his life. An hour ago, he'd been a normal guy with some odd bowel movements. Now, he was 99 percent sure he was some sort of therianthrope.

But what kind?

He went back to the sofa, picked up some of the hair. Long, grayish, fluffy.

Was he a weresheep?

No. He ate people. Had to be a carnivore of some sort.

So what gray animals ate other animals?

Wolves, obviously. Coyotes. Dogs. Cats. Were elephants carnivores?

The Internet told him they were herbivores, which was a relief. But then Weston thought of another gray carnivore.

Rats.

Weston didn't want to be a wererat. He *hated* rats. Hoarding nuts was one thing. Swimming in the sewers, eating garbage and feces and dead animals, that was awful. He held his armpit up to his face and sniffed, seeing if he could detect any sort of sewage smell. It seemed okay. Then he checked the time and saw he had two hours to get to the SA meeting. So he hopped in the shower, dressed, and got on his way.

It had snowed during the night, making Naperville seem even more Winter-Wonderlandish. The cold felt good on Weston's bare face. He attributed the slight fever to his condition: Google told him wolves had an average body temperature of 100.5.

His first stop was Dr. Waggoner's, to pick up the silver cross. Weston didn't want to keep it for himself, but it was evidence of a murder, so it was best to get rid of it.

The nurse handed it to him in an envelope.

"Are you going to put it on?" she asked, eyes twinkling.

"Not right now."

But when he stepped outside, he did open the envelope to take a look. It was, indeed, silver. But all of the movies, all the books, said silver killed werewolves. Weston took a deep breath and dumped it into his palm. It didn't burn his skin. Or was that only with vampires?

He was bringing it up to his face, ready to touch it to his tongue, when he remembered where it had been. Besides, it had already passed through his system without killing him. Obviously the legends were wrong.

He tucked the cross into his coat pocket and walked into town, toward the bakery. On his way, he passed a man dressed as Santa Claus, ringing a bell for some charity. Thinking of the cross, Weston approached and dropped it in the steel collection pot.

"Beware," Santa muttered, voice low and sinister.

Weston wasn't sure he heard correctly. "Excuse me?"

"There's a killer on the loose in Naperville." Weston could smell the NyQuil on Santa's breath. "Not an ordinary killer either. Only comes out when the moon is full."

"Uh, thanks for the warning."

Weston began to walk away, but Santa's hand reached out and snatched his wrist, pinching like a lobster claw.

"Naughty boys get what they deserve," Santa intoned.

"Okay . . ."

Santa's eyes suddenly lit up, burning with some internal fire.

"They will be torn limb from limb! Their heads severed from their unholy bodies! Burned to ash on sacred ground! BURNED! *BUR-RRRRRRRRNED!!!!!*"

Weston pulled free, then walked briskly to the other side of the street, badly shaken. What kind of charity allowed cough syrup–crazed psychotics out in public? Wasn't there some kind of screening process for volunteers?

He glanced once over his shoulder, and Psycho Santa was talking on a cell phone, still pointing at him like Donald Sutherland at the end of the first *Invasion of the Body Snatchers* remake. It gave Weston the chills.

The uneasy feeling stayed with him all the way up to Russoff's Bakery, where he bought a dozen assorted donuts and a black coffee. When he stepped back onto the street, Weston considered taking another route home so he wouldn't have to see Looney Claus again, then chided himself for being afraid. After all, he was a werecreature. What did he have to fear? If that Santa was really a bad person, chances were good that Weston's inner therianthrope would eat him tonight during the full moon. Weston allowed himself a small smile at the thought of seeing a white beard in his toilet tomorrow morning.

So he steeled himself, and walked the regular path home. But when he passed the spot where Psycho Santa had been, he saw the volunteer was no longer there. Crazy Kringle had packed up his charity pot and left.

Weston walked to his apartment parking lot, hopped into his car, spent a minute programming his GPS, and headed for the suburb of Schaumburg. During the drive, he tried to get his mind around the events of the past twenty-four hours. But he wasn't able to focus. He kept seeing Santa's face. Kept hearing his threats. Once, in the rearview mirror, he swore he saw someone several car lengths behind him in a pointy red hat.

"You're being paranoid," he said to himself, refusing to drink any more coffee.

Just the same, he drove a little faster.

Ten minutes later he was at Saint Lucian's, an unassuming Catholic church with a 1970s vibe to the architecture. It was orange with a black shingle roof, shaped like an upside-down V. Two large stained glass windows flanked the double entry doors, and a statue of someone, possibly Jesus, perched atop the steeple. There were only six cars in the parking lot, which Weston appreciated because he wasn't good at remembering names, and no one would be short a donut. He parked behind an SUV and took a deep breath to calm his nerves. It was 11:46.

"Here goes nothing."

Bakery goods in hand, he approached the double doors and let himself into Saint Lucian's.

The church was dark, quiet. It smelled of scented candles, many of which were burning on a stand next to a charity box. Weston looked down the aisle, to the altar, seeing no one. Then he caught a handwritten sign taped to the back of a pew that read, SA MEETING IN BASEMENT.

He did a 360, opened a storage closet, then a confessional booth, before finding the door to the stairs next to a baptismal font. The concrete staircase wasn't lit, but at the bottom he heard voices. Weston descended, the temperature getting warmer the lower he went. At the bottom he walked past a large furnace, down a short hall, and over to a meeting room.

A bored-looking man whose gray hair and loose skin put him somewhere in the sixties, peered at Weston through thick glasses. He wore jeans and a faded turtleneck sweater. From his stance, and his severe haircut, Weston guessed he was ex-military. He stood guard over the doorway, preventing Weston from seeing inside.

"Sorry, sir. This is a private meeting."

The conversation in the room stopped.

"This is SA, right?"

"Yeah. But it's invitation only."

Weston was momentarily confused, until he remembered the hotline conversation.

"Talbot," he said.

"Tall what?"

"Talbot. Isn't that the password?"

"No."

"It's last week's password," someone from in the room said.

"Sorry, buddy." Old Guy folded his arms. "That was last week's password."

"That's the one I was told to use."

"By whom?"

"The SA hotline woman. Tina or Lena or someone."

"Sorry. Can't let you in."

"I brought you donuts." He meekly held up the box.

Old Guy took them.

"Thanks."

"So I can come in?"

"No."

Weston didn't know what to do. He could call the hotline back, but he didn't have the number handy. He'd have to find Internet access, find the website, and by then the meeting could be over.

"Listen." Weston lowered his voice. "You have to let me in. I'm a thespianthrope."

Several snickers from inside the room.

"Does that mean when the moon rises you start doing Shakespeare?" someone asked.

More laughs. Weston realized what he said.

"A *therianthrope*," he corrected. "I'm the Naperville Ripper."

"I don't care if you're Mother Theresa. You don't get in without the correct password."

Weston snapped his fingers. "Zela. Her name was Zela. She liked to grab people's nuts."

Old Guy remained impassive.

"I mean, she said she was a weresquirrel. She hoarded nuts."

"I'll call Zela." It was a woman's voice. Weston waited, wondering what he would do if they turned him away. For all of his Googling, he'd found precious little information about his condition. He needed to talk to these people, to understand what was going on. And to learn how to deal with it.

"He's okay," the woman said. "Zela gave him the wrong password. Said he's kind of a schmuck, though."

Old Guy stared hard at Weston. "We don't allow for schmuckiness at SA meetings. Got it?"

Weston nodded.

"Oh, lighten up, Scott." The woman again. "Let the poor guy in."

Scott stepped to the side. Weston took his donuts back and entered the room. A standard church basement. Low ceiling. Damp smell. Fluorescent lights. Old-fashioned coffee percolator bubbling on a stand in the corner, next to a trunk. A long, cafeteria-style table dominated the center, surrounded by orange plastic chairs. In the chairs were five people, three men and two women. One of the women, a striking blonde, stood up and extended her hand. She had apple cheeks, a tiny upturned nose, and Angelina Jolie lips.

"Welcome to Shapeshifters Anonymous. I'm Irena Reed, chapter president."

The one who called Zela. Weston reached his hand out to shake hers, but she bypassed it, grabbing the donuts. She brought them to the table, and everyone gathered round, picking and choosing. Irena selected a jelly filled and bit into it, soft and slow. Weston found it incredibly erotic.

"So what's your name?" she purred, mouth dusted with powdered sugar.

"I thought this was anonymous."

Irena motioned for him to come closer, and they walked over to the coffee stand while everyone else ate.

"The founders thought *Shapeshifters Anonymous* had gravitas."

"Gravitas?"

"You know. Depth. Sorry, I'm a schoolteacher. That's one of our current vocab words. When this group was created, they thought *Shapeshifters Anonymous* sounded better than the other potential names. We were this close to calling ourselves *Shapeshifters 'R' Us.*"

"Oh. Okay then." He looked at the group and waved. "My name is Weston."

Weston waited for them all to reply in unison, "Hi, Weston." They didn't.

"You're welcome," Weston tried.

Still no greeting.

"They aren't very social when there's food in front of them," Irena said.

"I guess not. So . . . you're a therianthrope?"

"A werecheetah. Which is kind of ironic, being a teacher."

He stared blankly, not getting it.

"We expel cheetahs." Irena put a hand to her mouth and giggled.

Weston realized he was already in love with her. "So who is everyone here?"

"The ex-marine, Scott Howard, he's a weretortoise."

Weston appraised the man anew. Long wrinkled neck. Bowed back. "It suits him."

"The small guy with the big head, that's David Kessler. He's a werecoral."

Weston blinked. "He turns into coral?"

"Yeah."

"Like a coral reef?"

"Shh. He's sensitive about it."

"How about that older woman?" Weston indicated a portly figure with a huge mess of curly black hair.

"Phyllis Allenby. She's a furry."

"What's that?"

"Furries dress up in animal costumes. Like baseball team mascots."

Weston was confused. "Why?"

"I'm not sure. Might be some sort of weird sex thing."

"So she's not a therianthrope?"

"No. She likes to wear a hippo outfit and dance around. Personally, I don't get it."

"Why is she allowed into meetings?"

"We all kind of feel sorry for her."

A tall man with his mouth around something covered in sprinkles called over to them.

"You two talking about us?"

Irena shot him with her thumb and index finger. "Got it in one, Andy."

Andy strutted over, his grin smeared with chocolate. He shook Weston's hand, pumping enthusiastically.

"Andy McDerrmott, wereboar."

"You . . . become a pig?" Weston guessed.

"Actually, when the full moon rises, I change into someone vastly self-interested, and I talk incessantly about worthless minutiae going on in my life."

Weston wasn't sure how to answer. Andy slapped him on the shoulder, hard enough to rock him.

"A *bore*! Get it? *Were-bore!*" Andy laughed, flecking Weston with sprinkles. "Actually, kidding, I turn into a pig."

"You mean a bigger pig, right, Andy?"

Andy shot Irena a look that was pure letch.

"God, you're so hot, Irena. When are we going to get together, have ourselves a litter of little kiggens?"

"On the first of never, Andy. And they wouldn't be kiggens. They'd be pities."

"Snap," Phyllis said. "Shoot that pig down, girl."

"So who's the last guy?" Weston asked. "The big one?"

The trio glanced at the heavily muscled man sitting at the end of the table, staring off into space.

"That's Ryan."

"Just Ryan?"

Andy wiped his mouth on the sleeve of his sports jacket. "That's all he's ever told us. Never talks. Never says a word. Comes to every meeting, but just sits there, looking like the Terminator."

"What does he change into?"

"No one knows. Has to be something, though, or Zela wouldn't have sent him here." Andy faced Weston. "So you're the Naperville Ripper, huh? What kind of therianthrope are you? Wererat?"

Andy frowned. "I'm not sure. I think I'm a werewolf."

This provoked laughter from the group.

"What's funny?"

"Everyone thinks they're a werewolf at first," Irena explained, patting him on the arm. "It's because werewolves are the most popular therianthropes."

"They get all the good press," Andy said. "All the books. All the movies. Never gonna see a flick called *An American Wereboar in London*."

"Or *The Oinking*," Phyllis added.

Furry or not, Weston was starting to like Phyllis.

Irena's hand moved up Weston's arm, making him feel a little light-headed.

"Because we can't remember what we do when we've changed, we all first assume we're werewolves."

"So how can I find out what I change into?"

"I set up a video camera and recorded myself." Andy reached into his jacket, took out a CD. "We can pop it in the DVD if you want."

"Don't say yes," Phyllis warned. "The last time he put in a tape of himself and some woman doing the nasty. And it was real nasty."

"An honest mistake." Andy leaned closer to Weston and whispered, "She was a college cheerleader, studying massage therapy. I was bow-legged for a week afterward."

"She was an elderly woman," Phyllis said. "With a walker."

"Mind your own business, you furvert. You're not even a real therianthrope."

Phyllis stuck out her jaw. "I am in my heart."

"When there's a full moon, you don't turn into a hippo. You turn into an idiot who puts on a hippo outfit and skips around like a retarded children's show host."

Phyllis stood up, fists clenched.

"I'm 'bout to stick an apple in your talk-hole and roast you on a spit, Ham Boy."

"Enough." Irena raised her hands. "We're adults. Let's act like it."

"Does anyone want the last donut?" It was David, the werecoral, talking. "Weston? You haven't had one yet."

Weston patted his stomach. "No thanks. I just ate my neighbor and her dog."

"I ate a Fuller Brush Salesman once," Andy said.

"Did not," Phyllis countered. "You ate your own toilet brush. And a pack of them Ty-D-Bowl tablets. That's why your poo was blue."

"So I can have the last donut?" David had already taken a bite out of it.

Weston looked at Irena, felt his heart flutter.

"Other than video, is there another way to find out what I am?"

Irena's eyes sparkled. "Yes. In fact, there is."

The group, except for Ryan, gathered in front of the chest sitting in the corner of the room.

"Testing equipment." Irena twisted an old-fashioned key in the lock and opened the lid.

Weston expected some sort of medical supplies, or maybe a chemistry set. Instead, the trunk was filled with dried plants, broken antiques, and assorted worthless-looking junk.

"Hold out your hand."

Weston did as told. Irena held his wrist, and then ran a twig lightly across his palm.

"Feel anything?"

Other than getting a little aroused, Weston felt nothing. He shook his head.

"Catnip," Irena said. "It's a shame. You would have made a cute kitty."

She brought the branch to her lips, sniffed it, and a tiny moan escaped her throat. Andy took it away from her and tossed it back in the trunk.

"If we let her, she'll play with that all day, and the meeting starts in five minutes. Here, touch this."

Andy handed him a longer, darker twig. Weston touched it, and immediately felt like his entire arm had caught on fire. There was a puff of smoke, and a crackling sound. He recoiled.

"Jesus! What the hell was that, a burning bush?"

Andy cocked his head to the side. "It was wolfsbane. I'll be damned. You are a lycanthrope."

Everyone's expressions changed from surprise to awe, and Weston swore that Irena's pupils got wider. He shrugged.

"Okay, so I'm a werewolf."

"We've never had a werewolf in the group," David said. "How did you become a werewolf?"

"I have no idea."

Weston recalled the masturbation scare tales from his youth, many of which involved hairy palms. He almost asked if that may have caused it, but looked at Irena and decided to keep it to himself.

"Is your mother or father a werewolf?" Scott, the weretortoise, asked. "I inherited a recessive gene from my mother, Shelly. Been a therianthrope since birth."

"No. This only started three months ago."

"Were you bitten by a therianthrope?" David asked. "That's how they got me."

Weston didn't think that coral could actually bite, but he didn't mention it. Instead he shook his head.

"How about a curse?" Irena asked. "Were you cursed by a gypsy recently?"

"No, I . . ." Then Weston remembered his evil next-door neighbor. He'd been wondering about her ethnic background, and now it seemed obvious. *Of course* she was a gypsy. How could he have missed the signs? His shoulders slumped.

"Oh, boy. I think maybe I was cursed, for brushing my teeth too loudly."

"You're lucky." David smiled. "That's the easiest type of therianthropy to cure."

"Who wants to be cured?" Scott's eyes narrowed. "I like being a weretortoise."

"That's because when you change, all you do is eat salad and swim around in your bathtub," Andy said. "I root through the garbage and eat aluminum cans. You ever try to crap out a six-pack of Budweiser tall boys?"

David put his hands on his hips. "I'm saying that Weston's a carnivore, like Irena. They eat people. It has to weigh heavy on the conscience."

"Do you feel guilty about it?" Weston asked Irena.

"Nope." Irena smiled. "And I have the added benefit of not having to put up with any bad kids in my class for more than a month."

Weston wondered if it was too soon to propose marriage. He squelched the thought and turned to David.

"So, assuming I want to go back to normal, how do I do it?"

"Just go back to the gypsy that cursed you and pay her to take the curse off."

Oops.

"That might be a problem, seeing as how I ate her."

Andy slapped him on the shoulder. "Tough break, man. But you'll get used to it. Until then, it's probably a good idea to get yourself a nice, sturdy leash."

"It's time to begin the meeting. Let's get started." Irena leaned into Weston and softly said, "We can talk more later."

Weston sincerely hoped so.

"Let's begin by joining hands and saying the Shapeshifters Anonymous Credo."

Everyone around the table joined hands, including the silent Ryan. Weston noted that Irena's hand was soft and warm, and she played her index finger along the top of his as she talked. So did Phyllis.

Irena began.

"I, state your name, agree to abide by the rules of ethics as set forth by Shapeshifters Anonymous."

Everyone, including Weston, repeated it.

"I promise to do my best to use my abilities for the good of man and therianthrope kind."

They repeated it.

"I promise to do my best to help any therianthrope who comes to me in need."

They repeated it. Weston thought it a lot like being in church. Which, technically, they were.

"I promise to do my best not to devour any nice people."

Weston repeated this verse with extra emphasis.

"I promise to avoid Kris Kringle, the dreaded Santa Claus, and his many evil helpers."

"Hold on," Weston interrupted. "What the hell does that mean?"

"Santa Claus is a therianthrope hunter," David said. "He kills shapeshifters."

"You're kidding. Right?"

An uncomfortable silence ensued. Everyone stopped holding hands. Scott cleared his throat, then pushed away from the table and stood up.

"No one is sure how our kind got started. Some say black magic. Some say interspecies breeding, though I don't buy into that malarkey. Some say therianthropes date back to the very beginning, the Garden of Eden, where man and werebeast lived in harmony. But the Bible doesn't tell the whole story. Certain religious leaders over the years have edited it as they see fit. Entire books were taken out. Like the Book of Bob."

Weston looked around to see if anyone was smiling. All faces were serious.

"The Book of Bob?"

"The Book of Bob is a lost chapter of the Old Testament, dating back to the Hellenistic period. It tells the story of God's prophet, Bob, son of Jakeh, who is the first werewolf mentioned in the Bible."

"The first? There aren't any."

"They were edited out. Pay attention, son. You'll learn something. See, Bob was a werewolf, blessed by the Lord with the gift of lycanthropy to do His work by eating evildoers. But after eating his one-thousandth sinner, Bob became prideful of his accomplishments, and that angered God."

"Why would that anger God?"

"This was the Old Testament. God got pissed off a lot. Didn't you ever read Job?"

"I'm just saying—"

Irena shushed him. Scott continued.

"So to put Bob in his place, God granted one of Bob's enemies—Christopher, son of Cringle—a red suit of impenetrable armor, and ordered him to smite all therianthropes. God also blessed domesticated beasts with the power to fly through the sky, to pull Christopher's warship of destruction throughout the world."

Weston again looked around the room. Andy was examining his fingernails. Ryan was staring off into space. But David looked like a child listening to his favorite bedtime story.

"Bob and Christopher fought, and Bob proved victorious. Upon triumphing, he begged God to forgive his pridefulness, and God agreed. But Christopher, God's chosen avenger, felt betrayed. So he turned to the other side, begging for assistance."

"The devil?"

"Lucifer himself, the Son of the Morning Star. Lucifer gave Christopher a fearsome weapon, shaped like the talons of an eagle, forged in the fires of hell. He called the weapon Satan's Claws. And Christopher recruited an army of helpers to rid the world of Bob and his kind, claiming he was bringing about salvation."

"Let me see if I got this right," Weston said. "Kris Kringle and his magic red suit are using Satan's Claws—which I'm guessing became *Santa Claus* over time—to kill therianthropes with the help of . . . *the Salvation Army*?"

Everyone nodded. Weston laughed in disbelief.

"So how did this whole toy thing get started?"

"Kringle has killed millions of therianthropes, leaving many children orphans. He began to feel some remorse, so after he slaughtered their parents he began to leave toys behind, to take away some of the sting."

"And this is for real?"

Scott reached up and pulled down his collar, exposing a terrible scar along his neck.

"Kringle gave this to me when I was seven years old, right after murdering my parents."

"I thought he gave orphans toys."

"He also gave me a train set."

Weston shook his head. "Look, I can accept this whole shapeshifting thing. And touching the wolfsbane, that was creepy. But you want me to believe that every volunteer on a street corner with a bell and a Santa suit is out to murder us? I just saw one of those guys this morning, and while he was kind of odd—"

Scott reached across the table, grabbing Weston by the shirt. His face was pure panic.

"You saw one! Where?"

"Back in Naperville."

"What did he say to you?"

"Something about naughty boys and being beheaded and burned on sacred ground. He was obviously out of his mind."

Irena clutched Weston's hand. "The only way we can die is old age or beheading."

"Think carefully, Weston." Scott actually looked frightened. So did everyone else. "Were you followed here?"

"I don't think so. I mean, maybe I saw him talking on a cell phone. And maybe there was someone in a Santa suit a few cars behind me on the expressway—"

A shrill whistle cut Weston off. It sounded like a teapot.

But it wasn't a teapot. It was an alarm.

"They've found us." David's voice was quavering. "They're here."

* * *

"Battle stations!" Irena cried, causing everyone to scurry off in different directions.

Scott hurried to the coffee table, pushed the machine aside, and pressed a red button on the wall. An iron gate slammed closed across the entry door, and three TV monitors rose up on pedestals from hidden panels in the floor.

"Jesus." Phyllis squinted at one of the screens. "There have to be forty of them."

Weston looked, watching as the cameras switched from one view to another around the church. Santa's helpers, dozens of Santa's helpers. Wielding bats and axes and swords. They had the place surrounded.

"We need to call the police." David's voice had gone up an octave.

Irena already had the phone in her hand. "Line's been cut."

"Cell phones?"

"We're in a basement. No signals."

Scott knelt before the trunk, removing the top section and revealing a cache of handguns underneath. He tossed one to Weston, along with an extra clip.

"Are guns safe to throw?"

"Safety is on. Ever used a nine millimeter before?"

"No."

"Thumb off the safety on the side. Then pull back the top part. That's the slide, loads the bullet into the chamber. Now all you have to do is pull the trigger. Those red suits they're wearing are Kevlar, so aim for the face."

Weston had more questions, but Scott was too busy distributing the guns.

"Place your shots carefully, people. We don't have a lot of ammo. Ryan! Can you fire a weapon?"

Ryan remained sitting, staring into space.

"Dammit, man! We need you!"

Ryan didn't move.

"Can't we escape?" Weston asked Irena.

Irena worked her slide, jacking in a round.

"That's the only door."

"But those are steel bars. They can't get through it."

"They'll get through." Phyllis pointed. "See?"

Weston checked out the monitor, saw a group of Santa's storming down the stairs with a battering ram. The first CLANG! made everyone in the room jump.

"The table! Move!"

Weston helped Andy and Scott push the cafeteria table in front of the door. Then the group, except for Ryan, huddled together in the back of the room, guns pointed forward.

"I hope we live through this," Weston told Irena, "because I'd really like to ask you out."

"I'd like that, too."

"Living through this, or going out with me?"

"Both."

Another CLANG! accompanied by a CREAK! which shook the table.

"Wait until you see the whites of their beards, people."

CLANG!

CLANG!

The table lurched forward.

CLANG!

They were in.

The room erupted in gunfire. It was louder than anything Weston had heard in his life, and he'd seen Iron Maiden in concert when he was seventeen. The kick of the gun surprised him, throwing off his aim, but Weston kept his head, kept sighting the targets, kept pulling the trigger.

The first Santa only made it a step inside.

The next three only made it two steps.

Then it got bad. A dozen of Santa's helpers burst into the room, swinging their weapons, their HO HO HO! war cries cutting through the cacophony of gunfire.

Weston fired until his pistol was empty. He tried to tug the empty clip out of the bottom of the gun, but it didn't budge. He wasted valuable seconds looking for the button or switch to release it, and then a helper tackled him.

His eyes were crazed, and his breath smelled like cough syrup, and Weston knew that this was the Santa who'd threatened him on the street corner in Naperville.

"Naughty boy! Naughty boy!" he screamed, both hands clasped on a curved dagger poised above Weston's eye.

Weston blocked with his elbows, trying to keep the knife away, but the crazy old elf possessed some sort of supernatural strength, and the knife inched closer and closer no matter how hard he resisted. Weston saw his terrified expression reflected in the polished steel blade as the tip tickled his eyelashes.

"Hey! Santa! Got some cookies for you!"

Weston watched, amazed, as someone jammed a gun into the Santa's snarling mouth and pulled the trigger. Psycho Santa's hat lifted up off his head, did a pirouette in the air, and fell down onto his limp body.

Weston followed the hand that held the gun, saw Irena staring down at him. She helped him to his feet.

"Thanks."

She nodded, taking his pistol and showing him the button to release the empty clip.

"Where did you learn how to shoot?" he asked.

"I teach high school."

Weston slammed the spare clip home and pulled the slide, firing six times at a Santa's helper swinging, of all things, a Grim Reaper scythe. The neck shot did him in.

"Hold your fire! They're retreating!"

As quickly as it began, the attack stopped. The gun smoke cleared. Weston winced when he saw the piles of dead Santa's helpers strewn around the room. At least two dozen of them. A Norman Rockwell painting it was not.

"Everyone okay?" Scott asked.

Everyone said yes except for Ryan, who remained sitting in the same chair, and David, who had a nasty gash on his shoulder that Phyllis was bandaging with duct tape and paper towels.

"Well, we sure kicked some Santa ass." Andy walked next to one of the fallen helpers and nudged him with his foot. "Try climbing down a chimney now, shithead."

"It's not over."

Everyone turned to look at Ryan.

"Did you see something, Ryan?" Irena asked.

Ryan pointed to the monitor.

They all stared at a wide-angle shot of the parking lot and watched eight reindeer racing down from the sky and using the blacktop like a landing strip. Behind them, a massive sleigh. It skidded to a stop, and a hulking figure, dressed in red, climbed out and stared up at the camera.

"It's Santa Claus," Ryan whispered. "He's come to town."

Weston watched, horrified, as Santa headed for the church entrance, his remaining helpers scurrying around him.

"My God," Phyllis gasped. "He's huge."

Weston couldn't really judge perspective, but it seemed like Santa stood at least a foot taller than any of the Salvation Army volunteers.

"Who has ammo left?" Scott yelled.

"I'm out."

"Me, too."

"So am I."

Weston checked his clip. "I've got two bullets."

It got very quiet. Scott rubbed his neck.

"Okay. We'll have to make do. Everyone grab a weapon. Kris Kringle is a lot more powerful than his helpers. Maybe, if we all strike at once, we'll have a chance."

From the sound of Scott's voice, he didn't believe his own words.

Andy didn't buy it either. "David is wounded. Ryan is sitting there like a pud. You think three men and two women can fend off Kringle and his Satan's Claws? He's going to cut us into pieces!"

"We don't have a choice."

"But I don't want to get sliced up!" Andy said. "I'm too pretty to die like that!"

"Calm down, son. You're not helping the situation."

Andy knelt next to one of the helpers and began undressing him.

"You guys fight. I'm going to put on a red suit and pretend to be dead."

Weston locked eyes with Irena, saw fear, wondered if she saw the same in him.

"There's a way."

It was Ryan again, still staring off into space.

"You actually going to get up off your ass and help?" Phyllis asked.

Ryan slowly reached into his pants pocket, pulling out five tiny vials of liquid.

"I've been saving these."

Andy grabbed one, unscrewed the top. "Is it cyanide? Tell me it's cyanide, because I'm so drinking it."

"It's a metamorphosis potion. It will allow you to change into your therianthrope forms, while still retaining your human intellect."

Scott took a vial, squinting at it.

"Where did you get these?"

"I've had them for a long time."

"How do you know they work?"

"I know."

"Guess it can't hurt to try." Irena grabbed the remaining vials. She handed one to Weston, and one to David. She also held one out for Phyllis.

"But I'm not a therianthrope," Phyllis said. "I'm just a furry."

"You're one of us," Irena told her.

Phyllis nodded, and took the vial.

"Are you taking one?" Scott asked Ryan.

Ryan shook his head.

Scott shrugged. "Okay. Here goes nothing."

He downed the liquid. Everyone watched.

At first, nothing happened. Then Scott twitched. The twitching became faster, and faster, until he looked like a blurry photograph. Scott made a small sound, like a sigh, dropped his gun, and fell to all fours.

He'd changed into a turtle. A giant turtle, with vaguely human features. His face, now green and scaled, looked similar to his human face. And his body retained a roughly humanoid shape; so much so that he was able to push off the ground and stand on two stubby legs.

"I'll be damned." Scott reached up and tapped the top of his shell. "And I can still think. Hell, I can even talk."

Irena had already drunk her vial, and her clothes ripped, exposing the spots underneath. While in final werecheetah form she retained her long blond hair, and—Weston could appreciate this—her breasts. He could suddenly understand the appeal furries saw in anthropomorphic costumes.

"You look great," Weston told her.

Her whiskers twitched, and she licked her arm and rubbed it over her face.

An oink, from behind, and Andy the wereboar was standing next to the overturned table, chewing on the cardboard donut box.

"What?" he said. "There's still some frosting inside."

"This sucks."

Weston turned to David, who had become a greenish, roundish ball of coral. Weston could make out his face underneath a row of tiny, undulating tentacles.

"I think you're adorable," Irena told him. "Like Humpty Dumpty."

"I don't have arms or legs! How am I supposed to fight Santa?"

"Try rolling on him," Andy said, his snout stuck in the garbage can.

"I guess it's my turn." Phyllis drank the potion.

Everyone waited.

Nothing happened.

"Well, shit," Phyllis said. "And I don't even have my hippo suit here. At least give me the damn gun."

Weston handed it to her, then looked at his vial.

"You'll be fine," Irena said.

She walked a circle around him, then nuzzled against his chest. Weston stroked her chin, and she purred.

"Better hurry." Scott was eyeing the monitor. "Here comes Santa Claus."

Weston closed his eyes and lifted the vial to his lips.

* * *

It was kind of like being born. Darkness. Warmth. Then turmoil, sensory overload, a thousand things happening at once. It didn't hurt, but it didn't tickle either. Weston coughed, but it came out harsh. A bark. He looked down at his arms and noted they were covered with long, gray fur. His pants stayed on, but his clawed feet burst through the tops of his shoes.

"Hello, sexy."

Weston stared at Irena and had an overpowering, irrational urge to bark at her. He managed to keep it in check.

"Remember," Scott said. "He's wearing armor. It's claw-proof. Go for his head and neck, or use blunt force."

They formed a semicircle around the door, except for the immobile David and the still-seated Ryan. Then they waited. Weston heard a licking sound, traced it to Andy, who had his nose buried between his own legs.

"Andy," he growled. "Quit it."

"Are you kidding? I don't think I'm ever going to stop."

Then the crazed Santa's helpers burst into the room, screaming and swinging weapons. Weston recoiled at first, remembered what he was, and then lashed out with a claw. It caught the helper in the side of the head, snapping his neck like a candy cane.

Andy quit grooming—if you could call it that—long enough to gore a helper between his red shirt and pants, right in the belly. What came out looked a lot like a bowlful of jelly.

Phyllis fired twice, then picked up the scythe and started swinging it like a madwoman and swearing like a truck driver with a toothache.

Scott had two helpers backed up against the wall, using his enormous shell to squeeze the life out of them.

Even David had managed to get into the act, snaring a helper with his tiny, translucent tentacles. Judging from the screams, those tentacles had stingers on them.

Weston searched for Irena, and saw her hanging on to a helper's back, biting at his neck.

Two more Santa's helpers rushed in, and Weston lunged at them, surprised by his speed. He kept his arms spread out and caught each one under the chin. His canine muscles flexed, tightened, and their heads came off like Barbie dolls.

And then, there *he* was.

Kris Kringle was even bigger up close than he was on the TV monitors. So huge he had to duck down to fit through the doorway. When he entered the room and reared up, he must have been eight feet tall. And wide, with a chest like a whiskey barrel, arms like tree trunks. His long white beard was flecked with blood, and his tiny dark eyes twinkled with malevolent glee.

But the worst thing were his hands. They ended in horrible metal claws, each blade the length of a samurai sword. One of his helpers, the one Irena had bitten, staggered over to Kringle, clutching his bleeding neck. Kringle lashed out, severing the man into three large pieces, even with the Kevlar suit on.

It was so horrible, so outrageously demonic, that Weston had to laugh when he saw it. In spite of himself.

Scott waddled over to Kringle and pointed his stubby fingers at him.

"Your reign of evil ends today, Kringle."

Kringle laughed, a deep, resonating croak that sounded like thunder. Then his huge black boot shot out, kicking Scott in the chest, knocking him across the room and into the back wall. Scott crashed through it like a turtle-shaped meteor.

Andy said, "Holy shit," then tore ass through the hole in the wall after Scott.

Kringle took a step forward, and Weston had an urge to pee; an urge so strong he actually lifted a leg. There was no way they could defeat Santa Claus. He was a monster. He'd tear through them like tissue paper.

Kringle appraised Weston, eyeing him head to toe, and said, "Robert Weston Smith. Werewolf. You're on my list."

Then he looked at Irena, who'd come to Weston's side, clutching his paw.

"Irena Reed. Werecheetah. You're on my list, too. Want to sit on Santa's lap, little girl?"

Irena hissed at him. Kringle's eyes fell upon David next.

"And what the hell are you? A were-onion?"

David released the dead helper. "I'm David Kessler. Werecoral."

"David Kessler. Yes. You're also on my list. Now who is this crazy bitch?"

Phyllis put her hands on her hips and stuck out her jaw. "Phyllis Lawanda Marisha Taleena Allenby. Am I on your stupid-ass list, too?"

"No."

"No? You sure 'bout that, fat man?"

Kringle smiled.

"I checked it twice."

Phyllis's eyes went mean.

"You saying I'm not one of them? I'm one of them. I'm one of them in my heart, you giant sack of—"

"Enough!"

Ryan stood up and walked over to Kringle.

"And who are you, little human?"

"I'm tired of running, Christopher. I've been running for too long."

Kringle's brow furrowed.

"That voice. I know that voice."

"I had some work done. Changed my human face. But I'm sure you'll recognize this one."

Ryan's body shook, and then he transformed into a werewolf. A giant werewolf, several feet taller than Weston.

Kringle took a step back, his face awash with fear.

"Bob."

Weston watched, awestruck, as this millennia-old battle played out before him.

Kringle snarled, raising up his awful Satan Claws.

Bob bared his teeth and howled, a gut-churning cry that reverberated to the core of Weston's very soul.

But before either of them attacked, before either of them even moved, Kris Kringle's head rolled off his shoulders and onto the floor by Bob's feet.

Phyllis Lawanda Marisha Taleena Allenby, scythe in hand, brought the blade down and speared the tip into Kringle's decapitated head, holding it up so it faced her.

"Am I on your list *now*, muthafucker?"

Bob peered down at Phyllis, his lupine jaw hanging open.

"You just killed Kris Kringle."

"Damn easy, too. Why the hell didn't you do that five thousand years ago?"

Scott, a round green hand pressed to his wrinkled old head, stumbled back into the room.

"What happened?"

"Phyllis killed Kris Kringle," Irena said.

"You go, girl."

Scott gave Phyllis a high five.

"You all fought bravely." Bob stood tall, addressing the group. "Except for the pig. For your courage, you'll now have full control over your therianthrope powers. You can change at will, and will retain control of your inner creatures."

"So how do we turn back?" Irena asked.

"Concentrate."

Scott went first, morphing back into his human form.

Weston and Irena changed while holding hands.

David's face scrunched up, but nothing happened.

"It's not working," he said. "I'm still coral."

"How about me?" Phyllis asked. "I'm the one that killed that jolly old bastard."

"I can turn you into a werewolf, if you so desire."

"These guys offered me that before. But I don't want to be no wolf, or no cheetah, or no turtle, or no dumb-ass coral. No offense, David."

"None taken. I'm concentrating, but nothing's happening."

Phyllis folded her arms. "My inner animal is a hippopotamus. That's what I want to be."

Bob's shoulders slumped. "I'm sorry, Phyllis. That's the extent of my power. But . . . maybe . . . just maybe . . ."

"Maybe what?"

"I don't know if this will work, because he's dead."

"Just spill the beans, Lon Chaney."

"Try sitting on Santa's lap."

Phyllis raised a drawn-on eyebrow. "You serious?"

"He might still have some magic left. Try it."

Phyllis walked over to the fallen Kringle and sat on one of his massive thighs.

"Now what?"

"Make a Christmas wish, Phyllis. Make your most heartfelt Christmas wish ever."

She closed her eyes, and her lips whispered something Weston couldn't hear.

And then Weston felt something. Kind of like a breeze. A breeze made of Christmas magic. It swirled around the room, touching each of them, and then coming to rest on Phyllis.

But nothing happened. She didn't morph into a hippo. She didn't morph into anything. A minute passed, and she was still the same old Phyllis.

"I'm sorry, Phyllis." Bob helped her up. "I wish there was something else I could do."

A sad silence blanketed the room.

Then bad-boy rapper LL Cool J strutted into the basement, sans shirt. He took Phyllis's hand, gave her a deeply passionate kiss, and cupped her butt.

"Gonna take you back to the crib and make love to you all night, girl. But first we gonna stop by the bank, get your hundred million dollars."

LL picked her up and carried her out.

"See you guys next week," Phyllis called after them.

"Someone push me over to Santa's lap," David said. "This coral wants a house in Hawaii."

"What about all of these corpses?" Scott made a sweeping gesture with his hands. "The police are gonna have a field day."

"I'll take care of it." Bob rubbed his stomach. "I didn't have any of the donuts."

"Little help here." David wiggled in place.

Weston felt a tug on his hand. He stared into Irena's eyes.

"Want to, maybe, grab some coffee?" he asked.

"No."

Weston died a little inside. Irena's nose twitched, showing him a brief glimpse of her inner cheetah.

"Instead of coffee, I want you to come to my place. I've got a leash and a king-size bed."

God bless us, everyone, Weston thought as they walked hand in hand out the door.

AUTHOR'S NOTES

The Salvation Army is a wonderful organization with over 3.5 million volunteers, and I'm pretty sure none of them are cough syrup–swilling psychotics.

The names used in this story are all names of characters from famous werewolf movies. Unless someone tries to sue me, in which case I made all of them up. LL Cool J also did a rocking version of "Who's Afraid of the Big Bad Wolf."

While the modern Bible is missing many of its original passages, the Book of Bob isn't one of them. You're probably getting it confused with the lost Book of Fred.

Other than that, everything in this story is 100 percent true.

The Star of David

Patricia Briggs

Patricia Briggs is the #1 New York Times *bestselling author of the Mercy Thompson series as well as assorted other books. She lives in Montana with her husband and a menagerie of animals and kids in a house that resembles a zoo crossed with a library. The horses have to stay outside. And people wonder where the ideas for her stories come from.*

"I checked them out myself," Myra snapped. "Have you ever just considered that *your boy* isn't the angel you thought he was?"

Stella took off her glasses and set them on her desk. "I think that we both need some perspective. Why don't you take the rest of the afternoon off." *Before I slap your stupid face.* People like Devonte don't change that fast, not without good reason.

Myra opened her mouth, but after she got a look at Stella's face, she shut it again. Mutely she stalked to her desk and retrieved her coat and purse. She slammed the door behind her.

As soon as she was gone, Stella opened the folder and looked at the pictures of the crime scene again. They were duplicates, and doubtless Clive, her brother the detective, had broken a few rules when he sent them to her—not that breaking rules had ever bothered him, not when he was five and not as a grown man nearing fifty and old enough to know better.

She touched the photos lightly, then closed the folder again. There was a yellow sticky with a phone number on it and nothing else: Clive didn't have to put a name on it. Her little brother knew she'd see what he had seen.

She picked up the phone and punched in the numbers fast, not giving herself a chance for second thoughts.

*   *   *

The barracks were empty, leaving David's office silent and bleak. The boys were on furlough with their various families for December.

His mercenaries specialized in live retrieval, which tended to be in-and-out stuff, a couple of weeks per job at the most. He didn't want to get involved in the gray area of unsanctioned combat or out-and-out war—where you killed people because someone told you to. In retrieval there were good guys and bad guys still—and if there weren't, he didn't take the job. Their reputation was such that they had no trouble finding jobs.

And unless all hell really broke loose, they always took December off to be with their families. David never let them know how hard that made it for him.

Werewolves need their packs.

If his pack was human, well, they knew about him and they filled that odd wolf-quirk that demanded he have people to protect, brothers in heart and mind. He couldn't stomach a real pack, he hated what he was too much.

He couldn't bear to live with his own kind, but this worked as a substitute and kept him centered. When his boys were here, when they had a job to do, he had direction and purpose.

His grandsons had invited him for the family dinner, but he'd refused as he always did. He still saw his sons on a regular basis. Both of them had served in his small band of mercenaries for a while, until the life lost its appeal or the risks grew too great for men with growing families. But he stayed away at Christmas.

Restlessness had him pacing: there were no plans to make, no wrongs to right. Finally he unlocked the safe and pulled out a couple of the newer rifles. He needed to put some time in with them anyway.

An hour of shooting staved off the restlessness, but only until he locked the guns up again. He'd have to go for a run. When he emptied his pockets in preparation, he noticed he had missed a call while he'd been shooting. He glanced at the number, frowning when he didn't recognize it. Most of his jobs came through an agent who knew better than to give out his cell number. Before he could decide if he wanted to return the call, his phone rang again, a call from the same number.

"Christiansen," he answered briskly.

There was a long silence. "Papa?"

He closed his eyes and sank back in his chair feeling his heart expand with almost painful intentness as his wolf fought with the man who knew his daughter hated him: didn't want to see him, ever. She had been there when her mother died.

"Stella?" He couldn't imagine what it took to make her break almost forty years of silence. "Are you all right? Is there something wrong?" Someone he could kill for her? A building to blow up? Anything at all.

She swallowed. He could hear it over the line. He waited for her to hang up.

Instead, when she spoke again, her voice was brisk and the wavery pain that colored that first "Papa" was gone as if it had never been. "I was wondering if you would consider doing a favor for me."

"What do you need?" He was proud that came out evenly. Always better to know what you're getting into, he told himself. He wanted to tell her that she could ask him for anything—but he didn't want to scare her.

"I run an agency that places foster kids," she told him, as if he didn't know. As if her brothers hadn't told her how he quizzed them to find out how she was doing and what she was up to. He hoped she never found out about her ex-boyfriend who'd turned stalker. He hadn't killed that one, though his willingness to do so had made it easier to persuade the man that he wanted to take up permanent residence in a different state.

"I know," he said, because it seemed like she needed a response.

"There's something—" She hesitated. "Look, this might not have been the best idea."

He was losing her again. He had to breathe deeply to keep the panic from his voice. "Why don't you tell me about it anyway? Do you have something better to do?"

"I remember that," she said. "I remember you doing that with

Mom. She'd be hysterical, throwing dishes or books, and you'd sit down and say, 'Why don't you tell me about it?'"

Did she want to talk about her mother now? About the one time he'd needed to be calm and had failed? He hadn't known he was a were-wolf until it was too late. Until after he'd killed his wife and the lover she'd taken while David had been fighting for God and country, both of whom had forgotten him. She'd been waiting until he came home to tell him that she was leaving—it was a mistake she'd had no time to regret. He, on the other hand, might have forever to regret it for her.

He never spoke of it. Not to anyone. For Stella he'd do it, but she knew the story anyway. She'd been there.

"Do you want to talk about your mother?" he asked, his voice carrying into a lower timbre, as it did when the wolf was close.

"No. Not that," she said hurriedly. "Nothing like that. I'm sorry. This isn't a good idea."

She was going to hang up. He drew on his hard-earned control and thought fast.

Forty years as a hunter and leader of men had given him a lot of practice reading between the lines. If he could put aside the fact that she was his daughter, maybe he could salvage this.

She'd told him she ran a foster agency like it was important to the rest of what she had to say.

"It's about your work?" he asked, trying to figure out what a social worker would need with a werewolf. Oh. "Is there a—" His daughter preferred not to talk about werewolves, Clive had told him. So if there was something supernatural, she was going to have to bring it up. "Is there someone bothering you?"

"No," she said. "Nothing like that. It's one of my boys."

Stella had never married, never had children of her own. Her brother said it was because she had all the people to take care of that she could handle.

"One of the foster kids."

"Devonte Parish."

"He one of your special ones?" he asked. His Stella had never seen a stray she hadn't brought home, animal or human. Most she'd dusted off and sent home with a meal and bandages as needed—but some of them she'd kept.

She sighed. "Come and see him, would you? Tomorrow?"

"I'll be there," he promised. It would take him a few hours to set up permission from the packs in her area: travel was complicated for a werewolf. "Probably sometime in the afternoon. This the number I can find you at?"

Instead of taking a taxi from the airport, he rented a car. It might be harder to park, but it would give them mobility and privacy. If his daughter only needed this, if she didn't want to smoke the peace pipe yet, then he didn't need it witnessed by a cabdriver. A witness would make it harder for him to control himself—and his little girl never needed to see him out of control ever again.

He called her before setting out, and he could tell that she'd had second and third thoughts.

"Look," he finally told her. "I'm here now. Maybe we should go and talk to the boy. Where can I meet you?"

He'd have known her anywhere though he hadn't, by her request, seen her since the night he'd killed his wife. She'd been twelve and now she was a grown woman with silver threads running through her kinky black hair. The last time he'd seen her, she'd been still a little rounded and soft as most children are—and now there wasn't an ounce of softness in her. She was muscular and lean—like him.

It had been a long time, but he'd never have mistaken her for anyone else: she had his eyes and her mother's face.

He'd thought you had to be bleeding someplace to hurt this badly. The beast struggled within him, looking for an enemy. But he controlled and subdued it before he pulled the car to the curb and unlocked the automatic door.

She was wearing a brown wool suit that was several shades darker than the milk and coffee skin she'd gotten from her mother. His own skin was dark as the night and kept him safely hidden in the shadows where he and people like him belonged.

She opened the car door and got in. He waited until she'd fastened her seat belt before pulling out from the curb. Slush splattered out from under his tires, but it was only a token. Once he was in the traffic lane, the road was bare.

She didn't say anything for a long time, so he just drove. He had no idea where he was going, but he figured she'd tell him when she was ready. He kept his eyes on traffic to give her time to get a good look at him.

"You look younger than I remember," she said finally. "Younger than me."

"I was thirty-five or thereabouts when I was Changed. Being a werewolf seems to settle physical age about twenty-five for most of us." There it was out in the open and she could do with it as she pleased.

He could smell her fear of him spike, and if he'd really been twenty-five, he thought he might have cried. Being this agitated wasn't smart if you were a werewolf. He took a deep breath through his nose and tried to calm down—he'd earned her fear.

"Devonte won't talk to me or anyone else," she said, and then as if those words had been the key to the floodgate, she kept going. "I wish you could have seen him when I first met him. He was ten going on forty. He'd just lost his grandmother, who had raised him. He looked me right in the eye, stuck his jaw out, and told me that he needed a home where he would be clothed and fed so he could concentrate on school."

"Smart boy?" he asked. She'd started in the middle of the story: he'd forgotten that habit of hers until just now.

"Very smart. Quiet. But funny, too." She made a sad sound, and her sorrow overwhelmed her fear of him. "We screen the homes. We visit. But there's never enough of us—and some of the horrible ones can put on a good show for a long time. It takes a while, too, before you get a feel for the bad ones. If he could have stayed with his first family, everything would have been fine. He stayed with them for six years. But this fall the foster mother unexpectedly got pregnant and her husband got a job transfer . . ."

They'd abandoned the boy like he was an old couch that was too awkward to move, David thought. He felt a flash of anger for this boy he'd never met. He swallowed the emotion quickly; he could do that these days. For a while. He was going to have to take that run when he got back home.

"I was tied up in court cases and someone else moved him to his next family," Stella continued, staring at her hands, which were clenched on a manila folder. "It shouldn't have been a problem. This was a family who already has fostered several children—and Devonte was a good kid, not the kind to give anyone problems."

"But something happened?" he suggested.

"His foster mother says that he just went wild, throwing furniture, breaking things. When he threatened her, his foster father stepped in and knocked him out. Devonte's in the hospital with a broken wrist and two broken ribs and he won't talk."

"You don't believe the foster family."

She gave an indignant huff. "The Linnfords look like Mr. and Mrs. Brady. She smiles and nods when he speaks and he is all charm and concern." She huffed again and spoke very precisely, "I wouldn't believe them if all they were doing was giving me the time of day. And I know Devonte. He just wants to get through school and get a scholarship so he can go to college and take care of himself."

He nodded thoughtfully. "So why did you call me?" He was willing to have a talk with the family, but he suspected if that was all she needed, it would have been a cold day in hell before she called him—she had her brothers for that.

"Because of the photos." She held up the folder in invitation.

He had to drive a couple of blocks before he found a convenient parking place and pulled over, leaving the engine running.

He pulled six photos off a clip that attached them to the back of the folder she held and spread them out to look. Interest rose up and he wished he had something more than photos. It certainly looked like more damage than one lone boy could do: ten boys maybe, if they had sledgehammers. The holes in the walls were something anyone could have done. The holes in the ten-foot ceiling, the executive desk on its side in three pieces, and the antique oak chair broken to splinters and missing a leg were more interesting.

"The last time I saw something like that . . ." Stella whispered.

It was probably a good thing she couldn't bring herself to finish that sentence. He had to admit that all this scene was missing was blood and body parts.

"How old is Devonte?"

"Sixteen."

"Can you get me in to look at the damage?"

"No, they had contractors in to fix it."

His eyebrows raised. "How long has it been?"

"It was the twenty-first. Three days." She waved a hand. "I know. Contractors are usually a month wait at least, but money talks. This guy has serious money."

That sounded wrong. "Then why are they taking in a foster kid?"

She looked him in the eye for the first time and nodded at him as if he'd gotten something right. "If I'd been the one to vet them, I'd have smelled a rat right there. Rich folk don't want mongrel children who've had it rough. Or if they do, they go to China or Romania and adopt babies to coo over. They don't take in foster kids, not without an agenda. But we're desperate for foster homes . . . and it wasn't me who approved them."

"You said the boy wouldn't talk. To you? Or to anybody?"

"To anybody. He hasn't said a word since the incident. Won't communicate at all."

David considered that, running through possibilities. "Was anyone hurt except for the boy?"

"No."

"Would you mind if I went to see him now?"

"Please."

He followed her directions to the hospital. He parked the car, but before he could open the door, she grabbed his arm. The first time she touched him.

"Could he be a werewolf?"

"Maybe," he told her. "That kind of damage . . ."

"It looked like our house," she said, not looking at him, but not taking her hand off him either. "Like our house that night."

"If he was a werewolf, I doubt your Mr. Linnford would have been able to knock him out without taking a lot of damage. Maybe Linnford is the werewolf." That would fit, most of the werewolves he knew, if they survived, eventually became wealthy. Children were more difficult. Maybe that was why Linnford and his wife fostered children.

Stella jerked her chin up and down once. "That's what I thought. That's it. Linnford might be a werewolf. Could you tell?"

His chest felt tight. How very brave of her: she'd called the only monster she knew to deal with the other monsters. It reminded him of how she'd stood between him and the boys, protecting them the best that she could.

"Let me talk to Devonte," he said, trying to keep the growl out of his voice with only moderate success. "Then I can deal with Linnford."

The hospital corridors were decorated with garlands and green and red bulbs. Every year Christmas got more plastic and seemed further and further from the Christmases David had known as a child.

His daughter led him to the elevators without hesitation and exchanged nods with a few of the staff members who walked past. He hated the way his children aged every year. Hated the silver in their hair that was a constant reminder that eventually time would take them all away from him.

She kept as much distance between them as she could in the elevator. As if he were a stranger—or a monster. At least she wasn't running from him screaming.

You can't live with bitterness. He knew that. Bitterness, like most unpleasant emotions, made the wolf restless. Restless wolves were dangerous. The nurse at the station just outside the elevator knew Stella, too, and greeted her by name.

"That Mr. Linnford was here asking after Devonte. I told him that he wasn't allowed to visit yet." She gave Stella a disappointed look, clearly blaming her for putting Mr. Linnford to such bother. "What a nice man he is, looking after that boy after what he did to them."

She handed Stella a clipboard and gave David a mildly curious look.

He gave her his most harmless smile and she smiled back before glancing down at the clipboard Stella had returned.

David could read it from where he stood. Stella Christiansen and guest. Well, he told himself, she could hardly write down that he was her father when she looked older than he did.

"He may be a nice man," Stella told the nurse with a thread of steel in her voice, "but you just keep him out until we know for sure what happened and why."

She strode off toward a set of doors where a policeman sat in front of a desk, sitting on a wooden chair, and reading a worn paperback copy of Stephen King's *Cujo*. "Jorge," she said.

"Stella." He buzzed the door and let them through.

"He's in the secured wing," she explained under her breath as she walked briskly down the hall. "Not that it's all that secure. Jorge shouldn't have let you through without checking your ID."

Not that anyone would question his Stella, David thought. Even as a little girl, people did what she told them to do. He was careful not to smile at her, she wouldn't understand it.

This part of the hospital smelled like blood, desperation, and disinfectant. Even though most of the scents were old, a new wolf penned up in this environment would cause a lot more excitement than he was seeing: and a sixteen-year-old could only be a new wolf. Any younger than that and they mostly didn't survive the Change. Anyway, he'd have scented a wolf by now: their first conclusion was right—Stella's boy was no werewolf.

"Any cameras in the rooms?" he asked in a low voice.

Her steady footfall paused. "No. That's still on the list of advised improvements for the future."

"All right. No one else here?"

"Not right now," she said. "This hospital isn't near gang territory and they put the adult offenders in a different section." She entered one of the open doorways and he followed her in, shutting the door behind them.

It wasn't a private room, but the first bed was empty. In the second bed was a boy staring at the wall—there were no windows. He was beaten up a bit and had a cast on one hand. The other hand was attached to a sturdy rail that stuck out of the bed on the side nearest the wall with a locking nylon strap—better than handcuffs, he thought, but not much. The boy didn't look up as they came in.

Maybe it was the name, or maybe the image that "foster kid" brought to mind, but he'd expected Devonte to be black. Instead, the boy looked as if someone had taken half a dozen races and shook them up—Eurasian races, though, not from the Dark Continent. There was Native American or Oriental in the corners of his eyes—and he supposed that nose could be Jewish or Italian. His skin looked as if he had a deep suntan, but this time of year it was more likely the color was his own: Mexican, Greek, or even Indian.

Not that it mattered. He'd found that the years were slowly completing the job that Vietnam had begun—race or religion mattered very little to him anymore. But even if it had mattered . . . Stella had asked him for help.

Stella glanced at her father. She didn't know him, didn't know if he'd see through Devonte's defiant sullenness to the fear underneath. His expressionless face and upright military bearing gave her no clue. She could read people, but she didn't know her father anymore, hadn't seen him since . . . that night. Watching him made her uncomfortable, so she turned her attention to the other person in the room.

"Hey, kid."

Devonte kept his gaze on the wall.

"I brought someone to see you."

Her father, after a keen look at the boy, lifted his head and sucked in air through his nose hard enough she could hear it.

"Where are the clothes he was wearing when they brought him in?" he asked.

That drew Devonte's attention, and satisfaction at his reaction slowed her answer. Her father's eye fell on the locker and he stalked to it and opened the door. He took out the clear plastic bag of clothes and said, with studied casualness, "Linnford was here asking about you today."

Devonte went still as a mouse.

Stella didn't know where this was going, but pitched in to help. "The police informed me that Linnford's decided to not press assault charges. They should move you to a room with a view soon. I'm scheduled for a meeting tomorrow morning to decide what happens to you when you get out of here."

Devonte opened his mouth, but then closed it resolutely.

Her father sniffed at the bag, then said softly, "Why do your clothes smell like vampire, boy?"

Devonte jumped, the whites of his eyes showing all the way round his irises. His mouth opened and this time Stella thought it might really be an inability to speak that kept him quiet. She was choking a bit on "vampire" herself. But she wouldn't have believed in werewolves either, she supposed, if her father weren't one.

"I didn't introduce you," she murmured. "Devonte, this is my father, I called him when I saw the crime scene photos. He's a werewolf." If he was having vampire problems, maybe a werewolf would look good.

The sad blue-gray chair with the ripped Naugahyde seat that had been sitting next to Devonte's bed zipped past her and flung itself at her father—who caught it and gave the boy a curious half smile. "Oh, I bet you surprised it, didn't you? Wizards aren't exactly common."

"Wizard?" Stella squeaked regrettably.

Her father's smile widened just a little—a smile she remembered from her childhood when she or one of her brothers had done something particularly clever. This one was aimed at Devonte.

He moved the chair gently between his hands. "A witch's power centers on bodies and minds, flesh and blood. A wizard has power over the physical—" The empty bed slammed into the wall with the open locker, bending the door and cracking the drywall. Her father was safely in front of it and belatedly she realized he must have jumped over it.

He still had the chair and his smile had grown to a wide, white grin. "Very nice, boy. But I'm not your enemy." He glanced up at the clock on the wall and shook his head.

"Someone ought to reset that thing. Do you know what time it is?"

No more furniture moved. Her father made a show of taking out his cell phone and looking at it. "Six thirty. It's dark outside already. How badly did you hurt it with that chair I saw in the photo?"

Devonte was breathing hard, but Stella controlled her urge to go to him. Her father, hopefully, knew what he was doing. She shivered, though she was wearing her favorite wool suit and the hospital was quite warm. How much of the stories she'd heard about vampires was true?

Devonte released a breath. "Not badly enough."

On the tails of Devonte's reply, her father asked, "Who taught you not to talk at all, if you have a secret to keep?"

"My grandmother. Her mother survived Dachau because the American troops came just in time—and because she kept her mouth shut when the Nazis wanted information."

Her father's face softened. "Tough woman. Was she the Gypsy? Most wizards have at least a little Gypsy blood."

Devonte shrugged, rubbed his hands over his face hard. She recognized the gesture from a hundred different kids: he was trying not to cry. "Stella said you're a werewolf."

Her father cocked his head as if he were weighing something. "Stella doesn't lie." Unexpectedly he pinned Stella with his eyes. "I don't know if we'll have a vampire calling tonight—it depends upon how badly Devonte hurt it."

"Her," said Devonte. "It was a her."

Still looking at Stella, her father corrected himself. "Her. She must have been pretty badly injured if she hasn't come here already. And it probably means we're lucky and she is alone. If there were others, they'd have come yesterday or the day before—they can't afford to let Devonte live with what he knows about them. Vampires haven't survived as long as they have by leaving witnesses."

"No one would have believed me," Devonte said. "They'd have locked me up forever."

That made her father release her from the grip of his gaze as he focused his attention on Devonte. The boy straightened under the impact—Stella knew exactly how he felt.

"Is that what Linnford told you when his neighbors came running to see why there was so much noise?" her father asked gently. "Upscale apartment dwellers aren't nearly as likely to ignore odd sounds. Is that why you threw around so much furniture? That was smart, boy."

Devonte was nodding his head—and he straightened a little more at her father's praise.

"Next time a vampire attacks you and you don't manage to kill it, though, you shout it to the world. You may end up seeing a psychologist for the rest of your life—but the vampires will stay as far from you as they can. If she doesn't come tonight, you tell your story to the newspapers." Her father glanced at Stella and she nodded.

"I know a couple of reporters," she said. "'Boy Claims He Was Attacked by Vampire' ought to sell enough papers to justify a headline or two."

"All right then." Her father returned his attention to her. "I need you to go out and find some wood for us: a chair, a table, something we can make stakes out of."

"Holy water?" asked Devonte. "They might have a chapel here."

"Smart," said her father. "But from what I've heard, it doesn't do enough damage to be worth running it down. Go now, Stella—and be careful."

She almost saluted him, but she didn't trust him enough to tease. He saw it, almost smiled, and then turned back to Devonte. "And you're going to tell me everything you know about this vampire."

Stella glanced in the room next to Devonte's, but, like his, it was decorated in early Naugahyde and metal: no wood to be found. She didn't bother checking any more but hurried to the security door—and read the note on the door.

"No, sir. She lived with them—they told me she was Linnford's sister." Devonte stopped talking when she came back.

"Jorge's been called away, he'll be back in a few minutes."

Her father considered that. "I think the show's on. No wooden chairs?"

"All the rooms in this wing are like this one."

"Without an effective weapon, I'll get a better chance at her as a wolf than as a human. It means I can't talk to you, though—and it will take a while to change back, maybe a couple of hours." He looked away, and in an adult version of Devonte's earlier gesture, rubbed his face tiredly. She heard the rasp of whisker on skin. "I control the wolf now—and have for a long time."

He was worried about her.

"It's all right," she told him. He gave her the same kind of keen examination he'd given Devonte earlier and she wondered what information he was drawing from it. Could he tell how scared she was?

His face softened. "You'll do, my star."

She'd forgotten that he used to call her that—hated the way it tightened her throat. "Should I call Clive and Steve?"

"Not for a vampire," he told her. "All that will do is up the body count. To that end, we'll stay here and wait—an isolation ward is as good a place to face her as any. If I'm wrong, and the guard's leaving isn't the beginning of her attack—if she doesn't come tonight, we get all of us into the safety of someone's home, where the vampire can't just waltz in without invitation. Then I'll call in a few favors and my friends and I can take care of her somewhere there aren't any civilians to be hurt."

He looked around with evident dissatisfaction.

"What are you looking for?" Devonte asked so she didn't have to.

"A place to hide." Then he looked up and smiled at the dropped ceiling.

"Those panels won't support your weight," she warned him.

"No, but this is a hospital and this is the old wing. I bet they have a cable ladder for their computer and electric cables . . ." As he spoke, he'd hopped on the empty bed and pushed up a ceiling panel to take a look.

"What's a cable ladder?" Stella asked.

"In this case, it's a sturdy aluminum track attached to the oak beam with stout hardware." He sounded pleased as he replaced the ceiling panel he'd taken out. "I could hide a couple of people up here if I had to."

He was a mercenary, she remembered, and wondered how many times he'd hidden on top of cable ladders.

He moved the empty bed away from the wall and climbed on it again and removed a different panel. "Do you think you can get this panel back where it belongs after I get up here, boy?"

"Sure." Devonte sounded thoroughly pleased. If anyone else had called him "boy," he'd have been bristling. He was already well on the way to a big case of hero worship, just like the one she'd had.

"Stella." Her father took off his red flannel shirt and laid it on the empty bed behind him. "When this is over, you call Clive, tell him everything, and he'll arrange a cleanup. He knows who to call for help with it. It's safer for everyone if people don't believe in vampires and werewolves. Leaving bodies makes it kind of hard to deny."

"I'll call him."

Without his shirt to cover him, she could see there was no softness in him. A few scars showed up gray on his dark skin. She'd forgotten how dark he was, like ebony.

As he peeled off his sky-blue undershirt, he said, with a touch of humor, "If you don't want to see more of your father than any daughter ever should, you need to turn your back." And she realized she'd been staring at him.

Devonte made an odd noise—he was laughing. There was a tightness to the sound and she knew he was scared and excited to see what it looked like when a man changed into a werewolf. For some reason she felt her own mouth stretch into a nervous grin she let Devonte see just before she did as her father advised her and turned her back.

David didn't like changing in front of anyone. He wasn't exactly vulnerable—but it made the wolf edgy and if someone decided to get brave and approach too closely . . . well, the wolf would feel threatened, like a snake shedding its skin.

So to the boy he said quietly, "Watching is fine. But wait for a bit if you want to touch . . ." He had a thought. "Stella, if she sends the Linnfords in first, I'll do my best to stay hidden. I can take a vampire . . ." Honesty forced him to continue. "Maybe I can take a vampire, but only with surprise on my side. Her human minions, if they are still human enough to walk in daylight, are still too human to detect me. Don't let them take Devonte out of this room."

He tried to remember everything he knew about vampires. Once he changed, it would be too late to talk. "Don't look in the vampire's eyes, don't let her touch you. Unless you are really a believer, don't plan on crosses helping you out. When I attack, don't try and help, just keep out of it so I don't have to worry about you."

Wishing they had a wooden stake, he knelt on the floor and allowed himself to change. Calling the wolf was easy, it knew there was a fight to be had, blood to be shed, and in its eagerness it rushed the change as if called by the moon herself.

He never remembered exactly how bad it was going to hurt. His mother had once told him that childbirth was like that for women. That if they remembered how bad it was, they'd lack the courage to face the next time.

But he did remember it was always worse than he expected, and that somehow helped him bear it.

The shivery, icy pain slid over his bones while fire threaded through his muscles, reshaping, reorganizing, and altering what was there to suit itself. Experience kept him from making noise—it was one of the first things he learned: how to control his instincts and keep the howls, the growls, and the whines inside and bury them in silence. Noise can attract unwanted attention.

His lungs labored to provide oxygen as adrenaline forced his heart to beat too fast. His face ached as teeth became fangs and his jaw extended with cheekbones. His eyesight blurred and then sharpened with a predatory clarity that allowed him to see prey and enemy alike no matter what shadows they tried to hide in.

"Cool," said someone. Devonte. He-who-was-to-be-guarded.

Someone moved and it attracted his attention. Her terror flooded his senses like perfume.

Prey. He liked it when they ran.

Then she lifted her chin and he saw a second image, superimposed over the first. A child standing between him and two smaller children, her chin jutting out as she lifted up a baseball bat in wordless defiance that spoke louder than her terror and the blood.

Not prey. Not prey. His. His star.

It was all right then. She could see his pain—she had earned that right. And together they would stop the monster from eating the boy.

For the first few minutes after the change, he mostly thought like the wolf, but as the pain subsided, he settled back into control. He shook off the last of the unpleasant tingles with the same willpower he used to set aside the desire to snarl at the boy who reached out with a hand . . . only to jerk back, caught by the strap on his wrist.

David hopped onto the bed and snapped through the ballistic nylon that attached Devonte's cuff to the rail and waited while the boy petted him tentatively with all the fascination of a person touching a tiger.

"That'll be a little hard to explain," said Stella.

He looked at her and she flinched . . . then jerked up her chin and met his eyes. "What if the Linnfords ask about the restraint?"

It had been the wolf's response to seeing the boy he was supposed to protect tied up like a bad dog, not the man's.

"They haven't been here," said Devonte. "Unless they spend a lot of time in hospital prison, they won't know it was supposed to be there. I'll cover the cuff on my wrist with the blanket."

Stella nodded her head thoughtfully. "All right. And if things get bad, at least this way you can run. He's right, it's better if the restraint is off."

David let them work it out. He launched himself off Devonte's bed and onto the other—forgetting that Devonte was already hurt until he heard the boy's indrawn breath. David was still half operating on wolf instincts—which wasn't very helpful when fighting vampires. He needed to be thinking.

Maybe it had only been the suddenness of his movement, though, because the boy made the same sound when David hopped through the almost-too-narrow opening in the ceiling and onto the track in the plenum space between the original fourteen-foot ceiling and false panels fitted into the flimsy hangers that kept them in place. The track groaned a little under his sudden weight, but it didn't bend.

"My father always told us that no one ever looks up for their enemy," Stella said after a moment. "Can you replace the panel? If you can't, I—"

The panel he'd moved slid back into place with more force than necessary and cracked down the middle.

"Damn it."

"Don't worry, no one will notice. There are a couple of broken panels up there."

She couldn't see any sign that her father was hiding in the ceiling except for the bed. She grabbed it by the headboard and tugged it back to its original position, then she did the same with the chair.

She'd forgotten how impressive the wolf was . . . almost beautiful: the perfect killing machine covered with four-inch-deep, red-gold fur. She hadn't remembered the black that tipped his ears and surrounded his eyes like Egyptian kohl.

"If you'll get back, I'll see what I can do with the wall," said Devonte. "Sometimes I can fix things as well as move them."

That gave her a little pause, but she found that wizards weren't as frightening as werewolves and vampires. She considered his offer, then shook her head.

"No. They already know what you are." She gathered her father's clothes from the bedspread and folded them neatly. Then she stashed them—and the plastic bag with Devonte's clothes—in the locker. "Just leave the wall. We only need to hide the werewolf from them, and you might need all the power you've got to help with the vampire."

Devonte nodded.

"Right then." She took a deep breath and picked up her catchall purse from the floor where she'd set it.

Her brothers had made fun of her purses until she'd used one to take out a mugger. She'd been lucky—it had been laden with a pair of three-pound weights she'd been transporting from home to work—but she'd never admitted that to her brothers. Afterward they'd given her Mace, karate lessons, and quit bugging her about the size of her purse.

Unearthing a travel-sized game board from its depths, she said, "How about some checkers?"

Five hard-won games later she decided the vampire either wasn't coming tonight, or she was waiting for Stella to go away. She jumped three of Devonte's checkers and there was a quiet knock on the door. She turned to look as Jorge, the cop who'd gotten babysitting duty today, poked his head in.

"Sorry to leave you stuck here."

"No problem. Just beating a poor helpless child at checkers."

She waited for him to respond with something funny—Jorge was quick on his feet. But his face just stayed . . . not blank precisely, but neutral.

"They need you down in pediatrics, now. Looks like a case of child abuse, and Doc Gonzales wants you to talk to the little girl."

She couldn't help the instincts that brought her to her feet, but those same instincts were screaming that there was something wrong with Jorge.

Between her job and having a brother on the force, she'd gotten to know some of the cops pretty well. Nothing bothered Jorge like a child who'd been hurt. She'd seen him cry like a baby when he talked about a car wreck where the child hadn't survived. But he'd passed this message along to her with all the passion of a hospital switchboard operator.

In the movies, vampires could make people do what they wanted them to—she couldn't remember if the people were permanently damaged. Mostly, she was afraid, they just died.

She glanced down at her watch and shook her head. "You know my rules," she said. "It's after six and I'm off shift."

Her rules were a standing joke with her brothers and their friends—a serious joke. She'd seen too many people burn out from the stress of her job. So she'd made a list of rules she had to follow, and they'd kept her sane so far. One of her rules was that from eight in the morning until six in the evening she was on the job; outside of those hours she did her best to have a real life. She was breaking it now, with Devonte.

Instead of calling her on it, Jorge just processed her reply and finally nodded. "All right. I'll tell them."

He didn't close the door when he left. She went to the doorway and watched him walk mechanically down the hall and through the security door, which he'd left open. Very unlike him to leave a security door open, but he closed it behind him.

"That was the vampire's doing, wasn't it?" she asked, looking up.

The soft growl that eased through the ceiling was somehow reassuring—though she hadn't forgotten his reservations about how well he'd do against a vampire.

She went back to Devonte's bed and made her move on the board. Out in the hall the security door opened again, and someone wearing high heels click-clicked briskly down the hall.

Stella took a deep breath, settled back on the end of the bed, and told Devonte, "Your turn."

He looked at the board, but she saw his hand shake as whoever it was in the hallway closed in on them.

"King me," he said in a fair approximation of triumph.

The footsteps stopped in the doorway. Devonte looked over her shoulder and his face went slack with fear. Stella inhaled and took her first look.

She'd thought a vampire would be young, like her father. Wasn't that the myth? But this woman had gray hair and wrinkles under her eyes and in the soft, white skin of her neck. She was dressed in a professionally tailored wine-colored suit. She wore a diamond necklace around her aging neck, and diamond-and-pearl earrings.

"Well," said Stella, "no one is going to think you look like a cuddly grandma."

The woman laughed, her face lighting up with a cheer so genuine that Stella thought she might have liked her if only the laughter didn't showcase her fangs. "The boy talked, did he? I thought for sure he'd hold his tongue, if only to keep his own secrets. Either that or broadcast it to the world, and then you and I wouldn't be in this position."

She gave Stella a kindly smile that showed off a charmingly mismatched pair of dimples. "I am sorry you had to be involved. I tried to get you out of it."

But Stella had been dealing with people a long time, she could smell a fake a mile away. The laughter had been real, but the kind concern certainly wasn't.

"Separating your prey," Stella said. She needed to get the vampire into the room, where her father could drop on top of her, but how?

The vampire displayed her fangs and dimples again. "More convenient and easier to keep the noise down," she allowed. "But not really necessary. Not even if you are a"—she took a deep breath—"werewolf."

The news didn't seem to bother her. Stella fought off the feeling that her father was going to be overmatched. He'd been a soldier and then a mercenary, training his own sons and then grandsons. Surely he knew what he was doing.

"Hah," sneered Devonte in classic adolescent disdain. "You aren't so tough. I nearly killed you all by myself."

The vampire sneered right back, and on her, the expression made the hair on the back of Stella's neck stand up and take notice. "You were a mistake, boy. One I intend to clear up."

David crouched motionless, waiting for the sound of the vampire's voice to indicate she had moved underneath him.

Patience, patience, he counseled himself, but he should have been counseling someone else.

If the vampire's theatrics scared Stella, they drove Devonte into action. The bed he tried to smash her father with rattled across the floor. He must have tired himself out with his earlier wizardry because it was traveling only half as fast as it had when he'd tried to drive her father through the wall.

The vampire had no trouble grabbing it . . . or throwing it through the plaster wall and into the hallway, where it crashed on its side, flinging wheels, bedding, mattress, and pieces of the arcana that distinguished it from a normal bed.

She was so busy impressing them with her Incredible Hulk imitation, she didn't see the old blue-gray chair. It hit her squarely in the back, driving her directly under the panel Devonte had cracked.

"Now," whispered Stella, diving toward the hole the vampire had made in the wall, hoping that would be out of the way.

Even though Devonte's chair had knocked the vampire to her knees, Stella's motion drew her attention. The thing was fast, and she lunged for Stella in the same motion she used to rise. Then the roof fell on top of her, the roof and a silently snarling red-gold wolf with claws and fangs that made the vampire's look like toys.

For a moment she was twelve again, watching the monster dig those long claws into her mother's lover and she froze in horror. The woman looked frail beneath the huge wolf's bulk—until she pulled her legs under him and threw him into the outer wall, the one made of cinder blocks and not plaster.

With an inhuman howl, the vampire leaped upon her father. She looked nothing like the elegant woman who had walked into the room. In the brief glimpse she'd had of her face, Stella saw something terrible . . . evil.

"Stella, behind you!" Devonte yelled, hopping of the bed, his good arm around his ribs.

She hadn't been paying attention to anything except the vampire. Devonte's warning came just a little late and someone grabbed her by the arm and jerked her roughly around—Linnford. Gone was the urban smile and GQ posture, his face was lit with fanaticism and madness. He had a knife in the hand that wasn't holding her. She reacted without thinking, twisting so his thrust went past her abdomen, slicing through fabric but not skin.

Something buzzed between them, hitting Linnford in the chest and knocking him back to the floor. He jerked and spasmed like a skewered frog in a film she'd once had to watch in college. The chair sat on top of him, balanced on one bent leg, the other three appearing to hover in the air.

It took a moment for her to properly understand what she was seeing. The bent chair leg was stuck into his rib cage, just to the left of his sternum. Blood began spitting out like a macabre fountain.

"Honey?" Hannah Linnford stood in the doorway. Like Stella, she seemed to be having trouble understanding what she was seeing.

Muttering, "Does no one remember to shut the security doors?" Stella pulled the mini-canister of Mace her youngest brother had given her after the mugging incident out of her pocket and sprayed it in the other woman's face.

If she'd been holding Linnford's knife, she could have cheerfully driven it through Hannah's neck: these people had taken one of her kids and tried to feed him to a vampire.

Thinking of her kids made Stella look for Devonte.

He was leaning against the wall a few feet from his bed, staring at Linnford—and his expression centered Stella because he needed her. She ran to him and tugged him to the far corner of the room, away from the fighting monsters, but too close to the Linnfords. Once she had him where she wanted him, she did her best to block his view of Linnford's dying body. If she could get medical help soon enough, Linnford might survive—but she felt no drive to do it. Let him rot.

Mace can in hand, she kept a weather eye on the woman screaming on the floor, but most of her attention was on the fight her father was losing.

They fought like a pair of cats, coming together clawing and biting, almost too fast for her eyes to focus on, then, for no reason she could see, they'd retreat. After a few seconds of staring at each other, they'd go at it again. Unlike cats, they were eerily silent.

The vampire's carefully arranged hair was fallen, covering her face, but not disguising her glittering . . . no, glowing red eyes. Her arm flashed out in a jerky movement that was so quick Stella almost missed it—and the wolf twitched away with another wound that dripped blood: the vampire was still virtually untouched.

The two monsters backed away from each other and the vampire licked her fingers.

"You taste so good, wolf," she said. "I can't wait until I can sink my fangs through your skin and suck that sweetness dry."

Stella sprayed Hannah in the face again. Then she hauled Devonte out the door and away from the vampire, making regrettably little allowance for his broken ribs. Dead was worse than in pain.

It was working, David thought, watching the vampire lick his blood off her fingers. Though he was mostly focused on the vampire, he noticed when Stella took the boy out of the room. Good for her. With the vampire's minions here, one dead and one incapacitated, she shouldn't have trouble getting out. He hoped she took Devonte to her home—or any home—where they'd be safe. Then he put them out of his mind and concentrated on the battle at hand.

He'd met a vampire or two, but never fought one before. He'd heard that some of them had a strange reaction to werewolf blood. She seemed to be one of them.

He could only hope that her bloodlust would make her stupid. He'd heard that vampires couldn't feed from the dead. If it wasn't true, he might be in trouble.

He waited for her to come at him again—and this time he stepped into her fist, falling limply at her feet. She hit him hard, he felt the bone in his jaw creak, so the limp fall wasn't hard to fake. He'd wait until she started feeding and the residual dizziness from her blow left, then he'd take her.

She fell on him and he waited for her fangs to dig in. Instead she jerked a couple of times and then lay still. She wasn't breathing and her heart wasn't beating—but she'd been like that when she walked into the room.

"Papa?"

Stella was supposed to be safely away.

He rose with a roar, making an audible sound for the first time so the vampire would pay attention to him and leave his daughter alone. But the woman's body rolled smoothly off of him and lay on the floor—two wooden chair legs stuck through her back.

"Are you all right? Jorge left the security door open. I knew it when the Linnfords came in. We broke the legs off Jorge's chair, and Devonte used whatever he used to toss the furniture around to drive them into her back."

The soldier in him insisted on a full and quick survey of the room.

Linnford was dead, the abused chair was the obvious cause of death. A woman, presumably his wife, sobbed harshly, her face pressed into Linnford's arm: a possible threat. Stella and Devonte were standing way too close to the vampire.

They'd killed her.

For a moment he felt a surge of pride. Stella didn't have an ounce of quit in her whole body. She and the boy had managed to take advantage of the distraction he'd arranged before he could.

"Everyone was gone, Jorge and everyone." He looked at the triumph in Stella's face, not quite hidden by her worry for her friends.

She thought the vampire was finished, but wood through the heart didn't always keep the undead down.

"Are you all right?" Stella asked. And then when he just stared at her, "Papa?"

He'd come here hoping to play hero, he knew, hoping to mend what couldn't be mended. But the only role for him was that of monster, because that was the only thing he was.

He pulled the sheet off the bed and ripped it with a claw, then tossed it toward Linnford's sobbing woman. Stella took the hint and she and Devonte made a rope of sorts out of it and tied her up.

While they were working at that, he walked slowly up to the vampire. Stella had called him Papa tonight, more than once. He'd try to hold on to that and forget the rest.

He growled at the vampire: her fault that he would lose his daughter a second time. Then he snapped his teeth through her spine. The meat of her was tougher than it should have been, tougher than jerky and bad-tasting to boot. His jaw hurt from the hit he'd taken as he set his teeth and put some muscle into separating her head from her body.

When he was finished, the boy was losing his last meal in the corner, an arm wrapped around his ribs. Throwing up with broken ribs sucked: he knew all about that. Linnford's woman was secured. Stella had a hand over her mouth as if to prevent herself from imitating Devonte. When she pulled her eyes away from the vampire's severed head and looked at him, he saw horror.

He felt the blood dripping from his jaws—and couldn't face her any longer. Couldn't stay while horror turned to fear of him. He didn't look at his daughter again as he ran away for the first time in his long life.

When he could, he changed back to human at the home of the local werewolf pack. They let him shower, and gave him a pair of sweats—the universal answer to the common problem of changing back to human and not having clothes to put back on.

He called his oldest son to make sure that Stella had called him and that he had handled the cleanup. She had remembered, and Clive was proceeding with his usual thoroughness.

Linnford was about to have a terrible car wreck. The vampire's body, both parts of it, were scheduled for immediate incineration. The biggest problem was what to do with Linnford's wife. For the moment she seemed to be too traumatized to talk. Maybe the vampire's death had broken her—or maybe she'd come around. Either way, she'd need help, discreet help from people who knew how to tell the difference between the victim of a vampire and a minion and would treat her accordingly.

David made a few calls, and got the number of a very private sanitarium run by a small, very secret government agency. The price wasn't bad—all he had to do was rescue some missionary who was related to a high-level politician. The fool had managed to get kidnapped with his wife and two young children. David's team would still get paid, and he'd probably have taken the assignment anyway.

By the time he called Clive back, his sons had located a few missing hospital personnel and the cop who'd been guarding the door. David heard the relief in Clive's voice: Jorge was apparently a friend. None of the recovered people seemed to be hurt, though they had no idea why they were all in the basement.

David hung up and turned off his cell phone. Accepting the offer of a bedroom from the pack Alpha, David took his tired body to bed and slept.

* * *

Christmas Day was coming to a close when David drove his rental to his son's house—friends had picked it up from the hospital for him.

Red and green lights covered every bush and railing as well as surrounding all the windows. Knee-high candy canes lined the walk.

There were cars at his son's house. David frowned at them and checked his new watch. He was coming over at the right time. He'd made it clear that he didn't want to intrude—which was understood to mean that he wouldn't come when Stella was likely to be there.

He'd already have been on a flight home except that he didn't know how to contact Devonte. He tapped the envelope against his leg and wondered why he'd picked up a Christmas card instead of just handing over his business card. Below his contact information he'd made Devonte an open job offer beginning as soon as Devonte was eighteen. David could think of a thousand ways a wizard would be of use to a small group of mercenaries.

Of course, after watching David tear up the vampire's body, Devonte probably wouldn't be interested, so more to the point was the name and phone number on the other side of the card. Both belonged to a wizard who was willing to take on a pupil, the local Alpha had given it to him.

Clive had promised to give it to Devonte.

David had to search under the giant wreath on the door for the bell. As he waited, he noticed that he could hear a lot of people inside, and even through the door he smelled the turkey.

He took a step back, but the door was already opening.

Stella stood in the doorway. Over her shoulder he could see the whole family running around preparing the table for Christmas dinner. Devonte was sitting on the couch reading to one of the toddlers that seemed to be everywhere. Clive leaned against the fireplace and met David's gaze. He lifted a glass of wine and sipped it, smiling slyly.

David took another step back and opened his mouth to apologize to Stella . . . just as her face lit with her mother's smile. She stepped out onto the porch and wrapped her arms around him.

"Merry Christmas, Papa," she said. "I hope you like turkey."

You'd Better Not Pyout

Nancy Pickard

Nancy Pickard is a four-time Edgar® Award nominee, and a multiple winner of Anthony, Agatha, and Macavity awards for her novels and short stories. She has also won the Shamus and Barry awards for short fiction. One of her proudest accomplishments was seeing the first fantasy story she ever wrote selected for an anthology of the year's best fantasy and horror stories. She lives in the Kansas City area, where she was traumatized by a werewolf movie when she was a child.

MIAMI BEACH

"I'm telling you," Pasha argued, "it explains everything."

"Oh, come on," Serge scoffed.

The two vampires sat in their favorite booth in their favorite Cuban café, where the fluorescent lighting gave everybody a sickly blue-white glow, and not just them. Before it was a café, it had been a gay bar, and before that a boutique hotel, and before that a funeral home, and before that a mansion, and before that a coconut plantation, and before that a hunting ground for crocodiles, and before that, they didn't know. The 1700s were before their time. Of all the incarnations of the property, the café was their favorite. It was a place to go before supper, where they could spot gluttonous humans who'd eaten so much that it made them sluggish when they departed. Pasha liked to imagine he could taste a memory of fried plantains in their fatty blood; Serge just liked it that he didn't have to work so hard for a meal. A bloated human was a slow human.

"No, really, listen to me," Pasha urged him. "I'm telling you, Santa Claus is a vampire. It explains so much!" He snapped his fingers with both hands and then pointed his long pale forefingers at Serge. "For instance, how old is he?"

Serge wrapped his hands around his coffee cup, which a waitress had just brought over to him. It was his third one of the evening. The waitresses all knew that "refill" meant they had to empty the mug full of cooled coffee, and bring him back a full fresh hot one. Not for the drink. He never drank any of it. For the warmth.

"Old," he said, grudgingly.

"Nobody really knows how old he is, yes? But definitely more than one human life span. He's ancient," Pasha reminded him excitedly. "Eternal, like us. And he only works at night!" Or "nyight," as Pasha pronounced it, having never entirely lost his Russian "y."

"He's not *real*, Pasha!"

"Neither are we supposed to be."

That stopped Serge for a moment, even caused his handsome brow to crease.

They were both exceptionally good-looking vamps, having been turned in the prime of their royal Russian twenties. Pasha had been blond as a Hollywood mink long before there was a Hollywood. Serge still had hair as thick, dark, and curly as a Russian black bear's fur. Cousins then, they were related by more kinds of blood than family now.

In the course of Pasha's many "thyeories," over three centuries, there always came a moment that gave Serge pause until he could think his way around it. This time, he thought he had a perfect rebuttal: "But he gets into *houses*!"

"Yeah, because he's *invyited*."

"Invited?" Vampires had to be invited into homes; they couldn't just barge in like unwelcome dinner guests. "They're all asleep when he arrives. It's not like they wait by the chimney and holler up, 'Come on in, Santa!'"

Pasha smiled. He loved his theory. He always loved his theories.

"It's the cyookies," he said, with an air of triumph.

"The *cookies*?" Serge smiled at the unlikely word, then laughed out loud, which revealed his teeth.

In the booth behind Pasha, a little boy climbed up and turned around to look at them. He saw the pointed incisors, longer than they ought to be, and stared with big eyes. Serge growled deep in his throat, loud enough for the boy to hear, low enough to keep anybody else from hearing.

The child turned around again fast, and disappeared below the top of the booth.

"The cookies and the milk!" Pasha exclaimed, caught up in his enthusiasm for his own brilliance. "All those glasses of myilk, all those sugar cookies with sprinkles and icing, what are they but invitations?" His eyes narrowed as he whispered in a dark and meaningful tone, "'The stockings all hung by the chimney with care, *in hopes that Saint Nicholas soon will be there.*'" Pasha slapped the tabletop triumphantly with the palms of his hands. Silverware jumped. Human customers stared, then looked quickly away as if unnerved by something they couldn't put their finger on. "They're for *him*, Serge! He knows it. They know it."

"He brings *gifts*, Pasha."

"So?"

"When's the last time you gave a human anything but a real bad hickey?"

"Yeah, but what about all those people who die right after Christmas is over?"

"What are you talking about?"

"Psychologists think it's because people put off dying until after big events like their birthdays, or Christmas. But that's not it. They're dying after Christmas, because *he* comes *back*."

"Back?"

"Of course! That's the genius of it! Christmas Eve, he accepts the invitation into their homes, and creates the illusion that benevolent Santa Claus was there. That's the reason for the gifts. Duh. Then he's *in*. They've *invited* him. He can come back anytime he wants to, as often as he likes! I think what he does, see, is he feasts right after the holidays, which accounts for all those obituaries, but he doesn't kill all of them, of course—"

"Of course," Serge said, dryly.

"—because that would be—"

"Self-defeating?"

"—dangerous. And nobody could eat that much in one night anyway. So he saves most of them for return visits. I mean, why do you think he keeps a list?"

Serge leaned forward and said with quiet clarity:

"He. Goes. Down. Chimneys. Pasha."

Vampires could die in flames.

"They're not lit! You think people leave a lighted fire for Santa Claus to come down? Even if he wasn't a vampire, they wouldn't do that! They don't want to burn him, they want those gifts."

Serge feigned disappointment. "But gee, all those pictures of Santa. He's in the living room, by the Christmas tree, and there's always a lighted fireplace." He sighed as if a cherished illusion had been shattered, but then he perked up. "He leaves coal for the bad boys and girls. What's that all about?"

"Code."

"Coal."

"Code. Like a sign to other vamps. 'Bad blood here.'"

"What the hell *is* bad blood anyway?"

"You know. Old, sour, too salty, whatever."

"I don't know. Seems a little *thoughtful* to me. When's the last time a vampire did us a favor? And Pasha, answer me this. If he got into everybody's homes the first time, then why does he keep doing it *every year*? And how does he get around to the whole world in one night? We may be supernatural beings, but we're not supermen who can circle the globe a hundred times in a minute."

"I haven't figured that out yet," Pasha admitted, looking not at all abashed. "But I'm sure there's a reason."

Serge sighed and dipped a finger in his coffee. "I was afraid there would be."

This time he was the one who snapped his translucent fingers, which made coffee fly off his wet finger. When he got the waitress's attention, he pointed down toward his cup, commanding, *refill*. His fingers were freezing. Even in south Florida. It was what he hated most about being undead—the chill, the everlasting chill of the damned grave, like eternal Siberia. It was what he missed the most about blood—his *own* blood, surging, coursing, pumping, pulsing hot corpuscles that had kept his appendages as warm as a human woman's breast, right before she died in his arms.

"We should go," Pasha urged him.

Pasha didn't have the same problem with being cold all the time, which didn't seem fair to Serge since, of the two of them, he thought that Pasha had by far the colder heart.

"You slurped kids years before I did," Serge said, in an aggrieved tone.

"What the hell does that have to do with going?"

"Where?"

"The North Pole."

"Are you nuts? It's *cold* at the North Pole."

"Oh, come on, admit it, you miss the furs we used to wear."

Serge glanced down at his cotton running suit, the warmest he could dress in south Florida without drawing too much attention to himself. He wore long underwear beneath it, where nobody could see. It was true that he did long for the fur-trimmed caps, the ermine capes, the sable robes of his human youth. What a picture they'd made dashing through the snow! How very Dr. Zhivago they'd been. How toasty warm he'd felt under all those layers of thick white wolf fur . . .

"Where would we get the clothes?"

"We'll stop in Lapland."

"How would we find him?"

"We'll follow the red drops on the snow."

Pasha grinned, so that Serge couldn't tell if he meant it.

"Let's go get us some of that endless supply of red juice," Pasha urged his cousin, finally finding an argument that convinced even Serge. Going out for groceries only once a year sounded even easier than chasing overeaters.

THE NORTH POLE

"Africa," Nicholas informed the children, the ones whom human beings thought were elves. "This year we're going to concentrate on Africa. We need to convert more of those heathens into believing in me."

One of the little tykes piped up, "I don't like Africa."

"Of course you don't like it," Nicholas said, heartily. He had to practice "hearty," as it didn't come naturally to his personality, which tended more toward dour and homicidal. He also had to work on "jolly." "Old" was no problem, "fat" could be taken care of with a stuffed costume. He didn't even make a stab at "Saint," of course. Even an imitation of "Saint" was out of the question for him, like turkey and dressing and pumpkin pie with whipped cream. He made an effort to smile at the clutch of pale children sitting on the floor in front of him, but judging from the way they all scooted back, his attempt came out looking more like a maniacal grimace. "You don't like it because of what happened to Donder and Blitzen last year."

The little vampires shuddered.

It took a lot, Nicholas knew, to make a baby vampire shudder.

Thinking about the dead reindeers nearly gave him the creeps, too.

Nearly. Because a tinge of admiration also crept into his feelings.

Disemboweling a reindeer on the run! Now that took real talent. If he weren't so furious at the Wild Dogs of Africa for doing it, he'd have wanted to pat their ugly heads and praise them, "Good doggies, smart doggies!"

"Why can't you just kill them?" a pale tyke demanded.

"Because they're cousins to our friends the werewolves," Nicholas explained with exaggerated cheerfulness, the way he thought kindergarten teachers talked to their charges. "And you know what our friends the werewolves do when they're mad, don't you, boys and girls?"

Again, the baby vampires shuddered.

Baby vampires didn't like to be disemboweled any more than reindeer did.

"But what if they kill Dasher or Prancer?" a pretty little girl asked him.

It wasn't that the wee vampires were concerned about the fate of the animals, Nicholas well knew. They were concerned about their own fates, selfish little bloodsuckers. If he lost too many reindeer, it would take him forever to get home with their treats.

"I won't allow that to happen," he growled.

One brave toddler challenged, "How?"

He didn't yet know, but he wasn't telling them that. He had to figure out a way to destroy the wild dogs without incurring the inconvenient wrath of the werewolves. They weren't numerous in Africa, but all it took was one to spread the word all over the bloody world.

"You let me worry about the reindeer," he warned them, so sternly that they all inched back again. "You just worry about wrapping all those damned gifts."

The baby vampires groaned.

ZIMBABWE, AFRICA

Under the almost-full moon, Ingrid Andersen's long, curly red hair gleamed as if the gods themselves were shining a spotlight on her. If so, they must have had a hard time keeping up with the bouncing spot of red, because it was moving fast in the Land Rover driven by her assistant wildlife biologist, Damian Mansfeld.

"Slow down," Ingrid commanded. Instantly obeying her, he braked, propelling both of their bodies forward until their seat belts stopped them. "There's the park entrance."

He couldn't even see it, but he trusted her to know.

When she said, "Turn. Now," he turned. Now.

She had the slightest hint of an accent that might have come from her native Sweden, though privately Damian thought it was unlike any Scandinavian accent he had ever heard. When he'd asked her about it once, she'd reeled off a slew of Swedish phrases, as if that proved something. Because she was his boss, and because she could stare with yellow eyes that looked as level and challenging as the Serengeti Plain, he didn't ask a second time.

They bounced off the road that went from Bulawayo to Victoria Falls, and bounced onto the dirt road leading into Zimbabwe's Hwange National Park, where many of the world's endangered creatures roamed. Even in the park, the animals weren't safe. They were threatened by each other, the weather, and—the most dangerous predators—poachers and paramilitary thugs who liked to kill elephants for sport and salable body parts.

In the endless dark of the African night, illuminated only by the eerie moon with its flat shadows, Damian worked up the courage to protest, "It's 14,600 square kilometers, Ingrid. How are we going to find them?" He didn't add his most pressing question, as he slammed down on the accelerator again: *And why do we have to do this on Christmas Eve?*

In the uncanny and unnerving way she had of seeming to read his mind, his boss said, "Poachers are coming." And then she added, "I'll find them."

She would, too, Damian believed.

Somehow, through some sixth sense that he'd never witnessed in any other person, Ingrid would lash him on through the dark hours, over the primitive roads, until she located their target: a pack of wild dogs. Damian, who did not believe that all endangered species were created equal, loathed the creatures, as most sensible people did, in his opinion. They were the ugliest animals he'd ever seen. Worse, even, than hyena. They were so ugly they were scary to see. His own small son, upon first seeing one, had screamed and run to hide behind Damian's legs. They had unnaturally long legs, eyes that gleamed red in headlights, hideous coats that looked splattered with brown, black, and tan paint—giving them their other name, the Painted Wolves—and absurdly big ears. They looked as if some mad geneticist had mated a penful of hyenas, rabbits, and soldiers in camouflage gear, and these short-haired, repulsive mammals had emerged to scare the hell out of everybody who had the misfortune to watch them in action.

Ingrid claimed they were loving, social families.

They cared for their young and their wounded and sick, she said.

They let the young eat first after a kill.

The less able among them took on "jobs" like nursing and baby-sitting.

Damian called it running in packs—packs that hunted in moon-light, that brought down antelopes four times their size by disembowel-ing them on the run. They were ruthless hunters. They were also amazing runners, he'd give them that. What he'd also like to give them was the business end of a machine gun. Rat-a-tat-tat. There were maybe only five thousand of them left in the world, and almost all of those were in southern Africa. With only a few machine gun blasts, he could wipe their blight off the earth, and hardly anybody but Ingrid Ander-sen—gorgeous, brilliant, crazy Ingrid—would mourn them. Then they could concentrate on protecting species who deserved saving—the rhi-nos and elephants, the hippos and gorillas, the beautiful and the beloved, instead of the ugly and the reviled.

"Can't you go any faster?" Ingrid screamed above the roar of the motor.

Damian made a show of quickly lifting his right foot and then slam-ming it down again, but his real answer was: no. They couldn't drive any faster without killing themselves, and he was damned if he'd die in pursuit of the Wild Dogs of Africa. Especially not on the night before Christmas. He wanted to get home to watch his children open their gifts from Santa Claus.

THE NORTH POLE

"We have visitors, Nick!"

Santa looked up from his pleasant task of decorating a tree with little glass ornaments filled with sparkling blood. This century's wife, the eternally beautiful Victoria, stood in the doorway looking more excited than mere tree decorations should warrant—which told Nich-olas who his unexpected guests must be.

"Vamps, Vikki? Handsome ones?"

She sidled into the room, her long red velvet gown sweeping the floor.

"Don't touch my ornaments," he snapped, as her right hand sneaked gracefully out of a velvet pocket to do just that. "They aren't snacks."

"I don't want to touch your ornaments," she sniffed, and turned to leave.

"Or theirs, either," he warned her.

"At least you're dressed for it," Nick observed to his two visitors, who were all done up like dead Romanovs. He eyed the one who called himself Serge and whose teeth were chattering so hard that Nick thought it was a wonder he didn't set the glass balls on the tree to clinking. "I hope you won't think me rude, but you don't seem cut out for the job."

"J-j-job?"

"Of being dead."

"H-hate c-cold," Serge admitted.

"Then why are you here, of all places?"

Nick's tone was gracious, or at least he thought it was, his manner was open, and the goblets of crimson that he had offered them were warm enough to remove the chill from a vampire's heart.

The other one, the one called Pasha, spoke for both of them.

"Wanna hep."

His lips were blue and still frosty from being outside. Even after a few sips from the goblet, the blond vampire could barely get his mouth to move enough for him to speak.

"Really," said Nick. "How kind. You want to help how, exactly?"

"Big wor," Pasha mumbled.

"Ah, you're saying it's a great big world, and I must have my hands full trying to get around to every home on just one night."

"Thas w'sayin."

"Yes, well, since you have only my best interests in mind, you'll be glad to hear that I don't actually visit every home on Christmas Eve. I learned long ago that all I have to do is a few of them on any given holiday. The legend spreads from there. Word of mouth, don't you know. Still the best advertising."

He smiled widely, showing incisors so old they were hideously long and yellow.

He suspected these young vampires had never before seen fangs that looked like his, because they had never before met a vampire as old as he. Young vampires thought him doddering in his silly red fat suit—until they saw his yellow fangs.

The chattering one's frosty blue eyes widened.

The other one, who had cast Victoria a smoldering glance when she left the chamber, stepped back.

Apparently they weren't entirely stupid, Nick thought, laying a finger against the side of his nose.

Perhaps he could make use of them.

"So there's no job opportunity for you in that regard," he said with gentle regret on their behalf. "Neither paid, nor volunteer." He paused. Picked at something caught between a fang and a bicuspid, drew it out, and stared at it before flicking it—a bit of flesh?—away. Then he smiled his frighteningly gracious smile at them again. "What *can* you do for me?"

"Pasha," Serge whispered. Sufficient grog had warmed them up enough so that their limbs and lips worked again. "Except for Santa and his wife, there aren't any other grown-up vampires here. It's just those creepy kids. Why are we the only other grown-ups?"

Victoria had shown them the workshops and the dorms, and now she was taking them to the stables. Ahead of them, her red velvet butt swayed enticingly. Pasha was far too distracted to care about Serge's worries. "Because we're the only ones who've ever been smart enough to figure it out," he whispered back.

Victoria turned long enough to flash a toothy smile at him.

All other thoughts melted from Pasha's mind as they followed her into the warmest area in the castle. Serge nearly wept with relief when he felt the heat. But Victoria didn't stop there, to his dismay. She led them through the stable with its huge, empty, immaculate stalls, and back outside again, onto an enormous ice field.

"There they are," she said, and pointed toward the distance.

Her guests huddled together against the frigid wind, and squinted into it.

"Reindeer," Pasha muttered, sounding bored.

Serge said nothing. Opening his mouth to speak made his teeth hurt.

Pasha's boredom didn't last long. Even from so far away, the vampires could detect that there was something about the reindeer that was not like any other animal, not deer, nor elk, nor even moose. And then they found out what it was. At one moment Pasha and Serge were squinting at a herd far out in a frozen pasture, and in the next moment, all of the animals were standing in front of them, terrifyingly large, shaking their antlers, snorting and pawing the ground as if eager to get going.

"My god. Do they really fly?" Pasha asked Victoria.

"They do."

"How?"

"Research and development. Nick has the most incredible R&D department in the world." She giggled. "Literally, in the world. You'll have to meet Rudolph."

"There's really a Rudolph!"

"Oh, yes."

"Does he have a red nose?"

The lowered lashes rose, allowing Pasha to see the deliciously evil glint in her cobalt-blue eyes, and the flirtatiousness in them. "Yes, but Nick is trying to fix that. It was a mistake in the breeding."

"Mistake? But everybody loves Rudolph's red nose!"

"They wouldn't," she purred, "if they knew it came from heavy drinking."

It took a moment, but then Pasha burst out laughing, followed a moment later by frozen Serge, who quickly closed his mouth again for fear his tonsils would freeze.

Blood, she meant.

Rudolph the Red-Nosed Reindeer had a very shiny red nose because he drank blood.

"Are you saying that Rudolph is a vampire reindeer?"

"A prototype," she whispered. "Priceless. Nick's never been able to repeat that one success. Don't mention it to him. It makes him cranky to be reminded of it." She smiled, showing neat pointed incisors. "And we don't want to make Santa Claus cranky, do we, boys?"

"Noooo," agreed Pasha, fervently.

Serge shivered at the thought.

"Come on," Victoria urged them. "I'll show you our private quarters."

"I have just the job for you two," were the first words they heard when they entered the plush red chambers. Nicholas stood in the center of the room, dominating all he surveyed. "How would you like to accompany me on my Christmas Eve travels, as bodyguards?"

"Great!" Pasha forced his gaze toward the husband.

Serge felt such a rush of relief that for a moment he almost thought he was warm. He'd been convinced they were going to die, joining all the other adult vampires who were not there.

"You do know what tonight is?" Nick inquired of them.

Both of the visitors looked confused. There was something about the atmosphere that made people who were not accustomed to it lose all track of space and time.

"It's Christmas Eve," Nick told them, gently. "We leave in an hour."

ZIMBABWE, AFRICA

"Go," Ingrid instructed Damian.

"I can't just leave you out here by yourself!"

He sat behind the wheel of the Land Rover, staring out in disbelief at where she stood alone in the moonlight. There was nothing around them. Nothing visible, that is. He knew—as she must—that the deceptively empty landscape teemed with animals, most of which could kill a human who made such an inviting target.

Ingrid raised her cell phone in one hand and her rifle in the other. "I'm not alone."

"A lot of good those are going to do you against the whole pack of those damned dogs. Not to mention lions, or hyena."

"Go," she repeated, calmly. "Drive to the park station. See if anybody's left us any tips about the poachers. I'll be fine."

"You'll be meat," he said, bitterly.

As Damian peeled furiously away from his lunatic boss, he thought, *And I'll be blamed.*

Ingrid waited in the tall grass, watching the headlights vanish.

That will keep him busy.

Quickly, because the dogs had never before faced a predator as wicked and vindictive as the one they would face tonight, she shed her clothes, including her socks and shoes. Without even pausing to fold them neatly as she usually did, she stuffed them into the knapsack she always kept with her. Tossed in her cell phone. Zipped the bag. Slung it onto her back. Dug a long hole in the dirt with her bare hands and buried the gun there. Sniffed the air, listened to it, tasted it, and then started running. By the time she had gone ten steps, she was racing on all fours, her feet and hands protected by the thick pads that had grown there, her breasts drawn back into her chest, her long red hair turned to thick white fur that streamed behind her as she sped through the night. She had been born a werewolf. Her parents had put her out in the mountains to die. Instead, while she was still fur-covered and smelling of canine, a family of wild dogs had sniffed around her, nudged her up, taken her along with them, nursed her, raised her, even through the transformations, which came unpredictably and frighteningly until she learned conscious control of them.

When she was a child, she had longed to be only wolf.

Now that she was an adult, she still wished her life could be that simple.

Every few kilometers, Ingrid howled, sounding frantic to her own acute hearing, praying there would be no answer.

Finally, off in the distance, a chorus howled back at her.

Oh, my God! I was right! Dammit, dammit!

The dogs were returning to where they had so successfully killed the strange beasts the previous year. They were so smart! Their group brain knew it would be tonight. Knew where to go back to. They must be excited, anticipating another glorious kill unlike any kills they had ever made before, except for last Christmas Eve.

A second kill would never be allowed.

She had to arrive before they did. Their lives depended on it.

I'm coming, I'm coming, my dear ones!

"We thought you meant bodyguard *you*!" Pasha protested.

They had glided to an astonishingly silent and smooth stop on the empty, dusty street of an African village. Once out of the sleigh and on the ground, Nicholas turned with a merry wink and said, "If you let anything happen to any of these reindeer, I will dress you in suits of silver crosses, set you on fire, and dump your ashes in a holy water pool."

"You want us to guard the *reindeer*?" Serge said, dumbfounded.

He was also nauseous, having discovered that moving at supersonic speeds didn't sit well with a stomach full of "Blood, Yugoslavia, Christmas, 1242." Either it hadn't been properly stored, or else it hadn't been a very good year.

Nick laughed at the looks of outraged pride on their faces.

"Fancy yourself too good for this job, eh?"

When neither dared give him a truthful answer—*Yes! Duh!*—he leaned close enough for them to learn that yellowed teeth didn't smell good. "Any one of my reindeer is worth a thousand of your sorry dead carcasses." Then, laying a finger upside of his nose again, he pushed into the front door of the first hut, and said over his shoulder, "Watch out for the wild dogs. They'll disembowel you faster than my sled can fly." And with that he was gone . . . only to pop his head back out again. "You do see the problem, don't you? These huts don't have what you could call a proper roof, so I can't land up there. I have to park in the street. Which leaves my reindeer vulnerable to attack. That's why you're here. It's the only reason you're here. It's the only reason you're still alive. Protect them." He didn't mention they were there to be convenient scapegoats if killing the dogs got any werewolves riled up. "I had nothing to do with it!" he could claim. "It was those damned heartless young ones."

Then he was gone into the hut again.

"Why do I ever listen to you?" Serge wailed.

"Shyut up. At least it's warmer here."

They took up positions at either end of the sleigh with its huge harnessed animals: Serge took the Rudolph end, because the red nose gave off a rosy glow that he could read by—he was on *War and Peace*, in the original Russian, for the eighth time. Pasha hopped up to sit on the back of the sleigh while they waited for Nick to pop in and out of the huts that had put refreshments out for him.

Rudolph heard it first: the howling.

The big beast's ears perked up.

His red nose quivered. He snorted. He stamped the ground. Behind him, the other reindeer moved restlessly in their bridles and harnesses.

Serge stepped back and called quietly to his cousin, "What in the name of all that's holy was *that*?"

She was triangulating: her howl, their howls and barking, and the village where she knew it was all converging. If she hadn't been so frightened for them, she'd have been excited beyond words. *Beyond words.* That had been her life with them. Feeling loved, taken care of, taught, trained, encouraged, protected . . . and then nudged out on her own. She had to leave, because she was a female. In a wild dog family, only the dominant pair mated—the Alpha male and Alpha female—so the other females had to go off in search of their own new band, which would be made up of brothers who had broken away from a different parent pack.

That wasn't possible for her, of course.

She wasn't dog, she wasn't wolf, she wasn't human.

She was mutant, hybrid, half-breed, monster.

She'd been unbearably lonely without them.

Slowly, over the years, she'd grown accustomed to living as a human who rarely shape-shifted, and then only to protect the endangered. Now *they* were endangered. *Beyond words.* That was also why she couldn't have warned them ahead of time. In their brains, there was memory and there was *now*, but there was no future. There was no way for her to say, *Don't go there.*

North of the village the dogs came . . . running, running, howling . . .

Close enough to see their quarry—the huge succulent beasts so conveniently tethered and tied down—the dogs slowed, scattered, circling the village, surrounding it, crouching low as they secured their positions, hair rising on their necks, primed for attack, listening for signals, for danger, for the moment when they would all rush forward . . .

Silently, they moved, and then, muscles bunched, they waited until . . .

As one, as if the pack were one body with one brain, the dogs attacked from every direction, muzzles back, teeth bared, lunging toward their kill.

The reindeer, restrained by forces stronger than leather, shuddered in their halters and yokes, but they were not helpless. They were enormous, with murderous hooves and teeth, and jaws that could grab a dog and crack its head even as it was flung to the side. Between them and the dogs, on either side, Pasha and Serge were the ones who looked helpless, until their eyes glittered and their teeth showed. They, too, could grab and tear; they, too, had superhuman strength beyond anything the wild dogs possessed, the two vampires making up in strength and viciousness what they lacked in numbers.

The townspeople slumbered under the spell of Christmas Eve.

"No!" Ingrid cried, as she raced toward the village.

Massacre seemed laid out in front of her. Her family wouldn't stand a chance, mere natural predators against unnatural ones. Long, thick white wolf fur streaming behind her, she thundered into the midst of them, snarling, growling, pushing her own family out of the way so she could protect them from this force they could never understand.

She hurled herself toward the vampires at the heart of the fight.

Blood and fur flew all around her.

There were cries of pain, roars of fury.

And then a space cleared, and two bloodied but unbeaten vampires stared at this new attacker who was like none of the pack they had seen yet.

"What the . . ." exclaimed Pasha.

"Werewolf!" screamed Serge.

She pulled back into her haunches, primed herself to launch at them, pushed off with her great strength, and was airborne when the door of the nearest village hut flew open and the Old One stepped outside. He yelled at Serge and Pasha in a voice that quaked the ground around them, "Forget the dogs, you idiots! Don't let the werewolf get Rudolph!"

Ingrid shape-shifted while in mid-lunge.

Before their eyes, the white wolf changed into a nude and shapely young woman with red hair instead of white fur. The shift altered her speed, allowing her to hit the ground with her bare feet, right in front of the astonished vampires. As they lunged toward her throat, she crouched to pick up her knapsack that had fallen. With it in hand, she shoved between them, and then ran alongside the reindeer before the vampires could recover in time to keep her from going where she was aiming. The Unsaint figured it out first and screamed at Pasha and Serge to catch her, but they were all too late. Ingrid grabbed the reindeer halter she was seeking and with one great burst of strictly human power hauled herself up and astride of . . . Rudolph.

"Get *off* of him!" she heard the Old One yell.

Her answer was to pull her silver hunting dagger from her knapsack and to point it toward the jugular vein in the reindeer's neck. Rudolph, raised with vampires, barely registered the light weight of the woman on his back, and merely shook his reins a bit. Ingrid did not know why her foe was so determined to protect this particular reindeer out of all of them; she just knew that whatever the reason, it might be the leverage to rescue her family from him.

Her family!

The dogs had pulled back, at first frightened by the huge new fighter who had appeared, and then nearly hysterical with excitement as they recognized her. Out of respect for her greater size and power, all of them, including the female and male heads of the family, remained standing where they were, waiting, allowing her to take the lead. Their wounded crawled toward them, bleeding into the dust, whining with the pain of their terrible injuries.

A silence descended on the strange scene.

The Old Vampire didn't move from where he stood near the sleigh, but just quietly asked her in his deep voice, "How did you know?"

He sounded genuinely curious.

He also sounded as if he were humoring her, trying to calm her down so that she wouldn't use her knife.

"Dead reindeer," Ingrid said, wryly, from high on Rudolph's back, "don't show up in Africa all that often, Santa Claus." She pronounced his name with scathing sarcasm. "And reindeer this size don't show up anywhere unless they're supernatural. Besides, I'd always suspected—"

"Don't tell me. Because I work nights and live forever?"

"That, and your red suit." Ingrid pointed to it with her knife, then quickly pointed back at Rudolph. "That was a stroke of genius."

The Old One smiled, a facial change that made the dogs quiver with the desire to lunge and kill. Ingrid looked into the eyes of the dominant male dog and then the dominant female dog to tell them to control their pack.

They understood her.

Young dogs who needed nipping got nipped.

Nobody charged anybody. They stood in a standoff while young werewolf and ancient vampire confronted each other. Slowly, he took a few steps toward her. Careful steps, barely perceptible steps that a human with normal senses and eyesight might not have noticed.

"Yes, I thought it was inspired," Nicholas agreed, with no modesty.

"But why the white beard and white trim?"

He sighed. "I know. So stupid. Easy to hide blood on red, impossible to hide—much less get *out*!—on white. It was all red to start with. My hair, my beard, the fur trim. All red. Then the damned illustrators got hold of the legend, and turned me into a fat, ermine-trimmed fop."

Ingrid straightened her posture, and looked at him: yellow wolf eyes staring their challenge into old, cold vampire eyes.

"I'm not going to let you kill my family," she said.

"Your family?" He laughed, sounding nothing like the merry old elf of lore. Like her, he was suddenly alert, all banter gone. "So that's it. So that's why you defend them like this. You warm-blooded monsters! You should take a hint from those of us with nothing left to lose."

"Except—"

"My life?" He laughed again. "You think I'd be sorry to lose that?"

"No." She pricked the reindeer's neck, enough to draw blood, and yet no blood ran from him. At the prick, the beast flicked his monstrous head back toward her, displaying a gleam of a tooth like a rapier. Suddenly, at the sight of it, and no sight of blood from the wound, Ingrid understood the importance of this animal. "Not *your* life."

"No!" Nicholas roared. "Not Rudolph!"

"You fly away," Ingrid threatened him, "or I kill him."

"I've spent a bloody fortune on that reindeer!" And then his eyes turned crafty. Proudly, he thumped his red and white furry chest. "You can't kill him. You don't have any holy water or a wooden stake or a silver bullet."

Ingrid slid down off the opposite side of Rudolph and came up under his massive chest. With her hand that didn't hold her knife, she felt the sleek hide, gauging where a dead reindeer's heart must be. She peered out from underneath, at Nicholas. "Ah, but I have a dagger made *out* of silver bullets."

"No!" The old vampire's cry seemed truly anguished, but then his eyes turned sly again. "Even that won't do you any good. I can't leave without Rudolph. He guides my sleigh tonight."

"You have plenty of horsepower without him."

She moved the silver dagger closer to the reindeer's chest.

"All right, all right, but I want him back!"

"I'll let him go when I know you're far enough away."

"And how will you know that, little werewolf?"

In a mocking voice, Ingrid sang, "Jingle bells, jingle bells, jingle all the way . . ."

* * *

"He left us!" Pasha cried, in astonishment, as they watched the sleigh fly off.

Briefly, the whole sleigh—minus its lead reindeer—was silhouetted against the full moon. And then it disappeared into the Milky Way.

"He left us in Africa!" Serge screamed, and then he started stamping his own feet, just as the remaining reindeer had done before taking off. "What are we supposed to do in *Africa*?"

"You can be useful," Ingrid told them.

She slid down off Rudolph and gave him a mighty slap on his rump.

The great beast started running down the dirt road, and in only a few yards, he was airborne.

"Useful?" Pasha said it as if it were a bad taste in his mouth.

"Come on, boys," she encouraged them, as she donned her clothing again. "Someday, you'll thank me."

Before she showed them the better way, she got down on her haunches to say both hello and goodbye to her family. There was whimpering on both sides, from her and from them. There were licks and nuzzles, sniffing and pawing, but none of them lingered, not Ingrid, and not the dogs. For her, it was too painful to go through a farewell a second time. For them, there was hunting to do, to compensate for the loss of the splendid feast they had missed.

When she rose to her feet, Ingrid slapped off the dust.

She didn't glance behind her to see the dogs go, but she could hear them, could feel the pounding they made on the earth. If she looked, she thought her heart might break again.

"Follow me." She started to walk but then stopped. "No, on second thought, I'll follow you. Go that way."

When they got back to where her gun was buried, she used her cell phone to call her assistant. "Damian. Yes, I'm fine. No, I didn't locate them. What do you know about the poachers?" She listened for a few moments, then said, "Come get me."

Under the full moon, she pointed the vampire cousins toward the south.

"Keep walking. In about twenty-five miles, you'll come upon a band of soldiers. Paramilitary. They're awful people. They force young boys to join them. They rape women, cut off limbs, kill everything in their path. Last month, they murdered a lowland gorilla. They're all yours, boys."

"Twenty-five myiles?" Pasha whined.

"To a smorgasbyord," Ingrid reminded him, with a wicked smile.

When she could barely see the vampires in the distance, her assistant screeched to an angry stop beside her. Ingrid opened the door of the jeep, climbed in. Her face still held a remnant of the smile she had given the vampires. When her assistant got a glimpse of it, he caught his breath. Her face reminded him of how wolves looked after they had triumphed in a hunt and kill.

Damian, having nursed grievances all night and having intended to complain about them, felt the hairs rise on the backs of his arms. Instead of speaking, he shut his mouth, and drove home.

"Let's be Santa Helpers," Serge mocked bitterly as they trudged in the darkness. "Let's go join up with dear old Santa Claus and get ourselves a lifetime's supply of blood bank."

"Okay, so maybe my plan didn't work out perfectly."

"Perfectly! How about not at all?! How about nearly getting us killed by wild dogs and a werewolf, not to mention the world's oldest vampire?"

Their supernatural vision picked out a campfire in the distance.

"I think," Pasha said, soothingly, "that this night is not over yet."

"It better not be. I'm starved." As the cousins started to run, covering yards where humans could have covered only inches, Serge turned his pale, handsome, hungry face toward Pasha and yelled into the African night, "And don't you *ever* try to talk to me about the Easter Bunny!"

At the campfire, hearing something strange, men reached for guns that were not armed with silver bullets.

Rogue Elements

Karen Chance

Karen Chance grew up in Orlando, Florida, the home of make-believe, which probably explains a lot. She has since resided in France, Great Britain, Hong Kong, and New Orleans, mostly goofing off but occasionally teaching history. She is currently back in Florida, courtesy of Katrina, where she writes full-time in between dodging hurricanes (and occasionally drinking a few). Her USA Today *and* New York Times *bestselling Cassandra Palmer series has recently spawned a spinoff,* Midnight's Daughter, *following the adventures of dhampir Dorina Basarab.*

"There's no such thing as a half werewolf," I said, trying not to growl. I'd been dreading this conversation for six months. It figured my boss would wait until now to bring it up. Way to ruin my Christmas Eve.

Gil looked at me impatiently, his bald head reflecting the office fluorescents. The same shiny dome and lack of humor could be seen in the painting behind him: Reginald Saunders, the newly elected leader of the Silver Circle of light magic users. He was the magical community's version of a president, only without the pesky term limits. Gil was his older brother, and head of the Vegas branch of the War Mage Corps, the Circle's version of a police force. It was my luck to get transferred from a nice, nondescript department in Jersey to one where any screwup would be all too obvious.

"Your mother was a Were, Lia. House Lobizón."

"Clan Lobizón. And my mother was a *human* with a *disease*." God, I got tired of trying to get that simple idea through thick skulls. "Lycanthropy isn't a genetic trait, like eye color. It isn't passed on to children—"

"Except when it is." Gil regarded me narrowly, as if expecting claws to show themselves at any second.

It was the usual reaction. Dad was a de Croissets, from an old magical family with a tradition of service in the Corps. To counteract my human surname, my mother called me Accalia, meaning she-wolf in Latin. The combination was enough to get me a double take anywhere in the magical world.

"I'm a war mage, Gil," I said after a pause. My therapist had suggested deep breathing for my occasional anger management issues. So far, I hadn't seen a lot of improvement. Of course, working with Gil probably had something to do with that. "How many Weres do you know with magical ability?"

"None. But I know it has happened. They don't die after being bitten, like vamps, and therefore don't lose their magic." He gave me a not-so-nice grin. "I looked it up."

"I'm not a Were!"

"My point is that your connection to those . . . people . . . makes you perfect for this job."

His tone made it clear that for "people" he'd just as soon have substituted "animals." I seriously considered turning and walking out of the office. One reason I didn't was the certainty that another incident of "insubordination," as my superiors called anything other than unquestioning obedience, and I was out the door permanently. A second was the photograph of the girl staring up at me from the corner of his desk.

She was a pretty sixteen-year-old with china-pale skin and natural honey-blond hair. Her eyes—blue according to her file—were hidden behind Gucci shades, and her five-two frame was draped across the front of this year's trendy sports car. She didn't look like a typical runaway.

Of course, she didn't look like a werewolf, either.

"Daniela Arnou is the fifth Were girl to go missing on my watch in the last six months," Gil informed me, his complexion darkening to pre-heart-attack level. "The Weres never ask us for help, but they have this time. And the Circle is leaning on me to show results."

"The ransom demands should tell you something."

"There haven't been any ransom demands. Not for any of them."

"But . . . why take them, then? Attacking high clan members is tantamount to suicide. Even if they were returned unharmed, the insult would require blood. Why take that risk without a big reward?"

"There you go." Gil looked like he'd scored a point. "This is exactly what I'm talking about. You immediately guessed their status."

"Rank," I corrected, "and it wasn't hard. Arnou is currently the leading clan. It doesn't change the fact that I'm not the person you—"

His palm hit the top of his desk, cutting me off. "Do you have any idea what kind of flack I'm getting over this?"

Yeah, and that's the main concern here, I didn't say. It didn't take much to set Gil off. Usually, just my presence was enough. I look more like a Were in human form than do many of the real thing, or, to be more precise, I look like the stereotype: tall, with dark hair and gray eyes. Gil's prejudice against Weres was outweighed only by his dislike for women in the Corps. He'd hated me on sight. Of course, my service record hadn't helped. I really didn't want to remind him about certain all-too-recent issues, but I had to get him to see reason.

"Trust me. You do *not* want me on this case."

"I don't want you on any case!" he said tetchily. "But I don't have anybody else. No one knows the Weres like you do."

I gave up on subtlety, never my strong suit anyway. "Did you *read* my file?" I asked incredulously. The Circle might not know everything about my background, but they knew one thing for certain: no clan wolf was going to tell me a damn thing.

Lycanthropy is rarely contracted in the womb, and when it is, the child usually doesn't live. Most clan children are infected by their parents at age five or six, when their systems are strong enough to handle the change. But despite being from one of the higher clans, where respect for tradition was practically a religion, my mother had refused. The clan leaders assumed it was due to her husband's influence, and pointed out that I wouldn't be properly socialized if she didn't give in. That I would always be an outsider, always different.

She never told them that I already was.

I was born with Neuri Syndrome. It's named after an ancient Russian tribe said to have been able to change themselves into wolves. That's ironic, considering that changing is the one thing carriers of

Neuri can never do. It occurs occasionally when the mother is Were and the father is not, which is why female Weres are strongly discouraged from marrying outside the clan. Essentially, it is a milder version of lycanthropy, one that prevents the carrier from getting the full-blown disease.

Neuri is a major cause of concern for the clans. The higher clans usually intermarry among themselves, preferring to add to their numbers by reproduction than to "turn" humans, who understand nothing of the culture or hierarchy. But the lower orders aren't so picky, especially after a war or feud leaves their numbers depleted. If Neuri were to get into the mainstream population, it would render human recruitment increasingly difficult, as more and more people became immune. For that reason, tradition decreed that babies born with the "aberration" be killed at birth.

For a long time, my mother's status had been enough to protect me. There weren't many ahead of her in clan rank and thereby able to challenge her decision, and those who were chose not to do so out of respect or friendship. But two years ago, the old *bardulf*, the clan chief, died and his successor decided to push the issue. Mother managed to avoid a summons to court, and thereby a new ruling, by pleading illness. Unfortunately, it wasn't faked.

She was diagnosed with pancreatic cancer shortly after my twenty-third birthday. Long after the treatments failed, long after there was no hope left, she nonetheless went through every painful procedure, just to wring out a few more months, weeks, even days. Because every minute she lived was a minute that the clan couldn't touch me. A minute closer to twenty-five, the age of majority under Were custom, at which time I could formally declare my emancipation from the clan.

She missed it by less than a week. Two days after she died, I was attacked by eight clan members determined to bring Larentia Lobizón's only child into the fold before time ran out, whether I liked it or not. They forgot one little detail: I was Guillame de Croissets' daughter, too, and a war mage in my own right. Not to mention that, while Father is retired, he's far from helpless. Both of us were half crazy with grief at the time of the attack, which hadn't even waited for the funeral. The result was a bloodbath spread across three blocks, resulting in six dead Weres, two fires, over five million dollars in property damage, and headlines in all the local papers.

The Circle covered it up as a gang war, but I received a black mark on my record for letting the fight become public as well as a quick transfer. The result where the clan was concerned was still to be determined. I somehow doubted I was going to like the outcome.

Gil was looking at me expectantly, like I was supposed to spill my guts and give him all the sordid little details, as if there weren't enough already in my file. The only thing the Circle didn't know was why I'd been attacked. Thanks to Dad's quick thinking and the clan's refusal to discuss their business with outsiders, most people thought it was the result of some old family feud. And it was going to stay that way.

"Why are you expected to do anything? Sir," I added belatedly, in response to his scowl. "The Weres usually handle this sort of thing themselves."

"That's what I said when their council threw this mess in my lap, thereby buying myself a royal ass-chewing." He tapped the glossy photo. "And I mean that literally. This one happens to be the daughter of the king."

"There's no such thing. The leading clans do elect a *bardric*, an overall chief, in times of crisis, but Sebastian has to lead through consensus. It's not the same as—"

"I don't care what you people call it," Gil broke in irritably.

"There is no 'you people'! I am *not* a Were!"

"You're not going to be a war mage, either, if you don't find that little bitch," he said, shoving the file into my hands. "Now get out of here."

Two hours later, I was standing outside the velvet ropes cordoning off the high roller table at a local casino. Despite the stakes, the game was pretty boring, mainly because it was so one-sided. Not surprisingly, considering that one of the players was cheating like mad.

I'd been watching him for almost an hour, and I had to admit he was good. If I hadn't known what to look for, I might have missed it. It was a small thing, just the slight twitch and flare of a nostril. It could have been a nervous habit or a tell, only this guy was too good to have either. And there was the fact that it happened every time someone made a bet.

"I raise." The skinny blond kid at the end of the table, who looked really out of place in this gimlet-eyed group, threw in a handful of thousand-dollar chips. I guess he was too young to have heard the old saying: If you're at the table more than a few minutes and you can't identify the sucker, you *are* the sucker.

The brunet settled back in his seat, eyelids drooping over whiskey-colored eyes, handsome face as pleasantly blank as it had been all night. It went with the rest of the package: a well-muscled body done up in good-old-boy denim, cowboy boots, and a sleepy expression. Almost as if playing for a pot that rivaled my yearly salary bored him. He threw in a sizable chunk of his chips. "Call."

The blond's confident expression faltered as he turned over his hand: three jacks. It was good, but not great—not with a pot like that. He'd been bluffing, and I had a feeling his opponent knew it. The brunet let the tension draw out for a few long seconds, then casually flipped over a full house. "Better luck next time, kid," he said. It didn't sound much like he meant it.

He cashed out, probably afraid that winning any more would put his name on the casino's suspect list, and headed out the front door. I let him get a small head start, then followed. I needed help to crack this case, and odd as it seemed, he was my best chance to get it.

Fremont Street is where the locals go to drink and gamble, in that order. But despite living in Vegas for six months, I'd never been among them. There was too much temptation to do a spell to skew the odds in my favor, and thereby violate the ban on magical interference in human games of chance. Rigging the games risked letting the human authorities, who monitored them closer than terrorism, discover the existence of the supernatural community. As a result, it was a serious no-no. The kind that carried a possible death penalty.

It was the coercive potential of that little fact that had me following a werewolf through the holiday crowds, while huge, goggle-eyed faces stared down at us like neon gods from the psychedelic arch overhead. Despite everything, he'd never lost the loose-hipped saunter of the upper clans, the one that said the whole world was there for him to walk on. The stride looked casual, but it ate up a lot of ground. I lost him in the crowd around an aging busker belting out "Silver Bells" from the bed of a rusty pickup.

I dodged the cops converging on the illegally parked vehicle and stared around, grimacing. My quarry was nowhere in sight, meaning he'd probably ducked into one of the clubs. But which one? The buxom redheads or the fetish-clad blondes? I mentally flipped a coin and decided on the blondes. A pert version with black eyebrows and a twenties-era bob gave me an odd look, but let me in.

The lights were down in preparation for the next act, and there was enough smoke in the air to count as a screen, but I thought I saw him lolling at the bar. I was sure of it when he suddenly stood up as I approached, the scowl on his face visible even in the bad light. I decided not to take chances. The guy could move like quicksilver; it had been hard enough tailing him when he wasn't trying to evade me.

He slowly sat back down, eyeing his left hand, which was glued to the bar top by the remains of his whiskey glass. It had been a thick, substantial piece that made a nice puddle when it liquefied and then grew solid again almost immediately, serving as a makeshift handcuff. Along with his fingers, the spell had trapped a little Santa-on-a-stick that had decorated the now evaporated booze. It grinned cheerfully out at the world, like a bug caught in amber.

"Hello, Cyrus." I appropriated an empty stool on his right. "Miss me?"

"You owe me a drink," he said, trying to flex his fingers and failing. "I'll tell my lawyers to add it to the bill when I sue you for assault."

"Two bourbons, straight up." I slid a twenty over the sticky counter to the bartender, who thanks to the dim light, had yet to notice the mess. "It's on me. You'll need your money for bail."

Cyrus slammed his free hand down, shattering the glass and making several nearby patrons jump. He began digging chunks out of his palm. "I'm being arrested? On what charge?"

"You're a lone wolf, without clan protection. Do I need one?"

"The last time I checked, yes!"

"Hmm." I sucked on a pretzel while the bartender poured our drinks. "Then I guess I'll have to go with endangering the Secrecy Act."

"I don't know what you're—"

"Your little gambling problem?"

There was a slight pause. "It's only a problem when I'm losing."

"Or cheating. By the way, how'd you do it? Can you tell how much a person is sweating? Or does their scent change when they're bluffing?"

"If you don't know, you can't prove a damn thing," he said firmly, abruptly standing up. "I've had a wonderful evening, Lia. Too bad this wasn't it."

"If you're going to quote Groucho, at least get him right. And lone wolf, remember?" Where he was concerned, I wouldn't need much proof. What little I did, his unusual lucky streak would provide.

Cyrus' eyes were glittering, but his voice stayed level. "If you were at the game, why not arrest me there?"

"Too many norms."

"And there aren't any here?"

I glanced about the murky room. "I think we're safe," I said wryly, "unless you plan to make a—"

I turned back around to find my quarry gone and the bartender peering at the mess on the bar with a puzzled frown. I threw another twenty on the counter and headed for the back door. It led into a side street, where Cyrus was already disappearing around a corner. Damn it!

I sent a doppelgänger spell after him, hoping the low light would make the misty double believable, and headed around the opposite corner to cut him off. And found myself slammed against a hard concrete wall for my trouble. "Nice try," Cyrus breathed, "but you forget your roots. Spells don't have a scent, Lia."

Having Cyrus' full attention was like being the only rabbit in the world in front of a pack of starving wolves. If I hadn't had the wall behind me, I might even have taken a step back. Only Weres ever did this, walked right past arm's length and set up camp inches away from my chest. I'd never gotten used to it, and it didn't help that his knuckles were pressing against my throat.

But showing fear is the absolute worst way to negotiate with a Were. And since he hadn't yet snapped my neck, that's exactly what we were doing. "Would you cut it out? I'm not really planning to arrest you!"

"Why not?" The darkness had made his eyes liquid black, but I could still see the suspicion in them. "Surely not some leftover senti-ment?"

"I have to find some missing girls," I said curtly. "And I'm new here. I don't have the contacts I did back East—"

"And you think I do?"

"You always have contacts. If you help me, I'll forget what I saw tonight."

Violet-blue light filtered down from a neon sign, bathing him in strange shadows. It leeched away the good-old-boy vibe, leaving the harsh planes of his face clearly visible. For a moment, I almost thought I could see the wolf staring out at me. "And if I say no?"

I flexed my shields a little, slamming him back into a nearby Dump-ster. I wasn't the only one who'd forgotten who he was dealing with. "You haven't heard what I want yet. You might even like it."

Cyrus pried himself loose from the Dumpster's metal embrace. "If you're involved, I doubt it."

"Even if it could put you back in the king's good graces?"

He scowled as I stepped out into the street to hail a cab. "What king?"

"My boss is convinced that Sebastian is the werewolf king."

"You know damn well—"

"Yeah, but I kind of like it. I think I'll call him 'your majesty' if we ever meet. See how well that goes over."

"I can already tell you that," he said dryly. "And what, pray tell, is a lowly grifter and a disgraced war mage supposed to do for the almighty Sebastian?"

We got in the cab and I tossed the file onto his lap. "Save his daughter."

* * *

"You don't get it! If I don't find these girls, they could end up dead!"

We were back at his place, a seedy motel room considerably off the Strip, with the buzz of traffic clearly audible from outside. It mingled with the sound of the ice machine at the end of the hall, a couple of parents screaming at their kids, and a guy with a four-pack-a-day habit coughing up his lungs somewhere nearby. Merry Christmas.

Cyrus flipped on the TV and turned it loud enough to drown out our conversation, at least to human ears. "And if you do find them, you could. This smells bad, Lia."

"So do the Corps' prisons."

"You talk like a war mage."

"I am a war mage."

"No, the Corps is your job. I'm talking about what you *are*."

"Don't start this again, Cyrus."

He remained lounging in a threadbare recliner someone had squashed into the narrow space beside the bed. He'd taken off the garbage-stained shirt, and his white undershirt straps were bright against his suntanned skin, his dark hair just a little long and curling over the back of his neck. The flickering light from the TV gilded his lashes and highlighted a few places where he'd done a less than perfect job shaving. He was the image of a weary vacationer, tapped out, irritated, and ready to go home, except for his eyes, which didn't match.

"You want this job because it makes you feel human. You surround yourself with them, all day, every day. You bathe in their scent, thin though it is, and tell yourself that they're your true clan. That lycanthropy is only a disease—"

"Because it is!"

Cyrus smiled grimly. "Being Were has never been about genes; it's not even about the change. It's about being proud of what we are and what we stand for, the old ways, the honorable ways, in a world that no longer understands what that word means."

"This from a card cheat."

"You refuse to see what is obvious to everyone else. You're Were, like it or not. And you always will be." He lit up a cigar as he spoke, cupping the end in his big hands, flicking the lighter closed with a practiced flip of the wrist. It was the casual action that got me, the attitude of someone higher in clan status condescending to explain the obvious to an inferior. It was doubly maddening since no clan would have touched either of us.

I decided not to let him, or my temper, get me off point. "Are you going to help or not?"

He blew smoke in my direction. "I've done what I could. If it's not enough to make you reconsider, I don't know what will."

Cyrus had confirmed what I'd already suspected: not one, not two or even three, but all five of the missing girls were high clan—from Leidolf, Maccon, Tamaska, and Rand, as well as Daniela from Arnou. That much had been obvious from their names, but the file hadn't included the small matter of them all being the daughters of clan leaders. Somebody had a serious death wish.

"I need a name, a place, a *starting point*," I told him impatiently. "Not reasons to quit."

He just looked at me, implacability clear on that strong face. It made me want to scream, even though I'd known this wasn't going to be easy. Unlike me, Cyrus had been clan once. His wolf form had the distinctive black and tan markings of the Arnou itself. Moreover, he had the rare distinction of having been born wolf, which added a cache at any level. He'd had every advantage: marriage into the highest clans, guaranteed wealth from their investments, power, prestige, and the knowledge that if he got into trouble, the family would back him to the last.

Unless, as it turned out, he got into trouble with them.

I'd never found out what he'd done to be named *vargulf*, the Were equivalent of blacklisted. It must have been something pretty bad, as it's considered a fate worse than death. All the privileges of rank were forfeited, including clan protection. It wasn't quite the same as hanging a target on his back, but it was close. Anyone who had a grievance against him, including anyone jealous of the position he'd once held, was free to kill him without fear of clan retribution. He had no reason to do Arnou any favors.

"I thought you said that being Were is all about honor," I said a little desperately. Because I could haul him off to jail—maybe—but I couldn't force him to help me. "Was that more talk? Or did you mean it? Because if you meant it, I don't see how you can stand by while a girl of your own clan—"

"Ex-clan. And I didn't say I was going to stand by. I said you were better off out of it."

"Meaning what?"

"That whoever did this managed to overcome, not only the girls themselves, but their bodyguards. *Were* bodyguards," he said for emphasis, as if I'd thought they'd be something else. "Your superiors must really want to get rid of you, to send you on such an errand."

"The Corps is a little busy lately," I said dryly. There had always been animosity between the Silver Circle and its Black counterpart, a bunch of dark magic users with no scruples and less conscience, but it had recently erupted into full-scale war. This left the Corps seriously stretched for help and probably explained why they had yet to toss me out on my ear. "And no one else knows much about Weres."

"No one else has had a vendetta declared against them, either. Lobizón blames you for the deaths of their wolves."

"I know." It was old news, the proclamation being issued the day after the battle as custom required, "before the blood of the dead grew cold." It wasn't the vendetta itself that worried me, though. The clan had already seen what two mages could do; I doubted they wanted to be facing a whole cadre of us. What was keeping me up nights was the thought of what would happen if word leaked back to my superiors. If they discovered that I'd been marked for death by an important member of their vital new alliance, I'd be out the door in about a nanosecond. And that would leave Dad and me facing, not a handful of Weres, but the whole clan.

On our own.

I'd lived with what had felt like a hand clenched around my neck for seven months, knowing that it was only the Were dislike for speaking about clan business with outsiders that was saving me. Ironically, Lobizón's respect for tradition was currently my best defense. But it was anyone's guess how long it would hold.

"Lobizón isn't involved in this," I said, trying to sound as if the vendetta was no big deal. "And I intend to stay as far away from them as possible."

"That would be a good trick."

Something in Cyrus' tone worried me. "Why?"

"Because they're currently in town for the *Ulfhring*," he informed me quietly. "I thought you knew. It begins tomorrow."

"They're holding it *here*?" The clan leaders usually assembled in upstate New York for their yearly meeting, in Arnou's home territory. "Why the change?"

"The new alliance. They want to show solidarity with the mages, and they're based here. Every senior clan leader is either already in Vegas or will be soon, along with his or her entourage. You need to lay low until they leave, not go prying into their business."

"It's not prying if we were invited," I pointed out absently. No wonder Gil was nervous. All the clans with missing daughters were in town and were planning to chew his ass out. Possibly literally, if he didn't turn up something soon.

"You can try that argument on the families of the Weres you killed," Cyrus said quietly. "But I wouldn't give good odds on your success."

"You can't expect me to just sit around. The *Ulfhring* can drag on for days!"

"Then let your partner check things out for you."

"I don't have a partner."

Cyrus placed his cigar in an ashtray, then before I could blink, he'd crossed the room and invaded my personal space. "What happened, Lia? Did no one want to work with someone who smelled a little too much like clan?"

"I just transferred here."

"You've been here six months." It looked as if I wasn't the only one keeping tabs.

"I told you, we're shorthanded—"

Cyrus interrupted me by taking a deep breath right beside my ear. "I've met half-Weres before and they smell human. Just human. They don't smell familiar, like family, like *home*. Why do you?"

Before I could answer, his mouth came down on mine, warm with brandy and rich, sweet smoke, his hands sliding down to my hips, and for a moment, it was as perfect as if we'd never been apart. As if he'd spent the last six months mapping out my body every night. I'd never wanted anyone else like this, not even close.

It had been the original Bad Idea. I'd known it when I met him, known it when I kept going back, again and again, for glimpses into the Were world, for help with cases I couldn't crack, for that intoxicating sense of belonging I got every time we were together. Known it when I seduced him for the first time.

I'd agonized over it for weeks, never having been with a Were, knowing damn well I shouldn't be with this one, not even sure how to go about it as Were seduction techniques weren't something I wanted to ask Mom about. In the end, the answer was simple: Just kiss him and strip him and let him take me to bed. Sleep beside him afterward, my face tight against his neck, the wild, unmistakable scent of clan engulfing me. Kiss his temple in the morning before getting up and steal his last doughnut on the way out the door.

It would have been a great recipe, except that I was a war mage and he was someone who took the law as a not-very-serious suggestion. Eventually, after my life imploded, I'd done the right thing and walked away. Because Cyrus on the side of law and order wasn't happening, and I didn't want to have to put my boyfriend away someday. Because it was already so hard to leave that it scared me. Because Cyrus had taught me that it was possible to never stop being friends and yet to end up enemies. And that walking away is sometimes the only way to stay sane.

"Anyone else would have been paired up almost immediately," he murmured. "Why risk your life for the Corps? They don't care if you live or die."

"And you do?"

"Strangely enough, yes. Which is why you're staying here."

"I'm a *war mage*, Cyrus. I don't need protection!"

"You do from Lobizón. If they kill you in some back alley, with no witnesses, they can deny it to the Corps. In the current situation, they'd probably get away with it. Not to mention that you're a young woman who smells like clan: exactly the type going missing lately."

"And you're a Were. Just like those bodyguards that were killed!"

"Yes, except the only person I'm going to have to look out for is me."

"You need me. If Were resources were enough to deal with this, they never would have called us in!"

"I'll manage."

"I'm not staying here," I said flatly. And, fortunately, there was no way he could make me.

"You are if you want my help." Except that one.

I'd seen his mouth set in that hard, tight line before, and decided not to waste more time arguing. "When will you be back?"

"That depends on how forthcoming my sources are." Cyrus put a hand around the back of my head and rubbed his thumb along the side of my neck. "Don't do anything stupid while I'm gone. And keep your head down."

I waited until his footsteps had vanished. Then I waited some more, because there was a good chance that he was hanging around the parking lot to see if I'd follow. I switched channels to a Christmas special coming from somewhere with actual snow.

After sitting through two musical numbers, including a dog that barked "Jingle Bells" and an appropriately timed antacid commercial, I decided it had been long enough. A full moon illuminated the parking lot, but there weren't any wolves prowling around. Of course, there wouldn't have been even if Cyrus had still been there. The old stories are a myth, based on the writings of one screwy medieval monk: Weres can change at will. It's one of the things that makes them so deadly.

I caught a cab back to Fremont, where my Christmas present to myself was safe in valet parking. Fortunately, old habits die hard and I'd tagged Cyrus at the motel. The little spell caused me to turn my beat-up

Honda motorcycle, brand-new in 1983, in the direction of its faint tug from the East.

Tracking spells are useful but they only do so much. They usually get me to the right general area, but don't tell me exactly where a person is. But I didn't have a long search that time, because that road only led one place.

"Strictly Pleasure, where we're strictest about ensuring *your* pleasure. What fantasy can we help you fulfill tonight?"

The woman who answered the door of the plain brick structure was young, Asian, and extremely pretty. Or, at least, I assumed she was. The silk-clad body had elegant curves and the dark hair was long and sleek. But the face was covered in enough makeup to make a geisha jealous.

"I'd like a Were. Female," I said tersely.

"Of course." She waved me into a vestibule with an adjacent small office. "Would you like a dom or a sub this evening?" I just looked at her. "That would be a sub, then. Do you have a preference as to species?"

"Wolf."

"I'm sorry. We're a little short on those lately. Will a wererat work for you? They're very sturdy—can take almost as much pain as a wolf, and it's been my experience that they heal even faster."

That was a lie, but I didn't call her on it. "I don't know. Has she been here awhile?" I needed someone who might know what was going on.

The woman looked torn. She wasn't sure what I wanted to hear, that the sex worker with whom I was contemplating spending my Christmas Eve was fresh and relatively untouched, or experienced and skilled. "She's been here a few months," she finally admitted. "But with their healing abilities, honestly, you can't tell. She has almost no marks at all."

Anything that would leave a permanent mark on a Were would have been lethal to a human. I made a note to file a report on Strictly Pleasure's idea of safe working conditions. "I'll take her."

After the processing of my credit card and the reading of a few rules, which were repeated so fast that they were almost unintelligible, I was led down a corridor to "Jezebel's" room. She turned out to be a short, muscular brunette with a dark tan and a world-weary demeanor that didn't match her maybe twenty years. She didn't look submissive, but I guess these things are relative, and I *had* asked for a Were. The room was a surprise, too, with a cluttered, college dorm feel, complete with rock-star posters on the wall, clothes dribbling out of an over-stuffed wardrobe, and a Hello Kitty wall clock.

"You were expecting maybe a dungeon?" she asked, seeing my expression.

"Something like that."

"They're downstairs. Rent by the hour."

"I'm just here to talk."

"Dirty?" She sounded hopeful.

"Only if it includes information."

The hopeful look was replaced by a frown. "What kind of information?"

"About Weres. Wolves, in particular."

The frown became a scowl. "Why? What have they got that I don't?"

That was the big question. "There aren't any here, then?"

"Our last two wolf girls left a month ago."

"Left for where?"

She shrugged. "One day, I got up and new people were moving into their rooms."

"Is that normal?"

Her eyes narrowed. "Why do you care?"

"Is there any reason you shouldn't tell me?"

"Is there any reason I should?" I took the hint and got out my wallet. Fifty bucks did the trick, mainly because she didn't know much. "It was weird. Mostly, if someone gets lucky and a big shot wants to set her up on her own, *everybody* hears about it. One of the guys got a sweet deal a couple weeks ago, and he went on and on, like the rest of us were complete losers—"

"But these girls didn't?"

"Nope. One day they're here, next day they're gone." She snapped her fingers. "Like that."

Just like the high clan girls. I tried to look only mildly interested. "Lone wolves?"

"No. Felan." It was one of the smaller, lower-ranked clans in the area. That surprised me. Clans are close-knit, with what reflects on one reflecting on all. I had a hard time imagining any clan wolves being allowed to take up a profession that, while legal in the supernatural world, wasn't likely to improve their clan's standing.

"Maybe the leaders found out what they were doing and came for them."

Jezebel rolled her eyes and flopped back onto her messy bed. "Who do you think sent 'em here?"

"What?" I was certain I'd heard wrong.

"The leaders got a percentage of what they made. Mine do it, too. Lots of 'em do."

"Wait a minute. You're telling me that their clans forced the Felani girls to work here?"

Jezebel shrugged. "I don't know about forced. But you know how it is. Defy the leaders and you pay for it, and keep on paying. So does your family. I figured I'd do my time. Another year and I'm out of here, and nobody else from my family gets tapped. I got two younger sisters, you know?"

I nodded. A pretty little blackmail routine: do as we say or we take your sisters instead. Could that be why Daniela had been kidnapped? By parents outraged over Sebastian's indifference to the fate of their own daughters? As much as I wanted an answer, it seemed unlikely. A low-ranking family from a minor clan would no more attack Arnou than they would turn vegetarian. Humans might try it, if they were enraged enough, but Weres just didn't think that way.

"I need to find out where those girls went," I said after a minute. "Where are the records kept?"

I got a disdainful look. "You want to talk about stuff everybody knows, okay. We talk. But I'm not getting in trouble for—" I waved a hundred in front of her face and she stopped abruptly, but still looked mutinous. "That won't cover the beating I'll get if anyone finds out I helped you."

I added a second bill and fluttered them in front of her. "I can blank short-term memory. No one has to know."

"Yeah. I'm sure." Her eyes tracked the money, but she made no move to take it.

"I'm a war mage," I added.

The bills were suddenly gone, disappearing somewhere in the short, bright wrapper she wore. "The records are in Yuki's office," she told me briskly.

"The woman who checked me in?"

"He ain't no woman. But yeah, he runs the place."

"Is there any way to get him away from the desk for a minute?"

Jezebel shook her head. "He wants to make sure we don't bring any regulars in on our own and stiff the house. He guards that door like a hawk."

"Is he a mage?"

"No. Tsume."

"But that's a clan name." It meant "claw" in Japanese.

"Yeah. He's our last wolf. Acts like one, too. No offense."

"I'm not a wolf."

Jezebel wrinkled her forehead. "But you smell like—"

I held up a hand. "Don't, okay?" Yuki being a wolf constituted a problem. Unlike humans and most mages, Weres are very resistant to magical suggestions. There was a good chance I wouldn't be able to spell him to tell me anything, or to blank his memory afterward. And Weres don't frighten or intimidate easily. This could get ugly.

I stepped into the hallway and cast a privacy spell to let me call Gil without worrying about Were hearing. "I didn't give you my personal cell so you could ruin my holiday," he told me acerbically.

"It isn't Christmas for another four hours. And besides, you haven't heard why I'm calling yet. I might have a line on those girls."

"Like hell you do. You haven't even been on the case a day!"

"I said might have. But there's a chance I'll need to use a little . . . persuasion . . . to get my lead to talk."

"What lead?"

"Just a guy. It might be nothing. But I wanted to clear it with you first."

"You called me up on Christmas Eve to ask if you can torture someone?"

"It probably won't come to that." I stepped out of the way of a large dominatrix in a shiny PVC cat suit and the guy in chains who was crawling after her. They edged around me politely. "Although I appear to be in the right place for it."

"What? Where are you?"

I didn't answer, because a door had opened down the hall and a very familiar backside emerged. The guy it was attached to didn't see me, maybe because the half-dressed young woman lounging in the door had his whole attention. "I'll take care of you, Nissa," he said fondly. "Now what are you going to do for me?"

"I tell everybody, we no talk to the mage." Her voice was low and sultry, with a heavy Spanish accent.

"To any mages," Cyrus corrected, a finger to her lips. "But particularly to any with dark hair, spectacular legs, and homicidal tendencies."

She pouted. "Is she prettier than me?"

"She's more dangerous than you, which is what you need to keep in mind," he chided. Then he kissed her.

His shirt was unbuttoned with the tails hanging, leaving the hollow of his throat pale and vulnerable. I swallowed hard, trying to resist the alien desire to leap down the corridor and tear into that soft flesh, to feel his blood slick and hot in my mouth. For a moment, I could actually taste it.

"Lia!" Gil's voice in my ear made me jump. "Where the hell are you? What's going on?" I tried to answer, but the words wouldn't come.

I'd wondered why Cyrus had left Jersey at almost the same time I did. I'd been vain enough to think that it might have had something to do with me, although he'd made no effort to contact me. I'd also thought things might have gotten a little hot for him in Atlantic City, so he'd moved West to its bigger, badder cousin, where he wasn't as well known. But what if he'd had another reason?

Because I found it really hard to believe that all this had been going on and no one in the high clans had heard anything. And since no effort was being made to stop it, it was a good guess that they were being paid to look the other way. For that to work, they'd need someone to gather and channel the kickbacks to the leaders. Someone with lots of contacts and no reputation to lose, who could be a convenient scapegoat if things went wrong. Someone like Cyrus.

I slipped back into Jezebel's room and shut the door with a soft click, laying my forehead against it. The sudden adrenaline rush faded to leave me cold, sick, and shaking. I had to take a few deep breaths to catch up with myself, to remember that there was a procedure to be followed. If I was right and leading Weres were dirty, I needed proof. And for me to successfully bring a case like this, it had better be airtight.

"I'll call you back," I said, cutting into whatever Gil had been squawking. I put my phone away very deliberately and turned around so I wouldn't be tempted to put a fist through the door. "I'm going to go talk with Yuki," I said.

Jezebel took in my expression. "Huh. Think I'll go talk to him, too."

As a Were, Yuki was a sad disappointment. He started looking panicked before I even asked him anything, about the time I hung him from the chandelier in his office. It was wrought iron with lots of pointy bits and didn't appear to be all that comfortable. I smiled pleasantly like my trainers had taught me and pulled out photos of the missing girls.

"Have you seen any of these?" He started to shake his head and I held up a finger. "Think *real* hard. Because I know you'd hate to lie to me. Just like I'd hate to see you get overly intimate with the coatrack."

"I haven't seen them," he said. For some reason, all the lilt had gone out of his voice.

"He's telling the truth," Jezebel said. "I could smell it if he was lying."

"Then what about the two wolves who went missing from here? What happened to them?"

I could almost see Yuki trying to puzzle out how much he could plausibly get away with denying. I was about to apply more threats, but

Jezebel decided we'd talked enough. I got the feeling there wasn't a lot of love lost between those two, and she obviously thought it would be a shame to waste a good memory wipe. After she pulled a Taser out of her wrap and started waving it around, Yuki became positively voluble.

"The boss selected them for a private party," he said quickly. "The buyers specifically wanted wolves."

"And when they didn't come back?"

"No one comes back from those kind of parties," he said, his eyes tracking the Taser. "Some patrons like it extra rough, and we have rules about the extent of damage inflicted on-site. But elsewhere . . . things can get messy."

"And the clans do nothing?"

"We usually pick lone wolves for that kind of thing."

"But not this time." I poked him hard enough to set him swinging. "Why not?"

"Because we didn't have any! The bosses prefer to use clan wolves around here when possible, because if they run away, the clan will bring them back. But we employ lone wolves from time to time for jobs like this. The clans don't like it much if we return their people in pieces. Or don't return them at all."

"Then why didn't their clan object this time? If the girls die, there goes their cut of the profits."

"They were well compensated. Very well, from what I heard." He looked sulky, like maybe they hadn't offered to share.

As sick as his story was, it did sound possible, but only where the Felani girls were concerned. Because I couldn't see anybody capturing high clan members for some demented fun and games. It would almost ensure that they were caught, and Arnou wouldn't take cash in retribution. They would take blood. And everybody knew it.

"Who paid you?" I asked.

"I don't know. The names were obviously fake." Jezebel brandished the Taser again and he paled. "A lot of people don't use their real names when they contact us!"

"But they have to give a real address. What was it?"

Yuki shook his head frantically. "I can't tell you that!"

"I'll get it out of him!" Jezebel snarled. She was clearly looking forward to it.

"Give me the address and I'll blank all this from your memory," I said, holding her off. "If the clan questions you, you can deny any involvement and they'll believe it. Because you'll believe it."

Yuki just hung there, swaying gently, for a long moment. His heavy mascara had run, making tracks through his pearly cheek powder, like he was crying black tears. I put on my sympathetic face, and I guess it must have worked because he finally told me.

I glanced at Jezebel and she nodded. I wrote down the address, making him spell it twice so there couldn't be a mistake, and turned to go. I was halfway to the door when I heard the sound of tearing fabric and a thump behind me. Yuki caught me by the arm, his long, perfectly polished nails almost but not quite breaking the skin. "Wait! You haven't done the memory wipe yet!"

"That would be because there's no such thing. Not for Weres."

"But you said—"

"I lied."

"But they'll kill me!"

I thought about the two girls he'd callously sent to a horrible end. "That would be my guess."

"But you're a war mage! You can't—"

"I'm not a very good war mage," I told him sadly. "You should see my performance evals."

"I wouldn't worry about the clans," Jezebel added. "When I tell everyone what happened to those girls, and that you set it up . . ." She gave him a slow smile. Yuki looked at me, but I guess he didn't see anything helpful because the next minute he took the hint, hiked up his skirts, and ran. Jezebel sauntered out after him.

I called Gil with the address on the way there. It was a little hard to concentrate considering the traffic—it looked like most people preferred one more roll of the dice to visions of sugarplums—but it was a short conversation. "I'll meet you," Gil said when I finished, and hung up. I smiled. It had to be pretty major when a department head got out of a warm bed to sling a spell or two in the cold—and to hog the credit.

The address Yuki had provided led me to a large McMansion in one of the new, absurdly overpriced subdivisions that have been springing up like mushrooms all around Vegas. I don't know what I'd been expecting, but it hadn't been pale yellow stucco and a red tile roof, surrounded by a neatly swept lawn and a lot of cars. An SUV pulled up while I sat there, and a couple of people in sequins and Santa hats got out, carrying a bottle of booze in a shiny gold package.

I drove past and let my bike idle around the corner while I checked the scribbled instructions again. As strange as it seemed, the number was right, so I parked the bike and waited for my backup. And waited.

After twenty minutes, I called Gil again, but his cell went straight to voice mail. Where the hell was everyone? Traffic wasn't *that* bad. And unless the war had suddenly come to town, I found it hard to believe that another case had taken precedence.

I decided to move a little closer and at least find out what kind of wards we were dealing with. Only there weren't any. There also weren't any of the standard traps, snares, or other nasty surprises I'd been expecting. The door wasn't even locked, so either someone was superconfident or unbelievably careless. Or this was a trap. But it didn't feel like one. There was no sign of anything illicit going on, just a brightly lit vestibule with terra-cotta-tiled floors and a pine wreath with a big red bow. Music and laughter spilled out of a side room, which I couldn't see without going all the way in.

Damn it! It was no surprise that Yuki had lied, but I hadn't thought Jezebel would help him. And now he had an hour's head start. Even worse, Gil was on his way to raid some norm's Christmas party.

I pulled the door shut and started to turn, only to hear someone's voice from behind me. "About time you showed up," it said, and the world exploded in pain.

I woke up an indeterminate time later, feeling as if I'd run into a wall. I tried looking around but my eyes didn't seem to be working. My memory is usually pretty good, so it probably wasn't a positive sign that I had no recall of whatever had happened. Just fragments of conversation that didn't make sense.

. . . mother was a Were. I always suspected . . .
If she's human . . .
She's not. And we're running out of time.
I'll prepare . . .

I felt a needle prick my arm, and then nothing but cold creeping painfully over my body. I strained, desperate to move an arm, to open my eyes, to think, but for a long time all I felt was the dragging weight of a body that wasn't obeying my commands. And then feeling returned and there was nothing but agony.

When I finally forced my lids open, a terrible white light was pouring in, stabbing at my brain. I tried to block it, but I couldn't lift my hand. I also couldn't see straight, and all I could hear was an awful, inhuman noise coming out of my own chest. For one horrible second, I needed air and couldn't remember how to get it, my lungs refusing to work. There were suddenly voices all around me, blurry faces peering down, and a smug voice saying, *"I told you so."* Then darkness again.

I came around the second time mainly because of the absence of pain. It didn't feel like it was gone for good, more like it had taken a break and would be back to torture me again soon. But for the moment, I could breathe, although my ribs ached with each shallow attempt.

My wrist had fallen near my face, and my watch informed me that it was 12:05 A.M. Christmas morning. I'd have traded all the presents in the world for the ability to sit up, to know what had happened. I flexed a finger and it was stiff, like a dried twig that would snap if I pushed too hard. My brain was screaming at me to do something, to move, to get into a defensive position, but I couldn't manage it. I did finally lift my head, though, and saw that I wasn't in the foyer anymore. Not unless the owners had decided to renovate it in early industrial ugly while I was out.

I also wasn't alone.

"I've been looking for you," I croaked, and a blond head snapped up. The girl had been seated on the other side of the small cage we seemed to be sharing, staring at its iron bars. She stared at me now instead, blue eyes wide.

"You're alive." Daniela seemed surprised.

I licked my lips, but couldn't feel it. "The jury's still out."

She grabbed a water bottle that was hanging on the side of the cage. She couldn't stand up, the cage top was too low, but she scuttled over on hands and knees. "None of the others lasted this long," she said, as I tried to drink through numb lips.

I spit water all over my shirt. "What others?" I croaked.

"The other Weres who were here. They're all dead."

"How, why?"

"Failed experiments," she said angrily. "Some mages are planning to blow up the clan leaders at the *Ulfhring* tomorrow."

"What does that have to do with you?"

"I'm the bomb."

I tried to drag myself into a sitting position, but failed. "Come again?"

"They need me to get past security. That's why they took the daughters of highly placed members. If I say it's an emergency, security will let me in. They know me."

"And they think you're just going to carry in a bomb for them?"

"They plan to put me under a compulsion."

"That doesn't work on Weres," I pointed out.

"I know that! But they've come up with a potion that's supposed to help the suggestion to take."

"I've never heard of anything like that."

"Because it didn't work! All it did was kill everyone after a couple of hours. They've been trying to get the formula right, so I have time to blow myself up before I die."

"Let me guess. It killed the other high clan girls, so they started using low clan women to experiment on." The kind they thought no one would miss.

Daniela nodded. "They think they finally have the formula right. I get to find out in a few hours. But I've been thinking. I'm the only high clan girl left, and they don't have time to find a replacement."

I rolled over onto my side to get a look at her face. "What are you saying?"

"That you need to kill me."

"Come again?"

"I won't be responsible for killing my own father! I'd take care of it myself, only"—she glanced around, looking a little lost—"I'm not sure how . . ."

"I came to rescue you, not to kill you." I grasped one of the bars, and somehow managed to pull myself up with it. My strength ran out almost immediately, and I ended up slumped in a corner, limp as a rag doll.

Daniela eyed me skeptically. "Uh-huh. But seriously, we're dead anyway—"

"Seriously, I intend to live forever, or die trying," I told her, parroting one of Cyrus' borrowed sayings. Speaking of whom, how did he fit into this? Because, okay, he and the council were currently on the outs, but killing all of them seemed a little . . . extreme . . . for the guy I knew. And Daniela had said mages. "Who is behind this again? And why do I feel like I was run over by a convoy?"

"I don't know who they are. We don't chat a lot," she said sarcastically. "And you feel that way because they gave you the treatment. One last test, to make sure it works. And since you're still alive, they must have got it right." She gripped my arm. "We have to *do* something!"

I refrained from pointing out that I *was* doing something. And at the moment, not falling over felt like a major achievement. "It didn't work because I'm not a Were," I said instead.

"But you smell like—"

"I don't care what I smell like! Just tell me why they've targeted only women?"

"Because we're so much easier to control," Daniela said with a snarl. It pulled her lips back from her nice, white teeth. It should have looked comical, but somehow, it didn't. "That's what one of them kept saying, over and over, when anyone suggested bringing in a guy. We're weak-minded, more easily influenced. I'll show them weak, if I ever get out of here!"

"Why can't you?" The bars were steel, but with Were strength, that shouldn't have been a problem.

"Because the damn cage is warded!" She slammed her hands into the side, and it didn't even make the bars rattle.

"Shield charm. Pretty standard."

"For a mage! Too bad we don't have one."

"I'm a war mage," I informed her, right before I flopped onto my face. After a moment, I got my hands under me and pushed. Nothing happened. *Come on; you're tougher than this,* I told myself sternly. *War mage tough. Two-hundred-push-ups-before-breakfast tough. Full metal jacket, can't handle the truth tough. Shot a man in Reno just to watch him—*

"Really?" Daniela sounded doubtful.

"Really. Got the certificate and everything." I somehow got to my knees. "Do you ride?"

"What?"

"Bikes. Motorcycles. Because my piece of shit Honda is around the corner. To the left, after you go out the front. Get it and get out of here."

"And what are you going to do?"

I fumbled around in my jacket and found the keys. They'd taken my weapons, but left those. Guess no one had thought I'd be using them again. "Crash a party," I said grimly.

The corridor outside the basement wavered alarmingly. I tried shaking my head, but that only made it worse. I finally found the stairs by stumbling into them.

I gave up looking cool and climbed up on my hands and knees. Daniela had left the door open at the top and the guard dead, his neck slashed, the imprint of paw prints in the blood. Good girl. I took his gun and potion-belt, but didn't bother strapping either on. I didn't have enough coordination, and anyway, I was probably going to need them soon.

The telltale signature of the tag I'd left on Cyrus started licking at the back of my neck. It was louder at the end of the corridor, and alarm-like by the time I made it into a well-appointed living room filled with decorations, presents, and a lot of freaked-out party guests. The last probably had something to do with the man waving a gun around. He had his back to me, but I'd recognize that butt anywhere.

"The experiment was a failure," Gil was saying, his hands in the air. He was wearing a green Christmas sweater with brown reindeer on it, I noticed irrelevantly. "But that doesn't mean we can't come to an arrangement. I've heard about you. You fought your brother for the title and lost. They kicked you out of the clan, removed their protection, made you an outcast. Wouldn't you like to get a little of your own back?"

"Give me Lia and I'll think about it."

"I thought Were hearing was supposed to be sharp," Gil said disdainfully. "The bitch is dead. Like you're shortly going to be if you don't—"

I blinked, and in the space of time it took to get my eyes back open, Cyrus was gone and a huge black and tan wolf was tearing apart the living room. A moment later, five guards who must have snuck up on the outside of the house decided to hell with discretion and burst through the bow window. Gil dove behind the sofa, Cyrus followed him, and everyone else ran screaming for the door.

Within seconds, the Christmas tree went flying, the presents got mushed, and someone crashed into the cheerfully burning fireplace. It was a mage with his shields up, because he didn't get so much as singed, but he managed to fling firewood across the floor while climbing out. It turns out that wrapping paper is pretty good kindling, because the scattered presents were soon burning merrily.

A few guys managed to keep enough of their wits about them to try a spell or two, but I emptied the guard's clip into them. I couldn't see straight so my aim was off and most of them had shields up anyway, but at least it provided a distraction. Only one of the people it distracted was Cyrus, who glanced at me and then did a swift double take, which looked really strange in wolf form.

It wasn't much of a slip, but it allowed a couple of mages to get a net spell on him. Only that spell usually takes a minimum of three people, which might explain why, when Cyrus reared back, they both went sailing over the couch. The unraveling strands of the spell trapped them and a pissed-off werewolf in a snarling, flailing ball.

Instead of trying to help his beleaguered men, Gil took one look and ran for the back door, taking him straight in my direction. I smiled and he put on the brakes. "Lia. You're . . ."

"Alive, yeah."

Sweat broke out on his bald head. "In the nick of time, I was about to say. What took you so long? Help me contain that thing!"

"Nice try. But spells have a flavor of the caster, Gil. And I broke through yours on the cage downstairs." Not to mention that, judging by the portraits on the mantel, the idiot had been running his scheme out of his own basement.

He changed tactics without so much as a pause. It was actually kind of impressive. "Don't be a fool. You're in as much trouble as I am. Help me and I'll return the favor. Otherwise, it will be my word against yours. And who do you think the clans are going to believe?"

The one who doesn't smell like a liar, I almost said. "Out of curiosity, what is the point to all this? I know you hate Weres, but—"

"I could give a shit about them. But the deaths of their leaders will cause chaos in the clan system, and make them look like the unreliable allies they are. It will also discredit my brother, who talked us into this alliance in the first place."

"And you would want to do that because?"

"Because the position should have been mine!" Gil snarled. "The coalition decided his youth and good looks would appeal to more voters, and ran him instead of me. He used *my* contacts, *my* political clout, to his advantage, and what did I get? A clap on the shoulder and a handshake, then left in this dead-end job! What do you think about that?"

"I think it's crazy," I said, and he relaxed slightly, although he didn't take his hand out of his pocket. "Youth and good looks? 'Cause, seriously, Gil, I've seen your brother—"

"The clans hate you, Lia!" he snapped. "Why do you think I chose you for this job?"

"Because you knew they wouldn't talk to me."

"Exactly. But if you join me, I'll shield you from them."

"Right. *You're* going to protect me. Someone so ignorant of Were customs that you don't even understand the hierarchy?"

"What?" And it was obvious that he really didn't know. That he'd killed seven people, maybe more, for nothing. It was sickening.

"Any of your test subjects could have told you," I spat. "Even if your plan worked, there's a clearly delineated line of succession, with an appointed second coming forward immediately to take the place of a fallen leader. And if he dies, there's a third, and so on, down to the last member of the clan. And the first thing each and every one of them would do on assuming power is to hunt you down. Protect me? Thanks, but I prefer to take my chances."

"Sure about that? Life without allies can be a bitch." He pulled his hand out of his pocket and pointed the weapon it held at me.

I didn't bother to reply, because in order to fire, Gil had to lower his shields. And as soon as he did, I threw one of the dead guard's potion vials in his face. He dropped the gun, screaming, as its corrosive properties went to work. I watched him trying to claw out his own eyeballs for a moment; it was oddly satisfying. "Yeah. Fortunately, so can I."

I staggered over to Cyrus. He'd gotten his hind legs caught in a bunch of tinsel that had fallen off the ruined tree. "I'd offer you a hand, but . . ." I tried to wave and fell on my ass.

He crawled over to me using only his front paws. It looked like his hind legs weren't just caught, they were useless. He collapsed by my side in a great furry heap.

We lay there quietly for a few minutes, listening to the crackle of burning gifts. On the plus side, the fires eventually went out on their own and no one else attacked us. Not too surprisingly as most of them didn't seem to be still in one piece. Even Gil had finally stopped screaming.

"How are you?"

I blinked blearily at him. Oh. He'd changed back.

"Can't move."

"Yeah." He swallowed. "I'm having the same trouble."

"Pretend we're drunk."

He huffed a short laugh. "I wish I was drunk."

"How'd you find me?"

"Jezebel."

"Ah."

"I passed Daniela coming in," he added. "She's gone to get help."

"Good." I still didn't know how he fit into all this, but at the moment, I didn't care. I snuggled into him, letting the smell of clan surround me—musky, earthy, and indescribably sweet—and relaxed in spite of myself. A moment later, I was asleep.

I opened my eyes to find someone bending over me. At first, I thought it was Cyrus. But there were no snug jeans, soft flannel shirts, or cowboy boots in sight. Instead, the man by my bedside in what appeared to be a hospital room was wearing a crisp shirt and tie, subtle cuff links, and pants with a crease sharp enough to cut yourself on.

He looked like Cyrus, though, except for a pair of pure blue eyes. As my vision returned, I noticed subtle other differences: a slightly broader jaw, a narrower mouth, and a more classic nose. His hair was dark, but not as curly, and was cut shorter. He looked older, too, by maybe four or five years. But, other than that, they could have been brothers.

"We are." He settled himself on the chair that a nurse quickly scooted into place, and I realized I must have spoken aloud. "Could we have a moment, please?"

There seemed to be a lot of people around: doctors, nurses, and a bunch of heavily armed types who were obviously Weres despite being in human form. None of them was Cyrus. "How is—?"

He held up a hand and we waited until everyone filed out and the door shut. "My brother is fine. As is my daughter, thanks to you."

It took a moment for the implications of that short sentence to register. It was a good thing Cyrus was still alive, I decided. That way I got to kill him. "So I finally get to meet the great Sebastian."

"And I am at last able to make the acquaintance of Larentia Lobizón's daughter. I have heard much of you."

"None of it good, I bet."

"Until today, I'm afraid not. Your clan was quite displeased with you."

"Was?"

"I took the liberty of acquiring you for Clan Arnou. My brother rather insisted upon it."

I was pretty sure I'd missed something. "Why?"

"The vendetta. Arnou outranks Lobizón. Once they discover that you now belong to us, I expect the dispute to be quickly resolved."

I didn't doubt it, and it was a huge relief. But it also brought up another issue. "About the change—"

"It is each clan's right to determine how aggressively rogues are pursued."

"I'm not a rogue."

"You are clan-born, yet refuse the change. By most clan's laws, that makes you a rogue."

"And in yours?"

"We have never forced anyone to undergo the change who does not choose to do so. For whatever reason."

The unspoken word hung in the air between us, like the large, full moon outside. He had to know. He must have wondered why I was affected by a spell designed for Weres when I had refused the change. It wouldn't have been difficult to have me tested for Neuri while I was out. But he said nothing, so I didn't, either. After a moment, he leaned over and kissed me lightly on the cheek.

"Welcome to the family, Accalia," he murmured, and left.

I just lay there for a few minutes, until a pressing personal matter insisted that I get up. I found that I could actually walk and that the room stayed satisfyingly steady around me. It seemed that my body had won the fight.

I came out of the bathroom to find Cyrus lounging on the bed without so much as a scratch on him. "My niece totaled your bike," he said, by way of a greeting.

"She said she could ride!"

"Normally, she isn't bad. But she was a little upset for some reason."

I sat on the bed and looked at him, alive and well and grinning cockily, and couldn't manage to feel too bad about it. "You're Sebastian's brother."

"I knew this was coming."

"And a dangerous outlaw who challenged him for clan leadership?"

"That might have been slightly exag—"

"And who, despite that, is able to call in favors from him?"

Cyrus sighed. "The other clan leaders viewed Sebastian as more of a diplomat than a warrior. He needed a show of strength before the vote for *bardric* to help him seal the win. Beating me in open combat provided that. Plus, we'd heard some disturbing rumors and he needed someone to investigate them. We thought that clans with secrets would be more likely to talk to someone who had been publicly disgraced than to a clan wolf who might turn them in."

"You've been investigating the club."

"Among other things. It's why I came to Vegas."

"But why not shut it down? Those girls might still be alive!"

Cyrus took another deep breath. I briefly wondered if we had the same therapist. "And a lot of others would have gone unavenged. This has been going on for years, Lia. Without an overall leader, too much has been allowed to slip through the cracks. We needed evidence against all of the clans that participated, even those who don't have members there at the moment."

"But when the girls started disappearing—"

"We thought there might be a connection, but shutting the place down would have meant forfeiting our best chance of finding them. And the club isn't the only dirty game in town—not by half. They were one suspect among many. It may take years to clean up the entire mess."

"And you didn't tell me this because?"

"You know why. I didn't want to take the chance that you might go missing, too."

"I'm a war mage. This kind of thing is my *job*."

"No. This was clan business. Sebastian should never have gone to the Corps."

"I wouldn't have reported anything! Not if you'd explained."

Cyrus cocked an eyebrow at me. "You're a war mage. It would have been your *job*." I glared at him and he did that thing where he hid a smile somewhere under the skin of his face. "I knew I couldn't trust you to leave it to me, so I asked my informants to keep you out of the loop."

"Including Nissa."

"Ah, yes. Nissa. The sacrifices I make for—" I pushed him off the bed. His head popped back up, still grinning. "You seem awfully energetic for an invalid. Ready to go?"

"Go where?" I wasn't looking forward to the screaming messages that were no doubt crowding my answering machine. The Corps had to have discovered by now that the Vegas department head had gone bad, and taken half a dozen other operatives with him. I was going to drown in paperwork for *weeks*.

"It's still Christmas for . . ." He checked his watch. "Another forty-seven minutes."

"So?"

"I got your present downstairs." He threw some heavy denim and motorcycle leathers on the bed. "But you have to get dressed to see it."

I pulled on the clothes so fast that I didn't manage to flash him more than a couple of times. We snuck out the back way, dodged the few staff members who weren't gathered around the nurses' station, and there it was. Gleaming under the parking lot lights was a tripped-out Harley-Davidson Night Rod with black chrome and bloodred accents. It was love at first sight.

"Ever see Red Rock Canyon by moonlight?" Cyrus asked, as I ran my hand possessively over its undented sleekness.

"No."

"You will tonight." He threw a leg over the seat of a black and silver version parked alongside. "Race you."

He was out of the lot before I even managed to scramble on board. But the powerful motor gladly leapt into the chase. The air was cold, the stars were out, and the Vegas skyline was lit up like a Christmas tree. It was like flying.

"It's a full moon!" Cyrus yelled, as we turned on to Blue Diamond Road.

"So? I'm not a wolf!"

"Really?" His mouth wasn't curved but he was smiling anyway. "Bet I can make you howl."

He shot away, eating up the open road. I gunned it and followed. I bet he could, too.

Milk and Cookies

Rob Thurman

Rob Thurman is the author of several books making up the Cal Leandros Novels: Nightlife, Moonshine, Madhouse, Deathwish, Roadkill, *and* Blackout *(March 2011); the Trickster Novels:* Trick of the Light *and* The Grimrose Path *(September 7, 2010); and the contemporary suspense thriller* Chimera. *Rob lives in Indiana, land of many cows, demanding deer, and wild turkey as savage as any wolf, Were or otherwise. Protecting the author's house and home is a hundred-pound rescue Lab—Great Dane mix with teeth straight out of a Godzilla movie and the ferocious habit of hiding under the bed when visitors arrive. Reach the author at www.robthurman.net.*

Christmas sucked.

The display windows covered in velvet ribbons and tinsel. The tinkle of ringing bells around every corner. The snow, the presents, the frigging good cheer.

Yeah, it sucked all right. Sure, it was only once a year, but that was one time too many. Carolers, months of Christmas music, candy canes, and all but Cindy Lou Who skipping down the sidewalk.

It was too much. Too damn much.

I was seven when I knew there wasn't a Santa anymore. I was thirteen when my sister started the whole "Is there really a Santa?" thing and "The kids at school say . . ." The usual stuff. And that she was seven, the same age I'd been, only made it worse.

So I lied. Sure there was a Santa. And when Mom told me to take her to see store Santa, I hadn't bitched too much. She and Dad both had to work. They worked hard. We weren't poor, but we sure weren't rich either. Dad was a good hunter and that put food on the table, but it didn't pay the electric or the mortgage.

Plus I remembered what it was like, how knowing had taken the magic out of Christmas. I didn't want to admit it. I was tougher than that. I didn't want to admit that even six years later I missed waiting to hear hoofbeats on the roof, the jingle of bells, the thump of boots hitting the bottom of our big, old fireplace.

Yeah, I didn't want to fess up to it, but it was true. Now Christmas was just another day. I wasn't into Jesus or church, mangers or angels. You got presents and, sure, that was cool, but the excited knot in your stomach, the blankets clenched in your fists, the listening for all you were worth that Christmas Eve night.

Gone.

It was stupid to miss it. I was way too old for that shit. You could ask anybody. If the kids at school found out, they'd laugh me out of class. If the teachers found out, they wouldn't know what to think. Probably send me to the counselor for soft words, ink blots, and a note for my parents. But they didn't know, and every teacher would tell you: I wasn't a dreamer. No way. I was a smart-ass kid. My dad told me so, my teachers, the principal . . . who spent more time lecturing me than my teachers ever did. He told me at thirteen I was too young to get into trouble, too young to be cynical. And definitely too young to have such a foul mouth.

He didn't get out of the office much.

Smart-assed and foul-mouthed, you'd think there was no way I'd get glum every Christmas, but I did. Every single one. And no matter what had happened that one particular Christmas when I was seven—throughout the Christmas I'd first lost the spirit, I'd never get it back. I'd never get a do-over. No matter how much I wanted to.

Jackass, I said to my reflection in the display glass of the store. Suck it up. Get over it. You're not seven anymore. You're not a little kid. There are no do-overs in life.

I pushed the door open to the department store, the only one we had in Connor's Way, a town so small we had two stores, three restaurants, and one stoplight. It had been home since August now. It was one of those towns where everyone knew everyone and everything you did got around if you weren't careful. I was thirteen . . . there were *plenty* of things I did I didn't want getting around.

Tessa slid her hand into mine and I grimaced. Little sisters, what a pain in the ass. Big eyes the same brown as mine looked up at me and she smiled at me with that big-brother-worshipping smile. I sighed, squeezed her hand, and tugged her along. "Come on. Before the line gets too long." She was a pain, but she was my pain and family's what counts. Dad said that over and over again. People are people, but it's family that counts.

Along with the brown eyes she looked like me. Slightly dark skin, curly black hair. We were related all right. You could see that a mile away. Dead-on our dad.

"What kind of cookies should I make Santa?" Tessa chattered. "Chocolate chip? Peanut butter? Oooh, Snickerdoodles. Everybody loves Snickerdoodles. Right? You like Snickerdoodles, don't you?"

I rolled my eyes and was thankful the line wasn't that long. Santa was pretty much what I expected: fat enough to strain his big black belt and with a beard so fake and bushy that rats could've nested in it. He had glasses perched on the end of his red-veined nose and his lap was full of a sobbing, kicking-and-screaming two-year-old with a load in his training pants that had to weigh more than he did.

"Eww," Tessa said, tugging at my hand. "I don't want to sit there."

"Then just stand beside him and tell him what you want for Christmas," I said impatiently. "His balls could probably use the break." Hundreds of kids slamming down on them day after day, no way I'd want his job.

"Balls?" She wrinkled her nose. "I don't see any balls. Snowballs?"

Jesus. I was in for it now. "Hey, it's your turn," I said with relief, letting go of her hand and giving her a light shove. "Remember to hold still for the picture or Mom'll kill me."

She moved up beside and tiptoed up to whisper in his ear. The camera flashed, and even though it was a little early, it did make a cute picture. Then Tessa leaned back and bounced happily in shiny patent leather shoes that went with her best red velvet dress.

The fake Santa blinked at her, twitched a forced smile, and hurried her off with a candy cane. As we waited for the picture to pop out, I asked, "What'd you ask for?"

I let her take my hand again as she said solemnly, "You know."

We all wanted something we weren't going to get. This was Tessa's year for disappointment. The one thing she wanted and the one thing she'd never get. Feeling more guilty than I wanted to, I said, "You want to get a milk shake before we go home?"

Of course she did, and we went to the drugstore. They had an old-fashioned malt shop there. I didn't much know or care what an old-fashioned malt shop, like the sign said, was, but they served milk shakes and that was enough for me. I had chocolate, she had strawberry, and things were fine until Jed walked in. His parents had named him Jedidiah and he had a punch for anyone who called him that. It was supposed to be biblical. I guessed it didn't take.

I slid him a careful sideways look. Cold blue eyes stared back, then he gave a half snarl, half hateful grin. Jed was fourteen, big, and a bully. Christmas might suck, but so did bullies.

And Jed was of the worst kind. The worst in the school, that's for sure. He picked on kids who were smaller and younger. He thought that made him a badass. It didn't. It just made him a coward. He hadn't messed with me yet, but it was only a matter of time. I was close to his size, but not close enough for him to pass over me. Not by a good three inches. I was husky for my age, but a little short. Yeah, he was working his way up to me. He was a coward, but he was stupid, too. It wouldn't be long before he'd get over being careful of someone almost as heavy as him if not as tall. Between mean and stupid, stupid wins every time.

Tessa and I slurped up the last of our shakes and we left. She used both hands to try and peel the plastic off her candy cane. "You're smart," she announced.

"Oh yeah? What makes you think that?" The sidewalk was clear of snow, shoveled clean.

"That mean guy doesn't bother you." She popped the top loop of the cane in her mouth. "Wi-ly." She'd just learned the word when I'd been practicing for my spelling test and loved using it although half the time she didn't know what it meant.

Wily? Nah. I was about as wily as a Pop-Tart. This was just luck. And luck?

It only lasts so long.

"Nicky, are you paying attention or are you shooting for extra homework?"

I looked up from the history book I was only pretending to read. I was hungry. I didn't concentrate so well when I was hungry. My stomach growled as I lied, "Yes, Mrs. Gibbs, I'm paying attention."

She didn't believe me, but the bell rang, saving me and my stomach. I bolted for the cafeteria. It was burger day. Most of the kids were all about pizza day, but not me. I liked burgers and I paid for three meals to get three of them. When Mom had handed me my lunch money for the week, she'd ruffled my hair and said I was a growing boy. I might be three inches short of Jed, but I had shot up two inches in the past month. The boys in my family might hit their growth spurts late, but when we hit them, we *hit* them.

I was thinking that when he slammed his tray across from mine on the cafeteria table, his shaggy silver blond hair hanging in his eyes. "I hear you're in the Russian Club, geek."

I was, not that I cared much about it, but Dad insisted. Our grandparents had come from Russia. Roots and all that crap. Nicky was short for Nikolai, and I made damn sure no one in school knew *that*.

"Yeah, so?" I started on my first burger.

"That makes you a geek. A loser." Those eyes, pale as a snow-filled sky, stared at me. They were like the eyes of a husky, a wild one used to living on its own. Catching its own food. Killing because it could. Jed was twisted inside, *wrong*. The teachers didn't see it. They just saw parents who didn't care, maybe some sort of learning disorder, they didn't see what he really was, because they didn't want to. But I saw.

He was a monster. He was just a kid now maybe, but you could bet he was some kind of serial killer waiting to grow up. But wouldn't that be a lot of paperwork for the guidance counselor? Why not pass him on? Let him be someone else's problem.

"I don't like geeks." He leaned forward and bared teeth too big for his mouth. "And I definitely don't like losers." He reached over and took one of my burgers, daring me to do something about it.

But I didn't. Not there. Dad had taught me to fight, because everyone needed to be able to take care of himself. But he'd also taught me never to do it in public where you can get in trouble and never to hit first, at least not anyone smaller. It wouldn't be fair and it wouldn't be honorable. My dad believed in honor, pounded it into me from the time I could crawl. You can protect yourself, you can fight—that's the way the world was—but only the ones bigger than you.

Honor was a pain in the ass sometimes, but Jed *was* bigger than I was. I wasn't forgetting that. Still, there was the whole not getting into trouble thing . . .

Taking my burger back and smacking the son of a bitch over the head with his tray would definitely get me in trouble. So I ate my second burger and ignored him. He couldn't start anything either. Not at school. And I knew ways home to avoid him. I'd gotten to know the woods that stretched behind the school pretty good. Gotten detention for skipping class to explore them more than once. I deserved a lot more punishment than that, but Principal Johnson took it easy on me, no matter what he thought about my smart-ass ways and foul mouth.

Jed kept glaring at me while ripping into my burger with those snaggled teeth. Man, was that an orthodontist's dream. That was a car payment and a lap dance, right there.

How'd I know about lap dances? I had a cousin back East who had a friend and, boy, could she tell some stories. I was thinking of one of them and wishing twenty-one wasn't so far away when Sammy made the really bad choice of sitting next to me. He couldn't have been paying attention. Nobody sat at the same table as Jed on purpose. Sammy wasn't a bad guy. Not too smart and called Dog Boy by most of the kids at school, but he was okay. He had four dogs, big, shaggy mutts, who followed him to and from school. I liked dogs. Jed hated them and the feeling was mutual. One look of his freaky pale blue eyes and the dogs would bark until foam flew from their muzzles before eventually turning and fleeing with tails between their legs.

You know you're a shit when even dogs didn't like you. I kept hoping one would hump his leg or better yet piss on it, but it never happened. Probably for the best. I didn't want to think what Jed would do if he ever caught one of those dogs.

"Hey, Dog Boy," Jed sneered. "You think I want to eat my lunch smelling you? You stink like those damn mutts of yours. Get the hell out of here."

Sammy's eyes widened as he realized who was sitting with me and scrambled away, his tray shaking hard enough to spill his juice. He did smell a little like dog, but hey, we all have something. Jed was psycho and Sammy was a little doggy. I'd take a fur-covered pair of jeans over crazy any day. But today was a day crazy didn't seem to want to leave me alone. I'd started on my second burger, so Jed couldn't take that, but he did take my Jell-O. Cherry. It looked like fresh blood on his teeth as he wolfed it down. He narrowed his eyes at me as he licked a streak of red from his bottom lip. "You're not afraid of me, are you, asshole?"

I took another bite and chewed it. Bullies only heard what they wanted to hear. I wasn't going to waste my time.

He leaned in, his breath hot and smelling of meat and cherry. "I'll make you afraid. You got that? I'll make you so goddamn afraid you'll piss your pants." He snatched up his tray and stalked away.

Trouble, he was big trouble. Maybe the first trouble I couldn't get around. Crazy is crazy, and crazy never learns. He'd keep coming and coming until he caught me or backed me in a corner. I didn't want to be looking over my shoulder every minute. I didn't want him watching me. I stabbed my fork in my french fries. I was going to have to do something. That something being not letting Jed beat the shit out of me and stay out of trouble.

There was a trick.

"Hey, Nicky, you hanging out with Jaws?" Isaac sat across from me, chin propped in his hand.

Jed definitely had the teeth for the nickname, but no one had ever called him that to his face. "Nah, just my turn on his list." Isaac frowned. His parents had come over from Mexico and he'd already had his turn over that with Jed.

"Oh shit," he said, wincing. "Whatcha going to do?"

"Don't know yet." I dropped my fork. "Guess I'll have to think about it. Sneak through the woods home until he figures that out."

After the last class, I bolted into the woods. They were thick and deep, full of poison ivy and tangles of blackberry bushes that would tear you to pieces if you tried to push through. I managed. Scratches were scratches. They'd fade quick enough. And I'd avoided Jed.

This time.

The next afternoon I was at the store looking for a present for Tessa. I scowled at the Santa ringing the bell by the door. One more reminder . . . everywhere you looked. Skinny or with sagging beards and worn black boots or faded red pants. Fakes. It made the whole season fake.

But there were only two more days until Christmas Eve and I couldn't put off shopping anymore. I couldn't get Tessa what she really wanted, so I wandered up and down the doll aisle. It was amazing. They had dolls that walked and talked, crawled and cried, ate and pooped. Why would anyone want a toy that threw up on you while you changed its diaper? That was crazy. But Mom sent me out with a list and one of these nasty things was on it. I picked up the nearest one. It only talked and waved its arms, no puking involved. That was the one.

"Playing with dollies now," Jed purred from behind me. "Why not? You run like a goddamn girl. You might as well play like one, too." His hand circled my arm above my elbow so hard it cut the blood off. I felt the tingle in my fingers.

Jed had been behind me in the woods yesterday afternoon, but he didn't know them like I did. He'd come closer than I'd have thought, though. He just didn't care. Pain was nothing to him. Diving through blackberry bushes, sliding down ravines. He was one scratched, bruised mess now, and wasn't that too bad? I might try and stay out of trouble but there was no way I was sorry about that.

I ignored him, yanked my arm away, and took the doll to the check-out counter. He followed me every step of the way. "You can't run forever, *Nicky*," he whispered. I felt the hairs on the back of my neck ruffle in the god-awful stench of his breath. "No one's ever gotten away. And when I'm done with you and you hide like a little bitch every time you see me, I'll make your little sister sorry, too. Her and her dolly."

And that was that.

I'd put it off. I'd tried to stay out of trouble. I'd tried not to piss off Mom and Dad. But you couldn't let the assholes win, even crazy ones like Jed. I sat in a plastic chair by the door, eyes on the floor, until Jed gave up and left. And I never said a word to him.

There were kids that hated Jed. Lots of kids. If I could get all of them to join together and stand up to him, Jed might not be as tough as he thought he was. I could give it a try, but the thing about being beaten down . . . it's hard to get back up. I'd been to four schools now, Dad's job kept us traveling, and each school had a bully. Sometimes the bully would get caught and punished, but half the time it didn't matter. In weeks he would go back to doing what he did. The kids wouldn't stand up for themselves and hardly any of them would tell. They just took the bullying, sure the teachers couldn't help them. They were right. If the principal kicked the bully out of school, then he'd simply wait outside it.

My dad said in life there were sheep and wolves, and most of the time they couldn't cross over.

I sighed. Jed damn sure seemed like he thought he was a wolf. He was nuts as they came. He'd keep coming after me, going after the others, start messing with Tess. I folded the top of the bag the doll was in and got up. Nope, it probably wouldn't work, no matter how many kids Jed had given reason to hate him, but I'd give it a shot. There had to be some that'd band together against Jed. Hell, it always worked in the movies.

Right?

* * *

Wrong.

Isaac peered through black bangs at me in disbelief. "The guy's not human, okay? When he stomps you, it's like he's never gonna stop. He could take on Frankenstein, the Mummy, and the Werewolf all at once and go out for pizza after." Isaac was a huge fan of horror movies. He'd seen ones made before I was born, before my *parents* were born. The inside of his locker door was covered with pictures of monsters. Snarling, crouching, flying, sucking blood. They papered every square inch. I liked Isaac but he was a little weird.

"Come on." I stood at his locker and snorted, "He's not all that."

"Yeah, Nicky, he *is* all that. He caught me in the woods and he broke my arm, okay? And he said if I told anyone how it happened, he'd break the other one. I believed him because he *meant* it." He slammed the locker shut. "No way. Leave me out of it. He's crazy, and if you had any sense, you'd be watching behind you every minute." With that he hurried down the hall.

I gave up on Isaac and went on to Dog Boy . . . Sammy, I meant. Sammy. Five words out of my mouth and he was gone, fast as any of his dogs. It went that way all day. I'd expected it, but I'd hoped it'd be different.

Isaac had said Jed had caught him in the woods, the same ones Jed had chased me in. Jed didn't do his fighting on campus. That'd get him expelled and he knew it. Yeah, it would get *him* expelled—him, not me.

He didn't have the little *in* that I had with Principal Johnson. Good old Principal Johnson, not the brightest man to choke on chalk dust.

So I went to Plan B. That day when Jed, who was dependable as Cs in math, sat down opposite me in the cafeteria and took my slice of pizza, I picked up my tray, dumped the food off of it, and whacked him hard on the side of the head with it.

It knocked him sideways, almost off the seat, but he caught himself with one hand on the table. His eyes were ice, his teeth bared, and violence shivered under his skin. "Who's the bitch now?" I asked quietly. "You gonna roll over and take it? Or you gonna stand up and do something about it?" He'd been barely smart enough not to fight in school before, but this was a whole lot of different.

As plans went, it wasn't as idiotic as it seemed. There were teachers already moving toward us. They'd pull him off me before he got me too bad. And then out he'd go. Maybe it'd only be outside the school itself but that was something.

He shook with black anger, but as crazy as he was, he wasn't as stupid as I thought. I might not get expelled if there was a fight, but he knew he would. And I had a feeling his daddy would be a whole lot more disappointed than mine. I had a feeling Jed was a chip off the old block.

He stood and hissed, "Dead. You're dead."

He left the cafeteria and I sighed. Another plan shot to hell. Glumly I sat back down and waited for a teacher to come drag me off to Principal Johnson for a few weeks of detention.

It was actually two months.

After a lot of clutching at his comb-over of black hair and warnings on how he couldn't cover up things like this—he simply couldn't—he did. Like I knew he would. I was going to have to call Mom to go fetch Tessa from the bus stop and she wasn't going to be happy at the reason why. Understanding maybe, but not happy.

The same day, after two hours of detention, as I slid through the woods, I heard Jed behind me. This time was the first time I actually heard him howling with fury as he chased me. I might've been chunky and short, but I was quick. I had hit that gym door running. Jed hadn't been as fast.

"You son of a bitch! You son of a bitch! Where are you?" All that was followed by screams of rage. Incoherent animal sounds. Isaac was right. Jed did sound like a monster . . . a movie monster anyway. I slid under a thick overhang of dead blackberry vines and thought how I definitely hadn't made things any better. Not to say whacking him with a tray hadn't felt good, but it hadn't gotten me out of the trouble I thought it would.

Although, it really, *really* had felt good.

Finally I climbed a tree, my brown jacket blending in with the bark, and held still as he passed like a rabid Doberman beneath me. Swear to God, there was foam flying from his mouth as he screamed for me.

You skip a few Ritalin and things just go to hell.

Right. Like you could blame that kind of nuts on a little ADHD. I hugged the tree, rested my head against it, and stayed there for an hour. It was cold, but I didn't mind the cold. And it got dark, but I didn't mind that either. As far as monsters went, Jed's night vision must not have been too hot. He didn't hang around. I heard his last howl nearly a half mile away and then nothing again.

I finally climbed down and went home to face two things a lot worse than Jed: Mom and Dad. Dad ripped me a new one over detention. It didn't matter why I got it. Skorazys didn't make waves, didn't get noticed. Our grandparents and their grandparents had learned that over in Russia. Keep your head down or lose it altogether.

After the yelling was over, the worst came. Mom wanted me to help her and Tessa make Christmas cookies for Santa. When I wandered into the kitchen, Tess turned out to be making her "Merry Christmas, Santa" note in her room, all tongue and crooked crayon writing, as Mom roped me in. "You'll have a good time, Nicky," she said, smiling. She was a great mom, a pretty one, too, even with flour streaked across one cheek. Dark blond hair worn in a braid just past her shoulders, violet eyes, and a scar that bisected one eyebrow that only made her look curious all the time. I loved my mom. I know I was thirteen and not supposed to think things like that, but I did.

But she wanted me to make cookies for Santa? "You know there's no Santa, Mom," I grumped. "This whole Christmas thing"—I opened a bag of chocolate chips—"it's a waste of time."

A spoon smacked my hand. "The holiday spirit is in your heart. It's not about presents and shiny paper. Christmas is in you." She poked a finger in my chest. "And Santa is everywhere you look. If only you *would* look." She shook her head, smiled again, and dabbed my nose with cookie batter. I rolled my eyes and wiped it off with a finger, which I licked clean. "Now," she said firmly, "make your sister happy and help with the cookies. She'll be out here any minute."

And it wasn't so bad. I didn't believe in any of it anymore, but Mom and Tess laughed. Dad came in and we ended up having a cookie batter fight. It might've not been the real thing, but it was as close as you could get.

Right then, that was good enough.

The next day was the day before Christmas Eve, our last day of school before break. And my last day, I had a feeling, to figure things out with Jed. But first Mary Francesca tried to figure out things with me.

I'd seen her around, Mary Francesca . . . never just Mary or Fran . . . Mary Francesca. She was in some of my classes. She seemed nice, funny. She had red hair that fell in a mass of curls past her shoulders, bright red freckles, even brighter blue eyes, and she was smart. Definitely smarter than I was. No Cs in math for her.

She cornered me outside English, smiling. Her teeth were so bright I swore I could see my reflection. "Hey, Nick."

Nick. Not Nicky. I liked that.

"Hey," I said back. That was about it for me, conversation-wise. I mean, a pretty girl. What do you say?

She didn't have any problem. "I was wondering . . ." She leaned a little closer and I could smell strawberries and cream shampoo. "I was wondering if maybe you'd want to go to the Christmas dance with me?" I felt crushing disappointment and utter relief all at the same time. On the one hand, I wouldn't have to worry about clothes and flowers and talking and dancing. I'd seen what they did on MTV. No way I could do that and not get a boner right on the floor.

On the other hand, I liked Mary Francesca.

Not that it mattered how funny or smart she was or that she smelled like strawberries. There was no way my parents would go for it. It went back to the bad old days when persecution was everywhere. You couldn't trust strangers, secret police were around every corner, and you never knew who might turn you in. It was a lesson no one in the family had forgotten. We were Orthodox all the way and we didn't date outsiders. Which was going to make finding a prom date pretty damn hard. There were lots of us in Russia, not too many here. But those were the rules.

I added that to Christmas and bullies in the whole sucking category.

"Sorry." I shifted my backpack from one side to another, and I really was sorry. "I have detention for two months. My parents won't let me go anywhere. I'm grounded, damn, forever."

She frowned in disappointment—real disappointment, which made me again think how rules sucked. "Well, okay, I get that." Sighing, she unhooked a pin from her sweater and pinned it on mine. "Maybe by Spring Fling then." She looked around quickly, then leaned in to give me the quickest of kisses.

I was wrong. It wasn't her hair that smelled like strawberries; it was her lip gloss. I was still tasting it as she disappeared down the hall and around the corner. Then I looked down at the pin. Santa grinned up at me, mittened hand waving automatically.

Ho frigging ho.

Every class dragged minute by minute. No one stared at me like I was going to die, so no one knew this was the day Jed was coming after me. It didn't matter. I knew. I passed him once in the hall and his eyes had never been paler. He didn't grin, he didn't smirk. He just stared, flecks of spit at the corner of his mouth. That was it. Jed had gone off the edge and there was no coming back for him. Did a teacher notice? No. Did big men in white coats come drag him off to a big looming building with the baby eaters and mailman killers? No. No one wanted to know.

No one ever wanted to know.

A Plan C would be good now. Really good.

Jed was a year older, but he'd been left behind. He tripped me in math class on my way up to the board, his almost white eyes daring me to say something about it. I went on, did the calculation, and circled back another way to sit down.

When I ate lunch, he ate at a table next to mine and watched me. Watched my every move, my every bite. Half-chewed food fell from his mouth as he kept his eyes on me, but he didn't notice. Or care. I'd thought he'd grow up to be a serial killer, but I was wrong. He was already there and he had me marked as victim numero uno.

What do you do then? Go out kicking and screaming? Not me. I so did not plan on that.

Next time I passed him in the hall, I murmured, "Tomorrow. Northeast edge of the woods. By the bridge." I didn't wait on an answer. For all I knew, he'd chewed his tongue off already and wasn't going to give me one anyway. Then I went straight to the nurse's office, faked a stomach cramp and a little dry heaving, and had my mom picking me up in twenty minutes. Today was taken care of. Jed wasn't going to jump me early. And tomorrow . . .

A man's gotta do what a man's gotta do.

A guy on an old Western had said that once. He was right. I wasn't a man, but it still counted for me, too. I spent the night in my room thinking. I took off that silly Santa pin Mary Francesca had given me and almost tossed it, but at the last minute I laid it on my desk. The mitten continued to wave at me and I wondered how long until the battery ran out.

I went out once to the garage after the folks were asleep then came back and watched the stars and sliver of moon through my window. The cold air made them brighter, closer, until you could see the teeth in the moon's sly grin and the cold patience behind the stars' eyes.

After an hour of that, I went back in and stared at my closet. My last real Christmas was in there. It made me sad, proud, and had me pining all at the same time. Finally I put on my boxers and T-shirt and went to bed. I dreamed of cookies, presents, and a thousand lighted trees, and behind each tree was a Santa. He was laughing, cheeks red, stomach bouncing. A thousand Santas wherever you looked.

When I woke up in the morning, I had one of those things . . . oh shit, what is it? . . . an epiphany. A big word for a big idea. I knew what to do, how to do it, and if I did things just right, just so, it would turn out even better than I thought yesterday. It would be better than okay. It would.

It had to.

I ate lunch with Mom, Dad, and Tess. Let Jed freeze his ass off in the woods waiting for me. I was in no hurry. Afterward I grabbed my coat and backpack and said I'd be back. Grounding was grounding, but my dad thought that roaming in the woods was good for kids. Taught them things. Toughened them up.

I set off down our gravel road. The sky was white and gray and blue. Might be snow, might clear up. That was the fun thing about winter: it was always a surprise. I wore faded jeans and my rattiest sneakers. You never knew what was going to happen to them, not with someone like Jed. I liked the sneakers. We'd got them in San Antonio . . . they were orange with the black outline of a coyote howling at the moon. It was the same kind of moon we'd had last night. Narrow and hungry.

I hefted the backpack and tried not to think about that. I had to do what I had to do. Thinking about things like that—it wasn't good. It wasn't good for the plan or for Tess or for me. I kept on walking, new snow crunching under my rubber soles. We'd had lots of snow lately, at least a few feet of it. Blue Water Creek was the size of a small river now. You could toss a stick in that and it would be gone before your eyes could follow it.

Thirty minutes later I reached where I'd told Jed to meet me. He was there. Like he wouldn't be. If I was stupid enough to walk right up to him, he wasn't going to turn me down. He looked up from the struggling bundle of fur he had at his feet. The grin he gave me was colder than the snow under my feet. "Brought you a present, shithead."

Tied to a tree he had a dog. From the smell of the wet fur, it was soaked in paint thinner and Jed was trying to get a lighter to spark. He was trying to catch a dog on fire . . . on *fire*, just to piss me off before he finished me. That was the kind of sick asshole he was.

"I like dogs a lot," I said flatly. "I don't like you at all."

Jed had parked his bike on the edge of the swollen Blue Water Creek. I turned and kicked it into the flood. The bike was carried away instantly. That was why the adults told us to stay away from the creek: it was over the banks, it was icy cold, and it could drown you in an instant.

"Whoops," I said cheerfully. "You should've listened when they said stay away from the water."

He growled, "You goddamn son of a bitch. You don't know who you're dealing with, asshole. I'm going to make you wish you were dead. Hell, I'm going to *make* you dead." The pale eyes glowed with hatred as he shoved the lighter in his pocket. He picked up a baseball bat that had been hidden in the brush and rushed me, Louisville Slugger swinging. I caught it before it landed, ripped it out of his hands, whirled, and swung for the bleachers. He went down like Ms. Finkelstein on Principal Johnson.

Hard and fast.

Like I said, I got sent to the principal a lot, and he didn't always lock the door. Grown-ups could be stupid, too. Which was why skipping class and zero tolerance for violence were a little less zero for me. Principal Johnson was good with the excuses for the school board, and Ms. Finkelstein, the secretary, handed candy out to me like she was trying to make me diabetic.

I was hungry and getting hungrier—one lunch was never enough for me. My family . . . we liked to eat. I pulled one of Ms. Finkelstein's Tootsie Rolls out of my pocket and chewed on it while I nudged Jed with my sneaker. He was still breathing. That was good. He mumbled and started to twitch, his arms moving and hands digging at the dirt. I smacked him again with the bat at the base of the skull. A tap this time . . . just enough to do the job. Then I untied the dog. It had tags that said it lived and was loved only about five blocks from the woods. It knew its way home. First it dropped and bared a submissive stomach. I rubbed it lightly, washed off the paint thinner with snow, then let it jump up. I smiled as it bounded off homeward. I did like dogs . . . yapping, jumping, leg humping. It didn't matter. All dogs were good dogs.

I duct taped Jed's ankles, wrists, and mouth before waiting until long after dark to carry him through the woods. I didn't want to leave drag marks, and I scuffed my feet and doubled back enough times that no one could've made heads or tails of our trail. Jed was easy enough to haul even though he weighed more than me. Really easy. Shit floats. I guess assholes did, too. He woke up again. I was almost home, so I let him stay awake. He moaned, snarled, and tried to yell under the tape. That was Jed for you. A complainer. Bitch, bitch, bitch.

And dumb as a box of rocks. I'd given him every chance and he'd never taken one of them.

Our house was only a mile or two from the woods at the end of our long gravel lane. The nearest neighbor was half a mile away. It was nice. Quiet. Private.

Really private.

"They'll find your bike in the creek," I said to the struggling Jed. "They'll think you drowned. Think your body got wedged under somewhere. Who knows? Maybe it took you all the way to the river. Everyone will pretend to be sad." I looked back at him and smiled. "But no one will be."

Christmas Eve. I pulled Jed through the door into the blinking lights of the Christmas tree, the stockings on the mantel, the milk and cookies sat oh so carefully on the table. Tessa had left out milk and cookies for three years now. Third time's the charm.

Mom and Dad sat waiting on the couch for me. It was almost eleven—close to Christmas. Close enough. Tess would've long gone to bed. "That's where you've been." Mom shook her head affectionately. Boys will be boys.

"Anyone see you?" Dad demanded bluntly. "Any trouble?"

"Come on, Dad, you taught me better than that." I dumped Jed at the bottom of the fireplace before going to my room. I opened my closet door and rummaged through softball mitts, balls, games I'd outgrown but never thrown away until I found it buried in a corner: the polished skull. It had been pretty stinky for quite a while, but it wasn't the kind of stink my kind minded. I pulled the dusty red cap with the pom-pom off of it and shook it out, trying not to sneeze. These were the only things left. The reindeer venison was long gone. Around the base of the skull were handfuls of white hair, once curly and soft, now wiry and sparse. It didn't matter. It'd work. I also picked up a tattered white trimmed red jacket. At the last I grabbed the glue from my desk and went back to the living room.

"You're a good brother." Mom smiled, pleased.

"Yeah, yeah." I ducked my head in embarrassment as I jammed the Santa hat on Jed's head, draped the red jacket over the top of him, and glued the hair to his chin and jaws. He wasn't too helpful there, whipping his head back and forth. But I got the job done. I even pinned Mary Francesca's Santa pin to the jacket. It was the perfect touch.

Hungry, hungry, hungry, but he wasn't for me.

I picked up three cookies, ripped the tape off his mouth, and jammed them in there before he could get a word or a scream out. He turned slightly blue as he choked and coughed. I thought it'd keep his mouth shut long enough.

"Tess," I yelled. "Come on. Hurry up. He's here!"

After a second there was the sound of feet in footie pajamas hitting the floor and she came flying out, eyes as wide as they possibly could be when she spotted Jed. "Santa! Santa! I asked you to come and you're here! You're *here!*"

Six years ago I saw Santa. Seven years ago I'd made my first kill. It soured me on Christmas when I realized there wouldn't be any more Santas. No more surprises from the chimney. I'd finished that job. Kids, you don't realize how permanent things are. I was sorry afterward. Sorry I hadn't waited for my little sister to be old enough to join in on the fun. Sorry she could never have the thrill I'd had.

I watched as my little sister grinned big as her pajamas tore away and her skin twitched until fur rippled over her twisting, changing body from muzzle to tail. Her pumpkin orange eyes bright with Christmas spirit as her teeth were suddenly bright with something else as she tore into her present.

Mary Francesca's pin went flying. Wolves were Orthodox. We did only date our own kind. It was too bad. She was cute.

On the couch a buff-colored wolf tucked her head under the jaw of a larger black one. Their eyes were brilliant with pride and affection and the spirit of the holiday. Their baby's first kill. It was always special. I rested my muzzle on my paws and watched as Christmas came back to me.

Mom said Christmas wasn't in presents and trees, glitter and bows. She said it was in your heart and so was Santa if you want him to be. If I really wanted him, I could find him again.

Mom was right. Christmas *was* in your heart. And Santa was everywhere. If you only knew where to look.

Keeping Watch Over His Flock

Toni L. P. Kelner

Toni L. P. Kelner is the author of nine mystery novels and numerous short stories, including the Agatha Award–winning "Sleeping with the Plush." Though she's written about carnivals, fan conventions, high school pranksters, circuses, family reunions, vampires, and lingerie shops, this is her first werewolf story. Her personal pack includes her husband, fellow author Stephen P. Kelner; two daughters; and two guinea pigs. Unfortunately, none of them recognizes her status as top dog.

Maybe half the members of the pack were in wolf form, with the others still human, and Jake wasn't sure which he would rather look at—the bared teeth or the stern frowns. So instead he aimed his answers at the Christmas tree with its twinkling lights. There was something unreal about having his whole life decided in front of a Christmas tree, but that's what happened when you broke virtually all of a werewolf pack's rules on Christmas Eve.

"Look, I didn't mean to go solo without permission," Jake said.

"Was I unclear in denying you permission?" Though Brian was one of those who'd stayed human, the growl in the pack leader's voice could just as easily have come from a lupine throat.

"No, but—"

"Had you proven yourself ready by successfully taking a form deemed appropriate for your surroundings?"

"No, but—"

"Then what exactly did you mean to do?"

He swallowed. "Okay, I guess I did mean to. Look, can I tell it from the beginning?"

There was a murmur, and he risked a glance at the pack. Nobody looked particularly friendly or willing to listen, but Brian said, "Proceed. But Jake, don't lie again."

The message was clear. If he didn't tell the truth, he could kiss his place in the pack goodbye. He swallowed hard. He hadn't been in the pack long enough to know what it meant to be ejected, or even if he'd survive the experience.

The thing was, Jake wasn't sure that telling the truth would help. Even when Felicia, Brian's wife, had caught him sneaking into the house, he hadn't realized just how much trouble he was in until Brian started calling in the other pack members to judge him, right then and there, even though it was getting close to midnight. What with the holidays, not everybody could get to Brian's house, but enough were there to make whatever they decided official. And final.

"Okay," Jake said, "this is what happened."

"Are you excited about tonight?" Ruby asked.

"Duh! Who wouldn't be?"

"Me, too," the little girl said. "I just love Christmas."

"Oh yeah, Christmas." Jake rolled his eyes. It wasn't sugarplums running through his head, not with the full moon only hours away.

"What did you ask Santa for, Jake?"

"Huh?" He looked away from his game of WarCraft for a second, which was enough to blow his chance for a high score. "Shit!"

"Language!" said a voice from the kitchen.

"Sorry," he muttered.

"I'm sure Santa won't mind you saying one bad word," Ruby said, trying to make him feel better.

"Yeah, maybe not," Jake said, wondering if she was jerking his chain. Did the kid really still believe in the guy in the red suit? She was nearly nine, for freak's sake. Of course, Ruby had been raised in a real house with a real family—so real it was scary—while he'd been shuffled from foster home to foster home. It hadn't taken him long to realize that he didn't need to bother sending change-of-address cards to the North Pole.

"So what did you ask him for?" Ruby persisted.

He hadn't asked for anything. It hadn't occurred to him. "Um . . . It's kind of a secret."

"Like when you don't tell anybody your birthday wish?"

"Yeah, like that."

"Mom said it's okay to tell Christmas wishes, because sometimes Santa Claus can't get me everything on my list, so Mom and Dad have to help. Didn't your mother tell you that?"

"Ruby!" the voice from the kitchen chided.

Ruby put a hand to her mouth. "I'm sorry, Jake. I forgot!"

"It's okay," he said, and it was. "I don't really remember her anyway." The only memory he thought he had was a vague one of her scent. "I'm used to it."

"Besides, you have us now," Ruby said, putting her hand on his arm. "We're going to have the best Christmas ever!"

"Dam . . . Darned straight!" He wasn't some loser on his own anymore—he had a home, and a pack to watch his back. The full moon was on the way, and with it, his first honest-to-God, away-from-school-grounds run. Knowing that had been making him antsy all day long—if he'd been in wolf form, his tail would have been whipping around like crazy.

Felicia, Ruby's mother, came out from the kitchen with a well-filled plate. "Cookies!" she said brightly.

One whiff, and Jake was happy to put down the joystick. He reached for an iced gingerbread man and chomped on the head with even more gusto than he would have before finding out what he really was.

"Do you want to watch *Rudolph the Red-Nosed Reindeer* with me, Jake?" Ruby asked around a mouth of crumbs.

"Yeah, as if I wanted to watch a prey species prancing around." Reindeer were for eating.

Felicia didn't have to speak, just gave him a look, and he saw Ruby was looking half-confused, half-troubled.

"I mean CLAY species," he said. "You know, made of clay. That's why they call it claymation."

Ruby still wasn't convinced, and Felicia said, "No time for Rudolph right now. We're going to put out the manger scene. You can help, too, Jake."

. "Sure, if you want." Not only did she make awesome cookies, but it was always a good idea to stay on the good side of the pack's alpha female.

Brian came down the stairs from his trip to the attic, carrying a dusty cardboard box, and Jake was amazed once again that anybody could look so boring in human form, yet so freaking cool as a wolf. He was just this guy, in a college T-shirt and jeans.

"Are you ready for me?" Brian stopped at the archway into the living room, trying for casual.

"Mistletoe!" Ruby exclaimed and rushed over. He put down the box to pick her up and plant a kiss on her cheek.

Then Felicia joined Brian under the mistletoe, and after she'd been thoroughly kissed, she turned to look at Jake. He held up one hand and said, "Thanks, but I'll pass."

Brian just grinned. Despite being pack leader, he was a pretty good guy. He'd been the one to track Jake down and spring him from the system to get him into Dogwarts, the boarding school where packs taught the young werewolves the ins and outs of their world. Of course the school had some innocuous formal name to throw humans off the scent, but none of the kids used it.

Jake had been seriously stoked when Brian invited him to join his family for the Christmas holiday. He was the only kid at Dogwarts who hadn't been raised in a pack, and even though everybody was friendly enough, he hadn't been around long enough to establish himself. He figured hanging with the pack leader and his family ought to earn him a few dozen coolness points.

Brian moved the box next to a long table along one wall that Felicia had cleared off that afternoon, and opened it to show a pile of bundles wrapped in newspaper.

"I want to help," Ruby said.

"Gently now," Felicia warned her.

"I know, they were Grandma's. I'll be careful."

The way they slowly unwrapped each piece, Jake was expecting something extra cool, but all he saw was a bunch of decently painted ceramic figures of the usual suspects included in Nativity sets: Mary, Joseph, the kid, the Kings, some shepherds, and an assortment of camels, donkeys, sheep, and cows.

It looked as if they'd emptied the box when Ruby said, "Where's the wolf?"

"Must be in here somewhere," Felicia said, and rummaged around until she found one last wad of newspaper. "You do it, Jake."

The three of them were looking at him like it was a big deal, so he took it and peeled off the newspaper to reveal another figure.

He looked at it, and then at their expectant faces. "It's a dog."

"It's not a dog!" Ruby said. "It's a wolf."

"It looks like a dog," Jake said. "Kind of mangy, if you ask me."

"Jake doesn't know the story," Ruby said. "Tell him, Daddy!"

Brian cleared his throat. "In those days, Caesar Augustus sent word that all the world was to be taxed, and each—"

"Dude, I've seen *A Charlie Brown Christmas* three times this week. I know how it goes."

Felicia frowned, but relented when Ruby giggled.

Brian said, "Then you know that an angel appeared to the shepherds in the fields around Bethlehem, who were keeping watch over their flocks. And of course, shepherds always had dogs with them."

"Then it *is* a dog."

"Not exactly. Even now, there isn't that much difference between a dog and a wolf—"

"Yeah? So why doesn't anybody in the pack turn into a Chihuahua and party with Paris Hilton?"

"Just listen!" Felicia said sharply.

"Whatever."

Brian went on as if he hadn't been interrupted. "Back then, the differences between types of canine were even less. So it turned out that these shepherds had a wolf to guard their sheep."

Jake wanted to ask why the wolf didn't just chow down on mutton one night, with shepherd's pie for dessert, but from the look in Felicia's eye, he figured he better not go there.

"When the shepherds went to Bethlehem to see the Christ child, the wolf went with them, and when they were struck with the glory of the Lord, so was the wolf. Being a wolf, he wanted to give praise the best way he knew how. So he howled."

Jake blinked. He was pretty sure Linus hadn't said anything to Charlie Brown about a howling wolf.

"Naturally, the other animals were afraid," Brian continued, "and the shepherds were going to chase off the wolf. But the baby smiled at him, and waved His hand, and suddenly a man was standing there. And he bowed down with the others to praise the child. It was Jesus' first miracle."

"Turning a wolf into a naked guy?"

Felicia frowned again, but Ruby giggled and said, "Jake! They gave him something to wear."

Brian nodded. "When the shepherds went back to their flocks, the wolf went with them, still in human form, and they welcomed him. He married one of their daughters, and was a man in every respect. Except that he was stronger and his senses were those of a wolf."

"Like us," Ruby put in. She was too young to change, but she had the other werewolf gifts.

"That's right," Brian said. "Since the werewolf had those superior senses, he was able to recognize the danger when Herod's men came to Bethlehem to kill Jesus. It was the night of the first full moon after He was born."

"Like tonight!" Ruby said. As if Jake needed to be reminded about the full moon.

"The wolf warned Mary and Joseph to take Jesus to Egypt, and he went along to keep Herod's men from catching them. Once they were safe, an angel appeared to the wolf and offered him a reward. The wolf told him that while he was happy to be human, he still missed his old life. So the angel told him that every month, when the moon was full, he'd be able to return to his wolf form, and all his children would have the same gift."

Brian took the figure from Jake and placed it into the Nativity scene. "This was the first werewolf."

Jake stared at the statue, then at Brian, waiting for the punch line. Nada. But before he could say anything, the phone rang in the kitchen.

"I bet it's Aunt Ronnie!" Ruby said, and skedaddled away, with Felicia following, laughing.

Brian looked at the Nativity scene again, and said, "You're kidding, right? No offense, but Spider-Man has a way cooler origin story."

"Offense taken," Brian said, and just like that, the nice guy was gone and the alpha wolf was in charge. "I know you're new to the pack, Jake, but this is our tradition, and I expect you to show respect."

"Do the other packs believe this stuff about angels making us werewolves?"

"Each pack has its own myths," Brian admitted, "but they've all got some story. How do you think we became werewolves?"

Jake shrugged. "I don't know. Some kind of evolution thing, maybe."

"You think this is purely survival of the fittest?"

"Yeah, man. I mean, look at us. Stronger, better senses, like you said. We're wolves!"

"Wolves are endangered, and have been for years. That doesn't sound like a good evolutionary strategy to me."

Before Jake could argue the point further, Felicia called from the kitchen. "Brian!"

The pack leader patted him on the shoulder before heading into the kitchen.

Jake picked up the mangy sheepdog figurine again. He couldn't believe it. His first Christmas with the pack, and they were telling Bible stories. It was more like Christmas with Hannah Montana or some other lame Disney show than with a freaking wolf pack!

He realized the voices in the kitchen were sounding a lot more serious than they should have for a phone call from Brian's sister, so he drifted that way. Brian was listening and scribbling notes onto a pad while Felicia gathered junk from the cabinets.

"What's up?" he asked Ruby, who was watching it all with wide eyes.

"Mom's going tracking," she said.

Brian hung up the phone. "Dave will be here to pick you up in fifteen minutes," he said. "Have you got everything?"

She looked at the pile on the kitchen table. "Leash, harness, flashlight, cell phone, emergency kit. Yeah. I'll go change." She trotted up the stairs.

"What's going on?" Jake asked Brian.

"A little girl in town is missing. Felicia and David are going to join the searchers."

"Why not you?"

"Felicia is a better tracker, and the people in town are used to Dave handling her. I'll stay here with you and Ruby."

It only took a second for the implication of that to sink in. "What about the full moon?" The plan had been for Felicia to stay with Ruby, while he and Brian went for a good long run in the woods.

"I'm afraid we're not going to be able to go out tonight. We can't leave Ruby alone. The moon will still be full tomorrow night."

"Yeah, but tomorrow is the pack Christmas party. There won't be time for a decent run!" Jake knew he was whining, and in a bratty kid way rather than the way a submissive wolf was supposed to, but he couldn't help it.

"Jake, a little girl is missing! Isn't that more important?"

"She's human, right? Not a member of the pack?"

"What difference does that make?"

"Are you kidding? If she's human, let the other humans worry about it."

Felicia came back into the kitchen, having changed into all black. As in a black Labrador retriever. She padded over to Brian, who put the harness on her, and fitted the phone and other things into the harness pockets.

"Good hunting, Mom," Ruby said, putting her arms around the big dog.

"Thanks, sweetie," Felicia replied in the odd voice some werewolves were able to muster, even while in other forms. Jake hadn't even come close to mastering the technique himself. "I'll be back before Santa comes. You go watch *Rudolph*."

"Jake," Brian said, "will you keep Ruby company for a few minutes?"

"Yeah, sure." He followed the little girl back into the living room, but stayed close enough to the door to the kitchen to listen in. He'd learned years before that he was good at eavesdropping, without knowing why his hearing was so much sharper than normal. Than normal *human* hearing, he corrected himself.

"Can you believe that?" Felicia said, half-growling. "More worried about a run than a lost child?"

"He's a teenager," Brian said. "He thinks the world revolves around him."

"I think you're wasting your time with him, Brian. He's not right for the pack."

Jake silently flipped her the bird, even if she couldn't see it. See if he ever helped her put up her junky manger scene again.

"Give him time," Brian said soothingly.

"I won't let him ruin Ruby's Christmas!"

"Ruby likes him."

She snorted, though it was more of a snuffling while she was in that form. "That's something in his favor anyway."

A car horn sounded from the driveway.

Brian said, "There's Dave. You better go. Good hunting, love."

Felicia barked in response, and Jake heard Brian opening the door for her to bound out to the car. He scooted over to the television so he could pretend to care about a singing, candy-ass reindeer.

Brian came to the doorway. "Jake, could you come in here?"

"Sure."

He followed the pack leader, and the two of them sat down at the kitchen table.

"Look," Jake said, "maybe I could go out by myself. A lot of the guys are taking their first solo tonight."

"I talked to your teachers about that possibility."

"Really?" he said eagerly. "I'm ready, I know I am."

"What's the pack's first rule for a run?"

"Stay away from humans."

"And if you can't?"

"Don't interfere with them in any way. Stay out of their sight."

"And if you can't?"

"I won't go anywhere near a human, Brian, I swear."

"What's the rule if you can't stay out of a human's sight?"

He sighed, and quoted, "If you are seen, make sure to be in a form that will not cause alarm."

"Have you managed to take another form?"

"Not exactly."

"Which means what, exactly?"

Jake looked down at his hands. "It means I can be a different-colored wolf," he said, thinking about his classmates' snickers when the best he could do was to morph into a wolf with a deep purple coat, while they were successfully changing into German shepherds, Rottweilers, cocker spaniels, even an enormous Maine coon cat.

"That's not good enough. You're not ready for a solo."

"Why can't I just run as a wolf? Even in that story you told me about the angels and crap, you said we didn't start out as dogs, right? We aren't poodles or terriers or freaking opossums. We're wolves! For the first time in my life, I know what I am!"

"You're a werewolf. And if you've paid attention in class, you know that means man-wolf. The human comes first, and humans make choices. We can change into anything we choose to."

"I tried changing into something else. It didn't work."

"Keep trying. You just need to choose a form you're comfortable with. Felicia runs as a Labrador retriever most of the time, and I'm a pretty convincing Newfoundland."

"I'm not comfortable as anything but a wolf."

"Maybe you just don't want it badly enough."

Jake looked Brian right in the eye. "Well, maybe I don't. Maybe I like being a wolf, and maybe I don't want to change into anything else."

"Then you're not going to solo. It's okay if you want to change tonight, but you have to stay in the house."

"Yeah, whatever." As if he'd feel any less trapped as a wolf. It'd be even worse, to smell more of the outdoor world he was missing.

He started to slouch his way back to the living room.

"And Jake," Brian added, "if I catch you eavesdropping on me and Felicia again, you won't get a solo run until you're thirty!" Jake didn't know if it was the leader's voice or the way he held himself that suddenly made him seem more lupine than most of the pack was under a full moon.

Son of a bitch! How had he known? Jake threw himself down on the couch, glaring at the TV screen while the dumb reindeer moaned about being a misfit. He should try being the only outsider in the pack. Jake had been used to always being the new guy when he was moving between foster homes. He hadn't cared then. Now he was finally someplace he wanted to stay, someplace he wanted to belong, but he was going to be stuck being the new kid forever. Not being able to tell the guys at the Christmas party about his run was only going to make it worse. Maybe he could make something up. He grinned, imagining himself chasing after Rudolph and making more than his nose red.

The only good part of the evening was that Brian mostly ignored him. Instead he and Ruby laughed their way through watching Christmas videos, eating gingerbread men, and actually hanging a row of piece-of-crap stockings by the fireplace. Felicia stayed gone, and though she and Dave called in a few times, he didn't bother to ask what was happening and he sure as hell didn't eavesdrop.

When Jake finally escaped into the guest room, he refused to look out the window at the fat moon hanging in the sky, calling to him. What was the point of changing in the house? What was he supposed to do then? Curl up like a puppy on a tweenaged girls' poster? Maybe Brian had a Santa hat for him, and would take cutesy pictures for next year's Christmas card. Hell, why didn't they just get him fixed?

Finally he couldn't resist it any longer, and drew the blinds to at least see the moon. That was all it took, the one look, and he lost it. Jake knew the change felt different for different people—for him it felt like the best stretch anybody could ever have, the kind where you feel longer and looser when you're done. Ten minutes after that, without ever actually making a decision, he was downstairs, pushing the specially designed back door open to escape into the night.

He scurried off quickly, but once he was safely out of earshot, he stopped to breathe in deep. This was the life he was supposed to lead. Out in the wild, hearing and smelling and tasting things he'd never notice as a human. Why would he want to choose any other form when he could be a wolf? Hell, if it hadn't been for computer games and McDonald's, he'd have chosen to stay a wolf forever.

Of course, he was still going to obey pack laws, more or less, and that meant getting farther from the house. Fortunately, the house edged onto an open area and it was easy enough for him to lope through the woods, avoiding houses and roads and any humans who might spot him. Then he let himself go, running and howling and chasing rabbits. Okay, he didn't catch any, but it was early yet. He'd show Brian he was ready to solo, and was imagining telling the other young wolves at the next night's Christmas party when he ran right into a clearing. And smelled humans.

He skidded to a halt in the leaves, unable to stop himself from giving off a puppyish whimper. Standing stock-still, he listened and looked and sniffed. There was no sign that anybody had seen him.

Funny place for people to be on Christmas Eve, he thought. It was just an old shack, and he didn't think the place even had electricity hooked up. There was no fire, either, and while it was plenty warm for a wolf, it was awfully cold for humans.

Car trouble? Nobody was outside or looking out the window, so he crept around to the front of the shack, where a new-looking SUV was parked on a narrow dirt road. He got close enough to feel that the engine was still warm, and the tires intact.

What did he care anyway? The humans could handle their own problems. He was about to go back to the woods when he smelled something else. Somebody in that shack had a hard-on. He'd been surprised, and more than a little embarrassed, when he'd realized that arousal had its own smell, but there was no way anybody attending a coed school full of randy teenagers wasn't going to learn that smell.

Jake grinned the closest he could get to a grin as a wolf. Though he'd been way too nervous to try to spy on any of his amorous classmates at Dogwarts, this was different. He bet he could get a better show than anything on YouTube, and wouldn't the guys be jealous when they heard about it? He couldn't smell the guy's partner yet, but she had to be in there. Nobody would go to the trouble of sneaking out to the woods just to jerk off.

He was still within the rules, he told himself. The humans didn't know he was there, and wouldn't see him if he was careful. Chances were that they'd be too busy to notice anything but what they were doing.

He scouted around and found an old woodpile near a window that had some of the glass in place, and carefully put his front paws on it so he could peer inside. The humans had thoughtfully set out a couple of kerosene lanterns, making it easy for him to see them and hard for them to see him. And what he saw nearly made Jake bark with laughter. Standing with his back to him was a guy in a freaking Santa Claus suit! The hat, the beard, the whole nine yards. Yeah, this was going to be something to see.

Then Santa moved to one side, and Jake saw who it was with him. It was a kid. A little kid, a girl who looked even younger than Ruby. She was staring up at Santa with big brown eyes, and saying, "I thought there'd be snow at the North Pole. And reindeer."

"Don't worry about that, Cindy," the guy said in a creepy voice. "Just come sit on Santa's lap." Then the son of a bitch started to pull down his pants.

Jake knew a pedo when he saw one. He'd seen too damned much of that kind of thing at the foster homes he'd been stuck in, too many crying kids and smirking old men. One dude had made a play for him, but Brian had gotten him out in time. That guy still showed up in his bad dreams every once in a while.

Well, he'd be damned if this guy was going to get away with it. Every pack rule was forgotten as he howled and threw himself through the shreds of glass remaining in the window frame and onto the back of the pervert.

The phony Santa screamed as Jake snapped at him, ripping at the fake fur collar and drawing blood. The guy twisted around and managed to push Jake from him, then grabbed a piece of broken furniture to club at him. Jake backed off, but was tensing himself to spring when he felt the little girl tugging at his tail with all her might.

"Don't hurt Santa Claus," she yelled. "Bad dog, bad dog!"

Santa was on his feet by then, waving the chair leg, and Jake smelled the acrid piss as the man wet himself.

God, he wanted to rip at his throat, or better, tear into his crotch so he'd never hurt another kid. But the girl was still holding his tail, keeping him from his prey, and even as a wolf, he couldn't bring himself to bite her. All he could do was growl at the man backing toward the door.

Damn it, he was going to get away. The kid realized it, too, and sobbed, "Santa, don't leave me."

The bastard kept moving backward, ignoring the girl's pleas. She was crying so hard that her grip loosened, and Jake threw himself forward and toward Santa. At the last second, he felt her grab hold again, and his teeth closed on nothing more than the cheesy beard as he ripped it off the man's face.

Then Santa was gone, scrambling for his car while the kid held Jake back. All he could do was let loose a howl of frustration while the bastard drove away.

The little girl was still crying hysterically. When she finally let go of Jake's tail, she curled up into a ball of misery, her hands over her head as if to fend off the attack she was sure was coming.

Jake stared at her. What the hell was he supposed to do now? He couldn't just leave her. What if the pedo came back? Even if he didn't, how would the kid get home?

He got down on his belly, the same as he would for a superior wolf in the pack, and crawled over to her. She jerked when he touched her, but he didn't move any closer, just lay there on the warped wooden floor as her crying slowed. She must have finally realized he wasn't going to bite her, because she sat up. Though she scooted away from him, she didn't scream or try to hit him.

After a long moment, she said, "You bit Santa Claus."

Jake shook his head vigorously, wishing he could talk in wolf form the way Felicia could. Inspiration struck, and he grabbed the beard with his teeth and put it down in front of the girl.

"His beard?" she said, picking it up. Then she found the strings that had held it on to the guy's ears. "It's not real." She breathed a little gasp. "He wasn't the real Santa."

Even as a wolf, Jake could roll his eyes. After all that, the kid *still* believed in Santa Claus. But he shook his head again, confirming what she'd said.

"Then where am I? How am I going to get home?" Tears flowed again, and Jake wanted to cry with her. He didn't know the answers, either.

Though he wasn't sure how far they were from other houses, he didn't think she could walk very far. For one, now that Santa and his noxious scent were gone, he could tell that there was something funny about her smell, as if she'd been drugged. Belatedly, he realized that this must be the missing child Felicia had gone to search for, and he wished to God it had been she who had found her, instead of him.

Maybe he could carry her. He lay down in front of her, then tried to point at his back with his muzzle, to show what he wanted her to do. But she shrank from him. Jake didn't really blame her—if he'd seen a wolf attacking somebody, even somebody who deserved it, he wouldn't be all that eager to hop on the wolf's back afterward. He rubbed a paw across his muzzle and realized the fake Santa's blood stained his fur.

Okay, then, the thing left was to go for help, and get back as quickly as possible. And he got two feet beyond the door before he heard her crying for her mama and daddy.

Jake sat down. He just couldn't leave her. He couldn't leave her, and they couldn't stay there. That meant she had to come with him, but short of dragging her by the scruff of the neck, he couldn't figure out how to convince her he was harmless.

If only he didn't look so damned scary, so damned . . . So damned WOLF. Hell, she'd called him a dog—maybe she was afraid of dogs, too. Or maybe she was now. Even if he could change to some other canine form, or even just give himself puppy dog eyes, they'd be stuck. Human wouldn't be much better—after Santa, the last thing the kid needed to see was a naked teenager. Not to mention what would happen if anybody saw a naked teenager giving a little girl a piggyback ride.

If only he'd been able to learn the trick of changing to some other form. What had Brian said? That he could take any form he chose. All he had to do was choose some form that could carry the kid without scaring her. When he thought about what a kid Ruby's age would like, it only took him a second to decide what to go for. Hell, it couldn't hurt to try.

He was wrong. It did hurt. It hurt like hell. It was nothing like changing from human to wolf, or even from wolf to human. The worst part was not being able to let loose the grunts of pain he wanted to for fear of scaring the kid even more. It took twice as long as it should have taken to change, and twice as long after that to recover enough to wobble back into the shack.

Cindy gave that little gasp again when she saw him. "You're real!"

He nodded.

"Have you come to take me home?"

He nodded again.

"Are we going to fly?"

A shake.

"Why not?"

He did his best shrug, given the circumstances, and snorted.

"Is it because you're alone?"

He nodded, relieved that she'd come up with an explanation.

She approached him gingerly, and patted his head. Then she started to climb on top, Jake standing as still as he could to make sure he didn't startle her. Once he was sure she had a good grip on him, he started out the door and down the road.

It wasn't too bad at first—even though he wasn't used to carrying anybody, at least she was skinny. But he got awfully tired after a while, what with the extra weight, keeping an eye out for danger, and as Cindy got sleepier and sleepier, making sure she didn't slip off his back. All of that was even harder because he was still trying to figure out how the body was supposed to work. Whose idea was it to make the legs so long and spindly? At least the hard feet were useful—he didn't have to worry about stepping on broken glass or sharp rocks.

The first couple of houses they came to were dark, and Jake wasn't going to risk leaving her until he was sure there was help around. Only when they got to a well-lit house, with plenty of cars parked nearby, where he could see people talking and laughing inside, did he carry her to the front porch. He had to kind of kneel down so she could get off. As she stood, rubbing her eyes, he nudged her toward the door. He didn't back away until she hit the doorbell, and he could hear somebody coming.

He was starting to leave when she called out, "Wait! Which one are you?"

He should have known it was coming. So he made one final choice, and his nose glowed red in the moonlight.

"After that," he said to the assembled pack, "I headed back here. And Felicia caught me."

"I see," Brian said. He'd stayed quiet during the whole story, and the expression on his face hadn't changed a bit. "Felicia, do you have anything to add?"

"He didn't try to deny that he'd been out, if that's what you're asking."

"Can you explain how he found that child before an experienced team like you and Dave could?"

Felicia looked abashed, something that normally Jake would have been delighted to see. "We did track her to the road, but once she got into the car with the phony Santa, we couldn't follow any farther. We were working a spiral, trying to pick her scent up again, when we got the word that she'd been found unharmed at a house on the edge of town. She barely stayed awake long enough for her parents to get her, and nobody knows what happened."

"I see. Dave, I understand you investigated Jake's story."

Felicia's tracking partner stood. "I changed to track Jake and the little girl back to the shack. Everything there was just like he said."

"Will you be able to find the pedophile by scent?"

"Without a doubt."

Brian nodded. "Jake, do you have anything else to say?"

A million things ran through Jake's mind: He could point out that the kid was safe because of him, or that it was Christmas, or that he was new to the pack. Or he could just apologize and throw himself on their mercy. But it all stuck in his throat. They knew the story—what they decided to do was up to them. "No, sir."

"Very well." He turned to the pack. "Jake has broken several pack rules tonight. Normally, any of these transgressions would be reason to eject him from the pack, but since he is still young, he may remain if a pack member takes responsibility for teaching him better. Will anyone vouch for Jake?"

Jake didn't want to look up, didn't want to see the faces of the pack members, most of whom were basically strangers, after all. Then he heard a voice say, "I will."

It was Felicia.

"I will, as well," Dave said in his deep wolf voice.

Other voices chimed in, some of them the parents of his school friends and others he didn't even know the names of. Finally Brian waved them down. "As pack leader, I also vouch for Jake, and for now, will keep him with my family so that I can attend to his learning—and punishment—personally. Therefore the matter is settled, and the meeting is adjourned." He looked at his watch. "You all better get home to get those stockings filled. Merry Christmas!"

Jake was so choked up he could barely return the greetings and handshakes and hugs as the pack left. It was probably just as well, he decided later. If he had been able to speak, he'd probably have gone all Tiny Tim on them and said things that would have embarrassed him for the rest of time. Not cool, especially when it was looking like he'd be with the pack for a while. Maybe he'd wanted something for Christmas after all.

He was feeling pretty damned good until Brian said, "Now, about your punishment."

Jake nodded. Whatever it was, he could take it.

But Brian flashed a grin. "It can wait until after Christmas. You better head on up to your room and get what sleep you can. Ruby will be dragging us all out of bed in an hour or two to see what Santa brought her."

"No problem," Jake said. "I don't want to mess up Christmas any more than I already have."

"You haven't messed up anything, Jake. We're lucky to have you around—especially that little girl," Felicia said, then actually kissed him on the cheek. At his surprised look, she pointed upward. "Mistletoe."

He grinned. "But I'm still not kissing Brian."

"Thank the Lord for small favors," Brian said. "Now go to bed."

Just before he headed upstairs, Jake stopped at the manger scene and looked at the figure of the dog or wolf or whatever it was. Then he reached over and moved him closer to the baby Jesus, where he could keep a better eye on him. Just let Herod's men or anybody else try to mess with that kid, and they were going to get themselves one big, hairy, scary Christmas surprise. Nobody messed with kids while his pack was around.

COPYRIGHTS

"Introduction" copyright © 2008 by Charlaine Harris, Inc., and Toni L. P. Kelner.

"Gift Wrap" copyright © 2008 by Charlaine Harris, Inc.

"The Haire of the Beast" copyright © 2008 by Donna Andrews.

"Lucy, at Christmastime" copyright © 2008 by Simon R. Green.

"The Night Things Changed" copyright © 2008 by Dana Cameron.

"The Werewolf Before Christmas" copyright © 2008 by Kathleen Richardson.

"Fresh Meat" copyright © 2008 by Alan Gordon.

"*Il Est Né*" copyright © 2008 by Carrie Vaughn, LLC.

"The Perfect Gift" copyright © 2008 by Dana Stabenow.

"Christmas Past" copyright © 2008 by Keri Arthur.

"SA" copyright © 2008 by Joe Konrath.

"The Star of David" copyright © 2008 by Hurog, Inc.

"You'd Better Not Pyout" copyright © 2008 by Nancy Pickard.

"Rogue Elements" copyright © 2008 by Karen Chance.

"Milk and Cookies" copyright © 2008 by Robyn Thurman.

"Keeping Watch Over His Flock" copyright © 2008 by Toni L. P. Kelner.